TIGER DRIVE

a novel

TIGER DRIVE

a novel

one family
too many secrets
four people who want to matter

TERI CASE

BZCE PUBLISHING

Tiger Drive is a work of fiction and the characters, places, and incidents are products of the author's imagination or are used fictitiously. Any similarities or resemblance to actual events, locales, or persons, living or dead, are coincidental or due to archetypal characters who behave in common and anticipated ways.

BZCE Publishing, Ithaca, New York
Publication Date: February 2018

Hardcover ISBN: 978-0-9997015-5-3
Paperback ISBN: 978-0-9909175-6-4
ebook ISBN: 978-0-9909175-7-1

Cover art by Olya Vynnychenko
original photo © Walter Baxter (cc-by-sa/2.0)

To Karsen, Adam, and Crystal. It has been my honor and privilege to be your older sister. Given a chance, I'd do it all over again.

HARRY

Hello, my name is Harry.
—Sobriety meeting

Saturday morning, April 1, 1989

Harry opened his eyes and waited for his vision to clear. He was dressed and lying in bed—his bed. He recognized the quilt pattern on the damn twin mattress Janice had moved into their room six months before—and after seven kids and thirty years of marriage. The finality behind her action had made it one of the worst days of his life. They hadn't slept together since.

So he'd made it home, but how and when? He rolled onto his back and stared at the bedroom ceiling.

Another blackout.

What did he do last night? Or was it more than one night? He was no stranger to drinking binges and running blackouts that could last up to a week at a time. They had become part of his genetic makeup and bad habits over the past several years, increasing at a disastrous rate. He looked at his watch: April 1. So one night was lost forever, and he was waking up on April Fools' Day.

He was a fool.

What had he done between the blackout and bed? Part of him wanted to know, and part of him didn't. Nothing good ever came out of being so drunk he couldn't remember a damn thing.

His head pounded, and his ulcerated stomach gurgled with acid, rushing heat up his esophagus and burning his dry throat. His breath smelled and tasted of vomit and putrid mistakes. Waking up from a time warp was the worst feeling; he dreaded putting the pieces together because they were always wrapped in regret and guilt. Without fail, he'd always said or done something he shouldn't have. Something he could never take back.

Why did he keep doing this to himself? To his family?

The last thing he remembered was drinking beers at the Creek Bar.

Harry lifted his hand to his chest and then curled his fist over his heart. The skin over his knuckles stretched tight and began to burn.

What in the hell?

His knuckles were busted wide open, and dried blood caked his skin. A trail of bruises and scratches ran from his wrist to his elbow. His other arm didn't look any better.

He fought escalating panic. What happened last night? Who did he hurt? He eyed his hand. His best-case scenario would be that he had hit something, and his worst-case scenario would be that he'd hit someone. The scratches on his arms indicated the worst.

Janice was asleep in her bed, and her blankets pooled around her waist.

He eyed the plump skin of her upper arm. No obvious bruises. What a relief. Leaning across the two-foot chasm between their beds, he shook her shoulder.

"Janice. Janice," he said around small gasps of air. He cleared his throat and stroked her arm. "Janice."

"Leave me alone." She shrugged her shoulder away from him and buried the side of her face deeper into her pillow.

"Did I hurt you?"

"No, I was in bed when you came home and passed out." She tensed and started to turn to look at him. "Why?"

He nudged her shoulder to keep her in place. "Nothing to worry about, go back to sleep."

She tilted her head enough to squint at him. "Heard that before."

He couldn't bear to alarm her before he knew any details. Busted fists couldn't be good news, and it'd be best to let her remain oblivious, at least for now. He lay back on his bed. He looked again at his right hand and flexed his fingers, opening and closing them several times. Both hands were swollen and aching, but his dominant right hand was worse. Squeezing his eyes shut, he tried to remember. Waited. Nothing.

Think. Think. Think.

Okay. So he'd gone to the bar straight after work. He was stressed out, and he'd needed a drink because Janice would leave him for good if she found out about his gambling debt. And the damn debt had gone past due as of Friday morning. Anytime now, the asshole might call or show up on his and Janice's doorstep and claim the roof over their heads and take their cars. His stomach tightened as if he had just gone from cold to hot in that game his kids played. "Hotter," they'd say as he moved closer to what he needed to find.

Was that it? Was he getting hotter? Did his injuries have something to do with the pawnshop owner and lost titles?

He'd have to call Scotty at the Creek Bar to retrace his steps, and he prayed he hadn't brought more damage to his family than he already had. Had he gotten in a fight at the bar? No. He would've woken up in jail, or Janice would have heard about it. She was always there for the karaoke contest on Saturday nights. At one point, he'd thought he could scrape by and use her contest winnings to stay ahead of the loan, but she always told him she'd used the money to settle past due bills or buy groceries. He couldn't say, "Oh by the way, honey, I pawned our home and vehicles in a poker game." But one crisis at a time, he thought. First, what had he done?

Harry looked down at his T-shirt. It was splattered with reddish-brown stains. Blood—he hoped from his own damaged hands. His pants looked similar. He rolled over to the side of the bed. His top shirt was crumpled in a ball on the floor. He grabbed it, and an iron-like smell permeated his senses. Harry shook the shirt open. It was covered in dried blood—too much blood. He gagged and dropped it to the floor.

Invisible hands encircled Harry's neck. He struggled for oxygen. Spots blurred his vision. He sat up, putting his feet on the floor and dropped his head low between his knees.

Oh mother. What did he do last night?

As soon as his vision stopped spinning and he could breathe like a normal human being, Harry grabbed the bloody shirt and stumbled to the bathroom. He shoved the shirt in the small trash can, whipped off his T-shirt and pants, and added them to the garbage before tying the bag closed. He turned to the sink and scrubbed his face with soap and warm water. The yellow soap burned his wounds. He grabbed a towel from the floor and braced his hands on either side of the sink.

"What have you done?" he asked his reflection, a reflection he'd come to know as the self-sabotaging Jekyll to his broken-spirited Hyde. He reached for the glass of dentures on the counter. His upper teeth were soaking in the container. He ran his tongue around his toothless mouth. Where was his lower set of teeth? He shuffled toiletries around on the counter. They had to be there somewhere, but they weren't. He couldn't afford to lose those. Literally.

Damn it.

It wasn't funny how the sight of himself without his teeth could bring him to tears. He used to be a handsome man. A man going somewhere. A man people stared at for all the right reasons as he walked by.

Not anymore.

He turned his face from side to side. He just looked tired and old. Worn out. In trouble.

So he had hurt someone, lost his teeth, and gone to bed in bloody clothes. He glanced at the plastic boats and toy cars deserted in the drained tub. *Please—not his boys . . .*

Morning light from the windows guided his way as he raced in his boxers down the hall and through the living room to look for his four children who still lived at home. No one had fallen asleep on the couch. He made his way toward the two rooms at the far end of the main trailer. Nineteen-year-old Lisa was asleep in the first room, and he didn't see anything strange. He cut through the Jack and Jill bathroom to the second room.

His dog, Star, named after the white shape between her

eyes, was lying on the bath mat and growled at him—nothing new about that. Star had been growling at him since they'd brought her home as a puppy. He'd grown up on a farm in Minnesota and had once been a natural with animals, but that was a long time and too many bad decisions ago. He ignored her and stepped into the adjoining bedroom. The bunk beds his nine- and ten-year-old boys treated like a fort were empty.

Oh God.

He pushed on and stepped over to the bedroom window. His station wagon was parked outside. So, yeah, he had either hurt someone, lost his teeth, and driven home; or driven home, lost his teeth, and hurt someone he loved. Where were Justin and Tommy?

His self-loathing grew with every step.

His college-bound daughter, Carrie, was asleep in her room. As usual, she had cotton stuffed in her ears to block any noise.

No sign of the boys. There was nowhere left to look.

Oh, shit. Harry spun on his heel and headed back to the Jack and Jill bathroom.

Star was a terrier mutt with a white belly and caramel-colored coat. She was fifteen pounds if she was lucky, but she stood to her full height and then bared her teeth like a mama bear.

If dogs could talk.

He forced her to the side. Her bark had always been bigger than her bite. With his heart doing a *thump-de-dump*, he opened the vinyl shower curtain.

Justin and Tommy were huddled sound asleep beneath a pile of ThunderCats blankets in the porcelain bathtub. Their heads were on opposite ends of the basin and lying at awkward angles. Their bare, twig-like legs stuck out from their cartoon-pic skivvies, and Justin's foot rested under Tommy's chin. Tommy hugged a yellow plastic Wiffle Ball bat to his side. A dying flashlight glowed under Justin's hand, creating a translucent pink glow between his pudgy fingers. The pajama shirt at Justin's wrist was smudged with blood.

If he had hurt them, he'd never forgive himself. Harry curled his lips and choked on a sob. "Boys? Boys. Wake up." He leaned over the tub and squeezed their shoulders.

His touch startled his children. Justin's eyes widened, and he shrank back. He hugged the flashlight to his chest, casting an eerie glance over his face.

"Get away!" Justin cried.

Tommy gripped the bat and struggled to his knees. Cocking his elbows, he lifted the bat just like Harry had taught him for Little League baseball.

Hell—they were scared of him.

Harry put up his hands and took a step back. "It's okay. I'm not going to hurt you. Justin, show me your wrist." He sat down on the toilet to be at their eye level. "Did I do that?"

Justin nodded and pulled back his sleeve.

"Oh no," Harry said.

Justin's small wrist and forearm had bruises matching the sizes of Harry's thumb and four fingers. "Does it hurt? Rotate your wrist for me."

Justin stuck out his lip. He wiggled his wrist and flinched. "You scared me."

It took Harry a few minutes to find his voice. Every time he tried to speak, an anguished keen threatened to escape, and he'd have to clear it like a bad cough. "I'm so sorry. What happened, Tom?"

Tommy's scrawny arms were shaking, but he tightened his hold on his bat. His lips quivered. "You said if we didn't get out of your way, you'd kill us. We ran, but Justin tripped. You grabbed his arm and swung him over there." He pointed across the room.

Harry leaned forward until he was kneeling next to the tub. "I'm so sorry. I didn't mean it." He tried to take the bat, but Tommy wouldn't let go.

"Okay, keep the bat until you feel safe. That's your right." He turned to Justin. "Did I do anything else?"

Justin nodded. "My shoulder hurts."

"Nobody hates me more than I do right now, son. It won't happen again. I swear on my life."

Star started to whine, and she put her front paws on the bathtub.

Harry smoothed the hair between her ears and looked at his sons. "See, I know how to be gentle and nice now. Star's forgiven me this time, and she doesn't even like me. Tom, I'm real proud of you for sticking up for your little brother. Now, how about we go to Winchell's and get some hot chocolate and donuts? Just us boys. Will that help?"

"With sprinkles?" Justin asked.

"Anything you want. Come on, let's get dressed."

The boys crawled out of the tub and shied away from Harry's helping hands.

As soon as Justin's bloodstained pajama top hit the floor, Harry wadded it up and shoved it under his arm.

Tommy asked, "What did you do that for?"

Harry couldn't look him in the eye. "I'm going to get him a new pair of PJs."

"But I like my Superman jammies," Justin said.

"I will get you new ones. Let's get your shoes on." Harry took Justin's foot and pushed the tennis shoe past his heel. He was tying Justin's shoe when Tommy spoke again.

"You had blood on you last night."

Harry cringed and focused on Justin's shoe. His poor sons deserved so much better. "That was wine, not blood. Maybe I should get a Superman shirt to replace mine."

Justin giggled. "You're too big for one."

Harry brushed the bangs off of Justin's forehead. *So forgiving.*

Crossing his arms and shaking his head, Tommy said, "It wasn't wine. I know what wine smells like."

"I know you do," *Jesus Christ, he was the worst dad ever,* "but let's not talk about it anymore. It's our secret, and we have some donuts to eat. I think I'll have sprinkles too."

Justin laughed again. "You're too old for sprinkles."

"No one is too old for sprinkles," Harry said. "Let's go."

Two hours later, Janice was waiting for him on the back porch when they returned with full stomachs and Kmart bags.

Harry could tell by her pursed lips she was annoyed. He slowed his pace. There'd been a time when she looked at him as her hero. He'd sunk so far. Man, if she only knew how much trouble he was in. He wished he could tell her about the title to their trailers, but he couldn't until he came up with a solution. And he still couldn't remember last night.

"What have you three been up to? What's in the bag?" she asked.

"The boys and I went out for breakfast, and I bought them a gift."

"Why didn't you take the girls too?" she asked.

Because he hadn't scared the crap out of the girls.

"Boys, go in the house," Harry said.

The bags bounced off their skinny legs as they ran up the steps.

"You, Lisa, and Carrie were sleeping like angels," he said.

Janice squinted and looked hard at him. He hated it when she did that; it felt like she could read his mind. And after thirty years, she was damn good at it too. Drinking made him too predictable.

"You asked me earlier if I was okay. Did you black out last night?" she asked.

He nodded.

Janice rolled her eyes and reached for his injured hands. "What happened?"

It was the first time she had touched him in weeks, and he hated himself for needing to break the contact and pull away before she touched the sores. "I don't remember, but don't worry. It wasn't you, or the kids. But I scared them last night. I just wanted to make it up to them."

"By buying them breakfast and a present? Jesus, Harry. You didn't hit them? Can you even remember? You better be honest with me. I'll ask them anyway. Unlike you, they don't like to lie."

Harry was ninety percent confident he'd bought the boys' secrecy, but they were kids after all. "They're okay," he said.

She stared at him for an eternity, then she looked away and crossed her arms over her chest. Her stance reminded him of Tommy's defiance a few hours before. "They looked happy."

And he thought he'd gotten away with one more bad day, but he hadn't. Janice moved on to another topic he wished he could avoid.

Extending her hand, palm up, she said, "Give me the rest

of your money. Our lot rent is due this week. And we need groceries."

Harry hesitated. "Um, did you win anything at karaoke last night? Can you use the money for groceries?"

"Harry . . ."

He looked at his feet because they were the safest place to look.

"Damn it, Harry. You promised. I knew I shouldn't have trusted you with your paycheck yesterday, but I didn't have time to swing by the shop and pick it up. I was going to take it last night, but you left while I was singing. Please tell me you didn't blow it."

"Honey, I needed it for something else—"

"What for? Poker? Is that it? You never learn. What kind of a man are you? You want us to live on macaroni and government-issued cheese for the week? Don't you care if your kids have a roof over their heads? We need that money, Harry."

She was too close to the truth because, no, in the heat of the moment, he hadn't cared enough about a roof over their heads or food in their bellies. He'd been playing to win and to break even or at least catch up with the loan. He'd thought he'd win and nothing would be an issue. He clenched his jaw only to be reminded that he'd misplaced half his dentures. He hated how he looked without them. Nothing felt shittier than shame, and he felt what few hairs he had left on his balding head and the back of his neck rise like a damn dog who has been backed into a corner and is ready to fight his way out. His heart rate quickened, and sweat gathered on his forehead. "I can't handle this right now. Get out of my way!"

"Get out of *your* way?"

He didn't like the way she said "your"—like he'd been

keeping her from something better than her life with him. Because he knew he had been, and that he'd done so for years. She'd always deserved better. The truth hurts that way. He couldn't handle any more truth right now.

"You've become a pathetic excuse of a man, do you know that? I wish I'd never met you!" Janice yelled.

And he definitely couldn't handle that.

Over the years, they'd argued more and more, and they often said stuff they didn't mean, but dammit, her eyes told him she meant it this time. She did think he was pathetic. He snapped. He grabbed her neck, slamming her against the side of the trailer, creating a rumble and vibration through the thin metal. It echoed, and shouts and running footsteps told him the children had heard. The folds of Janice's chin were like silk under his bruised and calloused hands, and he felt her throat spasm as she tried to swallow and suck in air all at once. As she struggled with him and his hands tightened, images of another person flashed through Harry's mind. A different struggle. He shook his head to try to clear his thoughts. *What was happening to him?*

Janice clasped his hands and raked her nails across his injured knuckles.

Harry swore, released her throat, and slapped her. The force of his beefy palm threw her off balance, and she landed on the porch with a scream and a thud. Harry jumped back. Appalled by his own actions, he cried, "Janice. No, Janice." He took three steps back and looked from his hands to his wife.

He'd never forget Janice's expression, his betrayal radiating from her blue eyes. The set of her lips and jaw spoke of a finality that far surpassed any divide between a set of twin beds. He'd never laid his hands on Janice's neck before.

She'd made him promise not to touch her neck years ago because it made her feel vulnerable. He'd never known her reason, but her fear had been reason enough for him. And now, he'd broken his promise to her.

A fragmented memory of his two hands choking some man flashed again. Was it from last night? Had he strangled someone? Shit. What had he done? Was he both a murderer and an abusive husband now? His forehead was dripping sweat now. Janice and his home swam before his eyes. His anxiety almost overwhelmed him.

"Janice, I need your help—"

"Leave. God help me, but I never want to set eyes on you again." Janice curled her lip in a sneer and climbed to her feet. She rubbed her hand over her neck and then her cheek. "You promised never to touch me like that." Her voice reverberated between clenched teeth. "Never. Come. Back." She walked away from him, and without sparing him so much as another glance, she went into the trailer and slammed the door behind her.

Harry heard the distinct click of the lock, and Janice's voice carried through the cracked window as she called the police. Numb inside, he turned and stumbled to his car. He drove around town for a few hours in a daze and then began to retrace his steps from the night before. With each step, he knew he had lost his family forever. He registered for a kitchenette on Green Street, his usual location of exile and the one place that would let him pay in arrears.

A day later, there was a restraining order in place to stay away from his family, and Harry had figured out he'd beaten a man into a coma.

2

JANICE

Here's to those who wish us well and those who don't can go to hell.
—Patsy Cline

Saturday night, April 8, 1989

April showers bring May freedom, Janice hoped. There were eighty-eight trailers in Bengal Trailer Park, and most of them were as run-down as her own. The park was surrounded by sagebrush that smelled like urine when it rained or whenever the ragweed bloomed. Janice wouldn't miss it. She wouldn't miss any of it. Less than one month from now she could be happy again. And not just happy for a moment here and there, clinging to one handful of good memories, but really happy—the kind of happy that might make her glad to be alive. The kind that could give her goose bumps on a hot summer day for no other reason than the sun warmed her skin, the sky was blue, or the trees swayed in the breeze. The kind of happy she hadn't been in years.

She hadn't seen Harry in a week, not since he'd tried to choke her and she'd filed a restraining order, and if she won the karaoke contest tonight, she'd only have to see him one more time before she got to change her life once and for all: when she'd be dropping her bombshell news that she was leaving the boys with him for a year, moving to Nashville to reclaim her dream, and filing for a divorce.

Standing before a mirror in the living room where the light favored her aging skin, Janice wondered how her forty-eight years had flown and dragged all at once. She smeared baby-blue shadow across a wrinkled eyelid and then leaned to her right to peer out the cracked trailer window at the darkening sky.

"The boys should be home by now," she said.

She went to work on her other eye, cursing when the lid twitched. She was so nervous, her stomach was flip-flopping the Hamburger Helper she'd made for dinner, and she wondered if she should make herself throw up. She couldn't afford to be woozy tonight. Though she'd won the karaoke contest several times before, tonight's cash prize would change her life—and, someday, her boys' lives too.

"I'll look for them if they aren't home in ten," one of her daughters, Lisa or Carrie, replied. After having seven kids, eventually they all sounded alike. Harry liked to say she should have been named "Fertile Myrtle," but if she could do it all over again, she would've practiced abstinence when she was seventeen and never had any children.

If she shared her thoughts out loud, Janice knew other mothers, including bad ones, would call her a horrible person. What kind of mother would say if she could do it all over again, she wouldn't have her children? An unhappy one, she'd tell them. A mother who had struggled day in and day out to provide for her family and failed them. A woman so stuck in life she felt like she was wearing shoes four sizes too small, and every step in her life was excruciating and unrewarding, circle after strideless circle. And, worst of all, someone who was one choice away from hating herself. She would hate herself if she ignored this last chance to go to Nashville.

Despite her honesty, she expected people would still condemn her for putting her happiness first and for loving herself first—they wouldn't care that she was decades overdue for both. Instead, they'd step on their decaying soapboxes and claim that being a mother was the best thing that ever happened to them. She wished this were always true of motherhood, but it wasn't. And that was that.

"Thank you," she looked over her shoulder to confirm which daughter was promising to help, "Lisa. Remind them to do their chores, will you?" She puckered her lips to apply Rocket Red lipstick.

Someone was storming down the hallway. Janice paused with lipstick in hand just as her youngest daughter, Carrie, stomped into the room. Having two teenage daughters who couldn't get along was annoying as all get-out. Everything was such a huge deal to them.

"Stop wearing my pants." Carrie swung the jeans at Lisa, slapping her across her chest.

Lisa curled into a ball on the couch and covered her head with her hands before the second swing landed.

"What now?" Janice asked. She could do without their drama tonight.

Carrie shook the dirty jeans in her fist. "She," Carrie pointed a finger at Lisa, "wore my jeans without underwear. Again! Disgusting."

"Prude," Lisa said.

"Tramp!" Carrie said.

"Enough." Janice tossed her lipstick in her purse and slung it over her shoulder, all the while shaking her head. Her bottle-induced platinum-blond curls didn't budge due to the can of hairspray she'd applied. She nodded at Lisa. "Well?"

"I didn't want panty lines," Lisa said. "Duh."

"Sounds reasonable to me," Janice said and walked toward the door. She could hear and feel Carrie marching behind her. The entire trailer park probably could.

"You've got to be kidding me. I paid for these with my money. I don't want her to wear my clothes. She doesn't show respect for anything. If she doesn't want panty lines, she should wear her own pants. She should buy a thong, for crying out loud."

"Have you ever seen a thong?" Lisa asked.

"Have you ever seen underwear?"

"Stop it." Janice turned on the two girls, fists on bountiful hips, and looked from one to the other. Lisa, with her voluptuous curves advertised in tight clothing, stood in stark contrast to Carrie's tall, lean figure disguised under layers of material. When Janice was Carrie's age, she'd been pregnant, and at Lisa's age, she'd had a one-year-old son, WJ. People might think her an unfit mother, but at least she'd had the common sense to take Lisa to Planned Parenthood and put her on birth control three years ago. And as for Carrie, well, her youngest daughter was a walking poster for abstinence with her mousy-brown frizzy hair pulled into a librarian bun, perpetual frown, and her ridiculous determination to never wear makeup. She knew Carrie had sizable breasts hidden somewhere under that tent of a T-shirt with the slogan *This is your brain on drugs* and a picture of fried eggs in a cast iron skillet splashed across the front, but leave it to Carrie to not flaunt her chest while she had something worth flaunting. Janice once had nice breasts, but nursing had deflated them, and while she hadn't put herself on display like Lisa, she certainly hadn't been wearing baggy shirts that resembled a public service billboard.

Carrie's rapid breathing was fanning the hair on Janice's temple, and it was more annoying than having a small hand tugging her wrist for attention, expecting a response to an adolescent fit. If Carrie would wear tighter pants, Janice thought, Lisa wouldn't be able to squeeze into them anymore. But Carrie had never been one to ask her for advice.

Janice pointed at Lisa. "Don't wear your sister's clothes anymore, but if you do, wash them before she finds out."

Carrie screamed. "You know what? I have normal friends with normal parents, brothers, and sisters." She jabbed a finger at Lisa and then Janice. "Only people like you," she waved her hand in a circle in the air, "living like this, think the way you do." Carrie turned her back on Janice and crossed the room, yanking open a door that opened into a second trailer Harry had added years before. "I wish Dad could come home."

Janice flinched. "Be careful what you wish for, girl, it might just come true." She turned and headed in the opposite direction, expecting Carrie to slam the other door and rattle the foundation just to annoy her, but she didn't. Carrie was waiting for the perfect time, Janice bet.

"Who are you singing tonight?" Lisa yelled after her.

"Patsy Cline."

"Boring. Isn't she dead? Go for a Bon Jovi song," Lisa said.

Janice paused at the door. "I'll have you know that Patsy

Cline is an icon and one of the most influential women in the history of country music, and as for her being dead, I'm not exactly living."

But soon she would be.

"Find the boys and make sure everyone does their chores. If no one calls me at the bar, I'll bring home artichokes for tomorrow." Just as Janice made her final move to escape through the door, Carrie slammed hers. Twice. So predictable.

Janice tugged on the door handle of the rusty yellow Ford Pinto, but it wouldn't budge. She tried again. Nothing.

She threw her fringed purse on top of the car and lifted her leg, anchoring the rubber sole of her red cowboy boot next to the front door. The loose plump skin around her stomach poked out between the bottom of her vest and the waistband of her skirt. She yanked on the door until it swung open. She was lucky she didn't fall down. She adjusted her clothes, grabbed her purse, and dropped into the front seat. Slamming the door for good measure, she turned the ignition, but the engine whined and stalled.

Janice's chest tightened, and her heart began to palpitate. What would she do if the car wouldn't start and she missed the contest? She stared through the windshield at the dilapidated brown and red trailer. No, two trailers—Harry's version of a double-wide. Heaven forbid she should have an actual prefabricated thirty-foot-wide mobile home. Instead, she lived with Harry's finagling ways and in two old trailers lined up beside each other, connected by a door. Janice remembered the day almost three decades before when Harry had shown her the place.

"That's not a double-wide, Harry. It's two junky trailers,"

she'd said. "You promised me a nice home if I stayed in Corbett City, not two piles of metal crammed together."

"Two trailers are better than one trailer any day. You told me we needed more space," he said.

Harry tried to pat her growing belly, but Janice stepped out of his reach.

"I'll build a shell around the trailers, and it will look like a house—better than any mobile home in this trailer park."

"On what planet, Harry? On what planet would this be considered a house? And it won't be mobile once you start attaching things. Why can't we just get a nice home for our family? I'd rather have a nice tiny house than these two . . . things." She started to cry.

"It's the best I can do. We can't afford anything else right now," Harry said. "But someday I am going to get you a real home. Trust me. For now, home is where the heart is, right?"

But it had been another empty promise—sincere in the moment but never delivered. Within the first year, he'd sold the trailers' wheels and axles out from beneath them, and it would require a Herculean effort to replace the foundation so they could sell the trailers and buy or rent a new place someday.

The trailers had deteriorated over the life of their marriage. At times, she wondered how the walls stayed erect. Janice had trudged through the place so many times; every depressing nuance was etched in her brain.

A porch carpeted with AstroTurf surrounded the trailers. Foot traffic had worn through the green plastic, revealing a black underlay. Careless smokers had melted the turf with cigarette burns. Fencing ran along three sides of their lot. None of the fences matched unless *not* matching matched.

The west fence ran the length of the trailer and was chain-link with two-inch plastic slats inserted through the vertical wire mesh. "For privacy," Harry had claimed.

The second chain-link fence ran along the back side of the trailer and spanned the length of Tiger Drive, beginning at Lot One and ending at Lot Forty-Four. It marked the boundary between the *Adults Only* and the *Families with Children* sides of the park. If she had a dollar for every time someone had complained about one of her kids walking on the park's adult side on their way to the laundromat to use the candy vending machine, she could have afforded to move to Nashville a long time ago.

A water-damaged plywood fence ran the length of the east side of the yard, and like the rest of the lots, the front portion remained open and exposed. Janice had never understood why she couldn't at least have a fully fenced yard. A darn gate would have been nice. Over the years, the kids' broken toys and Harry's discarded projects had littered the space, suffocating any chance of her grass or tulips returning each spring. Suffocating her.

Dear God—she wasn't a religious regular, but she knew whom to call on when it suited her, and tonight had to happen —*please, don't take this chance away. Amen.*

She deserved better, and she couldn't stay and die in those trailers. Both she and God knew it too. She counted to ten, pumped the gas pedal, and turned the key. The engine started.

Interrupting her tears of relief, Janice turned the rearview mirror until it framed her eyes. Tonight was her chance to start again—the night where she could pick up the dream she had lost when she was seventeen, when everything had changed and she'd left her grandparents' Minnesota farm.

As she lifted her foot off the brake, the gravel churned and cracked beneath the rolling tires. She pressed the gas pedal, and dust spewed on everything she left behind.

3

CARRIE

Word of the Day

C arrie stormed into her bedroom with her wadded jeans in her hand and paced the length of her room, slamming the white cupboards that, in place of a dresser, held her clothes overhead.

Her bedroom was once someone's kitchen. Sometimes she wondered whose kitchen it had been. Had they succeeded and escaped trailer life? Or were they rotting away in a different but equally stifling trailer park? Twelve years ago, her older brother, Bobby, had converted the stripped kitchen and designated junk room to a bedroom by covering the walls with wood paneling and nailing down carpet swatches he'd found in the dumpster at the local carpet store. Bobby moved out as soon as he finished the space, and now she only heard from him if he needed money—she guessed for drugs, so she always said no. Besides, she was trying to save for college, and she didn't have the resources or stomach to contribute to his stupid choices. Maybe her room was his parting gift since he'd always known she didn't like sharing a room with Lisa. She threw the dirty jeans across the narrow space.

She hated this place. She hated this life.

She yanked down the shooting star mobile hanging in her window, a stuffed white polyester star with silver strands. Her mom had made it for her in honor of getting her own room and had said, "Make your room a place where you can dream."

Her mom wouldn't know a dream if one slapped her upside the head, but at the time, Carrie had believed her. She also used to believe that her father would get sober.

Fat chance.

She knew now that he'd never stop drinking, but she also hated it when he wasn't home. Despite his addiction, Carrie felt he brought balance, or routine, to her home life. Well, at least when he wasn't binge drinking, which seemed to happen at least twice a year. Last time he came home from a runner, she asked him why he drank, but he just shook his head and said he didn't know.

Except during the binge weeks, he got up each morning at the same time and went to work every day. When Carrie woke up for school and trudged to the bathroom to shower, she could rely on him to be sitting at the kitchen table drinking his third cup of coffee before he headed to his dump truck. He always said good morning, sometimes with a desperate or needy ring to his voice, she thought. She always grunted in response because, despite her love of school, she wasn't a morning person. Every night, close to the same time, he'd park his work diesel behind the trailer. During the warmer months, he'd come in the house and grab his first beer and return outdoors, where he watered the only tree he'd ever planted. In the winter, he'd drink a six-pack of beer at the kitchen table and read crime magazines for hours. Monday through Friday he was predictable. On paydays and weekends, he wasn't. But five mornings a week for close to forty weeks a year, Carrie had routine thanks to him.

She was closer to him than she could ever remember feeling toward her mother, who liked to remind her she'd been the "nightmare newborn," crying nonstop and robbing her of any sleep. Carrie once read that the first three months of a child's life is the strongest period for bonding between a mother and baby. She guessed colic, or maybe bad luck and timing, had closed that window of opportunity for her and her mom.

Perhaps for the same reason but with opposite results, she'd once been close to her oldest brother, WJ.

According to her mother, who'd shove Carrie into his fourteen-year-old arms when he came home each night from his first job at the gas station, Carrie would stop crying and fall asleep as soon as he held her. Carrie suspected her slumber had less to do with WJ's care and more to do with the gasoline fumes permeating the fabric of his uniform. Details had never been her parents' strong point. Who knows how many brain cells she'd lost as a gas-huffing newborn.

Her dad, on the other hand, would sit with her and tell her stories about his life. She'd once been embarrassed that he was so much older than her friends' fathers, but his memories were worth it to her now. All his best tales were those from before he met her mom and moved to Nevada. Carrie liked to imagine her life would blossom once she moved away from Tiger Drive forever. Her dad gave her useful advice, and the fact that he didn't follow his advice lent legitimacy to his guidance. He was walking proof of the consequence of ignoring his own counsel.

She remembered the day they were sitting on the front porch, and between drags on his cigarette, he'd told her, "Assume you're an alcoholic. Play it safe. You've got my genes, both good and bad. Let's hope more of the good ones, but just in case, when you grow up, never drink alcohol when you're too happy, too sad, too mad, too worried, or need to make a decision."

She was seven at the time. "I don't get it."

Her dad had patted her back. "For now, you don't need to understand, just remember what I said when you get older."

Once she started junior high school and her friends began experimenting with alcohol, she understood.

She'd made the mistake of joining them once when she was fifteen. Her parents had split up. Again. Feeling worried had been an understatement. It was a Saturday and her friends, Samantha and Tammy, had sneaked two bottles of gin from their parents' stashes, and they'd all gotten plastered. She'd been in ninth grade at the time, and a few guys from school ended up joining them. That Guy, as she preferred to think of him, was there too. One minute she was laughing, eating chocolate chip cookies, and enjoying her first buzz, and the next . . . well, she couldn't remember. She recalled bits of being in a room with That Guy and crying about her messed-up life, and she sort of remembered him patting her back and repeating, "You're okay."

When she'd woken up the next day with a pounding headache and heaving stomach, Samantha and Tammy horrified her with a play-by-play of her first and final blackout.

"He came and got us when you started crying," Samantha said.

"Was I crying just a little, or a lot?"

Samantha handed her a mirror. "Bawling."

Carrie looked at her puffy face and eyes. "How long?"

"How long were you crying?" Tammy asked.

"No, how long was I alone with him?" She turned her back on them and lifted her shirt. Wait, this wasn't her shirt. Her bra was gone. She angled the mirror so she could see her full breasts. She closed her eyes and prayed, then opened them. No marks. She lifted the mirror and turned her chin from side to side. Her neck was clear too. No hickeys. She had slept in her jeans. She squeezed her legs together but felt no soreness. Thank goodness! She was still a virgin, and still *not* like her mom and sister.

"Not too long," Tammy said.

Carrie turned back to face them, blushing. "Long enough. Samantha, why am I wearing your shirt? Was I dressed when you found me? Or did you have to dress me?"

"Oh, you were dressed. Nothing happened. Believe us, we asked him. You're wearing my shirt because you had vomit on yours."

Carrie froze. "What?" She covered her face with her hands and groaned. "Please tell me I didn't throw up on him. And please tell me I didn't throw up in front of him."

Samantha scrunched up her face. "A little. He mostly got the tears. I got the vomit."

Her life was over. He'd tell everyone at school. "I don't even remember going into the room with him. Why did you let me?"

"We tried to stop you, but you got a little nasty with us."

"Great. I'm more than a drunk. I'm a mean one. Did I tell him anything?"

Tammy rubbed her shoulder. "Well . . ."

"Tell me."

"He said, 'She has a rough life.'"

Carrie's shoulders drooped, and she hung her head. "I'm never drinking again."

It was difficult enough to wrap her head around the fact that she'd gone to a room alone with That Guy to do Gawd Knew What when she hadn't so much as held a guy's hand before, much less that she'd disclosed horrible stories about her family while tears and snot ran down her face. Carrie trusted Samantha and Tammy to guard her secrets, but she had no idea what to expect from That Guy. Would she arrive at school on Monday and find out he'd told everyone that he'd tried to hook up with her and she'd been a sobbing drunk? How much had she confessed about her home life? At least he hadn't taken advantage of the situation from what she could tell. Maybe he was just a nice guy, or maybe she'd made it impossible to get her clothes off between her sobbing and vomiting. She felt so humiliated and exposed, though. Shame stunk. She couldn't believe that she'd done it, and to herself.

He singled her out at school on Monday.

"Carrie, can I talk to you?"

She wanted to bolt, but Samantha and Tammy pushed her toward him. She looked everywhere but at him and squeezed her books against her chest. "You don't have to say anything. I'm sorry. Sorrier than you know. Just please don't tell anyone what I said and stuff."

"I'm not going to. I wouldn't. I just wanted to make sure you're okay."

His voice enveloped her like a heavy down comforter on a cold night—its sheer weight inviting her to pull the warmth tight, bury her head in a cocoon of darkness, and welcome the concern she thought she heard.

For the first time, Carrie looked him in the eyes. They

were blue and full of concern and sadness. *No, not concern. Pity.* She didn't need his pity.

She stiffened and stood tall. "I know I told you a bunch of stuff about me, but don't think my alcohol-induced verbal diarrhea gives you any right to feel sorry for me." She turned and left before he could respond.

It had taken two uneventful weeks at school before she began to believe That Guy was keeping her blubbering to himself and wouldn't gossip with his buddies and the rest of the freshman class. She started forgiving herself and making the commitment to never, ever drink again, much less draw any attention to herself. She had to do everything she could to avoid turning out like her older brothers, sisters, and her parents, and to break the pattern for her little brothers. It was about this time she started keeping lists and wearing baggy clothes. List item number one came straight out of her dad's mouth: "Assume you're an alcoholic." She should have listened to him. He would know the dangers of drinking and making a fool of oneself.

Dos & Don'ts List:

- *Do assume you're an alcoholic, and don't drink when you're too happy, too sad, too mad, too worried, or need to make a decision. Better yet, don't drink. Period.*

Now, three years later, she still refused to drink, and her dad hadn't been home for a week. Carrie was babysitting across the street the morning her mother kicked him out, and although Carrie wasn't certain what had happened between her parents this time, she assumed from experience that alcohol and money were involved. She'd asked Justin and Tommy, but they went on and on about Superman and donuts. None of it made sense to her. Her mom wouldn't tell her, and she couldn't reach her dad at the place he rented whenever he split up with her mom for a week here and there. Too bad they wouldn't stay apart. It was the back and forth, the breakups and makeups, that exhausted Carrie.

She'd been in the fourth grade when she first confronted her parents. "You're always making up when you should be breaking up." They laughed and said something stupid about how clever she could be. She glared at them. "It's not funny." She thought they could all have a chance at happiness if her parents would divorce, but her mom and dad often said they stayed together for the kids, which made her feel horrible for all of them.

Carrie wished she had a normal family with loving parents. She once told this to her oldest brother, WJ. He'd said, "If you could wish in one hand and shit in the other, which do you think would fill up faster?" The realist in her accepted that though he was crude, he wasn't wrong.

Now Carrie swiped her fingers below her eyes. *Tears are for quitters. Don't be a quitter.*

She sat down on her bed and leaned over to pick up the mobile from the floor, running the soft, silver ribbons across her palm. She rehung it and let it sway back and forth.

She'd rather be a dreamer than a realist, though.

She took long, slow breaths, counting to ten. She thought about her lists. She liked to keep lists of Dos & Don'ts, Worries, and Goals. Expanding or even reading the lists calmed her and gave her hope. Her mother and Lisa liked to tease her.

"Go write a crazy list, Carrie."

"Go read your anal lists, Carrie."

"Add me to your complaint list then, Carrie."

They didn't understand the lists were her roadmaps to a different life. Each list was a reminder of how to differentiate herself from her family, their failings, and their depressing lives. As far as she was concerned, her mother and sister should take a page from her book and start writing lists of their own. They could use a dozen, more like one hundred. Outside of the lists, Carrie knew an education was her one-way ticket away from Tiger Drive.

She reached for her Word of the Day calendar:

anneal \ə'nēl\ *vb 1 : To make (glass, steel) less brittle by heating then cooling 2 : Strengthen, toughen*

Some days she felt as fragile as glass and other days stronger than steel. She'd rather feel like rubber—letting everything bounce off her, or rolling with changes and rebounding with abandon. On the days she felt vulnerable, like she was the sole person at her pity party worrying about everything under the sun, she imagined what it would feel like to be one of her friends, able to anticipate her future at college all the while obsessing about makeup, clothes, guys, dating, and prom. Not obsessing about the future of her little brothers or feeling the weight of being their only promising example.

She just needed a chance to live her life the way she wanted to, and for a scholarship committee to pull her name out of a crowd of applicants. But so far, she'd had no luck.

If she entertained her worst-case scenario of not being able to afford college, or if she contemplated a single day of her little brothers' lives once she deserted them for the first year of school to move to Reno, she would implode into one million sharp-edged shards of glass, tearing apart everything in reach. It would be too late for her to "anneal."

Her backpack sat on the end of her bed. Carrie removed her textbooks and binders and rifled through her notebook, pulling out the guidelines for the scholarship essay her English teacher, Mr. Hill, had given her: *Review your parents' bookshelf. Identify a common theme of the books there. In one thousand words or less, demonstrate how this theme is, or is not, reflected in your life.*

Carrie thought of a few books off the top of her head that she'd seen her parents read. She didn't think the scholarship committee would be impressed; she sure wasn't.

The Rotary Scholarship was the largest of the scholarships she'd applied for and would pay for the majority of her tuition at the University of Nevada, Reno. It was also the last one up for grabs. She'd been accepted for UNR's fall semester, but it was already April. She'd hoped she would win a scholarship from the university itself. The application deadline was back in February, and some of her classmates had already received award letters in the mail.

Carrie preferred speaking to Mr. Hill, rather than the school counselor, about her funding concerns. He'd once kept her after class and told her his father was an "alcoholic too." She was never quite sure how he knew about her dad, and she didn't ask. She wondered if one day she might intuit if a person loved an alcoholic parent or family member.

Mr. Hill had offered to proof her essay for the Rotary Scholarship, and he'd advised her to be candid and write about her family and circumstances. He also recommended that she open up more in the interviews.

If Mr. Hill was correct, and if the sordid details of her family life were to be the best content, then the themed essay would be a slam dunk for the award. Short of pretending her parents were illiterate, or faking a reading list for the scholarship essay, she'd be sharing personal insights with the scholarship committee for sure. But only some. She couldn't share all the details about her family. She lived in constant fear that Child Protective Services would take Justin and Tommy away. Besides, she'd been raised and ordered by her parents to never share family secrets, and WJ's recent choices pretty much demanded censorship.

Carrie grabbed her notebook and headed toward her parents' room. She'd have to cross the living room, which meant dealing with Lisa again, but if things worked out the way she hoped, she wouldn't be dealing with Lisa in five months. She'd be moving into a dorm.

Lisa sat on the couch, eating a bowl of ice cream and watching *Urban Cowboy*.

Carrie wrinkled her nose. "How can you watch that movie over and over? Don't you get enough of that story at home?"

Lisa didn't take her eyes off of the television. "What do you mean? They're soul mates, and they can two-step."

Carrie snorted. She pointed at John Travolta and Debra Winger. "They live in a trailer—check. They get drunk—um, check. They lie and beat each other up—check, check."

"Be quiet." Lisa shoveled another spoonful of ice cream into her mouth.

"You should be a better role model for the boys and me.

You're a legal adult living at home and watching the same movie over and over. Gawd, do something with your life. I can't wait to get out of here."

Lisa groaned, walked over to the television, and turned the volume up.

"Hey," Carrie raised her voice over the volume, "it's your life! Become a loser like everyone else in this family, but don't come knocking on my door in ten years asking for handouts!"

"Shut up," Lisa said. "I'm going to move in with Charlie soon. So there. Add me to one of your crazy lists if you want. Or better yet, add 'Stop being a know-it-all' to one."

"That's your aspiration? Shacking up with a guy? I'll add 'Don't move in with a guy when you're nineteen.' It might be the best tip you've ever given me."

She left Lisa to her stupid movie and stomped into the kitchen where the sink was overflowing with dishes. After cleaning up the mess, she scratched her chore off the list that was hanging on the freezer door and held in place by two alphabet magnets. A chores list was the only list her mom ever kept, and certainly her single expectation. Her mother sure knew how to help her children aim high. Carrie picked up her notebook and headed to her parents' room, which was located on the far side of the trailer, past the laundry closet overflowing with clothes, and at the end of the hallway.

"Lisa," Carrie shouted, "you'd better get started on the laundry. It's your chore!"

Her parents' bedroom door was closed out of necessity. The top hinge was broken, and the brown composite wood hung an inch from the doorframe. A hole had been kicked through the bottom. She lifted the door up by the knob, used her weight to push it open, and leaned it against the wall.

Four plywood planks and six cinder blocks served as a bookshelf between two twin beds. Carrie was glad she'd been babysitting the night her dad came home to see his marital bed had been swapped.

Her parents' closet door was open, and she rolled her eyes. Was it so hard for them to do the right thing and keep the dang thing closed? Carrie knew her parents kept a gun on the top shelf of their closet. She didn't think the boys knew about it, and she'd like to keep it that way. Too many times she'd heard of young kids killing themselves with their parents' gun after mistaking it for a toy. Sure, her parents had told them they weren't allowed in their bedroom, but still, they should just keep it closed to be safe. She slid the plywood door closed for everyone's sake and returned to her task.

Two of the bookshelves were cluttered with unopened bills and paperwork. Carrie recognized the envelope for the Federal Pell Grant application she had asked her parents to complete two months before. She kept finding it and would hand it to her mother, who would just stash it in another to-never-do pile somewhere else in the house. She pulled it out and was disappointed, but not surprised, to see it remained blank. She placed it on top. When the counselor asked her this week about the status, and he would, she'd have to tell him the truth; her parents were too lazy to complete it. Or even better, she could say, "Sorry, my mom was too busy at karaoke, and my dad was drunk." She wouldn't, though. She'd have to find a way to persuade them to complete it and make another excuse for them with the counselor for the time being.

Carrie looked at the minimal book collection on the remaining two shelves. She recognized her mother's books and slid the tips of her fingers across the spines: *Gone with the Wind*, *The Clan of the Cave Bear*, *Jane Eyre*, *King James Bible*, *The Mists of Avalon*, and *The Thorn Birds*.

The old copy of *Jane Eyre* had a library index label affixed to the spine. Carrie opened it, and the inside flap showed the book belonged to a library in Lincoln County, Minnesota, and was due in April of 1959.

Nice. Her mom was a book thief.

Except for *Jane Eyre* and the Bible, Carrie read the back covers and jotted in her notebook:

Martyrs; strong women who end up lied to, haunted, widowed, or deserted; Mr. Rochester loses his eyesight and is completely reliant upon Jane (has a secret wife in the attic); Jesus Christ is crucified, and Mary doesn't leave his side; Priest falls in love with a little girl, and Irish Catholic husband beats his wife. Women struggle for power. Theme: Men leave, die, are arrogant, abusive and controlling, crippled, or perverted. And family secrets!

She moved on to the next shelf: *Ted Bundy: The Killer Next Door*, *Nevada Ghost Towns and Mining Camps*, *Twelve Angry Men*, *To Kill a Mockingbird*, and *True Crime* magazines. Carrie took a deep breath and released it. At least he didn't have *The Catcher in the Rye*. Boy, the scholarship committee was in for a real treat.

Dad: death, desperation, deception, justice/injustice, mysteries.

A streetlight kicked on, spilling light through the bedroom

window. Carrie hadn't heard the boys return home. Tommy and Justin knew the house rule: be home before the streetlights came on. She closed her notebook and left her parents' room. Lisa hadn't budged.

"We need to look for Tommy and Justin."

"The movie is almost over."

"Lisa."

"Fine, fine. I'll call around to the other houses."

"I'll walk through the park. I'll take Star." Carrie grabbed a sweater and pushed open the back door. "Star," she called. "Come here." But the little terrier didn't respond with a bark or an appearance. She clapped her hands together. "Star, where are you?"

Carrie stuck her head back in the trailer. "Have you seen Star?" she asked Lisa.

"The boys probably have her."

Carrie turned on the porch light and closed the door. The evening chill of the desert was settling in, and she shivered. The raised porch allowed her to see over the slatted fence; no sign of the boys. She walked toward the backyard and the empty playhouse her dad had thrown together with scraps of wood and metal he had pulled from the landfill.

Carrie walked around the trailers, pausing at the mailbox in front to see if she had any mail, but again, no scholarship letters.

She heard the creaking of a large vehicle as it slowed and rolled over one of the yellow speed bumps. The truck belonged to her neighbor across the drive. Barry and his wife, Dot, had three kids, and Carrie often babysat for them. Barry's trailer was one of the nicer homes in the park. Carrie liked that he kept his stairs painted. She made a mental note to add "Keep stairs painted" to a dream house list.

Barry pulled his truck into his parking space. He climbed out with a bucket of fried chicken in his arms.

"Hey, Barry."

"Hey there, little missy," Barry drawled, impersonating John Wayne. If his arms were empty, Carrie knew he would put one hand on the truck cab and angle his hips, mimicking The Duke's stance. Barry's pride and joy was his self-recorded VHS collection of John Wayne movies. She knew because when VCRs came on the market, Barry had stayed home three weekends in a row to record every Western on television, and he hadn't needed her to babysit.

"I'm looking for my brothers. Did you see them while you were driving in?" Carrie asked.

"Some kids are playing around Lot Nineteen."

"Thanks."

Carrie walked down the drive and followed the shouts of, "Tag, you're it."

"Tommy? Justin? Are you there?"

"They're not here."

"Jody?" Carrie used to babysit Jody and her sisters, but now that Jody was twelve, her single mother left them alone while she was working. "Have you seen them?"

"They went out to the fields," Jody said.

Ugh. The sagebrush-covered fields stretched for miles. If her brothers were still out there at this time of night, they could get lost. "Did they have the dog with them?" Star might get them home in one piece.

"Yeah," Jody said, "but they said they were taking her home because she doesn't like the gun." Jody gasped and covered her lips. "I wasn't supposed to tell."

"Gun? Did you see it?"

"Yes."

Carrie turned and ran home as fast as she could. She dashed up the back steps, through the back door, and shoved open her parents' bedroom door.

"Lisa!"

Carrie went to the closet, pushed it open, and patted her hand across the top shelf, feeling for the steel ammunition box. Why hadn't she made sure the boys didn't know about the gun? Or why hadn't they all taught them to be afraid of guns?

Epic failure as a big sister.

She inched the box forward with the tips of her fingers until she could grab it. She set it on one of the twin beds, snapped the box's green levers, and yanked it open.

"Thank Gawd." Carrie sat on the bed and dropped her chin to her chest.

"What's going on?" Lisa came into the room.

"Never mind. Jody told me the boys went to the field with a gun. But it's here." She patted the open Army-issue box. "It's right here."

"Oh no," Lisa said.

"What?"

"There were two. Dad brought another one home a few weeks ago."

They ran to the phone. Carrie grabbed it and dialed the Creek Bar. "Pick up the phone. Pick up the phone." It rang several times. Carrie disconnected and punched in the number for the manager at her dad's motel.

His landlady answered. "Yeah?"

Carrie thought she sounded drunk. "Can you get Harry Sloan in Number Twenty-Two for me?"

"This isn't an answering service."

"It's urgent," Carrie said.

The line went dead.

Carrie stared at the receiver. "You awful woman!" She thought for a second. "We have to call the police."

"We can't," Lisa said, taking the phone. "If we call the cops and tell them little boys are missing and have a gun, CPS might take them."

"Tommy and Justin could be hurt. They could be lost in the dark with a gun."

"Let's call WJ. He can go by Dad's. Maybe Dad took the gun with him, and we're worrying about nothing," Lisa said.

"They'll just fight. WJ can't know about the restraining order." As far as Carrie was concerned, WJ had become useless as an older brother, but she didn't want CPS involved. Was Lisa right that they would take her brothers away? Take her away since she wasn't an adult? Could this interfere with her scholarship? Could they all be put in the orphanage on Fifth Street? There were too many unknowns!

"Do you want to try to do something about it, or not?" Lisa asked.

"Anneal," Carrie said. "Strengthen or toughen glass or steel by heating and then cooling."

"Carrie." Lisa tapped the receiver against Carrie's forehead.

Carrie yanked her head back and bit her fingernail. She chewed until the skin turned pink and started to bleed. "Call him. But if he doesn't answer, I have to call the cops."

4

WJ

All kids are me frens.
—Popeye

WJ stood before his open bathroom door, which had a full-length mirror mounted on the inside. Every damn space in the thirty-foot RV served a dual purpose, and he hated each claustrophobic inch of it. Past his reflection, he could see Shelly's bare foot shaking and bumping against the green microfiber sofa where she'd fallen when he slapped her.

When he first started dating her three years ago, he'd promised himself he'd never treat a woman the way his dad did, but Shelly hadn't given him a damn choice today. He was as pissed off at her for forcing his hand as he was sorry for having to teach her a lesson. He could feel her hurt and anger in the air, crackling with the tension of unspoken apologies, and he didn't want her to pack up her clothes and leave him alone. Straight men had girlfriends. Gay guys didn't. He needed her to stay for the sake of appearances.

He should turn on his charm and make her laugh like he used to.

"Hey, Shelly. You know what the ladies say about Wranglers, don't you? 'Wrangler butts make me nuts.'" He wiggled his butt. "Does my butt make you nuts?"

But instead of laughing, she groaned and mumbled under her breath.

"Huh?" he asked. He moved her foot aside and sat down beside her on the narrow cushion to pull on his black steel toe boots. He stomped his feet until his boots were on tight, shaking the entire trailer. He glanced at her face and cringed. Dammit, he'd hit her harder than he wanted.

Shelly pressed her fingertips to her cheekbone and her swollen lip and then showed him the blood. "Why'd you do that? You've never hit me before."

He looked away, down at her paint-chipped toenails, and patted her ankle. "Don't talk if it hurts." He went to the kitchen and returned with ice cubes wrapped in a dishtowel. "Put this on your face." He frowned and pointed at her. "You asked for it, and I could have done a lot worse."

He opened a small drawer and pulled out one of several black-and-white bandanas, which had been folded into two-inch-wide bands. He'd started wearing bandanas after seeing the leader of the Hells Angels wearing one on the news. The guy looked like no one would ever fuck with him, and WJ had been tired of being fucked with. After parting his dishwater-blond hair down the center, he tied the bandana around his forehead and pulled his shoulder-length hair forward until it covered his ears. "Are my ears covered, hon?" He hated his big ears. When he was little, kids at school had called him Dumbo. He should have grown his hair out a long time ago.

Shelly nodded and looked away.

Leaning over her, WJ caressed the ball of her chin between his thumb and index finger and turned her to face him.

"You could've avoided all of this. Do you think I want to be in this position? It hurt me more than it hurt you."

"But the guy bought me a drink without asking."

"Then you should've sent it back. He told the bartender to 'give that faggot's girlfriend a drink.' And you took the drink." He worked so fucking hard to make sure no one could tell he was gay. Shit, sure the guy was guessing or just trying to push buttons, but if his own girlfriend didn't shut that shit down, then what? He'd become a laughing-stock. His gang would kick him out, and he'd have to watch his own back and defend himself. He'd be fucking alone again.

"But you're not a queer! What do you care if it's not true? Way you're reacting I'm beginning to wonder." Shelly spat at him and then cowered as WJ's eyes darkened.

Why the hell did she have to push him like this when he still had adrenaline rushing through his blood? He slid his fingers from her chin to both sides of her jaw and rubbed Shelly's head into the bench until she cried out.

"Is this man enough for you?"

The veins running from his elbow to his wrist thickened and bulged, and the tattoo on his forearm moved with each pump of blood. His original tat had been a naked voluptuous woman with long dark hair leaning against an anchor, but he'd had the tattoo altered one year ago to cover her head with a knight's helmet. The woman's hair poured from beneath the armor. A buzzard, twice her size, now perched on her bare shoulder, its talons indenting, but not puncturing, her skin. But the woman didn't buckle under the weight of the large beast, and instead, a strand of her hair tethered the bird's ankle, holding him in place.

WJ shoved himself away from Shelly, grabbed his leather belt, and swung it against the wall. The whip-like sound released some of his anger. He counted to ten before sliding the belt through the loops of his jeans until the gold rodeo-sized buckle engraved with the name "Buzzard" was centered above his crotch.

Shelly sobbed. "He was just a stupid, drunk kid turning twenty-one and showing off in front of his stupid friends. He didn't know who you are. Whichever kiss ass told you is the one you should be taking your anger out on, not me."

"Damn it, Shelly!" He kicked the bathroom door closed. "That's the fucking problem. He disrespected me in front of people who do know me. And those people respect me for not taking any shit from anyone. By disrespecting me, he is disrespecting my club, and they expect me to do something about it, and if I don't, then I look like a fucking coward. Do you think I want to beat up the little asshole like my dad used to beat me? What he gets is your fault, but you know what? He's lucky. He's lucky it was me that he insulted. It's best he learns now that he shouldn't shoot his mouth off like that, or he will get himself killed before he turns twenty-two."

"You shouldn't have friends who like you for those reasons. Why do you stay with the Right Knights? You don't need them. I swear they're cannibals, eating you from the inside out. Sometimes I don't recognize you anymore."

He'd never told Shelly how he used to have to fight for his life every fucking day or how alone he'd felt before Bender and the Knights walked into his life. "You don't get it," he said. "They saved me."

"Bullshit," she said.

That was the problem with Shelly—she needed everything fucking spelled out.

"Like I said, you don't get it." And he hoped she never would. When he'd met Bender and the Knights the first time, he'd been sitting in Mable's Bar waiting for his usual drink after work. A man had started a fight with him, something that happened to WJ so regularly he was used to standing up for himself. He liked to think jerks singled him out because of the stench of his uniform after a long day's work across the street at the sanitation company, but he figured most of them had some sixth sense and knew he liked men as much as women, so they wanted to punish him for it like his dad used to, and like the Navy did when they kicked him out. WJ had taken the larger man outside for a bare-knuckled fight and won. He had nothing to lose except future trouble from the guy. His number one rule in life was *show no fear*. When he'd returned to the bar, the five guys in leather jackets with patches approached him and ordered him a shot.

The apparent leader spoke first. "Bender's my name."

WJ turned in his stool to nod at Bender.

"In the past week, I've seen you get in more fights than any guy I've ever laid eyes on. You're a magnet for assholes." Bender chuckled and shook his head.

WJ knew they were some kind of gang with their bikes parked out front, but they had never intimidated him. WJ's second motto was *don't mess with me, and I won't mess with you*. He figured they felt the same.

But he couldn't lie. He'd watched them. Nobody ever messed with them. They came in as one, and they left as one. Hell, he bet they fought as one. Once upon a time, WJ had believed joining the Navy would create that community, that sense of belonging for him. If it had, he sure as shit wouldn't be sitting here now.

Bender eyed WJ's buzz cut. "Buzzard, if you're tired of dealing with assholes on your own, follow me."

WJ glared at him and ran his palm over his head. "If you make fun of my hair again, I'll take you all outside and kick all your asses."

Bender laughed and slapped his back. "Relax man. Buzzards are survivors. You're a survivor. Know a good thing when you see it. Come on." He turned and walked out the door with his cronies.

WJ had never had someone give him a nickname he liked before. A few seconds later, he followed them out the door, and he'd never looked back. He hadn't been in a one-on-one fight since. For once, he had people that not only cared about him; they protected him. And if that meant doing things he'd never imagined, it was worth it. Things like hitting Shelly. Things like punishing a fool turning twenty-one, and who was stupid enough to call him a faggot and hit on his girl.

He peered at the bookshelf hanging above Shelly and ran his finger along the seams of the *Popeye* comic books resting between two bookends. He straightened one that was sitting cockeyed until it was aligned with the rest of the hundred-fold collection. Popeye had never taken shit from anybody. "You're kind of like Olive Oyl, Shelly. Pitting men against each other to get what you want."

"Then who does that make you? Bluto or Popeye?" she asked, smoothing an ice cube across her cheek.

"Who do you think?"

"Bluto."

"Hmm." She was wrong. He was Popeye, and he dealt justice for the Right Knights the one way he knew how, the one way that had worked for him and for Popeye—with his fists. He pressed his palm across the top of the books and then along the bindings until they were flush against the wall and shelf. When he was satisfied the bookends were snug, he took a step back and surveyed his work.

The phone rang.

"You're lucky I still want to be with you." He grabbed the phone and stretched the cord until he reached the scarred nightstand, littered with beer cans and overflowing ashtrays.

"Hello?"

"It's me," Lisa said.

WJ took a deep breath to switch mental gears. "Hey, sis."

"We can't find the boys, and we think they have a gun. Do you know where Mom and Dad's second gun is?"

His heart skipped a beat. No, he didn't. He didn't even know they had two guns. WJ clenched his jaw and frowned but gentled his tone. "Slow down. Don't ever ask me something like that on the phone. When did you last see the boys?" WJ pushed the trash around on the nightstand and grabbed his money clip and switchblade.

"I don't know. I was watching *Urban Cowboy*," she said.

WJ liked that movie too. "Where's Mom?" he asked.

"Karaoke," Lisa said.

"Where's Dad?" WJ assumed Lisa's silence meant Harry was drunk and useless somewhere as usual. "Who else have you told?"

"No one, but Carrie wants to call the police."

WJ rolled his eyes and swore. Two lost boys who might have a gun and a younger sister who thought cops were the good guys were the last things he wanted to handle right now. "Tell Carrie to calm down and hold her horses. I'm heading into town and will find them." He let go of the receiver, and it bounced across the trailer and landed on the floor beneath the phone's cradle.

In a single stride, he reached his dresser and removed a mirror and a bag of crank. "Hello, Beautiful."

WJ understood his customers. He knew what he sold and why they wanted it. Crank—a methamphetamine—made people feel unbeatable. But, whereas WJ knew to limit himself, his customers couldn't help but overdo the shit. Most of his customers were impatient and greedy. They had their fucked-up junkie pride, thinking crank made them more hard core than people who drank, used cocaine, or smoked pot; they thought crank made them real people. They'd pay anything for the rush of happiness, fearlessness, and world-rocking invincibility, but too much of the shit, and crank could make anyone psychotic and toss them in a tinkering, paranoid, and perverted state of mind for hours. Crank wasn't a love drug, and he did his best to not sell it to parents. If any of his clients were raising kids, he didn't know about it. A crank whore would sell her kids for the shit if she wanted it bad enough, and he wanted no fucking part of that.

Even with the best quality, too much crank made him want to crawl out of his skin or chew off the inside of his cheeks until they were raw and his gums abscessed. With-drawals were a bitch, ten times worse than coming off of cocaine. Yeah, crank was coke's dirty fucking cousin. He'd give his clients a taste of cocaine if he thought they'd be able to afford it, but the stupid addicts didn't know how to pace themselves, and they left him no choice but to sell them cheaper shit so they could buy more and stay higher longer, which meant there was no use in keeping coke around, not even for himself. But if they could pay, WJ would play. It was all money in his pocket. He'd told Bender crank was the future of the gang, and he'd been right. Junkies couldn't get enough of it, and they always found a way to afford it. He was turning Corbett City into the crank capital per capita in the US. It earned him the favor of the Right Knights leader.

As far as WJ was concerned, the recognition was overdue. He'd been a prospect for the club, gophering all their necessary dirty work for two years before Bender made him a full-fledged member and patched him in. He refused to ride a motorcycle, but Bender had made an exception for him because certain duties just couldn't be taken care of on a bike. Jobs like ditching a stolen car or removing a scumbag's body. Now he had prospects of his own to send on shit errands and deals, or take along with him if extra fists were needed in certain relations or if someone had disrespected his crew. He'd earned his patch the hard way, and he was a bona fide Knight.

The club was growing, and if they played their cards right, the Hells Angels or a larger gang might absorb them and welcome them into the family some day. Even if Bender didn't care to merge, this was WJ's secret goal. He'd be set nationwide. Screw Corbett City. Fuck that hellhole RV. No one would trouble him again in the United Fucking States of America unless they wanted an entire family rat packing their ass in return. He'd once heard that if you did a Hells Angel a favor, they'd give you a card you could show anyone—even the police—and you'd be trouble-free and back on your merry way. That's what he wanted to be a part of—the don't-fuck-with-me-or-the-people-I-care-about club.

He tapped the clear baggie and created a small mound, nudging it into two lines. Holding his right nostril, he leaned down and snorted the first row. He shot back to a sitting position, and his head dropped back on his neck. "Hell, yeah."

He leaned forward and finished the second line, squinted, and squeezed the bridge of his nose until the burning sensation passed. The reason he was so good at dealing was because he knew how strong crank made a person feel—like a person who had life by the balls and not the other way around. When he was high, he felt safe because he could be the bad guy. The don't-mess-with-me-or-you'll-regret-it guy.

After he returned his stash to the drawer and closed the combination lock, he shrugged on his leather jacket. "Don't leave this trailer tonight, Shelly." He pushed open the front door and paused. "We can't fight no more. Okay?"

She didn't return his stare, but she nodded.

He jumped to the ground since the broken, aluminum doorstep hung to one side. The desert sand billowed around his boots and settled in the dog's water bowl.

"Hi, WJ," Billy, the teenage boy, called from across the narrow dirt road. A porch light cut through the dusk and illuminated him sitting on an upended milk crate, twirling a piece of curly hair around his finger. Behind him, a television flashed through a small trailer window.

WJ walked toward him and tossed his keys from one hand to the other. He grimaced at the boy's tight purple shirt and red-painted nails. "Shit, kid. You know dressing like that makes you a target, right? Not saying you're wrong, but you're asking for trouble. Your old man causing problems?"

He smiled. "Nope."

"Good. Have you eaten today?"

Billy shrugged his shoulders. "I'm okay."

WJ pulled out his wallet and handed him a twenty-dollar bill. "Walk to the market for me and get yourself some dinner. If they have the new *Popeye* comic, pick it up for me. But be real careful with it like always, okay?"

"Thanks, WJ. I will. I promise."

"Get going." WJ waited until the boy was halfway down the dirt road before yanking on the door to the boy's trailer.

"Are you in there, you piece of shit? The kid looks good, but you're not off the hook. My promise is still good. I will crush every bone in your hands if you touch him again. And don't think for a fucking minute I won't know if you do."

He slammed the door shut, and the trailer shook. He wound his way through the piles of auto parts and metal scraps and hopped into his shiny red pickup. The engine turned over, and he drove away from the junkyard.

He was in for a long night. Between teaching a lesson to a twenty-one-year-old fool and paying a visit to a dealer who'd been too stupid to pay his debt to Bender and had raised suspicions in the club that he was a narc, sometimes WJ felt like a fucking babysitter. But first he had two small boys to find before Goody Two-shoes Carrie called the cops. And if his brothers were hurt, if they had so much as a scratch on them, someone was going to pay.

5

JANICE

I can't miss a night's work and let my public down.
—Patsy Cline

D o, Re, Mi, Fa, Sol, La, Ti, Do." Janice sang as she turned into the Creek Bar.

Holy cow! It was early, but the parking lot was filled to capacity.

Thank the Lord. A full house just had to be a sign that she was meant to win tonight and follow her dreams.

She pulled around to the back of the building and parked. She pulled a can of Aqua Net out of her purse and retouched her hair. She was convinced volume complimented her profile, hiding her detested wrinkles and drooping chin. The fragrance of the hairspray comforted and excited her, as did the anticipated smells of perfume, bar smoke, and stale beer. She could imagine the heat of the stage lamps warming her face and shoulders as a cloak of glittering light floated through the air on dust particles and surrounded her, mesmerizing her audience. Pure heaven—

that's what being on stage felt like. A piece of heaven all to herself.

Customers seldom used the rear entrance, but her friend Scotty—who owned the place—always kept an employee at the door. Janice liked to pretend the back door was a secret entrance reserved for the star of the show—for her—as a necessary precaution against overzealous fans eager for her performance. Someday soon, she thought. Someday this would be true, and maybe even one day she'd perform at the Grand Ole Opry.

"Hi, Pete," Janice said to the bouncer as she approached the door.

He grunted as she passed by.

Inside, the soles of her cowboy boots peeled away from the sticky concrete floor. She made her way to the mahogany bar and dropped her bag on a vinyl stool.

"Scotch me, Scotty."

"Coming right up, Lady J." Scotty poured her two splashes of top shelf, tossed her a napkin, and handed her a drink. "Liquid bravery for you."

Bravery. Shoot. She had loads of it on her own.

She hooked a boot on the brass footrest and stared past his shoulder at the gilt mirror reflecting bottle labels and the larger-than-usual hazy outline of a crowd behind her. "What's the occasion? Not that I mind. The more the merrier."

"Take a closer look. It's a different crowd. Maybe you should take a break tonight?"

Scotty's tone rankled her nerves. Was he suggesting she shouldn't sing tonight because there were more people? That she had competition? Jerk had a lot of nerve. No way, nohow. She was too close to quitting this stupid town to become a wallflower now.

"Don't be an ass. Why would I skip a performance?"

He raised a brow and pointed behind her. "Like I said, it's a different crowd than you're used to."

She sipped her drink and looked over her shoulder. Several tables were pulled together in the center of the room, and more than a dozen twentysomethings were pooled together. Young, that's what was different from the usual crowd. Young and carefree, not serious or desperate like she was. For the first time that night, her faith in her destiny took a little hit—what if tonight wasn't her last night? She turned back to Scotty.

"Where did they come from?"

"The community college. Maybe my place is the new hot spot. Can't say I mind. They drink a lot and tip better than any of my regulars."

Janice turned on her barstool for a second look. Two girls were looking through the songbook and talking to the karaoke DJ. One girl had pouty lips and blond hair that hung past her bare shoulders. Even from a distance, Janice could tell her young skin was smooth and even-toned above her tank top. Three inches of a flat, tan abdomen showed above her jeans. Years ago, Janice had been prettier than the girl. Back then was when she should have become a country singer, not now when she was two years shy of fifty. But at the time, she hadn't known she was making the wrong choices. If she could talk to her younger self, she'd have a hell of a lot to warn her about.

Facing the bar, she ran her fingers over the creases surrounding her lips and adjusted her vest to cover her stomach. "Hope you carded them. They don't look a day older than my daughters."

Scotty frowned at her. "They're legal, and they aren't going anywhere."

"Do they know about the karaoke contest? About the money pot?" Dear God, please don't let them know about the contest. Not tonight. Not when she was so frigging close.

He nodded. "They've been practicing all week."

"That's bullshit!"

"Cool it," he said and filled her scotch glass with water.

Scotty was one of her only friends, and dammit, he knew this wasn't fair. And diluting her scotch—the one frigging drink she'd have all night like she was someone who couldn't control her liquor—added insult to the injustice of her life. She couldn't handle waiting another week, another contest, to at least know she could leave when she wanted.

"You can't include them. They can't just show up here one night and compete. Money doesn't mean anything to them. I've been working so hard—"

"Lower your voice," he said as people started to look their way.

"You wouldn't even have karaoke if it weren't for me telling you about it. No other bar in Corbett City has karaoke yet, and the contest was my idea too. The winner is supposed to be the best singer by popular vote. They'll just vote for each other like this is some stupid high school pageant, not based on talent. This is my gig. My night. My place. My fans."

"Fans . . . right. I'll tell you what—you can pick the order of your songs. Go before them, between them, after them, or over them. I don't care."

High-pitched giggles came from behind her. If their voices were as annoying as their laughter, the newbies would never win over her regulars. Time for her to suck it up and accept that they weren't going anywhere, so she might as well use her experience to her advantage. "I want to know what songs they sign up for too."

Scotty chuckled.

Like she was joking. "I'm dead serious."

"That's what's so funny," he said. "If it's that important to you, fine." He called for the DJ and gave him instructions to show Janice the playlist when she was ready.

The little creep rolled his eyes at her, but Scotty was the boss, so the dork could roll his eyes until they fell out of his head as far as she was concerned. As long as she could pick her slots, she didn't give a fig what the DJ thought of her. He didn't get to vote.

When they were alone again, Scotty asked, "What are you saving the money for anyway?"

She took a deep breath and a long sip of her drink. Scotty was holding a couple thousand dollars in contest winnings for her. Her money, not Harry's. Her karaoke stash. Her drunk of a husband wouldn't lay a finger on it, not here. If she confided in Scotty about her goals, would he help her out and forbid the newcomers from competing? No, she didn't think so. She couldn't believe she was so close to having enough money, and now she had to deal with a bunch of amateurs. She shook her head and remained silent.

"And how long are you going to continue to have those Sunday newspapers delivered to the bar?" he asked.

Why was he so nosy all of a sudden?

"It's none of your business. I told you that up front when I asked for your help. And if you think holding on to my savings and getting the papers for me makes it your business, then I'll find someone else to help me."

He groaned. "I don't mind helping you. I'm just curious."

He grabbed a towel, threw it over his shoulder, and leaned over to wash some glasses behind the bar. "I worry about you. You've been coming here a long time. A very long time. But times are changing. We're going to keep getting older, and newcomers," he nodded toward the crowd, "are going to keep getting younger."

"Spare me your sappy bartender wisdom. You're just another man, and those are more kids trying to get in my way."

"Hmph. It's what we're getting in the way of that has me curious." Scotty finished the dishes and tossed the dirty towel to the corner. "Speaking of which, where is Harry? Haven't seen him all week. He busts out of here a week ago Friday, all in a rush after some call on the bar phone, then nothing. Is he coming in tonight to hear you sing?"

"No." Janice stared at Scotty. "Not unless he wants to get arrested."

Scotty sighed. "I'll let Pete and the other bouncers know." He leaned his elbows on the counter. "It's too bad. You two used to have a lot of fun together."

She looked away from his penetrating stare. "Yeah, well, tell that to his fist."

"And now here's Janice, singing 'Crazy' by Patsy Cline."

Janice jumped onto the stage and cued the DJ. She'd decided to do a song now, while everyone was sober, and her second song later, after one of the girls sang "Like a Prayer" by Madonna. The nitwit didn't stand a chance—the regulars hated Madonna. She inhaled the scents of acidic cigarette smoke, body sweat, beer, and fried foods. She shook her hair and lifted her face to the warm lights.

"Testing. One, two, three."

A female in the audience repeated, "'Testing. One, two, three.' Nice outfit."

Little college twat didn't know squat and wouldn't recognize talent if it slapped her upside the head—something Janice might be willing to do before the night was over.

A deep voice shouted back, "Shut the hell up, or leave."

Janice smiled. *Take that, twat.* When the first chord played, Janice felt a shift in the room's energy.

The old-timers hooted and clapped.

The music vibrated the raised platform, pulsating through Janice's toes, up her legs, and to her pelvis.

Damn, she felt alive again.

Here. Now. Only she existed. Her heart throbbed, and she could swear she felt her blood flowing. She closed her eyes and began to sway from side to side. Janice imagined she was dressed like Patsy Cline: an emerald-green scarf tied around her neck, a button-down white blouse with a high collar, a wide belt, and a bell skirt. And then she sang her frigging heart out.

6

HARRY

Your best days are ahead of you.
—Sobriety meeting

H arry would never remember how he ended up meeting pawnshop owner Andrew Holt down at the river a week ago and beating him to a bloody pulp, but not remembering didn't change the truth. Over the last week, bits and pieces of the struggle had come back to him. The local news station and newspaper had kept him up to date on the man's condition and the investigation. "Key evidence" had been found at the scene. If he knew what the evidence was, he might remember more. Not like he could call and ask, though, and he wasn't going to confess.

Not yet, anyway.

He sure hoped the evidence wasn't his lower tray of dentures. He still hadn't found them. If God existed, he was the only one who knew where they were. Not long ago, he'd read in his *True Crime* magazines that forensics might be able to trace DNA in the future to solve crimes. Lucky for him, the science wasn't ready. But if they found his dentures and pulled up his past-due debt at the shop, it wouldn't be too hard to prove those dentures were his and that he had a motive.

It was just a matter of time—and the guy coming out of a coma—before the police would be knocking down his door and slapping handcuffs on him for attempted murder. Shoot, murder if the man died. Harry had lain low, sticking to work and the motel, wondering when the cops would point a finger at him. No matter what, the pawnshop had the legal right to yank his home and cars out from beneath his family's feet to cover his gambling debt.

They were gonna be homeless because of him.

He'd have no way to help them. No way to support them. Not from prison, anyway. So far, he'd managed to come up with only one solution for his stupidity that could change the outcome for his family.

He'd have to kill himself.

He'd saved himself until tonight, so he could see Janice sing. He'd missed her performance last Saturday, but he wouldn't tonight—restraining order be damned. When his oldest kids were still little and he'd tell them to stop doing something, like jumping off a chair, or when he'd sing them a song at bedtime, they'd say, "One more last time, Daddy." That's what he wanted. One more last time with his wife.

He pulled in next to her car at the bar. He leaned to his right and scrounged through the litter on the passenger side floor until he found the almost empty bottle of whiskey. Tilting his head back, he relaxed as the last drops splashed and burned the back of his throat. It wasn't enough, but it would have to be enough for now. Drops were like a damn placebo. He shouldn't have drunk the whole kit and caboodle earlier. As usual, he sucked at pacing himself.

As Harry walked toward the door, Pete stepped off the barstool and blocked his way.

Pete knows. He knows he choked her. Couldn't blame the guy for stopping him. What kind of husband strangles his wife? Harry's stomach turned. He looked down at his feet, swimming against the concrete. He stumbled forward, but Pete reached out and steered him to the brick wall beside the door.

"I won't hurt her again," Harry said. And if that wasn't the truth, nothing was. "Just came to see her sing, and then I'll get out of here."

Pete crossed his arms. "Not tonight, buddy. Go home and sleep it off."

Harry belched, covering his mouth two seconds too late. Damn it, he could use a big drink. His legs started to tremble, and sweat gathered on his brow.

No, no, no. Not a panic attack. Not now.

Harry slid down the wall to sit on the ground. Baked by the sun throughout the day, the brick and concrete warmed his backside. Much-needed cool air washed over him from the open door.

Keep it together, coward. Pass out now and they'll call an ambulance.

He'd end up in the same damn hospital as his victim. He wouldn't be able to do what he needed to do.

If he could've taken his own advice, at least once, to never drink if he was too happy, too sad, too mad, too worried, or needed to make a decision, this would've been the time because he was three-out-of-five right now.

"You look like crap," Pete said.

He sure as shit felt like crap. He'd never felt worse in his entire sixty-three years. Where had all the time gone? How had he made so many stupid mistakes? Have so many regrets? If he could go back in time, he'd meet Janice all over again and be a better man. He'd be the rescuer she thought he was all those years ago. Closing his eyes, he remembered the first time he saw her and the moment that sparked between them when their eyes met.

His heart slowed, and his breathing calmed. Magic. It had been pure magic.

"Janice used to tell me I looked like Dean Martin. You know that?"

"Nope."

Pete was his last hope. "She's my songbird. I have to see her sing."

"Don't care what she is—we know about the restraining order and don't want any trouble. I'll call you a cab."

Harry swung his keys around his index finger. "Have my own car. Let me see her, and I'll leave. Please. Man to man, I'm begging you."

Pete leaned down to where Harry was sitting and took his keys away from him like he was some damn kid. After removing the motel key, he tucked it in Harry's shirt pocket. "You can pick the rest up tomorrow."

"Come on. Let me in one last time?"

Pete snorted. "Last time? Janice will be here every Saturday for the rest of her life. You too."

"Please."

"No can do, Dean Martin. Stay put. I'll go call a cab."

"Pete!" A sob burst from his core as he reached out for Pete's retreating ankles. "I have to!" But he'd lost his chance, and he was alone again. He was so goddamn sick of being alone. He lowered his chin to his chest and cried. His shoulders shook so hard his spine chafed against the brick wall. He twisted his blue wristwatch and kissed its face. Janice had given it to him as a wedding gift. It no longer worked, but he wore it every day. Felt naked without it. Of all the things he'd lost a week ago, he sure was glad he hadn't lost her watch. He looked at the second watch ticking away on his other wrist. Janice liked to sing her first song around this time.

Harry heard the music start, recognized his wife's favorite song, and closed his eyes. Someone somewhere was looking out for him.

Thank you. Thank you.

The music brought his heart to aching, and he thought it might burst.

One stanza in, Harry felt Pete's steel toe boot nudge his feet, but it was one more stanza than he thought he'd get, so he'd take what he could.

"Don't fall asleep on me, Harry."

Harry dried his cheeks on his shirtsleeve. "No one sings like Janice. No one. Cuts me open," he pounded his chest, "every time."

Pete handed him a cigarette. "Stop crying and listen."

Harry took one puff and began to sing along with Janice's voice trailing from the bar. "Crazy for lo-oving youuu."

"You don't sound half bad," Pete said.

"I used to sing. It's how we met." When had they stopped singing together? It had been their thing. They should've never stopped.

"Cab's here," Pete said.

Harry sniffed. No, not yet. He couldn't leave her yet. "Please, Pete."

"Oh for Christ's sake." He held his index finger up to the cabbie.

Harry had just won the goddamn lotto. Life was complete. He'd accomplished what he set out to do tonight and hear his songbird sing one last time. Peace settled over him as he listened to her finish the song. Last time he'd felt this content and resolved was after sharing his first milkshake with Janice and WJ back at that diner in Minneapolis decades ago. Just the three of them, a young family, making plans for their future, intending to ditch Minneapolis and drive to Las Vegas to become entertainers and give WJ the world.

As the music faded and Janice's voice along with it, applause bounced off the walls and down the hall. Harry imagined her smiling, and pride and gratitude consumed him.

Damn, what a woman. What a woman. He was lucky to know her. To love her.

"You know what?" Harry flicked his cigarette and rolled onto his side onto his hands and knees. "That woman in there deserves the best. Better than me." He dragged his right foot forward and put his weight on it. He pulled his left foot forward and lifted his hips but began to pitch forward. "For the first time in a long time, I know I'm doing something right." And he did, it was a new feeling and a real first.

Pete grabbed him under the arms and helped him stand. "You might want to start with sobering up." He put some cab fare in Harry's shirt pocket and pulled open the cab door, shoving him into the back seat.

"Go home. Sleep it off. Don't come back tonight."

"Tell her I was here, Pete. Tell her she has never sang better."

Harry had tried to quit drinking. Many times.

Alcoholics Anonymous was a joke. Once, at a meeting, a sponsor had told him he didn't think Harry had hit bottom yet.

"What's the bottom?" Harry had asked.

"Only you can answer that question. The bottom is different for each alcoholic."

"How do I find my bottom then?"

"It will find you. You'll recognize it when it does. Just remember, H.A.L.T."

"H.A.L.T.?"

"Hungry. Angry. Lonely. Tired."

"What the . . . half the world is hungry, angry, lonely, and tired. It doesn't mean half the world has a drinking problem."

"Harry, it's alcohol-ism, not alcohol-wasm."

Harry had stormed out of the room, yelling, "You all make me apeshit crazy. I might as well drink."

He'd gone to the Walker Heights Crisis Clinic once. They told him he was suffering from depression.

"No kidding," he'd replied. "My dog could've told me that. What medical school did you go to?"

Why miss work and paychecks to have them tell him something he already knew?

Walker Heights wanted to admit him into detox, but his insurance didn't cover rehabilitation, and if he wasn't working, how was he going to feed his family? When he'd told his AA sponsor he couldn't afford the treatment facility, the sponsor had said it was just another excuse Harry was using to drink.

What an asshole.

Far as he was concerned, AA was a damn cult. AA wanted him to stand up in front of everyone and say, "I'm Harry, and I am an alcoholic." Shoot, wasn't it enough to try to stop drinking? He was more than these other people standing up and whining about addictions—okay with a label of alcoholic, recovering alcoholic, or recovered alcoholic—but always an alcoholic measured by chips and days sober.

The nuttiest conversation was when a lady in a meeting told him she had to give her first-year sobriety chip back because she'd had one drink one day. One drink out of 365 days, and that's what the fools wanted to count? One day?

Nope. AA wasn't for him. People clapped when someone said their own name, for crying out loud.

Their name!

He was more than an alcoholic. What was with all the "ics" anyway? People always wanted titles for everything. He was a workaholic, though. Nothing wrong with that, right? His boss Rudy had never complained, and Harry had never missed a day of work unless he counted his binges, and he used his two weeks vacation to cover those. No, he shouldn't be whittled away to a single thing: an alcohol-*ic*. He was also a husband, father, and hardworking man. Why couldn't he just stand up and say, "I'm Harry, and I'm a husband, father, and hardworking man who has alcoholism"?

But no, everyone just accused him of denial.

Harry knew other drunks who understood him better than anyone else, and he only had to buy them a drink from time to time to have a worthwhile and sympathetic conversation. So he had ditched both AA and Walker Heights.

Walker Heights had been right, though. Harry often felt depressed, but he didn't want to talk to a doctor about his past and the fuzzy memories and nightmares that gave him the damn shakes so bad that only booze settled his nerves. How was he supposed to tell anyone why he drank and what that man had done to him when he was eleven? What would people think of him? What would they call him? A homo? He knew one had nothing to do with the other, but people wouldn't get that. They'd think he'd had a choice in the matter, that he'd done something to deserve it, that he'd liked it. No one would understand. Decades later and he'd still never met another man who'd had this happen to him, or at least not one who blabbed about it. He was alone in his shame then, and he was alone in his shame and pain now. Never, ever, did he want anyone to know.

Besides, the memories came and went, so why talk about them, much less pay a doctor to listen? What was a shrink going to do for him anyway? He could go months sometimes without a memory or a nightmare, so he didn't always need to drink to escape. He would have normal days, days when he could just enjoy a six-pack of beer after a long day's work in the comfort of his home. He didn't always drink until he passed out or pissed his pants.

But every spring, the dark thoughts would come knocking at his door like some goddamn anniversary. Outside the time of year, he never knew what might trigger the warped memory. A few years ago, he was working at the landfill. He was on the ground maneuvering the truck levers to empty the large yellow dumpster. A bag had stuck to the bin, and when he pulled it free, the plastic tore open, and containers of spoiled milk dropped to the ground and burst. The curdled milk had sent him reeling backward, and in his mind he could smell the man's sour breath blowing over his shoulder and into his face while he forced himself on Harry, causing Harry to vomit on the pillow and struggle for breath—none of it stopping the monster. And that day at work, with rotten milk drying on his boots and pant legs, Harry had crawled up in his diesel cab and cried like that eleven-year-old innocent kid who had prayed to die that day. But he'd survived over fifty years so far. He cried so hard he couldn't catch his breath, and his hands and legs shook enough that Harry had to wait to drive the truck and finish working his shift. In those moments, Harry wondered why he kept hanging on, but then he'd think of his wife and kids and about how he had to protect them from other monsters.

Other times, the memory would visit him in a nightmare, and his own thrashing would startle him awake. He hated the night terrors. It was hard to distinguish between reality and dreams. He would spend the rest of the midnight hours alternating between drinking beer to numb his fears and sipping coffee to stay awake. But sometimes the memories were so vivid only a blackout could give him relief. But if someone tried to deal with him in those dark moments, he always came out fighting. Fighting for that little boy inside him who couldn't defend himself before.

As much as he hated to think about what had happened to him, he couldn't help but wonder if he'd suffered a memory during his blackout last Friday night, leading him to beat a man with a baseball bat. But there was no excuse for what he'd done, even if there was an explanation.

That poor man had been in the wrong place at the wrong time. No matter his line of work, that man had a family that was worried sick about him.

Come to think of it, almost everyone who'd ever met Harry had been in the wrong place at the wrong time.

"Get out, man. We're at your place," the cabbie said.

Some place. Some hell of a place.

7

HARRY

You've got to hit rock bottom.
—Sobriety meeting

Harry groped his way through the darkness for the door to his room—the fateful Number Twenty-Two—and fished for the key in his pocket. Metal scraped against metal as he struggled to find the keyhole.

He was either drunker than he thought, or keys were getting bigger.

He bent over and put his face close to the knob and focused on inserting the key. There was a click, and the door opened an inch. He kicked the door open the remainder of the way but waited at the threshold of the single room containing a twin mattress, a desk and chair, and a narrow kitchen counter with a single burner. The small space reeked of stale cigarette smoke and spoiled fast food. His sense of well-being from earlier fizzled away like a spilled beer.

He couldn't go in there again. He wanted to go home one more time.

He rubbed his palms over his face. Hard-earned calluses scratched his cheeks. The smoothest part of his hands was the nub of a finger on his right hand. He had lost three-quarters of the digit in the garbage truck compactor. His kids used to roll their eyes at him when he teased them, "I can't count to five because I only have four fingers to count on."

His lips trembled as he looked through the doorway at the small room devoid of life. Devoid of family.

How many times had he wished for a quiet house while he read the paper or when he tried to watch *Wild Kingdom* without one of the kids running in front of the television? He'd take back every wish if he could.

For the past week, finding the strength to enter the kitchenette each night had been the worst part of his day. The first few mornings he woke up rested, sober, and hopeful— hopeful it would be his last morning waking up alone. He'd fix his mistakes and find a way to apologize to Janice and the kids. He'd tell them that he loved them. Tell them he would not drink anymore. That he'd become the husband and dad they deserved. He would find a way to convince them, because in the face of each new day, he believed he could be a better man.

But none of that was even a choice anymore. Even if he could convince them to forgive him for gambling away their home, there was no fresh start that included him, and he couldn't run from the law forever. So every night he had ended up here. Alone and drunk.

And this morning had been different from any morning in his life. He hadn't felt hopeful when he woke up, only tired and resolved to do what he had to do. A lifetime of bad choices had caught up to him, and he knew he'd never be going home. Even if he wasn't facing prison time, he could never trust himself again—sober or drunk. He wished he'd never had a drink in his entire life. Where would he be now if he'd never started drinking or gambling? Or what if he'd found a way to quit that made sense to him?

Harry stepped into the motel room and closed the door behind him. He couldn't get any lower in his life.

Nope. He couldn't get any lower.

Well, damn.

He'd hit bottom. His AA sponsor hadn't been a complete idiot after all and was right about one thing. Harry didn't know what he'd expected, but there sure as heck weren't any bells, whistles, or cannons going off to recognize his rock bottom. No, it was more elemental, as if he could smell his rock bottom oozing from his pores, and his bottom smelled of . . . nothing. His bottom was blank, downright soulless. Gone was his recollection of the smells of his home; the thought created an avalanche of homesickness that made his knees buckle and left a void bigger than he could bear. Try as he might, he couldn't recall the safety net of smells he clung to in his darkest moments: Janice's lap as he lay his head in it to talk with her; the crook of her neck; the breath of his children as they burst with laughter or spoke a mile a minute; the metallic smell of his kids' dirty pudgy hands after playing all day; Janice's homemade bread and cinnamon rolls; an evergreen Christmas tree; coffee at his kitchen table; burnt marshmallows and Rice Krispy treats made by his children; the pillow and sheets on his bed; holiday meals on the table. He couldn't smell any of them. They all smelled of the same nothingness, and he was haunted by how it felt when his mother had died, and how over time he could no longer recall her voice or the once-familiar lines of her face.

All of it was gone. Blank. His rock bottom was empty.

No gentle smells and reminders of home because he could never go home again and reclaim them. He recognized the truth in every fiber of his being. Failure and isolation coursed through his veins, and homesickness turned him into a walking, raw, open wound where the only sensation was compassion and hope for those he'd betrayed.

H.A.L.T.

His rock bottom was devastating, and he wished he could have killed himself without finding it. It was one thing to think he was taking himself out of this world to protect his family but another to think he was a coward for hitting rock bottom and being unable to climb out. AA was wrong. It wasn't true that everyone could go up from their bottom. Sometimes, the bottom was too late.

It was more like he'd found out he had a terminal illness but too late to treat it or do anything about it.

He pushed himself away from the door and shuffled to the old chair. The wood creaked as he braced one hand on the back of the chair and sat down. The chair swayed under his weight, but he regained his balance with spread-eagled legs, squatting as he pulled the chair closer to the desk.

He'd been writing his suicide letter in his head all day. It was his last chance to say the right things. To be honest. To give his family what he should've given them all along.

Opportunity.

Freedom.

He sorted through the newspapers on his desk. He knew there was a pad of paper somewhere. A *Popeye* cartoon strip caught his eye, and he leaned close to read it. Never understood why, but WJ had always loved the spinach-loving sailor.

WJ. He'd done wrong by that boy. Maybe WJ would be

different and not involved with that gang if he'd had a better father than Harry. No matter how hard he tried, Harry had never understood him. Like this damn cartoon. Why did WJ care so much about the bulbous-nosed, toothless, bald, corn-cob–pipe–smoking albino?

He slid his finger over the comic strip. Popeye downs his spinach, blasts Bluto so hard he flies across the ocean, and Olive Oyl, friends, and kids smile and cheer.

Tears pooled in Harry's eyes. WJ was Popeye, dealing justice with brute force to Bluto. To Harry.

Sniffing, he tore the comic strip out, set it to the side, and then continued shuffling the pages on the desktop until he found a pad of blank paper.

Harry perched his dime-store glasses on his nose. He pulled a pair of scissors out of the desk and opened them wide to use one of the blades to whittle a dull pencil lead until it was sharp enough to write.

Harry wrote the date in the upper right-hand corner. It took him five minutes to write a list. He folded it in quarters and scribbled *My Kids* across the front.

Resting his cigarette on the edge of the desk, he took the second sheet of paper, and after a few seconds, he wrote fast before he forgot how to best say what had to be said. Tears dropped on the page, but he didn't have the time or desire to stop them. It was now or never.

Dear Songbird,

I'm a fool and a drunk. I loved you the best I could, but not the way you deserved. By the time you read this letter, I'll be gone. It won't be easy for any of you at first, but it will be easier in the long run if I'm out of the picture. I'm not trying to be wishy-washy either. You'll have a better chance in life without my drinking and gambling. I feel better about this decision than I have about anything in a long time. I was once a good man, and I aim to leave one by my last choice.

I've hit an all-time low. Hit that damn bottom AA warned me about, and I would have rather gone to my grave not letting those assholes be right about there being one. I've done a horrible thing I can't fix any other way. I hurt someone real bad. Worst of all, I screwed you over by doing it. I borrowed money from someone I shouldn't have, and I pawned the trailers and our cars. Last week, I blacked out. I beat up the pawnshop owner really bad, as in coma bad. He's been surviving on machines one day at a time. It's only a matter of time before someone comes to claim the roof over your heads, or before the police figure it out. I'm too much of a coward to turn myself in, and I can't go to prison. I'd die in there, and I'd be leaving you broke. Give the police this letter when they come knocking.

But I figured out how to take care of you. When I'm dead, you can collect my social security. Get your butt over to the social security office, apply for survivor benefits, and make all of those years of hard work mean something.

Can you grant me a dying wish? I did my children wrong. WJ most of all. Tell him about his real dad. I wish I could see his face when he hears he is Walter Whitworth, Junior. Oh, la-di-da—a junior. Let him find his family, and who knows, maybe he will become a better man than I raised him to be.

Harry had to pause to blow his nose and collect himself before he could write the rest of his letter. When he was finished, he slipped the letter to Janice, the list for his kids, and the comic strip in one envelope. He sealed it with a kiss. He rested the envelope on his desk, smoothing his beefy palm across the top and then wrote *For Janice*. When the police found him, he hoped they wouldn't open it before his wife had the chance.

His cigarette had burned to the filter, the ash stretching over thin air until the embers reached the desk and began to smolder. He kneaded his chest above his heart. If someone were to ask him how he felt right now, he'd tell them he felt sorry and regretful that he had to hurt his family more in order to help them. And he felt relieved because he'd written this letter with love and sincere apology. The second thing his sobriety sponsor turned out to be right about was that making amends was healing. He wished he had realized this sooner because then he could have said he was sorry in person to each and every one of his kids, and his wife.

"What's done is done," Harry said to the empty room. He stared across the small space at the rope piled on the floor and the bathroom door that would be the beginning of his end.

When one door closes, another one opens.

8

JANICE

I'm at that point again where it don't matter where he is to me anymore.
—Patsy Cline

J anice bowed, welcoming the applause and catcalls. She blew a kiss to the crowd and jumped off the stage. She hated how her breasts bounced against her ribs like two deflated water balloons and how the static electricity generated by her nylon-clad legs caused her skirt to bunch at the apex of her thighs. But by golly, they had loved her. Saggy breasts be damned. Her confidence was back. She had one more song to sing, and she could win.

No. She *would* win.

She stopped next to the DJ. She lifted her shoulder-length hair off the back of her neck and fanned herself. Maybe she'd grow her hair long enough in Nashville to wear an updo.

"When is my next set?" she asked. She needed time to cool down before she jumped back on stage. She wasn't worried about the order or the college kids participating anymore.

"You have three people ahead of you before your next *turn*," the peon DJ said.

What was this guy's problem? He could take his sarcasm and shove it in his ears. What did he know about music anyway? All he had to do was push some buttons on a machine. Wasn't her fault he wasn't good enough to be a radio DJ. Some people were just haters and blamers.

Scotty was waiting for her and handed her a tall glass of iced tea. "Good job."

"You know it!" Smiling, she took a long drink just as a man came to her side.

"Cigarette?" he asked.

Worrywart Scotty frowned at her.

What? She couldn't help it if she'd caught someone's eye. She sucked on her red straw, looking the stranger over from head to toe.

Jeepers. Another biker in the bar.

WJ liked bikers more than she did, so she tended to avoid them, but she felt high from being on stage, and being singled out warmed her cheeks. There was nothing wrong with a little flirtation, even though she was determined to swear off men once she left Harry and the boys. Strange men were one of the reasons the boys would be too distracting the first year in a new city. She had one last chance to focus on her life and pursue her dream, and she couldn't worry about Tommy's and Justin's safety while she got settled in Nashville and picked up any late-night gig she could get with who-knew-what kind of men who might not be kind to her boys. There were too many pervs and pedophiles out in the world for her to risk it. Harry would never get a Father of the

Year award, but so far he'd never laid a hand on Justin and Tommy. He'd gotten softer with the kids as he aged. Plus, Carrie would only leave the boys if she could afford college. They'd be better off with their father and sister at first. If Lisa stuck around, she could help too, but she wasn't too reliable.

"I never smoke while performing." Janice tapped her throat. "It's not good for my voice."

The biker tucked his lighter in the front pocket of his black leather vest, grabbed a nearby stool, and slid it close to her. "What's your name, sweetheart?"

Ack. Harry had called her sweetheart the first time he saw her. At eighteen years old, she'd thought the endearment was reverent, even adoring, but over the years, she'd come to hate the way "sweetheart" rolled off of some people's tongues in a condescending way. Besides, she didn't want to think about Harry right now. He'd made the choice to lose her, and she was making hers to leave him. She met the biker's brown eyes. She had always been partial to hazel. Without breaking eye contact, she called out, "Hear that, Scotty? This guy thinks I'm a sweetheart." But she liked the biker's wavy brown hair and well-groomed goatee. He smelled of old leather and metal, unlike Harry's exhausted Old Spice. "I'm not anyone's sweetheart, sweetheart."

She felt ten years younger talking to another man. She wasn't hurting anyone by dishing out a little fun.

He looked at her wedding band and raised his brows.

She set her drink down and waved her left hand. "This old thing? I'm a married woman, but only as far as the ring is concerned. I'd take it off, but my fingers are always so swollen I'm afraid it's till death do us part."

He chuckled. "What does your tattoo say?"

Janice showed him her wrist: *nothing changes if nothing changes*

She'd gotten the tattoo three years ago on her birthday. Harry had been furious that she'd permanently marked her body, and she had pointed out other ways her body had been forever scarred by stretch marks from pregnancies and frown lines from her stressful marriage. He never brought up the tattoo again.

For crying out loud. Why was she thinking so much about Harry tonight?

"I've heard that saying before," the biker said.

"Well, shoot," she said. "That's not a good sign."

"Why's that?"

"Because it's a sobriety slogan."

He nodded toward her iced tea and raised a brow.

"No, not me. Him." She tapped her wedding band. "I first heard it in Al-Anon years ago. I haven't been in years, but the saying has come to mean something to me. As for alcohol, I don't have more than one drink while I'm performing."

"I prefer 'Shit Happens,'" he said.

Of course he did. She was sick to death of hearing that saying. People would drawl it out: Sheeeeet Happens. Now, "Life Happens"—that was better. Life Happens could go either way, better or worse. But Shit Happens? Shit was always shit.

"You look too tidy to be a real biker. Jacket is new. No dirt under your fingernails. Are you one of those wannabes?" The best way to flirt with a man was to bust his balls. At least it worked in the romance novels she read from time to time.

"Friends and enemies call me Hawk. Bike is outside. Let's take a ride, and I'll show you where I wannabe," he said.

Corny. Good thing he had looks to fall back on. She eyed the studs running down the sides of his bike chaps. He was taller and leaner than Harry. She could use a little excitement, but in her limited experience with men, the talk was always more fun than the walk.

"You haven't even bought me a drink yet," Janice said.

"Bartender. Alcohol-free drink for the singer." Hawk pointed at Janice.

"What are you doing?" Scotty asked and refilled her iced tea.

Janice flicked her fingers at Scotty. "Shoo fly, shoo."

Hawk leaned near. "So what should I call you if you're not a sweetheart?" He put his large hand on the back of her neck and added pressure below her earlobe with his thumb.

One touch, one point of contact—even if she'd invited it by her teasing—changed everything for Janice. Nobody was allowed to touch her neck anymore. Not her kids, not her husband, and not some guy in a bar.

"Get your hand off my neck. Now." She leaned forward. The hair on her arms stood straight. She couldn't count the number of times a man had controlled her by the back of her neck. The first time was her Great Uncle Bo when she was nine years old, and she'd been forced to bury her underwear on that camping trip so her grandparents wouldn't find out what he'd done. It happened more than once. Sometimes he did nothing more than hold her face down in the dirt and threaten to violate her, but most of the time he followed through with his ugly promises. She would lie still and try to imagine she was anywhere else, but he seemed to prefer it when she fought. One time he gripped her neck and shoved her face in a bowl of dog food, but she couldn't remember the reason. He never seemed to need a reason.

Twice, Harry had grabbed her neck. The first time had been years ago by accident. He'd been trying to kiss her and didn't know she didn't like her neck touched. She'd set him straight, though. She never told Harry about her great uncle, but she'd made it clear that he was never to touch her neck again. She'd told him it scared her, and Harry said that was enough of an explanation for him. The second time Harry grabbed her neck was a week ago. She'd never forgive him. Maybe if she had confided in him a long time ago about her creepy uncle, he wouldn't have grabbed her neck again. Ever. But no matter what, he would have hit her a week ago. One had nothing to do with the other in his mind, only hers. But that was enough. The last straw for her. She was sick and tired of being controlled by a man and having a man dictate her future and her dreams.

Hawk kept his hand in place and squeezed.

Janice lifted her elbow under his arm and shoved him away. "I'm not kidding. Get your damn hand off my neck before I bite it off."

Oh, that's right. She remembered now why her Great Uncle Bo had forced her head in the dog bowl. He'd told her if she was going to bite him like a dog, she could eat like one too. Good thing for her, the monster was killed in an accident a few weeks later and the abuse died with him.

Chairs scraped the floor behind her, and she was grateful for the people prepared to come to her aid—even if they were some of WJ's friends. "Hands off, or we'll cut them off," one of them said.

Hawk clenched his jaw as he looked behind them, lifting his hand as if to say to the oncoming crowd, *There's no problem here.* Why couldn't the jerk just follow her demand? Why did it take another man for him to step back?

Pig.

"Make up your mind," he said to Janice.

"Not interested. Hands off." She turned away from him. "Mind made."

"You can't tell me—"

"I can tell you anything I want. It's my mouth. It's my body. Now get the hell away from me."

Scotty interfered. "That's enough." He pointed at Hawk. "Come down to the end of the bar, and I'll buy you a drink instead. You're messing with the wrong crowd."

Janice snickered and jiggled the ice in her glass to cover up for the fact that her hands were shaking. Scotty should throw the douchebag out.

"Old barfly. You're lucky I even tried," Hawk said. "Thought you'd be an easy screw." He followed Scotty.

Scotty returned to Janice. "You okay?"

Janice ignored his concern and shook her glass again. "Men," she said. "You all think because a lady talks to you, you're going to get laid. Who teaches you guys such baloney?"

"Lady J, you've been coming here for years, and I've never thought you would get in the sack with me." He wiped down the bar. "Come to think of it, I've never seen you leave with anyone but Harry."

Yeah, Scotty didn't miss much. She'd never been a cheater. "You're too ugly. It's best you never tried. I wouldn't want to hurt your feelings."

"Right," Scotty said.

She nodded toward the end of the bar. "Thanks for looking out for me." She placed a napkin over the top of her glass. She needed to step away and shake off the malaise that was dampening her earlier success, and she knew just how to do it. "Can I get my newspapers out of your office?" she asked.

Scotty pulled the keys from his pocket and tossed them to her. "Lock it up when you're done."

"Don't I always?"

Scotty's desktop was the perfect size to spread out *The Tennessean*. She flipped through the sections and pulled out the celebrity updates and classified ads. There were more apartments for rent than usual. Later, she would celebrate winning by combing through her choices. Her soft purse had barely enough room for the abbreviated paper, but she made it work. Buy the time she was done, she felt like it was Christmas Eve and Santa had just loaded up her stocking for being a good girl. She smiled as she locked up Scotty's office and headed back to the bar, the bulky papers in her bag giving her hope.

Watch out, Nashville.

9

WJ

I've had all I can stands, and I can't stands no more.
—Popeye

WJ always entered the Creek Bar through the front
door and paused for effect on the threshold. He liked
it when people noticed his arrival because, as far as he was
concerned, he owned this place and the people in it.

He was here. Beware.

He had two birds to kill with one stone. First, the place
served as a good rendezvous for the Right Knights because
Scotty was loyal and knew how to mind his own business.
And, second, he knew his mother was there somewhere.

His boots clicked against the concrete floor as he walked
toward the bar. He liked how the one-inch heels made him six
feet two, and how his leather jacket hugged his thirty-two-
inch waist. He was feeling lean and mean. Also fucking frustrated and helpless because he couldn't find his brothers.
He'd spent the last hour driving down dirt roads in the fields

surrounding the trailer park, calling for them. No luck. Dammit. He didn't have time for this shit.

The joint was packed, and he didn't recognize some younger faces. He'd turn them into customers in no time if they stuck around long enough. He took a closer look but didn't see the idiot kid from the night before who'd been dumb enough to buy Shelly a drink and call him a faggot.

Good.

He didn't have time to deal with the punk right now. In fact, he didn't have time to be worrying about his brothers. He had stuff to do for Bender tonight, and he wasn't about to let him down. But he'd messed up with his other siblings, and his little brothers were the only ones who still admired him. He wanted to be their hero, and right now they might need him, and he couldn't find them. But, shit, they shouldn't be his problem. And none of this would even be on his mind if his mother would just be a good mother. Instead, he had to hunt her down in a bar where she was a wannabe singer pretending to be footloose and fucking fancy-free. Why did he always have to take care of everyone and everything? If he'd wanted to be responsible for people, he would have had his own children.

Where in the hell was she?

"Hey, Buzzard," his brother-Knight, Hefty, called from the corner table, "where've you been, man? You're late."

Wrong. He was never late. He showed up when he goddamn wanted to, and the last thing he needed tonight was Hefty whining like a big fat baby. The dickhead answered to WJ, not the other way around.

Shit, this wasn't about his bulky and useful friend. Hefty was just ribbing him like always. WJ needed to calm the hell down and stop letting his family get to him like this. It was bad enough he was fighting with Shelly.

WJ flipped him off and smiled. "I was screwing your mother. You might as well call me Daddy from now on and buy me a beer."

Hefty laughed and placed his left palm on his right bicep and pumped his right forearm. "With all due respect." And that was just it. He knew Hefty respected him, and he respected Hefty.

"You wish, Buzz," Hefty's mother yelled from the table. She flashed the room a wide, toothless grin.

Ew—he looked away and ran his tongue over his own teeth—*all there and staying there.*

Missing teeth served as an ID card for his customers who overdid it. Druggies all acted surprised when their teeth started falling out, even though it was one of the first things he warned them about when they started using. He always gave new customers a chance to walk away. The trick was not to overdo it because once they started using, most wouldn't want to stop, and they'd be living in two hells. First hell, withdrawals were a motherfucker. Second hell, if they used too much for too long, they'd screw up their sinuses and lose their teeth—like Hefty's mom. He told every stupid idiot that their withdrawals from crank would be so painful they'd take the risk and gamble their teeth. No one ever believed him, and the freaks always acted surprised when their teeth started falling out in a bite of fried chicken or a hamburger.

But vanity served him well because whenever he craved more crank than usual, he thought about keeping his teeth. He'd kept his teeth through his dad's beatings. He'd be damned if he'd lose them to crank. He and his teeth had been through a lot together.

"Scotty, where's my mom?"

Scotty pointed.

She was just coming out of Scotty's office. Why Scotty would trust her with the keys to the office, WJ had no fucking clue. She was wearing a vest as a shirt and one of those stupid skirts with cowboy boots. Why couldn't he have a normal mother? One who wasn't obsessed with karaoke and dressing like a . . . a *Hee Haw* character.

He felt a twinge of satisfaction when she saw him and froze, hugging her purse to her chest. Mighty protective of a purse that couldn't have ten cents in it. He couldn't remember her ever being as protective with him, or any of her kids.

The sooner he told her the boys were in danger the sooner he could stop worrying about them and get on with his night. She could, should, and would find them herself.

"Mommie Dearest, I don't appreciate having to do your job."

"What are you talking about?" she said. She leaned and flicked the Right Knight patch on the back of his jacket. "I see you're in uniform." She looked over her shoulder. "Your 'friends' are over there."

He swatted her hand aside. She had no right to judge him or his friends. They'd been better to him than she had ever tried to be. Hell, they were good to her because she was his mom. What would she say if she knew his loyal friends went out of their way to vote for her every Saturday night whether she sang well or like crap? It was their way of helping her make extra money to feed her family. They made her sing for her supper. She liked to lift her nose at him and the Knights while she benefited the whole time from an association. She was winning, thanks to WJ. He'd never heard her sing. Not once. And he never would. Too fucking humiliating to watch her make a fool of herself.

"The girls called. The boys didn't come home." He leaned close to her ear. "They think the boys have a gun from your closet."

Her face screwed up, and she shook her head. "No," she said. "I checked earlier, and only the new BB gun was gone. Harry would have taken it. I wouldn't have left the house tonight if I thought the boys had it."

But the bitch blinked five times—what she'd always done since she'd started lying to him when he was little. She'd never given him enough credit for paying attention to every detail about her. Yeah, she would have left even knowing a gun was missing.

"Well, now you know. Get your stuff, and go find them." He reached for her bag, but she pulled it away from him.

"Don't touch my stuff. I can't leave. I'll be disqualified if I leave now."

In this moment, he hated her more than ever. "You can leave, and you will leave. What kind of mother is more worried about a stupid singing contest than her kids?"

"It's not stupid. And I told you—they don't have a gun. Besides, the boys know the fields like the back of their hands. And stop judging me. You're nothing but a thug doing dirty work for the crowd you run with, so don't pretend you have morals."

WJ's nostrils flared. "Don't talk to me about morals. And, yeah, I survived, but no thanks to you."

"I made you tough, didn't I? No one takes advantage of you, do they? I never babied you, and I'm not babying any of my other kids. You should thank me for not raising you, or any of them, to be as gullible as I was once upon a time."

Sometimes his hurt made him want to punch her. He hated how cold and unapologetic she could be. Nothing he said to her mattered. Why the hell did he keep trying? He couldn't teach her to be a better mother to his brothers and sisters. He couldn't change the past and make her a better mom to him. He was wasting his breath and time, but he couldn't walk away. "Gullible? You're nuts. Was letting Dad beat me about making me less gullible than you? That was your maternal goal? How long before Dad starts hurting Tommy and Justin, huh? They're about the age he started on me. What lesson are you teaching them by not protecting them as a mother should?"

Satisfaction rolled through him when she broke eye contact. She started to say something but then paused.

"Go away," she said. "You're ruining my vibe. I'm sure Harry has the BB gun. The boys are probably home by now."

But she didn't care enough to find out for sure, did she? He slammed his fist on the bar before her.

Shit. He'd drawn her attention to his knuckles, still red from when he'd hit Shelly.

She jabbed him in the chest with her index finger.

He wanted to grab it and break it.

"You can't go a day without beating someone up, so don't you dare lecture me on how to treat people, or pretend you're any better than your dad."

He was this close to throwing her across the room. "Don't you dare compare me to him. I've never hit a kid. And we're not talking about people. We're talking about my little brothers. Your sons."

"They're fine," she said and clenched her jaw.

"Sure, that's what you tell yourself about all of us, and all

of us older kids don't even talk to you or come around
no more."

She just didn't get it, did she? None of them were fine. He
didn't want his siblings to end up like him because she left
them no other choice.

And, shit, he needed to go and get on with his plans for
the night.

"I have a business to run, and I have somewhere to be.
Find Dad and see if the boys are with him. Or make sure he
has the BB gun. Don't let the boys hurt themselves, for shit's
sake."

She shook her head. "He won't be with them."

"Why? Where's the asshole at?"

"He'd be violating the restraining order." Janice popped
some peanuts from a bowl on the bar into her mouth and
turned to stare at him.

His mom always called the police when his dad did something to her, not someone else. Not him. "Restraining order?
You involved the police? Again? I told you I never want cops
snooping around the family, especially me. They are always
looking for an excuse to haul me in." He clenched his fist. His
blood pressure rose as he listened to her munch on the nuts.
His mom always put food in her mouth when she was
nervous. His dad had been the drunk, and his mom the
emotional eater. For years she had tried to make it up to him
after a bruising with what used to be his favorite treat, peanut
candy bars. The smell of peanuts turned his stomach now.

"Yeah, that would cramp your 'business,'" she said.

"It's paid your rent and fed my little brothers and sisters
more than once."

Janice turned away from him. "I had to call the police.
Harry was different this time."

His gut twisted. "What do you mean 'different'?"

"Let's just say last weekend Harry hit more than just me, and he has the torn-up hands to prove it."

WJ ground his teeth. "Did he hit the boys?" Out of the corner of his eye, he saw Scotty heading his way.

"That's not what I said."

"Are you letting him beat them? Like you let him beat me?"

Janice looked at him. "He hit you a couple of times, and we both know why. I'm not saying he was right, but he wanted you to know how to defend yourself. There are messed-up men out there looking for little boys to take advantage of, and with you being gay, your dad worried about you more than most. He thought it was for your own good."

"Shut. Up. Do not say that out loud. Never. Never say those words to me, or anyone else again."

Why did she have to be such a hypocrite? His mom and dad had forced him to pretend to be someone he wasn't, and then she just wanted to blab about it like it was a public message. What was it with the women in his life not protecting his secret?

"If beating me to a bloody pulp is what you call hitting me a 'couple of times,' let me tell you this—I thought he was going to kill me. I was a fucking kid, and I thought my own dad would rather I be dead." WJ turned at the bar. "And you didn't stop him."

"I didn't know how," she said and took another bite of fucking peanuts.

"You still don't."

"I kicked him out for good this time."

"For now." Why did he have to have her for a mother?

Scotty joined them and leaned in. "Lower your voices.

You're making everyone nervous. Harry stopped by earlier. We took his keys and sent him home in a cab. He was plastered. His wagon is out back. Take your family feud outside."

"Why didn't you tell me he was here?" Janice asked.

"Didn't want any trouble, but it's not easy with you around tonight," Scotty said.

"Hand me the phone," WJ said. He waited for Carrie to answer. "Did the boys come home?"

"You didn't find them?" Carrie said. "I need to call the police."

"Wait. Listen, if they have anything, it's a BB gun. I'm going to find Dad and make sure the boys aren't with him before I keep looking."

"Don't fight with him. Life sucks enough already."

"Don't worry about us. I won't do anything to Dad he doesn't deserve."

"WJ—"

He was going to tear the place down if he had to listen to Carrie defend their dad, so he cut her off and tossed the phone toward Scotty.

"Scotty, where's the dumb-ass from last night that bought Shelly a drink?"

Scotty waved him to the door of the bar, and WJ met him in the hallway. "He won't be around here again. We've eighty-sixed him, and Pete let him know in no uncertain terms who he'd been messing with and not to show his face again within a mile radius if he wanted to live a normal life."

"If anyone—I mean anyone—asks, I took care of him," WJ said.

"Understood. I'll talk to Pete."

"Good. Hefty," he yelled, "let's go."

WJ stormed to the back door to find Pete. "Give me Harry's keys."

Pete tossed the keys to WJ. "I told Harry I'd get his car to him tomorrow."

"No longer your responsibility. Where did the cab take him?"

"Green Street kitchenettes."

Of course, where his dad always went.

"Get in, Hefty." WJ climbed into his dad's car. It was a mess inside. Just like his dad.

"Why are we taking this car?"

"It's my dad's." Of all the Knights to have with him tonight, he was glad it was Hefty. His dad was still a strong man, and his drinking had always made him a ticking time bomb. WJ wasn't going to stand for it and risk the safety of his little brothers. His mom hadn't protected him, but goddamn it, he'd protect them. They'd all be better off without Dad, and WJ had enough guts to do something about the piece of shit.

10

JANICE

It seems that every time I stick my neck out, I get my foot into something else.
—Patsy Cline

April 1959—Lincoln County, MN

Janice rolled her lips between her teeth, trying to give Grandfather and Grandma time to adjust to her news. Like it or not, she was seventeen. She knew what she was doing, and she was going to marry Walter and have her baby whether they approved or not. She didn't expect them to be thrilled she was pregnant. Even she and Walter had needed a few days to get used to the idea, but they had always intended to start a family sooner or later. So it would be sooner. Big deal. They had it all worked out.

"Oh, Janice, what have you gone and done?"

She knew Grandma wasn't waiting for her to say more. Grandma smoothed her calloused palms over the yellow tablecloth covering the small table in their farmhouse kitchen.

Grandma always smoothed out materials when she was nervous: tablecloths, skirts, aprons, kitchen towels—just about anything Grandma could get her hands on.

Janice had inherited her grandma's nerves, but she liked to nibble on popcorn to soothe her nerves when necessary. Grandma always kept a big bowl of popcorn on the table, thanks to the corn in their garden. They teased each other when caught in their nervous tics. She'd say, "Grandma, you're making me so nervous by fiddling with that tablecloth, you're driving me to eat popcorn." Then Grandma would say, "The way you pick apart those tiny kernels has me itching to smooth some cloth." But this wasn't one of those teasing moments, so Janice was determined to ignore Grandma's obsession with the tablecloth and resisted scooping a handful of the popcorn within arms' reach.

Grandfather shoved back his chair, stood, and paced.

For as long as she could remember, she'd always called him Grandfather, never Grandpa. He'd always been more distant and stern than Grandma.

"Where are your values, girl? We raised you different."

Different than who? Her mother they'd never talk about?

"What made you do such a foolish thing as roll around in the hay with the Whitworth boy?"

Okay, that was enough. Walter was a man and would be her husband, and they'd made love, not rolled around in the hay like . . . actually, no barn animals did that either. What a stupid saying. Besides, if Grandfather only knew about awful, mean Great Uncle Bo. She shook her memories away. That monster was getting no space in her happy life.

No way, nohow.

She rolled her shoulders back and lifted her chin. "Walter is a gentleman. We've been going steady for months. We're in love. We want our baby, and we're going to get married."

Grandma reached over and covered her hand. "Lower your voice. He has the right to be disappointed."

Janice frowned. Why did Grandma always have to take his side? She pulled her hand free.

Grandfather stopped in his tracks, shaking his head. "Love? Marriage? What about respect? Why hasn't he once stopped by to visit with your grandmother and me while you were 'going steady'?"

She'd never liked that condescending tone he used when he was getting all uppity and judgmental. Sure, he'd raised her, but who did he think he was? As far as she knew, he'd never left Lincoln County, Minnesota, in all his years. Least not since he returned from World War I, anyways. Grandma always said he came back harder than before he'd left, and he went hard during the Great Depression when he struggled to care for his family. Not that she'd been born yet.

"Where's this fine gentleman now? Do you really think the largest landowning family in Lincoln County is going to pay for the dairy cow when the milk is free? You're ruining your life."

Dairy cow! Ruining her life? Walter was the best thing that had ever happened to her in this claustrophobic life.

She jumped to her feet, and emphasizing each word for good measure, said, "I am not a piece of livestock. Walter and I are going to have this baby. Together. If his parents aren't supportive, we'll do it on our own. And that goes for you, too. Whether you agree or not, we *are* going to be together."

"That easy, is it? Then where is he?" He glared down at her from his six foot three height and threw his arms up. "Why isn't he here to share his intentions?"

She wished she knew. He was supposed to be here by now to tell them the news together. It'd be a welcome, dramatic entrance if he knocked on their door just now. But he didn't.

"He promised he was speaking to his parents this morning, doing his chores, and coming over here to see you this afternoon as soon as he's done. I'm not sure why he isn't here yet, but Walter loves me, and I know he has a good reason for being late. I'll go and find him and bring him here. It's going to be okay. You'll see."

Grandfather rubbed his face like he did after a long day of working the farm. She regretted tiring him out when she knew time would show him how right she and Walter were together.

"I hope you're right. Dear God, let her be right." He pulled out a chair next to her at the table. He sat down so hard, her chair wobbled next to him. "What if his parents turn him out? What about your dreams to have a radio career in Minneapolis? You've always worked so hard in school. Times are slowly getting better for women, but there's still a long way to go, and you can't do a career with a baby. Even with a husband."

Yes, Grandfather was a stern man, but he supported the changes and flexibility growing for women in the fifties, and he had always encouraged her dream to leave Lincoln County after graduation and be a career woman. Despite his current lack of faith in her and Walter, she was sorry to worry him, but she wasn't going to let her grandparents' worries rub off on her.

"It won't be a problem. When we graduate in June, we're going to Minneapolis. I'll be eighteen. I'm going to get a job at the radio station, and Walter is going to write a novel and be home with the baby. And someday I'm going to be a famous singer and songwriter."

His jaw dropped. She wanted to reach over and push his mouth closed. Thank God she hadn't inherited his cynicism. For a fleeting moment, she wondered if he'd ever had a dream for his life.

Doubt it.

"Write a novel! Country singer? Stupid, idiotic kids, that's what you are. You think it's that simple? You don't even know how to take care of yourselves, much less a baby. Heck, you don't even know how to avoid getting pregnant!" He shoved his chair back and jabbed a finger in her direction and swallowed hard. "Your grandmother and I worked hard on this land so you'd have opportunities the rest of us didn't. Instead, you're having babies like a damn rabbit. Something anyone could do!" He got up and stormed out of the house.

She flinched when she heard the back door slam. None of this was going the way she and Walter had planned. They were supposed to see her and Walter together, happy and confident. Grandfather would have been impressed by Walter's determination to care for her, and Grandma would have been talking about sewing her a wedding dress that she could marry in.

"Oh, Janice." Her grandmother shook her head and incessantly smoothed her skirt across her lap.

"Stop it. Just stop it." Janice rose and grabbed her sweater.

Grandma sniffled and lifted teary eyes to her. "It's just we hoped life could be better for you than your . . ."

Janice's heart caught. Than her mother's? Because her mother had deserted her, leaving her with Grandma and Grandfather after giving birth? She held her breath, hoping

Grandma would give her something, anything, about the mother she'd never talked to or known. But Grandma clammed up as usual.

Janice wrapped her sweater protectively around her flat midriff. "I'm going to find Walter. We'll be back. You'll see."

Hugging her midriff, Janice sang Teresa Brewer's hit "Till I Waltz Again With You" as she walked toward Walter's farm.

She wondered what had held him up, and she hoped his discussion with his parents had been more supportive than the one with her grandparents. Through the fabric of her blouse, she fingered his class ring and the chain bouncing between her tender breasts. He'd never stood her up, and he had no reason to start now. Last night when they'd sat behind her barn, staring at the stars, making their plans, and pledging their lives to each other, there had been love and excitement in his hazel eyes. There was no faking what they shared.

Regardless of his delay, she decided to walk along Main Street, the longer route to Walter's. She needed to stop by the library anyway to return *Jane Eyre*. Someday she'd own a beautiful house in Nashville, Tennessee, with the grandest library ever. The first book she'd add would be this favorite.

Her neighbors, Mr. and Mrs. Christensen, came from behind and passed her on the narrow sidewalk.

Mr. Christensen tipped his hat. "Excuse us."

"Say hello to your grandparents," Mrs. Christensen said.

Janice. Say my name. It's Janice.

"Yes, ma'am," Janice said.

At the end of the block, she could see some classmates—the prissy girls, as she liked to call them—huddled in a circle. They'd never been rude to her but nor had they included her in anything in her entire life, despite growing up together in this small town. She'd always wondered if it was because her grandparents were raising her while the other kids had their mothers and fathers. In the end, she assumed it was that and because she had less money than most.

But most people respected her grandparents. At church or when someone came out to the farm to pick up milk or garden goods, people always took their time having a conversation with Grandfather and Grandma. They talked about the farm, politics, family, but never her mom. Never Janice. Sometimes she'd play a game with herself and hold her breath until someone asked, "And how is Janice coming along?" but *whoosh*, she always lost.

She'd always been invisible. But not to Walter.

June Black stood in the center of the group. Typical. Everyone—children, adults, even Grandma and Grandfather —fawned over June.

Well, everyone but Walter. Janice smiled.

Just wait until everyone heard their news. She wouldn't be invisible anymore.

June used to be Walter's steady, but he'd broken up with her when he started seeing Janice. June had thrown a fit and wanted an explanation, but even in this small town, Janice and Walter were able to keep their relationship a secret. No one expected Walter to see her—see that she mattered. Soon they'd be married, and June Black and the judgmental nosy busybodies could go to hell.

The prissy girls were hugging June and rubbing her arms and back.

As Janice neared the group, she heard June blubbering on about something. Tears streamed down her face.

Fake ones, for sure.

Who knew what she was crying about this time. June was spoiled, and Janice had never liked her for that very reason. Always crying about not being able to buy a new dress every day, or something equally silly.

Janice slowed her pace, hiked her book up under her arm, and prepared to cross the street to the library.

Mr. and Mrs. Christensen had reached the gaggle.

"Now girls," Janice heard Mrs. Christensen say, "why the tears?"

"Oh, Mrs. Christensen," June grabbed the woman's wrist, "it's Walter Whitworth. He's been killed in a tractor accident. The tractor rolled over, crushing his chest, and they said he drowned in his own blood."

Despite freezing in her tracks, Janice felt herself begin to sway. *Jane Eyre* fell to the street with a thump, and she frantically reached for her stomach before following her beloved book and crashing to the ground.

11

HARRY

Make amends.
—Sobriety meeting

Saturday night, April 8, 1989

Harry was going to hang. Lord knew drinking himself to death wasn't working, and he wasn't going to overdose on drugs. He was a lot of things, but he was no druggie. He had no intention of shooting himself and leaving a mess for someone else to clean up, and he didn't trust himself to jump from a building when the time came. Besides, he'd end up on the news, and that was the last thing his family needed. Anyway, the tallest building in Corbett City was the Riffle Blocks Casino, and it might not be tall enough.

He didn't know who'd find him, and he prayed it wouldn't be his family. Best for everyone if it was the police, but then they'd keep his letters to Janice from her until they were good and ready, and he was sorry she'd have to wait and be confused and angry till she could read his goodbye for herself. If he could figure a way to get the letters to her without raising suspicions, he would, but he couldn't, so it would all have to play out as it would.

Memories of fishing as a boy and his time as a merchant marine came in handy as he took the long yellow poly rope and made a hangman's noose fishing knot. He wasn't taking any chances with a bad knot pulling loose and mucking up his death. He slipped the knot over the top of the door and pulled the door closed. There was a tight fit between the rope and doorjamb.

That should do, but best make sure.

The noose rested against the face of the door over a foot above him. Of all the ways he might have worried he could die in his lifetime (car accidents, drunk driving, cancer, a sinking ship, fire, or lightning striking), never once had he thought he'd come to this. But no use crying over spilled milk because it was what it was. He'd made bad choices, and now he'd die with them.

Time for a test run.

He jumped up, wrapped his large hands around the noose, and picked up his feet to see if the rope and door could hold him once he kicked away a chair. The door didn't crack or fold, but it moaned with the force of his weight.

Damn, that'd be one hell of a mournful sound to die to, but so be it.

He kicked his legs to make sure any struggling wouldn't botch the job. The door moaned again. He sure hoped it would hold.

Letting go, he dropped to the floor.

Grabbing the bottle of whiskey he'd bought at the corner store, he sat on the mattress behind him.

There was no time like the present. No reason to drag this

out any longer than he had to. Best get busy drinking and dying.

Tugging at his shoestrings, he kicked off his work boots. He'd never meant to be a garbage man, and if there was a heaven and if he lucked out and got in, he damn well didn't want to take his mangy, stinking boots with him.

He'd read once in one of his crime magazines that people never committed suicide with their glasses on, at least not jumpers and hangers. Even though they'd be dead anyway, people didn't like the idea of cutting their faces.

Go figure.

Sometimes detectives could determine a staged death was foul play when they found smashed glasses on a jumper or lying near his landing. If there wasn't a heaven and he'd be reincarnated, maybe he'd come back as a detective. Wouldn't that be something?

Harry was vain enough that he'd remove his glasses just in case, but he was blind as a bat without them, and if there was one thing he was going to get right, it was going to be killing himself.

A man should be successful at one thing in his life, even if it was dying.

He'd just kicked off one boot when his doorknob rattled. Who in the hell was at his door this time of night? And why weren't they knocking?

"Who's there?"

He jumped up and opened the bathroom door to undo his handiwork. He grabbed the rope and threw it in the bathtub, pulling the plastic shower curtain closed.

Had to be his drunk-as-a-skunk landlord. Who else would want to see him? Rent wasn't due until tomorrow, but he'd heard she liked to enter people's apartments and steal cigarettes and booze—something most of the tenants had in common. He'd once seen her arrested outside Prescott's Drugstore across from the trailer park for shoplifting a pint of vodka. He might be an alcoholic, but he'd never had to steal his drink. Of course, almost killing someone was a whole lot worse than being a petty thief.

The knob jiggled again.

He flung the door open, ready to scare someone away. Now was not the time to be bugging him. Focus was key. But he could have fallen to the floor weeping like a willow with Neil Diamond at the sight before him.

His boys. Tommy and Justin. His beautiful boys.

He stared down at them in disbelief. They glowered up at him, their hands shoved in their coat pockets. Tommy's pocket protruded as if he had a gun pointed at Harry. They both wore plastic sheriff stars on their chests. Harry had bought them those stars last Saturday at the five and dime store next to the donut shop.

Other than a little shivering, they looked unharmed. What a damn gift to see their rosy cheeks. Had they walked here just to see him?

Harry wanted to grab them and hold them close—more than he'd ever wanted a drink in his life—to inhale the comforting smell of his children. A lost comfort he never expected to enjoy again. If he believed in a god, or a "higher power" as sobriety groups liked to say, for signs or validation, he couldn't help but believe the arrival of his young sons on this very doorstep could be anything but a sign.

Damn lump in his throat stopped him from saying anything right away. "Fearsome as you two look, I'm still so happy to see you. Are you all alone? It's late and dangerous out there."

At the sound of his voice, Star poked her head between Justin's legs and whined.

"We're here on business," Tommy said, rolling his shoulders back and lifting his chin.

Harry smiled. He'd taught Tommy how to puff up his chest like that when some kids at school had been bullying him. He'd told him, "Stand tall and proud, son. Makes you look bigger, and it will scare off those clowns. Call their bluff. Never throw the first punch." In hindsight, Harry wished he would have tried to toughen up WJ in the same way, but all those years ago, he didn't know how else to protect WJ other than to teach him to fight. Sometimes, in his darkest and drunkest moments, Harry wondered if he was any better than the man who'd raped him. Was it intention or action? WJ had been a little boy with no more control over being beat than Harry had over being raped. What if he had gotten WJ into a gym with real boxing lessons instead of hitting him with his own fists? Maybe WJ would be a frigging Muhammad Ali instead of a drug dealer.

"Business, eh? Come on in."

The boys didn't move from the doorway.

Star edged her way in and began sniffing the room.

"We'll talk from here," they said.

Harry sighed and stared at the skinny boys standing in the door. He was so damn happy to see them he felt his chest opening and expanding. For the first time in days, he could breathe. Really breathe. "Tom, is that finger loaded?"

"Yup."

"Be smarter than me. I've always learned the hard way. Forcing someone to listen, and with a weapon, is serious business. Someone might get hurt. Is that what you want?"

Tommy's shoulders slumped. He pulled his empty hands

from his pockets. "No, I don't want anyone to get hurt. I want everything to be fair. I don't want you to drink anymore and fight with Mom."

"Me neither," Justin said and tapped his badge.

"Me neither," Harry said. He squatted down before them, feeling both humiliated and gratified to see his sons standing up for their mother. He cleared his throat and wiped his cheek with his sleeve. "I'm proud of you for standing up to me. I can see you mean what you say. I promise you I'll never drink again, or fight with your mom again. I'm so sorry. Okay?" Harry stuck out his hand.

"Or anyone," Justin said.

"No more fighting. Period." Harry crossed his heart. He wished he could stay alive just to follow through on his promise to his boys.

Tommy stepped forward and shook hands. Justin was next.

Harry felt each of their small, trusting hands in the palm of his own, and the one-ton nightmare he'd been carrying on his shoulders lifted and floated away. He knew what he needed to do. They'd all be okay without him, and he was making the right choice.

"Okay," Harry said. His heart broke a little as their soft palms left his own. He put his palms on his knees and stood up. "Now then. Never pretend to have a gun again, okay?"

Tommy looked down. "We were kind of pretending. We had a BB gun. We took it to the field to practice, but some older kids saw us and stole it."

"They said they were going to shoot us if we didn't leave," Justin said.

"You made the right choice by leaving. But where did you

get the BB gun?" He knew already, but he'd better get their confession now.

The boys shrugged their shoulders and looked around the room.

"Did you take it from the closet?"

They nodded.

"Well, that's what some people call karma, boys. You took something that didn't belong to you, and someone took it from you. Now, what do you say the two of you get comfortable? I'll call the house and let everyone know you're with me. I don't have my car, so I can't take you home, but I can feed you some ramen and take you in a cab later, okay?"

"I'm Starvin Marvin," Justin said.

"Then we have a plan, Marvin," Harry said. "Let's make some Top Ramen."

"Can I have some raw noodles?" Tommy asked.

Harry grabbed a second package and tossed it to Tommy. "Share it. Fill up the pot on the burner. I need to go borrow the landlord's phone."

Harry closed the door behind him and stepped onto the creaky walkway. The desert night was cool, and the crisp air cleared his head. He knew his blood alcohol content must still be high, but he hadn't felt this sober in years. He walked past five doors to the manager's unit. Her lights were on, and he could hear her television. Hell, half the block could hear her television. He knocked.

"It's Harry. I need to use your phone."

She opened the door and swayed from side to side. "Come on in. Want to get high?" She pinched a joint between her fingers.

Harry shook his head. There wasn't anything he wouldn't have tried to get drunk. He'd drunk mouthwash, even vanilla extract for a buzz. One vice had been more than enough. "I need to use your phone."

He dialed the Creek Bar. Even with his good reason for calling, he didn't have high hopes that Scotty would hand Janice the phone, or that Janice would take his call. But he'd be a responsible dad this last time. As he expected, Scotty wouldn't budge, and that was okay because he liked knowing Janice had a protective friend like him.

"I understand, Scotty. Can you tell her the boys are with me and I'll get them home? And tell her they took the BB gun from her closet but they're okay." He hung up and called home.

"Hello?" Carrie answered.

Ah, Care Bear. His youngest daughter's voice, even full of worry, was music to his ears.

"It's me."

"Dad! I'm so glad. I tried to call you earlier, but your stupid landlord wouldn't get you. I can't find Tommy and Justin, and I think they have a gun. And WJ is looking for you. I'm freaking out!"

So he might get to see WJ tonight too. Any other night, he'd leave the room and avoid WJ. The fight had gone out of him the older he'd gotten, and he should never have tried to toughen WJ up the way he had. But damn, he was tough, and no one ever messed with him or took advantage of him, did they? But now he could say goodbye, maybe even sorry. He could give his oldest son the letter for Janice, a letter that would change WJ's life too.

"They're safe. They just got here. They have Star, and they don't have the BB gun anymore. I can handle WJ, don't worry."

"No. You guys can't handle being in the same room.

Please don't fight with him. We asked him to find the boys. He was doing me a favor. I was so worried about the gun, and I almost called the police."

"Everything is okay." And everything was going to be okay. He knew his decision might hurt Carrie the worst, but he also knew she was a hard worker and that she was resilient. He wished he could stay around long enough to see her go to college—the first of his kids to go to a university.

"When are you bringing them home? I want to see you."

"Can't right now, I've been drinking, but I'll figure out a way to get them home tonight. I'll ask WJ to take them if he shows up, or I'll bring them in a cab."

"Don't fight with WJ, okay?"

"I already said I wouldn't. Those days are over," he said. "It's Saturday night. Go and do something fun with your friends. Do whatever kids your age should be doing. Stop worrying."

"Right. Stop worrying. You and Mom don't make that easy to do."

Yeah, he got that.

"Dad?"

"Yeah?"

"Have you been eating? Are you doing okay? You always lose so much weight when this happens."

"I know, sweetie. I'm fine. I don't want you to worry about me."

"But Dad—"

"No 'but Dad,' Carrie. You're a smart girl. I couldn't be more proud of the young woman you've become. I know I've given you a million reasons to worry about me and to not trust me, but try to believe it when I say everything is going to be fine. Don't cry," he said when he heard her sniffle.

"If you get a place, Tommy, Justin, and I could come and live with you until I go to school," she said.

"I know you don't get along with your mother, Carrie, but of the two of us, she is the best parent to be with right now. She's not to blame for any of this. Sometimes you remind me of your mother when I first met her."

"Gawd, I hope not."

He chuckled. Whenever he had told Janice that Carrie reminded him of her, Janice always glared at him and said, "We're nothing alike."

But they sure were.

"I've got to go. I left the boys alone making soup."

"Wait, Dad, one more thing. I need to complete the Pell Grant application. I'm running out of time to get aid for college."

Harry closed his eyes. Right. "And I need to do it? What information do you need?"

"Your social security number, annual income, and information like that," she said. "Please. I gave it to you and Mom in February. You guys haven't touched it."

"Call the shop on Monday. I'll tell them to expect your call. They can give you the information."

"But when will I see you? You need to sign it."

"If the form is late and your Mom can't sign it, forge my signature. Okay?"

"That would be dishonest," she said.

She'd always been the one child he never had to worry about doing anything unethical or illegal, or becoming an addict.

"If you want the application completed then take matters into your own hands. I'm giving you permission to sign my name. Now, repeat after me: 'Stop worrying.'"

"I'll try."

Close enough.

"Good girl. I love you. Goodbye."

"I love you too. See you later."

See you later. He'd taught his kids always to say see you later and never goodbye. Goodbye was final. His heart warmed that he was able to say goodbye to her, but he was also grateful she hadn't picked up on his farewell. At least not yet. She was a smart cookie. When she calmed down, no longer worrying about the boys and the gun, his goodbye would come back to her, but by then he'd be gone.

He took a deep breath and called the office. He left his boss, Rudy, a message to answer all of Carrie's questions on Monday. He ended the call and walked past the landlord, and he almost made it to the door without dealing with her again.

"You owe me rent," she said.

Would she be the one who'd find him?

He didn't like her, but he didn't wish the job on anyone. "Get in line," Harry said. "I owe some people my life."

12

CARRIE

kakorrhaphiophobia \kak-ə-ˌraf-ē-ə-ˈfō-bē-ə\ *n : fear of
failure*

I love you too. See you later," Carrie said and gripped the
receiver. The phone was her lifeline to her dad right now.
She waited for him to hang up. She couldn't explain it, but
she'd gotten a wave of homesickness for him and didn't want
to be the one to end the call first. It was as if her waiting for
him to hang up sent him a silent message: *still here with
you, Dad.*

The line went dead.

When was the last time she'd felt homesick? She remembered how homesick she used to get when she was little and
was meant to stay the night at a friend's house. The regret
would start the second Mom or Dad dropped her off and
drove away. Those irrational and horrible feelings of *what
had she done*, or *how would she ever get home again*, had
been all-consuming. If she called her mom or dad to pick her
up, they wouldn't because they knew the feeling would pass

if she could just make it through one night away. So back then, she would pretend she was going to throw up (sick from something she ate or a stomach bug) until her friend's parents would call her parents and take her home. The last time it had happened was in the fourth grade, when she began to realize her family was messed up, but right now from her kitchen, she felt the worst ache for her dad to be with her, in the same house—a desperate need to see that he was okay.

Funny because now she couldn't wait to graduate and go to school so she'd never have to return home again. So she wouldn't have to deal with any of them unless she wanted to go out of her way to do so.

So what was bugging her? Nagging her?

She couldn't put her finger on it, other than she hated it when he was alone at that gross motel, even if it was his own fault.

Hated it. Hated it. It was good the boys were with him for a little bit.

Worry, worry, worry. All she ever did anymore was worry. Worry about school. Worry about her brothers. Worry about her dad.

Dad had said to "stop worrying" and "to go do what kids her age do."

As if.

Telling her to stop worrying and to act like her friends was like asking her to pretend she wasn't living this life and that Mom wasn't her mother, and he wasn't her father; to pretend that WJ wasn't quick to fight with him. Her friends—other kids—didn't have her same family problems.

It was literally all relative.

She needed new relatives. That's what she would need to

stop worrying and "to go do what kids her age do." Did he have any advice on how to do that?

Maybe she should find a ride to his motel to be with him and the boys. That way if WJ showed up, she could interfere. She'd thank him for his help, tell him the boys were okay, and send him on his way. WJ and Dad wouldn't even have to see each other. No fighting. No more trouble.

Five minutes ago, she was worried sick about the boys, now she was worried about Dad and WJ. Tomorrow it would be something else. It just never let up. Her stomach spasmed, and she began to feel hot. She'd love to be a kid. She'd love to be like her friends.

Calm down. Just calm yourself down.

She flipped open her journal. Thank Gawd for her journals and lists. She felt best when she was prepared for the worst-case scenarios on just about everything. If she was prepared for everything, she couldn't fail at anything.

Don't ignore problems, face them head-on and succeed.

She couldn't remember who told her that, but she was committed to the advice and had written it in her journal.

So what was the worse case scenario for Dad right now?

She thumbed through the pages until she found her Worries List and made some changes:

- *College money: What if I don't get a scholarship?*
- *Pell Grant application:* ~~*What if my parents don't complete the Pell Grant application?*~~ *What if I get caught forging Dad's signature?*
- *Essay and Rotary Scholarship interview*
- *A job during college*
- *How will I visit Justin and Tommy when I go to college? Get a car?*

- *How can I afford a car?*
- ~~*Boys and BB gun*~~

She added:

- *Dad: How can I help him? What if he and WJ*
  fight in front of the boys and someone gets hurt?
  Or worse, arrested and CPS gets involved?

Ever since she'd blacked out drinking three years ago, she'd felt sorrier for her dad than her mom. Bottom line, Carrie felt like her dad wasn't capable of changing his life without medical help, but her mom was able to change her life, their life, but she didn't, so it was unforgivable to Carrie that her mom hadn't at least tried to make a difference, even if it meant leaving her dad years ago.

How many years had he been drinking? Blacking out? WJ swore up and down that Dad had been drinking before WJ was born. He'd say, "Dad was born a mean-ass drunk." But he couldn't be right because she'd seen pictures of her dad, mom, and WJ when he was a baby. They were laughing, smiling. There was one picture of Dad and WJ when WJ was about two or three years old, and both of them had their heads thrown back with laughter. It was her favorite picture of them. Years ago, it went missing for a while until she saw it tucked in her dad's wallet.

Did her dad ever have anyone who tried to help him when he first started drinking? She'd never met her grandparents, and Dad avoided talking about his childhood like the plague, but maybe they had been alcoholics too, and what if one of them had never taken him aside when he was a young boy and told him, "Assume you're an alcoholic, Harry." And maybe if someone had, he would have learned the first time, like she did. He could have had a chance.

Right. Go and do what normal kids do.

Here she was on Saturday night, keeping a Worries List and contemplating the hypothetical unfairness of her dad's childhood.

Fun stuff.

She doubted anyone else at school was doing the same thing, at least she hoped they weren't. No, they would be talking about prom or what makeup to try or how to style their hair. When she was with them, they always begged her to wear more makeup and put gel in her frizzy hair. Sometimes she let them do makeovers on her. She liked the normalcy of the moment, just being one of the girls.

They were always frustrated the next day at school when she showed up her usual, makeup-free self. She didn't want to spend any of her money on cosmetics, and she still beat herself up for attracting That Guy to her when she was drunk. Best to avoid attention and not stand out in the looks department.

Once, That Guy had asked her why she didn't wear makeup when it would make her "so hot." Her guess was he'd never gone a day without anything he wanted. He could afford whatever he wanted too, including college. His parents owned real estate throughout the area. She'd asked him if he knew how much mascara, eyeliner, foundation, and blush cost. He didn't, of course.

"I can't afford to be hot," she'd told him. "I'd rather save my money for college."

He replied, "You'd find a way to afford being hot if you were ugly, I guess."

And she said, "Maybe if I were ugly *and* stupid."

He'd smiled and laughed. She liked the way his eyes twinkled whenever he thought she'd said something funny, but she didn't return his smile. She never did. She didn't want to encourage him or have classmates discover her crush on him. She'd had a soft spot for him since he'd thrown her family secrets in a vault, but she'd never told anyone she had feelings for him, and she would never tell anyone because her friends would freak out and encourage her to go for him. Besides, she spoke to him in English class, where they sat next to each other, but nowhere else. Not in the halls. Not in the cafeteria. When their senior year had started, she'd picked her seat first in class, and when he came in, he didn't hesitate —she noticed—to take the desk behind her even though there were plenty of open seats.

A month ago, he had mentioned the prom to her.

"Carrie, do you think I should rent a white or black tux for prom?" His warm peppermint breath tickled the back of her neck.

She suppressed a chill and turned in her chair just enough to see him from the corner of her eye.

Whoa! He was super close.

"You can borrow your dad's brown tuxedo from the sixties for all I care," she said.

Carrie expected a laugh, at least, and when she didn't get one or even a smile, she said, "I'm hardly fashionable, and I'm the worst person you could ask about clothing."

He tapped his pencil on his desk. "Yeah, but you see, the guy's supposed to wear a tux that complements his date's dress."

The faces of the perfect girls in their senior class flashed through her mind. No doubt one would swoon when he asked her to go. She snapped. "Ask your date, then." She turned forward in her seat. It wasn't until her teacher began speaking that it occurred to her that That Guy might have been asking her to prom.

Right. As if she could ever afford to go.

She watched the clock for fifty-two minutes and jumped up one second before the bell rang, all but running out of the classroom and hiding in the girls' bathroom nearby until she was sure he'd passed along.

Most of the girls in her class thought he was gorgeous, and she was no exception. She was focused, not blind. She had enough items on her Worries List—she didn't need to add a prom dress or an unrequited crush to her inventory.

She set her list down and walked to the mirror in the living room. She turned to the side and pulled her T-shirt tight. Her DD breasts sat high and firm. She let the cotton go, and it became a large lump of fabric once again. She didn't have time to worry about clothes. She had her metamorphosis to worry about, like becoming independent and going to college to change her life forever. Lisa thought she was jealous over the attention Lisa got from guys, but the truth was Carrie was scared. She could handle being overlooked by guys and classmates in a popularity contest, but she was terrified of being passed up for college and scholarships, even though the latter seemed to be happening anyway. If her clothes gave the impression she cared more about the books in her backpack than her appearance, then all the better. Besides, her mother and older sisters were perfect examples of how attracting the wrong kind of attention, dating, and messing around could derail aspirations.

She couldn't wait for the next chapter of her life. The University of Reno was a half-hour drive from Corbett City, and no one in her family lived in Reno. No one had graduated from high school, and no one would be moving near *her* university anytime in the near future, at least not until Justin and Tommy were ready to leave home, and by then she'd have every process and obstacle figured out for them.

Her best-case scenario would be to have a full-ride scholarship to UNR, take eighteen credits each semester, two classes each summer, and graduate with her bachelor of science degree in accounting in three years. The sooner she graduated, the sooner she could take her CPA exam and go to work. Then she could afford to have a place that could be a home to her little brothers if they ever needed one.

Her worst-case scenario would be if she didn't get enough financial assistance, and if she had to attend college part-time in order to work and support herself. It would take her several years to graduate, but she would and could make it work out.

At least now she could call her dad's employer on Monday to get information for her Pell Grant application.

Keep moving another step in the right direction.

Her dad was right—she'd take the process into her own hands and sign his name. If it turned out she was too late for the best grants, she could take out student loans. But without applying for the Pell Grant, she couldn't even borrow money for school.

Resolved, Carrie updated her Worries List.

- *College money: ~~What if I don't get a scholarship?~~ Talk to counselor about student loans.*
- *Pell Grant application: ~~What if my parents don't complete the Pell Grant application? What if I get caught forging Dad's signature?~~ Call Dad's work on Monday; sign & mail.*
- *Rotary Scholarship essay*

- *A job during college, ask counselor*
- *How will I visit Justin and Tommy when I go to college? Get a car?*
- *How can I afford a car?*
- ~~*Boys and BB gun*~~
- *Dad: How can I help him? What if he and WJ fight in front of the boys and someone gets hurt? Or worse, arrested, and CPS gets involved?*

She closed her journal. At least she didn't have to wait by the phone anymore. She could focus on writing the first draft of the Rotary Scholarship essay, but first she'd better let Lisa know the boys were fine. It was a stretch, but she might be as worried as Carrie.

As she approached Lisa's bedroom, Carrie heard grunts and moans. Wait a minute. Lisa wasn't worried, she was making out with her boyfriend.

Ew! Gross!

Lisa moaned again.

Carrie pounded on the door. "Stop it *Moan-a* Lisa! If Dad were here, you wouldn't have Jerk-face in there." Carrie ran back to the kitchen table, where she wouldn't have to hear anymore.

Lisa was more concerned about getting another hickey than finding her brothers!

If Dad brings the boys home and sees any marks on her neck, he'll freak out.

The last time it happened, Dad had accused Lisa of being no better than a fire hydrant and "allowing every dog to piss on you." Carrie agreed with him, and she knew she never wanted a hickey. She flipped open her journal to add to her Dos & Don'ts List:

- *Do assume you're an alcoholic, and don't drink when you're too happy, too sad, too mad, too worried, or need to make a decision. Better yet, don't drink. Period.*
- *Do get A's and B's in school*
- *Do finish all homework*
- *Don't miss school*
- *Do keep room clean*
- *Don't lie*
- *Don't do drugs*
- *Don't get a tattoo*
- *Don't wear cutoff shorts*
- *Don't smoke*
- *Don't gamble*
- *Don't yell all the time*
- *Don't swear*
- *Don't ride motorcycles*
- *Don't wear a lot of makeup*
- *Don't double pierce ears*
- *Don't take God's name in vain (Gawd is okay)*

And over the past several years, she had added:

- *Do go to college*
- *Don't wear Black Hills Gold or turquoise jewelry*
- *Don't wear skimpy clothes*
- *Do pay your bills*
- *Don't sing karaoke*
- *Don't sleep around*

"Don't get a hickey," Carrie said aloud as she added it to the list. She may not have control over her family, but she could at least follow her rules. Sometimes she slipped and cursed or took God's name in vain, and she would mess up and yell. But, come on, who could blame her? Still, the lists comforted her when she had no choice but to be home on weeknights and weekends.

She couldn't wait for this weekend to be over. She liked escaping to school and her work-study job with the county Monday through Friday. Her coworkers at the county personnel department were mature adults who cared about her, inspired her, and motivated her to focus on her future. She received constant accolades, things like: "You're the kind of person, Carrie, who will accomplish anything you choose." Every day, someone would ask her how her day was, what had she learned at school, how was the test she was worried about, had she received a scholarship yet?

"Don't worry," they'd say. "You'll get several."

She'd miss them—if she figured out financing—when she moved away for college. What would be the most meaningful way for her to show them her gratitude when the time came and she needed to tell them "See you later"?

Oh no, that was it. That was what had been bugging her!

Dad said "goodbye."

Dad never said goodbye. Never. Goodbye was final, and he had always taught them to say, "See you later," or "Until next time."

He'd say, "Never say goodbye unless you mean it."

He was a die-hard about "Never hitchhike" too. But he had said goodbye on the phone. Of course, he had also been drinking, so maybe he'd meant good night. And the boys were with him. And even if he'd said goodbye, where did he have to go? He had no money to leave or go anywhere. But . . . the words she'd overheard a few years ago when her dad left rehab came back to her. Words she could never quite shake away. Her dad had been explaining his reappearance at home to her mom. It was late, and Carrie had hidden outside the living room.

Dad had said, "I couldn't stay there. They told me I was suicidal. I'm not going to any insane asylum. What the hell do they know? Suicidal my ass. Drunk, yes. Suicidal, no. Proof they don't know what they're talking about." And then, "We can't afford for me to be out of work anyway."

She didn't think he was suicidal. Lonely and tired, of course. But she couldn't imagine he'd ever hurt himself like that, that he'd do anything permanent. He must have meant good night. He was probably distracted by the boys' appearance.

That was it, good night. Good night was what he'd meant to say.

If she could call him to make sure he was okay, she would, but she couldn't deal with the landlord again. There was no reason her mom would take her call at the bar—she hadn't the first time. She doubted any of her friends had to worry about their dad just because he said goodbye. They didn't have to wonder if it had been a slip of the tongue or if their dad would hurt himself. Carrie added to her list of worries and then turned to a blank page to write the first draft of her scholarship essay.

Just focus on school. Just focus on school. Just focus on school.

13

WJ

Avast there—Leave the kid alone, or I'll smack ya!
—Popeye

WJ couldn't wait for this shitshow of a Saturday night to end. So far, the only thing that had gone his way was that Scotty had blackballed the young dickwad who had called him a faggot last night. At least he didn't have to teach him a lesson by shoving that word up his ass. But every damn-thing-else that night had gone down the shitter.

As he turned into the driveway where his dad was staying, WJ glared at Hefty in the passenger's seat of his dad's car. It was the meathead's fault they were so behind schedule.

He could kill Hefty right now. Swear to God he could. But he had someone else to take care of first. His heart raced with adrenaline for what it was time to do.

He was going to kill his dad. Wipe the scumbag off the face of the earth. If he thought he could get his father to leave town and never come back, he'd give him the option and save himself the dirty work of killing him and covering his tracks, but his parents were two crazy magnets that wouldn't stay away from each other.

He couldn't trust either one of them to do the right thing. So he would.

WJ had survived those fists, but not many could. His little brothers couldn't. They were softer than WJ had been at their age. Or, hell, maybe they weren't. He'd once been sweet like them. It was just so damn hard to remember because his father had beat that innocent kid stuff out of him. When he was ten years old, he didn't have a big brother who could stand up to their dad, and he'd always sworn he'd defend his younger brothers. He hadn't had to protect Bobby; their dad never laid a hand on him probably because Bobby was straight. Nope, the abusive prick had saved all his "boxing lessons" for WJ.

Lucky him.

But the older his dad got, the drunker he stayed. He was a loose cannon, and no way was WJ going to let that cannon loose on his little brothers. He could stand a lot, but he couldn't stand for that.

There were many ways he'd like to kill his dad. He'd fantasized about them all his life, especially when he'd lain bruised and curled up on the floor, unable to get up long after his dad was done with a "lesson" that left the room spinning, his ears ringing, and pains—both from contact and intention—coming from so deep inside it hurt to breathe.

Why did his dad have to hate him so much? What had he ever done to deserve it? He couldn't help how he felt.

First time it happened, his dad had said, "Defend yourself, you little homo—because no one else will," and then he'd thrown a blanket over WJ's huddled form because he hated him so much he couldn't stand to look at him. That or he was too much of a fucking coward to witness his abuse.

Good old Dad was a monster, and when WJ was done with him, he wouldn't be covering him up with a blanket to hide his work, he'd be proud of it. Proud of protecting his siblings the only way he knew how—with his fists.

Taught me well, Dad.

With Hefty's help, he was going to suffocate the asshole with a pillow. He was probably passed out anyway. It would be for the best if there was no fight. No struggle. His mom would want to do something stupid and undeserving like a wake and a funeral. A bona fide send-off to shit knew where. But if there was a hell, that's where his dad belonged. And he couldn't send him there soon enough.

And if not for Hefty, WJ would be done with it. Seeing Hefty absently looking out the windshield beside him, WJ gave a swift right to Hefty's temple.

"Fuck, WJ! I said I'm sorry."

Sorry? Hefty didn't know what being sorry meant, not yet anyway. Bender was going to skin him alive.

They'd gone to collect debt from the deadbeat dealer on Bender's behalf and to scare the shit out of him if he was indeed narcing on his sources, Bender, and the club. WJ still couldn't believe that he had only stepped out of the room for one stupid second to get his cigarettes out of the car, and when he came back, the dealer was dead. A bloody lump in the center of the living room floor. Hefty had gone ballistic and smashed the man's face in.

"What the fuck did you do that for?" WJ had roared. There was blood sprayed all over the walls. They were supposed to rough him up, make sure he wasn't a narc, collect their money, and get out. He'd keep dealing drugs for them, making money, and from now on, he'd pay them on time. The plan was not to fucking kill him before they'd gotten any information or money, for Christ's sake. And damn, they'd have to find another dopehead to deal the area.

Hefty had flexed his hamburger-meat-looking fist, shaken his head, and said, "Lost my cool."

"Lost your cool? You can explain that to Bender, you dipshit."

He and Hefty had gloved up, gone through the house, and torn it apart like some pissed-off and desperate crankheads looking for a fix and losing their minds. Time would tell if the cops would fall for it.

Not likely.

Hefty losing his cool had cost them two hours covering their tracks, and WJ knew this wasn't over. Narc or not, the cops would already know the guy was a drug dealer—Corbett City cops knew everyone who was dealing. Not a single one of them hadn't been picked up at some point and asked to become a rat, but up until now, none had squealed about their source. They'd been more afraid of the Knights than the cops or ATF. But if this guy was a narc—something they couldn't confirm now since Hefty had killed him—the ATF would assume the RKs were involved. And if he wasn't a narc, ATF would still look at the RKs, because shit for sure, they were looking for any excuse to hand out warrants and search their homes. He and Hefty would have no alibi for the past two hours. Truck loads of shit were hitting the fan.

He parked his father's car in front of the motel. Carrie had said he was in Number Twenty-Two. WJ looked around.

Damn hell depressing place to die.

"Stay here," he said to Hefty. "Don't need you to fuck this up too."

Hefty frowned and added pressure to his bloody fist. "I think that guy lost a tooth in my knuckle."

"You idiot. He lost his fucking face in your knuckles."

Hefty curled his hand and flinched. "Buzz, we need to ditch this car. Someone may have seen it at the slimeball's house."

Oh, now the dumbass cared about a clean job?

"You're telling me what needs to be done? I'll always do what I need to do to defend the club's honor. The boss knows that. And you'd better figure it out too. We'll deal with your hand and the car next. Watch for my signal." WJ climbed out of the car.

Before he could reach the first step, his dad stuck his head out the front door, like he'd been expecting him. He was supposed to be passed out in bed, waiting for a pillow over the head and WJ's large hands grinding it into his face.

Dammit. He didn't want to draw any attention to himself outside the unit, from neighbors, but it was what it was. He took all of his pent-up anger from years of abuse, and the circus of his night, and let it loose toward his father. WJ leapt up the two stairs like a ferocious grizzly bear.

His dad stepped outside and pulled the door shut. "What are you doing with my car? Who's that with you?"

"Inside. Now." WJ shoved his shoulder.

"No," his dad said. "Is that one of your stupid friends? Your involvement with them is going to be your downfall."

"Fuck you. Inside." So much for being quiet.

"I don't want any trouble, and neither should you," his dad said.

"You are trouble. Trouble to my little brothers and sisters. Trouble drawing attention to the family. Trouble to me. I warned you the last time you hit me that I'd never let you abuse the kids." He took a final step forward and bumped his dad's chest with his own, expecting some resistance, but his dad just wilted.

"Stop acting like a damn cock. I haven't hit you for years, and I haven't touched the kids. I wouldn't. And I'm not going to fight you now," his dad said and put his hands up, palms facing forward.

Palms that used to curl into fists and slam into his little body.

"Lying sack of shit." He shoved his dad and gripped his dad's scabbed knuckles. He sure as hell had been hitting someone. "Why not? Scared? You weren't when I was a kid."

Harry stumbled and leaned against the wall.

WJ grabbed his dad's collar and twisted it into a noose around his neck, putting his face in his. His dad's breath reeked of stale beer. That heavy, hot breath had been shoved in his own face after a beating too many times to count. His dad would always lean down, spit flying with each word, and say, "Get up and fight me, pussy!"

"How does it feel, huh? How does it feel to be the 'pussy' now?" WJ twisted the collar tighter.

His dad's face started to turn red and then blue. He grabbed at WJ's hands. He wheezed. "Boys . . ."

What about the boys? WJ's hands were white as he clenched his dad's shirt. "Inside, now." He shoved his dad, gratified to see him stumble and bend at his waist to inhale air. "Time to die."

"Boys are here." His dad started coughing.

WJ stilled. Justin and Tommy? Here? Frantically, he looked to the small window, but it was empty. He was so relieved their little faces hadn't seen him choking their dad. No matter that his dad deserved it. WJ didn't want to be the one who snuffed out his little brothers' innocence. That was the entire fucking point. To protect them. Let them be kids.

He yanked his dad to a standing position. "Where?"

His dad rubbed his neck. "They showed up an hour ago. They're asleep. You want to beat me up? Kill me? Don't do it with them here. I'm too tired to fight you, or anyone else. Get in line. I'm done."

WJ paced away and then back. He flexed his hands. The force of his energy and his intention was almost more than he could handle. Good thing he'd wanted to be clearheaded and hadn't done another hit of crank.

Fuck! His dad was controlling his choices, even now.

"You're a pathetic excuse of a man." He'd never wanted to punch him more in his life, seeing that pansy-ass look on his face. He pulled back his fist, aiming for his dad's face, and was disappointed when his dad didn't even flinch.

Instead, his dad stared at his fist, the one he'd hit Shelly with.

"Your hands don't look any better than mine. Like father, like son."

That's what his mom had said too. "I'm nothing like you." His arm fell to his side.

"Once, you were nothing like me. I see that now. But it doesn't matter."

WJ frowned. "What the fuck does that mean? What in the hell are you talking about?"

WJ thought he might lose it. He'd come here to kill the asshole, and now they were talking in fucking riddles.

His dad turned toward the door. "Take the boys home, and I need you to give something to your mother for me too."

"What in the hell is wrong with you?" This was not the

way things were supposed to be going. But his dad only
ignored him and walked into the room.

WJ followed him and almost tripped over Star as she
darted between his legs.

Justin and Tommy were sprawled out on the floor, sound
asleep. Unharmed. Unmarked.

This fucking night had to end. Nothing was working out.

His dad walked over to the desk and picked up an envelope. "Take this and give it to your mom." He bent over and
picked up Tommy. "Get Justin."

WJ looked at the sealed envelope. "What the fuck is this?
A love letter? Who in the hell do you think I am? Cupid?"
But his dad still ignored him.

"Oh, for fuck's sake." WJ shoved the envelope in his front
pocket.

His dad put Tommy in WJ's arms and picked up Justin.
"Let's take them to the car, and you can take them home."

WJ held little Tommy in his arms. He was taking his dad's
orders as if he was a stupid kid again. Feeling helpless and
with arms full, he followed his dad out to the car.

Hefty jumped out. "Um, Buzz, is this the signal?"

If his arms weren't full, WJ would rip Hefty's head off.
"Does it look like a fucking signal?"

"Open the door," Harry said, glaring at Hefty.

"I'm confused," Hefty said, looking from WJ to Harry.

"Join the fucking club," WJ said and slid Tommy into the
back seat.

His dad laid Justin next to Tommy and waved Star into
the car. "Take them straight home. Carrie's waiting for them."
He pointed at Hefty. "And don't let that piece of shit
touch them."

WJ could only shake his head, fucking clueless about

what was happening, as his dad leaned in the car and caressed the boys' heads in a way he'd never touched WJ. He even touched the fat dog with more care. "Goodbye, boys."

WJ looked from the car to his old man. "I don't know what the fuck you're up to, but I'm coming back after I drop them off. This. Is. Not. Over."

"I wouldn't if I were you," his dad said. He ran a shaking hand through his silver hair. He sighed and frowned before reaching over and gently squeezing WJ's shoulder.

WJ flinched like the hand was a red-hot fireplace poker.

"But I'll be here if you do," he said and turned away.

WJ ran his hand over the envelope in his pocket. He stood beside the car until his dad disappeared into the room. No, not his dad, some fucking body snatcher he'd never met.

"What are you waiting for?" Hefty asked.

WJ's gut told him something was off, but given his intentions, he wasn't sure why he cared.

"Something's not right." He'd never seen his dad like this. Resigned. What had he said? "I'm done?" He pulled the letter out of his pocket and put it back. What if this was a suicide letter? Just when he was ready to kill his dad, was his dad going to do it for them?

No. No way. His dad was too much of a coward. Too selfish. Couldn't give up alcohol, much less life. He was probably just feeling fucking sorry for himself. He'd sleep it off just like he always did. But he still needed to die. By the time WJ returned, he would be passed out and easily taken care of, but it meant WJ had to stay revved up and furious to do the deed.

Hefty grunted. "Come on. My hand hurts like a son of a bitch."

"Shut your sissy mouth." He was never going to work

with Hefty again. Why the hell had he brought Hefty with him to kill his dad? He shouldn't bring him back with him when he returned.

He's still your father, a small voice whispered in his head, *maybe you wouldn't be able to kill him—that's why you brought Hefty.*

WJ shook his head and pushed the voice away. That man had stopped acting like a father years ago. WJ knew his father's fist and rejection better than he knew the man. His dad was too much of a wimp to hurt himself anyway. And if he did—one less problem to deal with.

"Get in. I'll take them home, drop you off at Doc's, and come back alone."

He hadn't realized it earlier, but he knew it now: there were some things a man should do alone. Like kill his dad.

14

JANICE

You're gonna have to learn to get out there in front of those cameras and hold your head up. Take charge when you're singing.
—Patsy Cline

April 1959—Lincoln County, MN

W alter, wait for me." Janice tried to yell, but her voice was a mere whisper as they ran through the field behind Grandfather's barn. How Walter managed to hear her, she didn't know, but he called over his shoulder, "I can't. You shouldn't have let go."

They were chasing three red helium balloons after the strings had slipped from her fingertips. At first they had laughed as they chased and jumped for the floating balloons, but with each step, Walter had gained distance, and he was getting too far away from her. She was desperate for him to return to her side and forget those blasted balloons.

"Come back," she called. Why couldn't she run faster?

Why was it so hard to breathe? The weight about her chest was unbearable, the pressure was squeezing her lungs, and her heart ached as if someone was wringing the hope out of it. Why, oh why, had she been so careless? She should have paid attention, held on tight.

"Come back!" she said again, but he kept running, and the weight in her chest became suffocating. The balloons started laughing at her, bobbing in the air in a happy dance as Walter chose them over her.

"Janice, wake up now," Grandma said.

What was Grandma doing here? She was afraid to take her eyes off Walter's retreating back. "Walter!"

"Wake up, honey."

Grandma again? Can't she see I'm busy?

"This thrashing isn't good for you or the baby."

The baby? She took her eyes off Walter for one second to turn in the field and face Grandma.

The baby.

Walter.

Janice trembled as Grandma smoothed the fabric over her shaking shoulders and started pulling her farther from Walter and the damn balloons he wouldn't stop chasing. She shrugged away Grandma's hands to turn back and look for Walter. She couldn't see him anymore, just the balloons floating higher, becoming specks on the horizon.

And then *whoosh*. The balloons disappeared. The field too. She was left in the dark.

She saw fluorescent red now as light danced against her closed eyelids. She curled her fists, gripping what felt like her bedsheets until someone . . . Grandma—she could tell by her calloused palms—gently uncurled her hands and adjusted the sheets underneath.

Walter was gone. Gone forever.

She could not, would not, open her eyes. She didn't want to see a world that didn't have Walter in it. Couldn't stand to lie in her bed and look up at her ceiling where she had once imagined the world beyond it and dreamt about their future. Opening her eyes made it real. Unlivable. But squeezing her eyes shut was not stopping the tears from falling down her face. Tears never lied. They came no matter what she didn't want to face.

She turned on her side toward Grandma's lemon scent, burying the side of her face in her pillow. *Let me back to the dream. Let me back to Walter.*

She couldn't take a life without him. What was she supposed to do now?

Her heart thumped slow and loud, echoing through her core and temples. *Thump. Silence. Thump. Silence.* How was her heart working at all? It was all wrung out.

Was he alone when he died? Was he scared? She should have been there with him. Maybe she could have saved him. Maybe if he hadn't been hurrying to do his chores to speak with Grandfather and Grandma, he'd still be alive. They should have waited longer to tell anyone. No, they should have just left and continued their lives together, and they would already be in the city—her, Walter, and her growing belly. No deadly tractors. No farm accidents.

The weight on her chest intensified. She curled her knees to her chin, feeling the chain with Walter's ring squeezed between her breasts. She'd been playing with the chain just before she heard June Black crying. Just before she fainted.

"Sweetie, come on now. Let me see those blue eyes."

A cool cloth was put against her temple. She took a deep, shuddering breath and looked at her new world.

Grandma blurred before her as she wiped at Janice's tears, but what was the point? Janice reached her hand up to stop her. There were too many tears to keep up with, and she wouldn't be stopping anytime soon. "Our baby?"

"The baby is fine. The doctor just left."

Janice grabbed the cloth from Grandma and covered her face and sobbed. Her baby was okay. She hadn't lost everything. She slid one hand down to cover her still-flat belly nestled behind her bent knees. She imagined their baby in the same fetal position she was in, grieving the loss of its father. Grieving for Walter, just like her. They had each other, and somehow, they'd both survive. They'd always have a part of Walter but never enough. She hugged herself and her baby tight and rocked back and forth, wishing they could sleep through the next several months of grief and that Grandma would let 'em.

A week later, Grandfather and Grandma went to Walter's funeral along with the entire community—except for Janice, of course. She was the most important person in Walter's life but was being told she couldn't go. It didn't make sense. Sitting up in bed, she challenged them both. "But what will you tell his parents when they ask about me?" she asked.

Darn it, she'd been invisible most of her life, but Walter's family would want to see her now. They'd lost their son but gained a daughter. A grandchild. She'd slept most of the week away. No doubt the Whitworths had been busy with the funeral arrangements, and she was only sorry she'd been too drained to help them out and be there for them, with them. She'd never interacted with them one on one, but like she'd promised Walter, she was ready to love his family as her own.

"You have to focus on yourself and the baby now. If anyone asks, we'll say you're ill," Grandfather said.

She frowned at him. He just didn't get it, did he? "Not just anyone. Most won't even notice I'm not there. They've never noticed me. But Walter's parents and brother will. That's who I care about now. I don't want them to think I'm ill and worry them on top of everything. Walter would want me to be with them."

Grandfather shook his head and rubbed his eyes. "I've been in town a few times this week. I'll bet my biggest hog he didn't say a word."

Oh no—she was having none of his doubt or putting up with him pretending to know Walter better than she did. Walter loved her. He loved their baby. He loved their plans. Surely Walter had talked to his parents before his accident. There was no reason he wouldn't have. "He told them. I know he did. You don't appreciate the man he was."

Grandma reached over and squeezed Grandfather's shoulder.

As empty and weak as she might feel, she wanted to go to the funeral more than ever. She wanted to be with Walter's family, near other people who understood the depth of her loss.

"Who's to say now? Maybe he did, but Janice, the funeral isn't the right time or place to find out. Consider the baby and the upset. I know what stress can do to a baby. I've seen my share of stillborn colts for less stress than this."

She was sick to death of being compared to animals, but Grandfather only had his farm animals he openly cared about. So if he wanted to compare her to his horses, that was as good as it could get with him. He was putting her and the baby first.

She caved. "Well, when you put it like that . . . it's what Walter would want, too—for our baby and me to be healthy." So it was settled; she'd stay home.

But while they were gone, Janice forced herself to get up, wash her face, change her clothes, and tidy her hair. She'd bet Grandfather's best hog that the Whitworths, upon seeing Grandfather and Grandma at the funeral, would surely ask them if they could follow them home. They'd want to see her and welcome her to their family just as Walter had assured her they would once he told them and gave them time to get used to the idea. That time had been shortchanged, but having lost their son, they'd be relieved to know she and the baby were okay—she just knew it.

But when Grandfather and Grandma returned, they looked pale and frustrated—and they were alone. She peppered them with questions about the funeral and Walter's family. "How are his parents? What did they say? When do they want to see me?"

"Oh, honey," Grandma said, sitting down and smoothing the skirt over her knees. "They don't know Walter was seeing you. When we gave our condolences to the Whitworths, they didn't bat an eyelash or ask for you. Walter must not have told them about you. Or the baby. I'm sorry, honey. You said he was going to tell them around his chores. Well, God had other plans, I suppose."

"Or Walter did," Grandfather said and clenched his jaw.

"Not now, Hugh," Grandma said.

Janice wasn't dumb, she knew what Grandfather was implying, but he was wrong. Walter didn't have other plans. Not for a second did she worry Walter had changed his mind. If he didn't tell his parents, he'd had a good reason. Something must have happened on the farm that caused him to forgo breakfast and talking to his parents.

What she didn't understand was why Grandma and Grandfather wouldn't have told them. Pulled them aside. Said something.

"But why didn't you tell them then?" she asked.

They just said, "Give us some time, everyone time, to recover."

Recovering would take her years. They'd all be feeling the loss of Walter for years to come, but their baby wasn't going to wait.

"I'm having this baby. My baby won't be invisible. They have the right to know. And my baby has a right to his or her family."

"Enough!" Grandfather roared so hard the glassware rattled. "This is not all about you. There are other people's lives to be considered. Lives that this news will damage. I will have your word that you will not leave this farm or tell anyone anything until I say so."

Over the next two months, Janice never left the farm. Grandma told the school that Janice had mono and would have to finish the year homeschooled and miss the graduation ceremony.

She didn't give a fig about missing graduation. She did her homework, obsessed about her baby's health, and waited for the right time to talk to Walter's family. At least the right time according to Grandfather.

The doctor was sworn to secrecy, and they'd told her more times than she could count that she'd best stay home and rest until they could figure out "what to do next about it."

As far as she was concerned, what she'd be doing next was having Walter Junior or Wanda Jane. When Walter had asked her what she would like to name their baby, she'd said, "Boy or girl, the initials will be W to honor you and J to honor me." He had loved the idea. She'd taken to the habit of calling her baby WJ while she talked to her stomach.

Grandma and Grandfather never mentioned her baby except in terms of "it" or "this news," but they also didn't press her to help with chores or ask her to stop talking about Walter to them, so she didn't try to press them to treat her unborn baby like their grandbaby just yet. They constantly fretted over her and wouldn't let her out of their sight most days. Truth be told, she'd never felt more loved by her grandparents. Or more suffocated.

Maybe Grandma and Grandfather thought she'd run off like her own mother did and leave them with a baby to raise. Or maybe on the days she couldn't get out of bed because she was so bereft, they thought she might never get up, but she was getting stronger. And she'd never leave her baby with them. No way, nohow.

Most days, she still couldn't believe that Walter was gone. How could they be so close to happiness and lose each other? He'd been buried for two months, and she hadn't been to the cemetery. She didn't want to think about him there. Her stomach was growing a little every day. Grandma said she was carrying high, and she was so skinny that in another few months "even the bats would see she was pregnant." She couldn't wait for the day he or she was born and brought love back to her life.

In July, Janice was sitting behind the barn in her and Walter's meeting spot when Grandfather's voice carried through the wind.

"Janice! Come inside!"

She stood and straightened her skirt. She plucked a foxtail from her anklet and pulled her sweater tight. She had worn the sweater the last time Walter held her. Sometimes, she could find a spot and still smell his scent.

When she entered the kitchen, supper wasn't on the table, and Grandfather and Grandma were sitting on one side of the table looking like someone had just run off with all the farm animals. Grandma had run into town today. Maybe she had bad news.

This didn't look good. Or maybe . . . maybe it was. Maybe they would finally take her to talk to the Whitworths, and they were just worried about worst-case scenarios and all that. Lord knew they were worriers.

Oh, how she was ready to tell the Whitworths!

Grandfather waved her to an empty chair across from them. "Your grandmother and I need to speak to you."

Finally! They were going to talk about her baby. She had so many things to get ready. A crib, colorful fabric for clothes, a pram . . .

"Janice, your grandmother and I've come to a decision."

The anticipation was killing her. Yes, a decision to let her share her "news" with all of Lincoln County and the Whitworths. She couldn't wait. She'd run down Main Street shouting, "I'm having Walter Whitworth's baby!"

"We will raise the child as our own," he said.

She exhaled sharply. *No, no, no.* They did not just say that. How dare they? Sucker punched by her own grandparents.

"It's the only way," Grandfather said.

She jumped to her feet, certain Walter was rolling in his grave, cheering her on to stand up for their family in his stead.

"Absolutely not. This is my child. I say what happens to him or her, not you."

"It's the only way," Grandfather said again, spreading his large palms flat on the table before him. "We've made arrangements for you to stay with your great aunt outside of Minneapolis until you have it. We'll raise it as our own. We'll say we are fostering it from a distant relative."

It. It. It. "You can't be serious." She looked to her grandma for support, but Grandma nodded.

"No," Janice said. "I won't allow it."

"Listen, girl. Soon, you won't be able to hide that you're pregnant. No one in town even knows you and Walter were sweet on each other. You and the child will be outcasts. We could lose our customers. You can't be an unwed mother in this town. Do you want people treating your child as a bastard? This community is too small."

"Not if we tell the Whitworths. People respect them. They have a right to know about their grandchild. They'll want to have our baby in their life. People will do what they ask. They always have!"

"You're assuming they would believe you, and it's a huge risk to take in this town. You have to think about the welfare of the child," Grandfather said.

"I am thinking about the welfare of my child!" Her baby was all she thought about. Why wouldn't they believe her and give the Whitworths more credit? Why did Grandfather always assume the worst?

Grandma leaned forward. "Janice, there is no easy way to tell you this."

There was more? What could be harder to say than what they just had?

Grandfather took Grandma's hand. "I'll tell her."

"No." Grandma shook her head. "It's best coming from me. I went to see Mrs. Whitworth today. To drop off the milk. June Black and her parents were there. It is Mrs. Whitworth's assumption that Walter was going to talk to her and her husband about a girlfriend, even hinted at the seriousness of the relationship. But then the accident happened."

Janice was so confused. This was good then. It proved Walter intended to tell them about her, not that she needed the proof. "So did you tell her? Did you tell her he was going to talk to her about me?"

Grandma sighed. "They think he was going to talk to them about June Black."

"What?"

Her grandparents just stared at her, and then Grandma said, "June showed up there just after the accident. It's a natural assumption."

"But he wasn't! He had no interest in her. She was always after him. But it was me. Me all the time."

"But they don't know that, and June isn't saying otherwise," Grandma said.

Janice jumped to her feet and pulled Walter's ring from her chest. "We have to tell them. I'll show them his ring. June is lying."

Grandfather stood to stare her down. "I believe you, but Walter is dead. Who are they more likely to believe? You or June Black? A girl he openly dated at one time. Come on, girl. You know. You're smart enough to know that there is not a happy ending here. I'm sorry the boy died and didn't get to talk to them about you. I'm sorry he left us all with this mess."

Mess. He thought her child was a mess to be cleaned up. Walter had not betrayed her. She knew that. June was another story. The Whitworths another story yet for not knowing Walter best of all.

"You'll go to your great aunt's tomorrow."

She sank into her chair, her legs no longer able to hold her. They all sat in silence for some time. Fix-its scrambled in her mind.

"But what about me, then? What am I supposed to do after I have my baby? I don't want to be separated." She wasn't her mother. She couldn't desert her child.

"That'll be up to you. You can return to the farm. Of course, you'll have to wait awhile so that people don't suspect the baby is yours. If you come back, the baby will be your cousin. Or," he said as he glanced at Grandma, "you can pursue your dreams in the city. A baby might be a lot of work for us alone, but we'll manage. Either way, the baby will be known as your cousin."

Her cousin? Her cousin?

Her hands went reflexively to her belly. She turned to Grandma. "There must be another way. You can't support this. You can't mean to do this again?"

Grandma looked down, and at that moment, Janice felt her heart breaking a second time.

Family secrets. She hated them. She hated her mother for creating a precedent. She hated her grandparents for allowing it. "The baby will be my baby. Is this how you managed my mother?" she asked. "Did you give her a choice without really giving her a choice to keep me?"

Grandma paled. "The situation with your mother was

different. She had already left Minnesota and was still married when she found out she was pregnant with you. We've always acknowledged you as our grandchild."

"How was it really different, though? I don't know my own mother. Why didn't she stay? I don't know my father's name! Has anyone in Lincoln County ever cared that you had to raise me?" But she knew the answer because she'd been invisible.

"Don't be naïve," Grandfather said. "This town is a Lutheran community, and having a child out of wedlock will not be accepted. You've always wondered why people were polite to you but remained distant. Even with your mother being wed, they were suspicious. But we did what we thought was best. Your mother made her choice to leave and not stay in touch. And that's all in the past. There's nothing we can do to change any of it now. This is the only way we know how to help you and the baby."

Janice had tried so many times to learn the truth about her mother's departure and knew from experience it was futile. But she would not perpetuate her family's secrets. She cradled her stomach. "Why would I want my baby to be treated politely but distantly then? If they were suspicious about my mother, they will certainly be judgmental about you raising a distant relative. And my baby will look like Walter. Have you thought of that? I can't have this baby and then pretend I'm not the mother. The baby is a part of me, a part of Walter. This baby is all I have! Don't you see that?"

"Without our help, you won't have anything," Grandfather said.

"Then I'll move to Minneapolis, and after I have the baby, I'll get a job, pay Great Aunt rent, and raise my baby. But please, please don't ask me to choose between you and my baby."

Grandma started to cry. It was the first time she'd ever seen Grandma cry. "There is only one choice, Janice. We've thought it through over and over."

Grandfather said, "We've got a little savings, and your grandmother's sister is willing to take you in for the year. She'll tell people you're a widow. You'll start showing soon. We're putting you on the bus tomorrow. When the baby is old enough, we'll come fetch it."

———

Eleven months later—Minneapolis, MN

June 12, 1960

Dear Grandfather and Grandma:

By the time you receive this letter, what I have to say won't be a surprise. I'm sure Great Aunt Bess has already called you.

Maybe life won't be easy, but Walter Jr. and I are going to figure it out together. With the money I earned waitressing while I was pregnant, I've secured an apartment for me and WJ in Minneapolis (That's what I call him, WJ). I have a flatmate who helps me babysit when she isn't working, and I have a new job at the local radio station. My dream is coming true after all. Baby and all. He's a healthy and happy eight-month-old boy.

Don't worry about us. We're better off together. I know

you thought you were offering the best option, but there's only one choice as far as I'm concerned, and my choice is to be a mother to my son. I'll write when I can.

With love and respect,
    —Janice

15

JANICE

*The one thing I wanted to do more than anything else was
sing country music.*
—Patsy Cline

Janice was so damn excited, her toes tingled. Soon she'd
be singing her last song at The Creek.

She could just hug herself.

Winning and saving enough money to go to Nashville was
the first goal she had set for herself in decades and, by golly,
with fingers crossed, she was doing it. People could call her a
lot of things, but in her heart, she could call herself a doer.
She was going to be someone who does what they say they're
going to do, someone who walks her talk. Happy tears stung
her eyes. When was the last time she'd had anything but sad
tears? She couldn't remember.

She hadn't been sure how she'd feel about her last night at
this bar that had played such a frequent role in her marriage,
both the ups and the downs. And the night had gotten off to
the wrong start when WJ showed up. But once he'd left and

had taken his hateful energy with him, the bar had livened up. Several newcomers had gotten on stage to sing, and in the end, had done her a favor; they all sucked and made her sound even better. She was going to win. She could feel it. Her last song tonight was her own private joke: "These Boots Are Made for Walkin'" by Nancy Sinatra. She freshened up her red lipstick and made her way back to the bar to wait for her turn on stage.

Scotty joined her. "Harry called. Your boys showed up at his place. Said something about a BB gun."

Her smile faltered. "Oh. Okay. Thanks," she said. She reached for the peanuts in the bowl in front of her and was surprised to find popcorn. Scotty must be trying something new, but the popcorn reminded her of her grandma, so she pushed the bowl away. She'd already eaten two bowls of nuts anyway, thanks to her nerves tonight. Despite what she'd said to WJ, of course she worried about the boys, but she knew they didn't have a real gun because she had checked the box before she left that night. She normally checked the guns every night before she went to bed, but the past week had been busy with her filing the restraining order and all, and tonight was the first time she had checked in a while.

So sue her.

Maybe she shouldn't have assumed that Harry took the BB gun. What if the boys had shot an eye out with a BB? She shivered at the thought. But what was done was done. So the boys had taken it. If they were with Harry, they'd be okay tonight. Besides, she would be leaving them with him very soon. It was best Harry got some practice putting out fires in her place. He was going to need that practice for this upcoming year.

However, given everything that was going on, she was

curious why Justin and Tommy had gone to Harry's motel. She'd explained to them what a restraining order meant and why she'd filed it. Tommy had asked her, "Are you scared of Dad, Mom?" She was honest and said she was sometimes.

"Are you afraid of Dad, Tom?" she'd asked. He had taken his time answering, and she held her breath—not so confident she'd be able to leave him for a year if he said yes. Harry had been horrible to WJ, but he had never hit any of the other kids.

But the cutie pie, who could set his jaw just like her grandfather used to, shook his head and said, "Nah, Justin and I can handle him. Right, Justin?"

While Justin and Tommy gave her the thumbs up, she let go of the breath she'd been holding and took those thumbs up as a sign. A sign that they would want her to follow her dreams if they were old enough to understand the *whys and hows*.

Harry had stayed at Green Street on enough occasions that she wasn't surprised the boys could navigate their way to the motel. They knew the fields well—they played in them most every day. But she really was curious why they'd sought Harry out when they'd never done so in the past—and why they took the BB gun. Perhaps it was another sign that the boys would be all right once she left them with their dad. She needed them to be. The more signs she was making the right choice, the better.

In a few weeks' time when she packed up her car and dropped off Justin and Tommy with Harry, she ran the risk that her small sons would never forgive her. If they grew up to loathe her, all of her children would officially consider her an abysmal failure of maternal love. But she had let this scare her into doing nothing, into making no changes, for long enough. She was no good to them like this—depressed, dying inside.

The greater risk was losing her mind. What kind of example was that?

She wanted one year, one year out of thirty, or twenty-eight, depending where she started counting—either when she'd had WJ or when she'd fallen in love with Harry—to pick up her dreams where she lost them. Just one year to remind her that life was worth living.

Was that so much to ask for?

She had no idea what to expect in Nashville. Maybe it was crazy for her to be forty-eight and dreaming about singing at the Grand Ole Opry, but she was going to try. With tonight's winnings, she would have enough money to get there and find an apartment. She didn't care if she had to sleep in her car between Nevada and Tennessee and survive on saltine crackers and jam. It would suit her just fine if her first apartment had to be a dive. She was willing to work two jobs to earn enough money to rent a recording studio, and if her first singing gig was on a sidewalk corner, fine. She could do it on her own.

No problem-o.

But what she couldn't afford to do, and downright refused to do, was worry about bringing her boys and being paranoid about the kind of people she would be inviting into her life in pursuit of her dreams this first year. What if one was a sexual threat to her children like Great Uncle Bo. A person—a mother—didn't get a second chance to correct that kind of risk to her kids. She would know. Harry had never done—would never do—anything sexually creepy to WJ. But he had beat him, and no matter what WJ believed, her regret for not interfering, not doing something about it, kept her up many nights.

She'd take that regret to her deathbed.

With Tommy and Justin in Nashville, she would have to worry about everything and everyone, something she'd been doing since the day WJ was born. She was prepared to do whatever was necessary to give one hundred percent to her dream, and that included forsaking Justin and Tommy for the time she deserved to establish her life away from Harry and Tiger Drive.

She'd be back for them once she had created a new life and when Harry agreed to a divorce. She didn't know when that day would be. Janice only knew for sure that she'd faced this same choice once before when she was pregnant with WJ, and she wasn't willing to make the same mistake.

When she left Lincoln County with her unborn child, it was the last time she saw her grandparents. She'd written them a few times, but she'd never fully forgiven them for asking her to choose between her baby and a home with them. Until now. Now she forgave them entirely. If anything, she was disappointed they hadn't pushed her harder to take their help, but she'd been stubborn, naïve, just like Grandfather had said. She'd thought it was best for her and her baby to have each other, that all a child needed was his mother's love, but now to look at her oldest son and the life he chose to live, in addition to the rocky one she'd given him as a child, she knew her stubbornness had only hurt them both.

Now she understood Grandfather and Grandma hadn't been trying to take her child away; they'd been trying to hand her an opportunity to live her life unencumbered. Maybe they'd offered her mother the same choice and her mother had been wiser to take the chance—she'd never know, since she never found her. At the time, Janice had seen their ulti-matum through the lens of control, secrecy, and sacrifice. Her sacrifice.

She'd been stupid and foolish. She'd sacrificed more in her lifetime than her seventeen-year-old self could've ever imagined.

She had chosen WJ and a husband over her grandparents. She'd thought Harry shared her aspirations. He was willing to raise WJ as his own, give him his name, and become her singing partner. Heck, even she had ended up creating secrets. WJ knew Harry as his father. He had no idea about Walter. Once Harry legally adopted him, WJ's revised and reissued birth certificate showed his name simply as WJ Sloan. She and Harry agreed to never tell WJ about his real dad, or his true given name.

It had taken her years to give up on Harry, and in the meantime, she'd kept getting pregnant. After WJ, she had Robert, a miscarriage, Michelle, another miscarriage, Lisa, Carrie, Tommy, and Justin. She trudged on day after day feeling like a butterfly trapped in a faulty cocoon with no escape, its wings damaged by stagnation. And all she had to show for her pain were seven children who didn't appreciate her sacrifices.

But not anymore. It was time to fly. She would show the people who thought they knew her that they'd never really known her at all.

Janice fingered her tattoo: *nothing changes if nothing changes*.

Well, she was making changes now.

"You okay?" Scotty tapped the bar in front.

She'd miss Scotty when she left. She hoped he wouldn't be one of the ones who ended up judging her for leaving.

She shook herself. "You bet I am." She lifted her purse across the bar. "Stash my bag, will you?" She took a sip of her tea and walked over to stand beside the DJ, waiting for the group of people on stage to finish singing "YMCA" by The Village People. This was it. This was her last song in Corbett City, Nevada!

Before the DJ reintroduced her, he updated the crowd: "Remember, the winner will be announced after the final entries. You must be present to win. Now, for her last entry, Janice will be singing 'These Boots Are Made for Walkin'.'"

The crowd cheered.

Janice knew from experience that the crowd got drunk and indiscriminate by this time of night. Most had been drinking for at least three hours, but some had been there all day. Some of the Right Knights were hanging about, as usual. She never understood why, given WJ had never once stuck around to hear her sing. She hoped her regulars would keep it together long enough to make sure she could win. If they disappeared, it didn't matter how bad everyone else sang, it would end up a popularity contest. She danced up the stage, grabbed the microphone, and turned away from the teleprompter.

She knew the words by heart, as any true performer should.

The music began, and she started snapping her fingers. She wished she had a tambourine. Her skirt brushed her calves, and she danced forward and back on the small stage, tilting the microphone stand with her.

The drunken college students pushed back their chairs and started dancing and singing along.

Janice wasn't expecting backup singers and missed a beat going into her next line. She skipped a few words to catch up and turned to the DJ, flailing her arm at him until she caught his attention. She hiked her thumb up above her head.

The DJ nodded and increased the volume, but the girls only raised their voices.

Oh well, what the hell? As a bona fide performer, she'd better get used to unruly fans. She improvised the last two lines.

> *And soon I'm gonna head your way*
> *And slap your mouths shut too!*

Janice pointed at the girls and bowed. The room exploded.

Scotty was waiting for her with a clean bar towel. She dabbed her forehead and décolletage.

"Always the entertainer," Scotty said. "Nice line. Glad you don't mean it."

"Scotty, if I don't win tonight, believe you me, I meant it. I'll be kicking some butt." She winked at him.

She was so so so so close to winning; she was almost afraid to believe the time was here. Sure she had a few hours to wait, but she had put her all into that song. "How did I sound? I could barely hear myself sing. I swear, if I don't win tonight, you're going to have to pay me out of your own pocket."

Scotty looked past her shoulder and said to someone behind her, "If you know what's good for you, stay away from this end of the bar right now."

Janice turned to see two girls, eyes wide.

"We just want to buy her a beer," they said in unison.

"She's done drinking tonight," he said.

Having Scotty for a friend was like having her own

personal bodyguard. Janice winked at the girls. This was the
first time that fans she'd never met wanted to buy her a drink.
If her smile wore pants, they'd be split at the seams. "Anything for my fans. I'll take that beer."

She nursed her beer over the next hour, not caring that it
turned warm and flat as she waited anxiously for the contest
to come to an end. She ignored the conversations around her
and couldn't take her eyes off the stage.

"What's gotten into you tonight?" Scotty asked. "Never
seen you so serious. It's not like you haven't been through
this process before."

If he only knew.

She spared him a glance. "I just really want to win
tonight. You know, with this young crowd and all showing
up. Claim my turf."

He seemed to buy it. But if she won—no, *when* she won
—she didn't care whose turf it became. In fact, for Scotty, she
hoped his spot would become a regular hangout. He deserved
steady business.

Finally, people were called to cast their votes with the DJ.
The suspense was killing her. With more contestants than
usual, the collecting and counting took longer than she was
used to. Scotty never knew who won until the DJ handed him
an envelope just before he hopped on the stage.

Janice thought she might get sick as she watched her
friend open the envelope and look out at the crowd. Stepping
up to the mic, he said, "And the winner tonight is my, and
now your, favorite lady." He turned to beam at her across the
room, and she thought she might faint. "Janice, get on
up here."

This was a true beginning for her. The last time she had
felt this hopeful, this believing, was when she met Harry all

those years ago, singing outside the diner. Her dreams with both Walter and Harry had, in their own way, been too good to be true, but this? This time the dream was all hers. She was in charge of her destiny now, and no one and nothing was going to stop her.

16

JANICE

I've become a captive of my own ambitions.
—Patsy Cline

August 1960

J anice pulled open the door on the large blue Post Office box. She paused and took a drag on her cigarette before tossing it in the gutter. She grabbed the letter she'd written to the Whitworths from her purse, but just like a dozen times before, she couldn't let it go. She half wanted the Whitworths to know the truth and was half afraid that they'd believe her and expect her to return home to raise WJ.

To small, suffocating Lincoln County.

She shoved the wrinkled envelope back in her bag. She'd wait until she was better settled with WJ before mailing anything.

Life had been much harder than she thought possible these past four months since they'd snuck out of Great Aunt's house. Yeah, being a single mom in the city was more difficult than she thought, but overall, she was happy with her choices. She loved WJ to the moon and back, and couldn't imagine being separated from him and not being his mama.

If not for her flatmate, Stephanie, she'd never have gotten an apartment. First hard lesson for Janice was finding out that even in a big city like Minneapolis, it was legal for landlords to deny housing to single women, widowed or otherwise. She'd met spunky Stephanie waiting in a temp agency. Stephanie had interviewed before her, and when she came out, she stuck her hands out to take WJ.

"What do you want?" Janice had asked Stephanie. "I'm not handing over my baby to a complete stranger."

"Honey, you can't go into an interview with this little guy on your lap. You'll never get hired." She dropped her purse in Janice's lap as she took hold of WJ. "Collateral—not that you're doing me any favors. While you and my purse are in the interview, this bundle of joy and I will be waiting out here for you to finish."

When they both got jobs, Stephanie invited her to move into her apartment. "It's small and I get the bedroom, but if you can sleep on the couch and keep the coast clear when I have a date, you can move in anytime."

So they did. And she loved the city. Hard as it was, and broke as she was, she could breathe here. The city was alive with people, cars, and theater—much better than farm animals and the curmudgeons in Lincoln County.

She took her time walking home and used her body weight to pull open the heavy wood door of her apartment building. The humidity caused the door to swell. Until the summer was over, she'd be getting her share of exercise just returning home each night if the blasted three flights of stairs in this heat didn't kill her first. She could hear Stephanie and

WJ giggling on the other side of the door as she inserted her key.

"I'm home, at last. I almost melted, it's so hot and humid."

Stephanie looked up from the floor, where she had just finished changing a diaper. She held the offensive cloth between the tips of two fingers. "As usual, WJ, your mama has perfect timing."

"Hardly." Janice dropped on all fours to kiss WJ before taking the dirty diaper. His hair was growing in, and he had a curlicue for a bang just like his dad had when he was alive. She brushed it from his forehead and smiled into the eyes so like Walter's. "Looking more like your daddy every day."

She stood and walked into the bathroom and washed the absorbent material in the toilet. Someday when she was rich and famous, she was going to own a washing machine. She hung it over the towel rack to dry.

"Oh no, you don't. Not tonight. I have a date," Stephanie said. "I don't want any diapers in sight when Mr. Right shows up."

"Again?" Janice sighed. "Same guy?"

Stephanie nodded while she pulled pink curlers from her hair. "How many Mr. Rights can there be?"

"You tell me. You seem to collect them." She settled on the sofa with WJ. "What's it like to date?" She held WJ under his arms and let him practice standing on her legs. His small fists reached for her nose and hair. He giggled when she pretended to swallow his fist.

"You should try it sometime and find out for yourself," Stephanie said.

"Not ready." Janice hugged her boy close. No, that wasn't true. Maybe she could make herself ready if she happened to meet someone with whom she felt a connection. Walter had been gone eighteen months now; it was hard to explain to someone like Stephanie who believed that "love is just in your imagination" that there was more to true love and how it could make a woman feel, how Walter had made her feel. She didn't want to settle. Plus she had WJ.

"Not ready, or not willing?" Stephanie asked.

Anyway, what did Stephanie know? She didn't have a baby to worry about. "I'll tell you what—if I ever meet an attractive man who will love me and WJ as his own, I'll let you know. Now, answer my question. What's it like to date?"

Stephanie stopped combing her curls. "When you find a good one, it's fun. But a lot of times these men are less intelligent than little WJ. That's why I choose the pretty ones."

Her son was going to be one gorgeous man, for sure. "You hear that, WJ? You're a looker. And I'm taking you on a date down to the corner diner so Jezebel here can get it on."

Stephanie laughed. "Have a milkshake on me."

Janice finished dressing WJ and grabbed her purse and her song notebook. She propped him on her hip and opened the door.

WJ's lips started to tremble. He stretched his arms toward Stephanie and grabbed fistfuls of air.

Janice scowled. She was his mama, not Stephanie. "No crying, WJ."

Stephanie cooed and walked toward him. She kissed him on his cheek. "It's okay, sweetie. I'll see you tomorrow." She pulled up his shirt and blew a raspberry on his belly.

He laughed, drooled, and pushed at Stephanie's red head with little chubby fingers. He started to blow little bubbles between his lips.

Janice wondered why he didn't miss her like Steph. He never cried when Janice had to leave him for work.

Jerking, she turned with WJ in her arms and grabbed his blanket to wipe his lips. "Don't spoil him. You'll turn him into a softie, and life isn't always easy."

Stephanie tilted her head to one side. "Sweetie, don't be so serious. He and I spend a lot of time together. You're working two jobs."

She felt two inches tall for being jealous of her friend, but that was the point. She was working so hard, and he couldn't even know it.

"I know. I know." She smoothed a hand over his soft hair. "And I appreciate your help. You know I do. It's just that . . . I don't know. What if his first word is 'mama' and he uses it on you? He doesn't know how hard I work so we can be together."

"Sugar, as my mom would say, 'Welcome to mother-hood,'" Stephanie said.

"I'm sorry. I guess we both need to stop being babies and toughen up like you."

Stephanie kissed her cheek. "Honey, I hope neither one of you toughens up like me." Stephanie had a cruel father and a hard life, and Janice could kick herself for reminding her of it.

Janice sighed. "Hey, don't keep us out too late, but have fun."

In vintage Stephanie fashion, she clapped her hands once, making a statement that she was moving forward. "I'll move the plant from the window sill when we leave so you'll know," Stephanie said. "Bye, bye, WJ."

Janice loved feeling WJ's weight on her hip as she walked down the flights of stairs and out onto the sidewalk. It was muggy, but the sky was clear. "Can you see the stars?" She pointed to the sky. "We can wish on shooting stars."

"Pppppp. Ga ga gaaaaaaaa."

"Huh? You wish that too?" She wrinkled her nose and gave him an Eskimo kiss. "Someday, we are going to live in Nashville, Tennessee, or sunny California. I'm going to be a famous singer. When we're on the road, we'll have a bus as big as our apartment building, and when we aren't on tour, we'll have a beach house and play together in the sand and ocean. Sound good?"

"Gag ga gaaa gaa."

"Keep that up, and you can be my backup singer," she said.

She'd lied to her grandparents in her letter. She wasn't working at a radio station. She'd had a few interviews, but the hours were demanding and unpredictable, and with WJ, she couldn't expect Stephanie to babysit him for hours on end. As it was, she relied too much on Stephanie to care for him while she worked as a typist and waited tables. But she wasn't giving up on her dreams. With the right timing and a little luck, she'd be back on track.

She pressed her lips against WJ's soft cheeks and hummed. Her steps slowed as she neared the diner on the corner. There was a crowd out front watching a barbershop quartet. She'd worked at the diner a few nights each week and had never seen them before.

What a pleasant surprise. Harmony made her heart sing.

WJ started bouncing in her arms and waving his fists.

She hugged him to her side. "Makes me want to dance too."

She nudged her way through the crowd, which wasn't

difficult. People tended to move out of the way when she had WJ with her.

There were four men singing, and she guessed they looked to be in their mid to late twenties.

Each man had his hair slicked back on the side with curls on top. One man, in particular, looked like Dean Martin. She'd always had a thing for Dean Martin. He was wearing slacks and a dress shirt. He had the sleeves rolled up on his arms, displaying his dark, hairy wrists. And she wasn't sure, but his eyes looked hazel. Hazel—just like Walter's and WJ's.

Dean Martin's doppelganger, a nice voice, and hazel eyes? *My oh my.*

That little buzz of attraction that she thought died with Walter resurfaced. Grandma used to say, "Be careful what you wish for," but Stephanie's words felt better "Life happens when you least expect it."

The men's voices were perfect together. As they snapped their fingers in unison, the four men swayed forward and back, feet tapping in a steady rhythm. The man who looked like Dean Martin was slapping his thigh with his free hand, and his baritone voice sent chills down her spine. She used to sing well with Walter, and she thought her voice might do a nice duet with this man too. She tapped the toe of her shoe to the beat and was disappointed when the song ended. She could've listened to them all night long.

The crowd applauded. Someday she'd find out what it was like to have an audience clapping for her.

"Time for a smoke, ladies and gentlemen," the Dean Martin look-alike said.

Janice stood still, watching people toss coins and bills in a hat on the sidewalk. Balancing WJ, she reached into her purse, but she had just one quarter to spare. Kind of. She'd been saving it for her Hershey bar and newspaper on Sunday, but they'd earned every penny. She could remember this harmony on Sunday instead of stuffing her face with chocolate or getting a cavity she couldn't afford to get fixed.

The crowd dispersed, and the men clapped each other on the back.

She watched as Dean Martin stuck a cigarette in his mouth. He let it dangle from his lips while he gathered their earnings. As he straightened the bills, he caught her staring.

She blushed and started to turn away. What had gotten into her? Stephanie was rubbing off on her.

Get ahold of yourself, Janice.

"Cute," he said around his cigarette.

"Oh," she stopped and turned back to him. "Thank you. He's my son."

"The kid's cute too, but I was talking about you. I bet your husband tells you that all the time."

Was he flirting with her?

"I'm a widow," she said.

"Then your husband was a lucky man. He had heaven on earth too."

What a flatterer. Janice smiled and tucked her face into WJ's crown to hide her warming cheeks.

The man stood and put the money in his pocket. He called back over his shoulder. "Back in ten, gents."

They nodded their heads, lit their cigarettes, and lounged against the wall.

"You sound real nice together." She nodded her head at Dean Martin, hoisted WJ higher on her hip, and reached for the diner door.

Dean Martin jumped forward and grabbed the handle. "Would the two of you like some company?"

She got goose bumps despite the blasted heat. To think she'd just promised Stephanie that if she ever met an attractive man who wasn't put off by her having a kid, she'd act on it. What should she say? How would Stephanie handle this?

"Suit yourself." She grinned and walked up the steps as he swung the door open.

"Ladies first."

The diner was empty, and she felt a little self-conscious as she walked ahead of him. Her heels clicked against the black-and-white checkered tiles as she headed toward the red booth in the back of the diner where she always sat on breaks. She looked over her shoulder. He was still there. He hadn't disappeared into thin air.

This was really happening.

WJ must've picked up on her excitement because he giggled, she thought, for no other apparent reason. Sometimes her son could read her mind, she could swear on it.

"Hi, Barry." She waved at the chef through the small serving window between the counter and the kitchen. "Hi, Charlene." She nodded at the head waitress behind the counter. Charlene would have a lot to say about Janice visiting with a man. "All good intentions, of course," as Charlene would always say before she dished out some unsolicited wisdom to Janice about waitressing or raising a child. Dating and men hadn't come up yet.

"Hi, sweetie. How's our big boy tonight?" Charlene's voice was raspy from years of smoking. She blew a kiss at WJ. She was wearing a brunette wig tonight, and Janice didn't know her true hair color since her eyebrows were drawn on, but whenever Charlene was feeling like a brunette, she got bossier and nosier than usual. But Janice liked her regardless of her choice of wigs. Her caked-on makeup emphasized the deep wrinkles at the corners of her eyes and around her mouth. Janice hoped she'd have laugh lines and wrinkles like Charlene when she was older and not the somber ones that Grandma always had.

WJ pumped his arms as if he was trying to fly from a nest.

Slow down, baby, you're not leaving my nest for a while. When she thought about WJ growing up someday, Janice was torn between relief at the idea that nothing would go wrong in his life and he'd grow to be happy and strong, and a fear that someday he wouldn't need her and she'd be alone again. But tonight, for the first time since she'd lost Walter, she felt more confident that she could meet someone again. Fall in love again. No matter if it happened tonight. Maybe Walter was up above and helping find her a new companion. She liked the idea of Walter having a hand in her life.

"Strawberry shake and a grilled cheese sandwich?" Charlene asked.

"You got it," Janice said. She slid into the booth with WJ and was getting ready to ask Charlene for a high chair when Dean Martin slid one up to the end of the table.

"Oh. Thanks. You read my mind," Janice said.

Charlene looked none too pleased as she walked up to the table and handed Janice a few saltine crackers and a banana for WJ. She slid a cup of coffee with cream and sugar toward her guest and said, "Hey, Harry. Been a long time. About two years, I think. You boys sound better than I remembered. Five people from the crowd came in to eat." Her glance slid from him to Janice. "But I didn't know the two of you knew each other."

Ah, so his name is Harry, and Charlene knows him. An interesting development.

Harry winked at Charlene and then smiled back at her.

"Charlene still doesn't let a man get a word in edgewise. We don't know each other, but I'd love a formal introduction to this beautiful young lady and her handsome son."

Charlene swatted him on the shoulder with her order pad.

"Formal, my wig. Harry, this is Janice and WJ. Our two favorite people. Let me say that again. Our two favorite people. Janice, this is Harry. He likes the ladies, so don't believe a word he says."

Harry laughed and grabbed Charlene's hand. "You still mad at me for breaking your heart? I didn't have a choice. Barry chased me away with his butcher's knife. Isn't that right, Barry?" Harry yelled across the diner.

Barry didn't reply, and from his expression, Janice could tell Barry wasn't too fond of Harry.

Charlene pursed her lips and turned to Janice. "I'll be back with your shake and sandwich." She pointed at Harry. "You behave."

Harry took a sip of his coffee and called after her. "Coffee is just the way I like it. Sweet and creamy."

"Mmm hmm," Charlene said but didn't turn around.

"How do you know Charlene and Barry?"

He sat back in the booth and spread one arm along the back. "The guys and I used to sing outside all the time."

As she reached for the saltine crackers, Janice looked at Harry out of the corner of her eye. "I'm surprised I haven't seen you before. I've been working part-time here for a while now." She broke up the crackers and banana and placed them before WJ.

WJ needed a few tries before he grabbed a chunk of banana.

"I used to be here every Thursday and Friday night." He pumped his thumb over his shoulder toward the quartet. "Two years ago we headed to Las Vegas. We did all right but had to get Jim back. He got into some trouble with the casinos. His wife and kids are in St. Paul. He was supporting them long distance, but if we'd stayed in Vegas much longer, he would've lost everything."

Grandma's words echoed in her mind again: *Be careful what you wish for.* She leaned back and crossed her arms. "And you? Are you a gambler?"

"Sweetheart, you haven't lived until you've gambled on the strip."

She was impressed when he moved his hot coffee out of WJ's reach and spooned an ice cube out of a water glass and placed it on her son's tray.

WJ chortled when the cold cube slipped from his grasp.

Harry sure knew how to keep an infant entertained.

"But I know when to stop. Jim doesn't. Didn't."

Grandma's warning floated away.

"Jim's family is lucky, then, that he has you for a friend. Do you have a family?" Janice nodded toward his left arm; his hand was resting out of her line of sight.

He lifted his ring-free left hand to rest it on the table. "No ring. No wife. No kids."

"Really?" She nodded toward WJ, who was playing with the ice cube. "You seem comfortable around babies."

"I'm the oldest of ten. Grew up on a farm. Learned to take care of kids early on."

"Me too," she said. "Well, I'm an only child, but I grew up on a farm."

"How did you end up in Minneapolis? Did your husband get a job here?"

Janice twisted Walter's class ring on her left finger. She nodded and said, "He died in an accident after we moved to the city and just before our son was born." She was so used to her story she almost believed it. After all, she felt like a widow.

"That must have been tough. So will you be staying in the city?"

"Actually, I'm trying to get a job at a radio station." She blushed. "I sing too. When I have enough money saved up for WJ and me, I'm heading to Nashville."

"No kidding? So you've got dreams, sweetheart?" His eyes darkened, and he leaned forward and stared into her eyes. "Like me?"

Janice's breath quickened. His eyes, when he said "dreams," lit up, just as she imagined hers did. Just as Walter's had. Eyes were the windows to the soul, and she thought she could see hers reflected in his. "Yes. And I'm going to make them come true. It's just a matter of time and determination." She patted her song notebook. "I write my own songs all the time."

"Maybe sometime you could sing one for me?" he asked.

He was so earnest, her heart leapt. She was about to say, "I'd like that," when Charlene slid a milkshake and sandwich across the table.

Janice waited for Charlene to refill Harry's coffee and walk away. She took a sip of her shake. Had she missed the moment to answer his question? Would he ask her again?

Harry leaned back and drummed his spoon against the table. "Las Vegas is the place to be if you want to become a star. We'll be heading back in a few months."

Oh no. Disappointment coursed through her. Just her luck to meet someone she clicked with, who shared her passion for singing, and he'd be leaving soon.

One of the quartet members stuck his head in the door. "Harry, come on."

"Listen, I've got to go. I'd ask you to stay until we're done, but I know this tyke will get tired. Meet me here tomorrow night?"

He was asking to see her again!

"I'll be working here tomorrow night, so yeah." She beamed.

Harry stood up and pulled out a few bills from his pocket. "This is on me." He laid the money on the table then leaned over and ruffled WJ's crown. "Take care of your mama for me, kid."

Janice watched Harry walk down the aisle. She wondered if he would glance back at her—something that always happened in her romance novels. When he was at the door, he turned back, lifted his chin, and winked.

Yes, he liked her.

She waved and then rested her chin on her fist. What a dreamy man and a dreamy night.

With impeccable timing, as usual, Charlene walked over to the table and interrupted the rosy feeling spreading through Janice's chest.

"I see that starry look in your eye. All good intentions of course, but be careful, sweetie. He may not look it, but he's almost twice your age, and he's straight-up trouble."

"Nah, Charlene, he's charming." She started writing a song about wishing on shooting stars with hazel-eyed men.

17

WJ

Pick on somebody yer size, ya big swab!
—Popeye

WJ's knee was bouncing so fast he was rocking the car, and he was irritating the shit out of himself. He was jonesing so fucking hard for a crank pick-me-up to get him through the rest of the night but didn't have any more with him. The one time he carried an extra stash would be the one time the cops pulled him over for something stupid. Number one way most dealers got busted. He wasn't going to give himself away on a silver platter. But, damn, he wished he'd made an exception tonight. But how could he? Not like he could have predicted this Saturday night shitshow.

By now he should've been drinking somewhere, celebrating that his dad wasn't his problem anymore. No one's problem anymore. He'd dropped off Hefty before taking the boys home. Now he'd just run to Tiger Drive, and get in and out. Get to what he needed to take care of once and for all.

He groaned when Carrie met him outside before he could

even put the car in park. She must have been in the window, waiting like a guard dog.

"It's almost midnight. Shouldn't you be sleeping or something?" He scowled at her as she scooped up Justin while he picked up Tommy. He didn't have time for her right now.

"What are you doing with Dad's car?" she asked, not giving him a second to kick the car door shut. Impatient. She was always so damn impatient.

"None of your business." He hadn't wanted her, or anybody outside the few who already knew, to know that he'd been driving his dad's car all night. If anyone tied the car back to the earlier fiasco, he was screwed.

"Are you taking his car back to him tonight?"

In other words, was he going to get in a fight with their dad? For sure. One of the things he'd never understand was how she could love their dad so much. Their family wasn't one for talking about anything, but she knew he'd had the snot beat out of him over and over. But she'd always been a loving kid, so maybe he should be glad because underneath all of her stuck-up ways, she loved him too. He knew that.

But she always asked too many questions and was too nosey. "You know, you could get yourself in trouble someday, asking the wrong person the wrong question."

"I'm never going to hang out with anyone I'd ever have to worry about that with," she said.

Yep. Stuck-up as stuck-up got.

"What about Dad's car?"

She didn't leave him any choice but to lie. "I'm just dropping it off out front. He'll be passed out by the time I get there."

"You promise?"

"You should worry more about loyalty than promises," he

said. When was she going to learn that promises from anyone weren't good for shit? Loyalty is what counted the most. Looking out for each other. Standing up for the people you respect or care about.

"What's that supposed to mean?" she asked. "I am loyal."

"If you were loyal, you wouldn't think about calling the cops just because you can't get what you want the second you want it."

"Are you nuts?" She just shook her head at him. "The boys had a gun!"

If his arms weren't full, he'd be tempted to squeeze her chin to hold her head in place. Make her listen and learn from him for a change instead of her always acting like she knew better than all of them about everything. He was the big brother, and her being better at school and going to college would never change that fact.

"I'm sorry you think it's a bad thing that I wanted to find our missing little brothers," she hissed.

"That's when you call me, not the cops."

"We did call you."

"But you thought about calling the cops first."

"Yes, because cops help people."

Stupidest thing she'd ever said. He snorted. "Not all of them. Just help me get them to bed. I've got my own life to live, you know."

"I'm not letting you leave until you promise you'll avoid Dad the rest of the night," she said. She put Justin in bed and covered him up.

WJ slipped Tommy into the top bunk and then pointed his finger in her face. "You're too fucking bossy for your own good."

"Don't swear." She slapped his finger away.

"I'm thirty years old—I can swear if I fucking want to." He thumped his chest as he turned to go. The envelope from his dad crackled in his shirt pocket. Whatever the hell it contained, he'd give it to his mom next time he saw her, and the further down the road that might be the better. He sure as hell wasn't going to leave it here with this nosy body.

"Real mature," she said.

"I've got to go. Be a normal teenager and go hang out with your friends or something." As he walked out, he heard her shout, "I swear to Gawd if one more dysfunctional person tells me to go do something 'normal,' I'm going to kill them!"

18

WJ

Now I'm go'ner pulvernize ya!
—Popeye

I t was close to midnight when WJ pulled up to his dad's place, but on the drive over, he'd made a decision. He wouldn't kill the SOB. He was tired of this shit and covering up everyone's fucking mistakes. If he killed him and one thing went wrong, one fucking thing, someone could link him back to his dad, and he'd not only be making a mess of his own life, he would draw attention to the Knights and give the ATF and the police the justification they'd been looking for to get a warrant to search his place. No doubt they'd "find" something there that might be enough for them to get warrants on Bender and everyone else. He was sworn to protect them and put them first, so that was what he'd fucking do. It was what he wanted to do.

But he was still going to get the final say on good old Dad's life. All those years of the jerk being in his face—he had reached the last straw. It was his turn to shout in Dad's face, push him around, and tell him how to act and what to do, make him feel like he was good for nothing and the sooner he got out of everyone's lives, the better off they'd all be—that he didn't matter for shit. He patted the wad of cash in his jeans pocket. He'd filled his dad's car up with gas—no excuses, no delays—and now he could wake the bastard up and chase him out of town.

It's leave-or-die time, Dad.

His dad could go back to Minnesota where he and his mom first met. He didn't give a crap where he went, but it would no longer be here. He had brass knuckles in his pocket and a knife in his boot. He was more than happy to use his fists to send the son of a bitch on his merry fucking way, and if he ever came back, his dad couldn't say he hadn't been warned, and WJ would get one of the Knights and finish him for good.

His dad's window was dark. Good.

He stepped out of the car and looked around. It was quiet; there wasn't a soul in sight.

There was no point in knocking. The knob turned without resistance. He opened the door enough to slide in, but the smell forced him back onto the porch. He yanked his bandana off his head to cover his nose. What the . . .

It smelled like a fucking sewer plant.

Face covered, he stepped inside. The room was silent and dark except for the light surrounding the closed bathroom door. Maybe Dad made it to the bathroom a second too late because he couldn't hear any heavy breathing coming from the dark corner where the bed would be, and that'd explain the God-awful smell. Squinting, he looked around. There was something on the floor in front of him he couldn't make out, so he pulled the front door wider to get some of the light from the parking lot.

Fresh air wouldn't hurt either.

His dad's socked feet poked out from his jeans where he kneeled before a chair. WJ stepped to the side of the doorway to let more light in. He wasn't about to start turning on all the lights.

The streetlight was enough. Enough to see a hangman's noose stretching from his dad's neck where his head rested on the seat of a wooden chair, his arms wrapped around it as if hugging the legs.

Sprawled over the chair, Dad's right cheek rested on the seat. Fully clothed, except for his shoes, he still wore his eyeglasses, though they were cock-eyed and the left arm sat at an angle from his head.

A yellow rope stretched several feet from the back of his neck and disappeared behind the top-splintered bathroom door. The weight of his dad's body must've caused the door to buckle and bust near the frame, letting the knot slide through. A second knot was held up on the other side of the hole.

A backup plan gone wrong.

A deep purple mark ran up the side of his jaw line, stopping behind his left ear.

Holy shit. He put two fingers against his dad's cool and stiff neck. Nothing.

He stood up and exhaled hard.

The motherfucker killed himself. Or tried to, changed his mind, and struggled until the rope slid free, but suffocated anyway. Couldn't even kill himself easy.

His dad looked pathetic wearing his glasses all crooked

on his face. Like he was passed out drunk instead of dead as a doornail.

Pathetic way to die, even for a pathetic man.

Without thinking why, WJ adjusted the left arm of his dad's glasses so it could tuck behind his ear. He pulled the knife out of his boot and sliced the noose at the back of his dad's swollen neck. He'd been dead long enough that his body didn't budge. WJ had seen DB's before, but never someone he knew outside of drugs. Felt like his dad might jump anytime from hugging that chair like a lifeline and sucker punch him. He got chills thinking about it.

His earlier idea that his dad was hugging the chair took on new meaning. Had he stood on that chair before kicking it away but fell back on it when the rope slipped?

He shook his head. Who was he, fucking *CSI*? Shit.

Earlier when he was leaving with the boys and wondered if Dad would kill himself, he'd dismissed it. It took balls to kill yourself, and his dad didn't have those. That's what he had thought. He'd been wrong.

"Old man, what have you done now?" He couldn't help but wonder how Carrie was going to take this news and who'd be giving it to her. Sure as shit wouldn't be him. He couldn't handle that. And the boys, what would they think?

While he'd been busy with his brothers, his dad had been busy dying. Dying the hard way. Dying the un-fucking-believable way.

Stepping back, WJ put his hands behind his head and looked up at the dark ceiling. He should be relieved and just get the hell out of there. But he was thrown off guard. No good would come of this—that's why Dad had needed to leave town instead of die. WJ couldn't have anything to do with this.

Fuck. Fuck. Fuck. What in the hell was he supposed to do now?

His dad must be laughing from his grave, saying, "I wouldn't come back if I were you."

And then his dad may as well have come back to life to punch him in the gut. WJ bent at his waist, hands on his knees. All those years of abuse, and he'd never get to throw it all back in his dad's face. His dad got the final say. His dad got the last word.

Anger and bile rose up in him so quick he began shaking, and his skin turned clammy.

Red. Red was all he could see now. *He* deserved the last word! Not his dad!

The hate boiled his blood as he leaned over and shouted in his dad's face, "You don't get the last word, motherfucker! You don't get the last word!" He kicked the chair so fucking hard it was satisfying to watch his dad and the chair fall to the side with a loud thud.

He turned and punched a hole in the wall.

His heart thundered in his chest, and he felt devastated. He'd been ready to face his dad for all of his abuse, pay him for all the pain by making him lose everything, and now he'd never get the satisfaction. He ran his hand over his chest, brushing the envelope in his pocket.

A suicide letter and more last words? He needed to get out of here and open it. Let someone else find his dad.

He looked around the stench-filled room. He shouldn't have touched anything: not the rope, not his dad, not the wall. He was sloppy like Hefty had been earlier. The cops might tie him to the scene. What the fuck had he been thinking? He hadn't been thinking, that was the problem. Shocked, that's what he was.

If he needed it, the letter would probably put him in the clear, depending what it said. He thought about leaving it in the room, but no, he should hold on to it in case someone had seen him there earlier. He could be honest about when and how he got it if anyone questioned him.

But swear to God, if he could stay clean of this mess and never need the letter to clear himself, he'd rip it into a million pieces. Never had he wanted to stifle someone's words more than he wanted to right now.

WJ used his bandana to wipe off the door handle, taking one last look at his dad before closing the door without a sound. It was still quiet out front. If anyone heard the noise he made earlier, they were ignoring it.

He climbed into his dad's car and drove five minutes to Swan Park and pulled up to a curb beneath a street lamp. His hands shook as he removed the envelope.

Two folded notes and a scrap of newspaper fell from his shaking fingers to his lap. One sheet was a list *For My Kids* that he scanned, only pausing when he saw the words:

- *It's okay if you're gay.*
- *It's okay if you're not gay.*

What? That was news to WJ, and he didn't believe it. Carrie kept lists too. What would she think of this one?

The second paper was a letter. He was still reeling from his dad's confession in the beginning that he was responsible for the pawnshop owner being in a coma, when his own name jumped off the page as he neared the bottom.

Can you grant me a dying wish? I did my children wrong. WJ most of all. Tell him about his real dad. I wish I could see his face when he hears he is Walter Whitworth, Junior. Oh, la-di-da—a junior. Let him find his family, and who knows, maybe he will become a better man than I raised him to be.

What? Harry wasn't his dad! Who in the hell was he? WJ's mouth turned dry, but he went on reading like he had no choice.

You know, I never cared if he was gay. I just didn't want him to be unable to protect himself, and who better than me to teach him to stick up for himself, teach him not to trust anyone. I know this was wrong now. I was the one who couldn't be trusted. Something happened to me when I was a boy, something I'm glad to take to my grave, but I think everyone would agree with me that WJ knows how to take care of himself. No one ever took advantage of him as a kid because of me.

The comic strip I included is for WJ too. I'll be damned if his crush on Popeye hasn't finally clicked. WJ is Popeye. I'm Bluto, the bully. WJ will get a kick out of me finally putting two and two together.

Janice, I love you. Go find your dream. When I first met you and WJ, you said . . .

The rest of the letter was about his mom. His mom who had lied to him his entire fucking life. He reread the parts about him again and again.

Harry wasn't his dad. The asshole who had crushed his

childhood and shamed him for feeling the way he did was never his dad. All those fucking years of wondering how his own dad could hate him so much meant nothing? All those years were just a waste when he should have been with his real dad? He reread.

Something happened to me when I was a boy, something I'm glad to take to my grave, but I think everyone would agree with me that WJ knows how to take care of himself. No one ever took advantage of him as a kid because of me.

What did Dad—no, Harry—mean? WJ remembered one time when he was ten. Harry made him help him with a side job cleaning out someone's yard. A creepy-ass man kept coming out on the porch and watching WJ. After a while, he asked WJ if he wanted to "come in and have a real Coca-Cola." He wanted the coke, but he didn't like something about the guy and knew better than to stop working or his dad would be pissed—he was supposed to be working and toughening up like a hardworking man—but the man paying them to do the work told him it was an order and to come inside. WJ didn't want to get his dad in trouble because that would end up in a spanking, or worse. Unsure, he started to put the rake down when his dad rounded the corner. Harry had taken one look at the man extending his hand to grab WJ's hand, and he had flown across the yard and punched the man right in the face. Knocked him out cold. Dad—no, Harry—had turned and shook the breath out of WJ. "Never go with anyone unless I tell you to. You hear me?" Then he'd yanked WJ to his chest and hugged him hard and tight. WJ had never forgotten it because he couldn't remember him ever hugging him before.

Then they grabbed their tools and went home. "We don't work for perverts." When they'd gotten home, his mom had asked why they were home early and started shouting when she realized the job wouldn't be completed and there'd be no money for food. WJ remembered watching and feeling helpless, waiting to hear Dad explain, but Dad never said anything. He just grabbed a beer from the fridge and said, "WJ, you go on and play now."

WJ refolded the paper and tucked it in his pocket with the list. He unfolded the newspaper clipping and read the scribbles on the comic strip. His dad—Harry—called him Popeye. Him. Popeye.

"Right. Right." His arm was shaking so bad that his elbow bounced on the windowsill. He brushed the corner of his eye against his shoulder, turning the fabric a shade darker. What was he supposed to do now?

Harry could have left the envelope in the room, but he'd given it to WJ instead. The man he thought was his dad may have gotten the last words, but WJ was going to do everything he could to make sure no one ever read what was inside.

No one could ever see. No one could know he was gay. If the cops got ahold of this, they'd ruin his life. They'd tell everyone. They'd tell the RKs, and WJ would lose everything. He'd become a laughingstock, a fuck-buddy, and he'd be forced to fight the men he considered his brothers.

The last time he felt so scared and at a loss was when he was nineteen, and he didn't think he could survive losing everything again.

19

WJ

I yam what I yam an' tha's all I yam!
—Popeye

1979—Camp Pendleton, San Diego, CA

WJ's entire body shook with anticipation. Goose bumps covered his bare arms as Joe caressed his wrist, then his upper arm, pausing to explore the curve of his bicep under his T-shirt with a fingertip. WJ couldn't make his lips stop shivering. His heart hammered between his ribs. He'd been so lonely, and no one had ever touched him with such care before Joe. He'd never get enough of it.

His first months in boot camp had been hell. He still didn't feel the loyalty and comradeship the recruiter had promised him when he enlisted in the Navy. Surrounded by the recruits of Company 012 day in and day out, running late-night drills, and all bunking in one room, he'd tried to belong, but he'd felt as different and isolated as ever. But then he met

Joe. The first time they made eye contact, he knew he wasn't alone. There was someone else like him.

Joe's tan fingers tickled WJ's collarbone and slid behind his neck, inviting his lips closer.

WJ lived for these stolen moments together. Was this what love was supposed to be like? Was he falling in love?

Yes. He was. He really was.

He focused on the strawberry-textured tongue darting between white teeth and settled his mouth against Joe's welcoming, soft lips.

"Privates! Attention!"

WJ's eyes widened. He could see his own immediate fear reflected in Joe's shocked eyes. They shoved each other away, and the force caused them to slip and slide on the hard shower floor. WJ covered his erection with his hands and struggled to his feet, snapping to attention. Heat and vulnerability crept up his chest and neck. He could feel and imagine his larger-than-average ears burning and jutting out from his crew cut. Their company was on leave. They'd been the two who hadn't left the base. They should have been safe. He focused on the medals on his captain's shirt. He was becoming light-headed.

Keep it together. Keep it together.

He hoped Joe was doing better than him but was afraid to look at him, knowing the captain watched them both.

WJ reached for the beatings and lessons he'd survived with his dad, never expecting that all those moments might prepare him for standing humiliated and naked in front of his captain. He'd get through this, and he and Joe would figure something out.

The captain stared at him with revulsion. WJ lifted his chin and stared forward. His dad's words echoed in his mind: *Never show you care. Someone knocks you down, you get back up and stare them down*. No matter that his dad knocked him down until he stayed down.

His captain's lips pursed, and his nostrils flared with each breath. A nerve ticked in his jaw.

"Men"—WJ didn't like the way he said "men," like they were anything but—"meet me in my office in five minutes." The captain exited the room without looking back. When he got to the open door, he spit on the ground.

He and Joe scurried for their towels and tied them tight about their waists. They were silent as they hurried to their bunks and lockers.

WJ kept looking at Joe, but Joe avoided eye contact.

"Joe, look at me."

Joe smoothed his hands over his shirt into the waistband of his pants until the shirt was wrinkle-free and military-tucked. His jaw was clamped, and sweat beaded above his upper lip.

"Babe," WJ grabbed his cap and went to stand before Joe, "look at me. We'll be okay. It's going to be okay. No matter what, we have each other." He extended a hand toward Joe.

"You fool." Joe shoved him hard against the locker then jerked away to punch air. He wiped the sweat from his brow. In a low voice he said, "We'll be discharged. It's never going to be okay. They don't let people like us stay in the military. This was supposed to be my career. My mom and dad will never forgive me." He swallowed hard and pointed at WJ's heart and then his own. "We both needed this opportunity. What else are we going to do?"

"We just keep getting back up, that's what we do. We'll figure it out, together," WJ said. He didn't care how desperate his voice sounded. He wanted to fix this for Joe and fix it right now.

Joe shook his head and looked down, then turned and left WJ alone in the barracks.

WJ hurried to catch up.

When they arrived as ordered, the captain was waiting with two MPs at his side.

"At ease." The captain spread their files before him. "The military does not tolerate homosexuality and acts incompatible with military service and security. I'll be recommending your separation from the armed forces via disability discharge." He looked from one to the other. "Private WJ Sloan and Private Joseph Morgan, you are hereby on notice for separation from service. You're now under the custody of the Military Police, who will escort you back to the barracks to get your belongings. You will wait in a holding cell until court tomorrow, where you will be formally discharged from the United States Navy."

Disability? And how was being gay incompatible with military security? WJ's gut tightened, and coldness clawed through his chest like someone was "wringing the life out of it," something he'd heard his mom say once, and it had stuck with him. He wasn't disabled. Every nasty thing his dad had ever called him came back to him, but nothing was more devastating than being told he was disabled for being human and falling in love.

"Sir," WJ said. "'Disability discharge,' Sir?"

The captain stood and walked around the desk until he stood before them. "Disability discharge. Be grateful, sailors, that this is a highly subjective and administrative decision up to each administrator's discretion and that you got me. Unless you can prove you were just being," he used his fingers to pantomime quotes, "'queens for a day' and that this won't happen again, which is impossible to convince me of after what I just saw, you're out of here. I could just as easily discharge you as dishonorable, undesirable, or for bad conduct. At least as a general separation due to disability, you can avoid fees and jail time. Dismissed!"

———

Corbett City, NV

WJ stepped off the bus and into the rain. He scanned the crowd but didn't recognize anyone. He straightened his white sailor cap and pulled his military-issue burlap sack high on his shoulder. Head down, his Adam's apple bobbed in synchronization with each step that took him closer to Tiger Drive.

Rain bounced off his shoulders and sprayed the sides of his face. He stared at the wet ground. The walk from the bus stop to his parents' trailer would take forty minutes. Too bad the bus hadn't broken down, given him more time to figure out how he was going to face his dad and mom.

He couldn't believe he was back in Corbett City. It was the last place he wanted to be. He swallowed a lump in his throat. He missed Joe and ached for him. He wondered if he was okay and what he was doing now.

He still couldn't believe that Joe had left the base and never looked back. WJ had hoped he would find him downtown at one of their favorite spots they went to on leave, but he couldn't. He had no way of finding Joe again because Joe didn't want to be found.

He was a failure.

He couldn't do anything right. He had destroyed Joe's

dreams and his own future. His parents would be disgusted with him. Again. Not too long ago, his mom and dad and little sisters had taken him to the Greyhound bus station to send him off to boot camp. Dad had slapped him on the back, telling him to be a man, which had been much better than his fists trying to drill manhood into him. Was also the only time his dad ever had looked proud of him. Mom had kissed him on his cheek as a goodbye. His send-off had been a single moment of hope for him and a Polaroid snapshot of a happy family he could tuck in his pocket and make up stories about.

Both of his parents were relieved he had joined the Navy. Enlisting had been his only choice, or so his dad said. He was failing high school and had barely passed adult education after his teachers and parents agreed to move him to the night classes, where he might get along better with the other "troubled" students. His send-off to the Navy had been the only time in his life he'd actually liked his parents. And he'd felt they liked him. At least that he could remember. But now, he was leaving the same bus station alone and in shame. He was only nineteen years old, and already he felt like a loser.

He assumed the MP had told his parents about Joe, about his "disability discharge," and that they knew when his bus would arrive, but they had left him to walk home in the rain. He didn't know what to expect other than they would be hypocrites and disappointed as usual. Fortunately, thanks to boot camp he was too strong for his dad to push around now.

He finally reached their block and headed through the backyard to the porch. He teared up when he saw his sisters' small faces and noses pushed up against their wet bedroom window, their breaths fanning out in a fog. Yep, clearly his family was expecting him. At least the girls were happy about it. He raised a hand, and their squeals bounced off the glass.

His mother opened the door for him. First thing he noticed was her bulging stomach. Pregnant again.

She smiled sadly. "You've gotten big. You look so like . . ."

She shook her head, pressed her fingertips to her closed eyes, and shook her head. He'd expected her to be mad at him, but not brought to tears. There was a lot he resented her for, but he'd never wanted to be the reason she cried.

"Hi, Mom," he said, not knowing what else to say. *Sorry* wasn't a choice. He was not sorry for meeting Joe.

"Come in before you drown." She squeezed his shoulder when he walked past.

He wanted to point out he was already soaking wet from having to walk home, but he didn't.

"Your father isn't home yet."

Fine, the more time he had, the better.

"WJ!" Lisa and Carrie ran into the room. "You're home!" They yanked on his rucksack. "Did you bring us souvenirs?"

"Little monkeys. The longer it takes me to get to the living room, the longer you'll have to wait and find out." He dropped his white cap onto Lisa's head.

They helped him carry the bag into the room and then dropped to the ground at his feet when he sat on the couch and began pulling items out of the bag.

"Hmm," he teased. "I thought they were in here." He pulled out shirt after shirt. "Maybe I forgot the gifts."

"WJ!" the girls said in unison.

"Oh, here they are." He handed each of them some candy and an orange Navy patch that read *Deck Ape* and had a picture of a gorilla wearing a Navy uniform and holding a mop.

They held the patches up to their shirts and modeled them for him and each other, making him smile for the first time in a week.

"I'm glad you came back," seven-year-old Carrie said. She jumped up and ran to the other room, yelling over her shoulder, "I have a welcome home present for you." She returned with a notebook and handed it to him.

"What's this?"

"Open it," Carrie said, leaning into his side.

"She's been making that since you left. I don't know what made her think to do it," his mom said.

WJ smiled and ruffled Carrie's hair. He opened the binder and found clippings of the *Popeye* comic strip roughly trimmed and taped onto notebook paper. Page after page, she had cut out every cartoon for most of the Sundays he'd been away. He swallowed hard, blinked, and cleared his throat. "Thank you." He tapped her forehead with his own.

Lisa pulled on his arm. "Who do you like more? Popeye or Bluto?"

WJ started to tell her, but Carrie interrupted.

"He's Popeye the Sailor Man." Carrie shook her head like Lisa was clueless.

WJ stilled. "You think I'm Popeye?"

She grabbed his sailor cap from Lisa and set it back on his head. "Yep."

WJ smiled and looked to see his mom's reaction, but her back was turned as she pulled out an ironing board.

The board whined as she opened it. She held her belly as

she bent over to plug in the iron. "Girls, go and pick out a piece of clothing, and we can iron on the patches."

WJ listened to their bare feet slap against the linoleum floor in the hallway. As soon as they were gone, he rolled his cap between his fingers and then finally found the courage to ask, "What do you both know?"

"Enough," she said.

Blood rushed up his neck and across his cheeks. "What's Dad been saying? Are you going to let me stay here until I can get a job and find a place to live? I don't have anywhere else to go, or I would already be there."

"He'll be home soon, and you can ask him yourself. He tried to warn you—about being obvious and that most people, especially in the military, won't stand for it."

Yeah, warned him with his fists. WJ ground his teeth together. "And you, can you still not stand for me to be me?" If any time in his life he needed her to be a better mom, it was now. Tears filled his eyes.

"I love you in my own way, WJ. Dad loves you in his. If I thought someone wouldn't beat you up over it, or use your sexuality against you, I wouldn't give a fig about who you like or love. But I am afraid for you."

"Dad beat me up over it, Mom. Over and over. You let him. What more is there to be afraid of? Love means accepting me the way I am," he said. And having met Joe, he now knew being lonely was the scariest thing of all.

"Love isn't perfect. The giver gets to choose what it looks like. Take it or leave it," she said. "I have enough to accept about my life and love." She tested the heat of the iron and leaned against the wall. She patted her stomach and pulled a cigarette from her breast pocket. "We all make choices."

"How I feel isn't a choice. A choice is the two of you

staying together. A choice is you not interfering and standing up for me. A choice is to keep getting pregnant."

"I don't expect you to understand, WJ, but there are times I really love your dad. He saved me when I met him. And now, well, the past always seems like the best time to break up."

Heavy footfalls echoed from the porch.

His dad was home, and WJ dreaded the confrontation.

The back door swung open. WJ watched his dad as he shrugged out of his wet jacket and dropped a case of beer on the table. He hung up his jacket and turned toward the living room. He froze when he saw WJ. After what felt like hours, his dad pulled out a chair and sat down at the table. He tore open the case of beer and set one can in front of him and another across the table. He pointed at the empty chair. "Get in here, WJ."

As WJ walked into the kitchen, the kids returned. "Go with Mom," he said.

His mom ushered them away and moved the ironing board to their bedroom.

WJ pulled out the chair and sat down as he was told, then pulled the tab on the can and took a sip.

"You really messed up this time, son. How many times do I have to tell you not to be a queer, huh? This time you got fired from the goddamn United States Navy. Next time you might get beat to death by someone."

"Don't you mean you?" WJ said. "Go ahead. Try."

"Taught you to fight, didn't I? Take it from me. There are men out there willing to do a hell of a lot worse to someone like you than I ever could," his dad said and took a long drink of his beer. "I'll be the first to admit I don't know how to be your father. The first time you got caught peeping on your classmates in the middle school locker room, I could only think to slap it out of you and teach you to defend yourself. But it didn't help, did it? You've just gone and done it again as an adult. I can't protect you anymore."

WJ pushed his chair back. "You've never protected me. I needed protection from you. I don't want to listen to you. And I don't have to."

"Stay there. I don't want to fight with you. Hell, I can't anymore. Look how big you've gotten. But you need to figure this out."

"Figure what out? I am who I am," WJ said. "I can't change how I feel."

"You're weak. You're sloppy. But you can damn well hide it. It's for your own good. Now listen. You can stay here until you get your first paycheck."

"I'll look for a job tomorrow," WJ said. His shoulders slumped. Hide it? He was so sick of hiding.

"It's done. I got you a job at the sanitation company," Dad said.

WJ couldn't believe his ears. "Why? Why would you do that?"

"You need a job. The military was your best bet, but this will have to be a close second. Don't screw this up. Keep your feelings to yourself this time. Be at the office tomorrow. The owner, Rudy, is expecting you at noon sharp."

"But why would you get me a job where you work? You're disgusted I'm your son. You're ashamed of me."

"You can't expect me to be fucking happy about it, can you? Besides, some day your mother and I need to have a talk with you, but it's not going to be today."

"What do you mean? Talk about what? You're confusing

the hell out of me."

"Do you want a job or not, Twinkle Toes?"

WJ ran his palm over his buzz cut. "Don't call me that. I want the job . . . but I don't understand you."

"It wouldn't matter if you did," his dad said. "Welcome to adulthood."

They stared at each other silently as they finished the beers.

His dad never asked about the other guy. About Joe.

"I don't know how to hide how I feel," WJ said.

"Whatever you want to say and do, just do the opposite," his dad said as he opened his second beer. "And if anyone ever confronts you—"

"Throw the first punch, yeah, I know," WJ said.

20

JANICE

I'm gonna be something one of these days. Sitting around the
house playing wife and mother is driving me crazy.
—Patsy Cline

Janice closed the door of her Pinto and paused to look at the trailers. In the dark, everything looked cleaner. The streets and neighbors were quiet. The stars glistened in the sky. The desert night air was crisp and eliminated the odor of sagebrush. Most of the lights in the trailers were turned off, and she couldn't see the tattered and frayed edges of the curtains that had always been symbolic of her unraveling life.

She hugged her purse close. The folded classified ads crinkled inside. Scotty was still holding her money where it was safe. She had learned from her mistakes over the years—well, most of them—and she never kept cash, much less the thousands she'd saved from the contest, in her home. Harry and her older children, whenever they came around, could sniff out money. It didn't matter where she hid it, they'd find it. And then came the invariable argument about who was entitled to the money, who was owed money. Hadn't everyone borrowed from each other at some point?

It didn't seem to occur to Harry and her grown kids that she had rent to pay and mouths to feed. Sometimes she looked at her adult children, thought of how she had changed slowly over the years, and wondered what they might regret someday or what their last straw would be—that last straw that could drive them to make a choice like she was making now to leave everything behind and start anew. But none of them had children—something they'd been smart or just plain lucky about. They'd never have to reflect on their own wins and losses as a parent or feel the angst she'd felt and carried over the years, and therefore, they'd never think of her as an individual navigating life without a how-to manual, only someone who'd been a bad mom. They could just sit and judge and constantly point and wag a finger: Bad Mom. Bad Mom.

Carrie was the worst. She took advantage of every opportunity to tell Janice when she sucked. But until Carrie had to walk a mile in her shoes, she wasn't going to let her daughter's opinion stop her. Carrie would be going to college soon enough, and she'd learn that making choices wasn't always easy when you couldn't blame someone else if the consequences sucked. Once Janice left, Carrie would have to decide if she'd move to Reno for school and leave her brothers in the sole care of their dad or if she'd stay home and commute. She wouldn't know Janice would be back for the boys in a year. She'd have to pick her straw and decide if she could leave them behind, just like Janice. Sure, Carrie could blame her for being put in the position, but in the long run, Carrie would have to live with her decision.

Just as Janice would have to live with hers.

She walked up the steps to the porch. She couldn't wait to spread the classifieds out on her bedspread and circle places she could live. Even though it was almost one a.m., her adrenaline was pumping, and she felt like it was the middle of the day.

When she opened the door, Star greeted her with a wagging tail. The good thing about Star was the pooch never needed more than Janice could give her. A bowl of food, a smile, and a pat now and then, and Star loved her right back.

A light was shining in the kitchen. It would be a miracle if anyone would ever turn off all the lights. As she stepped from the hall, she saw Carrie writing at the kitchen table.

Ugh—her daughter was the last person she wanted to see on such an important night of her life. And judging from the look on Carrie's face when she looked up, she wasn't too happy either.

Nothing new there. The less interaction, the better. Janice nodded, turned on her heel, and retreated down the hall toward her bedroom.

"Justin and Tommy are okay. Not that you care," Carrie called after her.

Janice stopped, rolled her eyes, and then retraced the few steps she had been able to take. She stopped at the end of the hall and stared across the five feet of worn linoleum.

"Not that I need to explain myself to you, but your dad left a message at the bar. They'll be fine for the night." *And the next year.* "I just drove by, but the lights were out, and I didn't want to wake anyone." And that was true. She had. But she'd been relieved when all was dark and quiet and she could keep driving.

Carrie shook her head and snorted.

Janice knew this was body language for "What kind of

mother are you?" Raising her eyebrows, she asked, "What? You think I should have woken everyone up just to bring them home?"

Carrie set down her pencil, pursed her lips, and jutted her neck forward.

Janice hated it when she did that. The gesture reminded her of the angry hens on her grandfather's farm just before they were killed, plucked, and roasted. Whenever she'd had an attitude on the farm, Grandfather would say, "You keep sticking your head out like a chicken and you'll lose it someday."

"They're home already. In bed. WJ brought them," Carrie said with a voice that sounded like a stretched out "Duh."

"Oh." That was a surprise. "Did he mention how things went when he saw your dad?"

Carrie gave her the look. The look that said a good mother wouldn't have to ask such a question because a good mother would have raised a son who didn't hate his dad so much. A good mother wouldn't have let a dad treat his son that way. The look covered a long list of disappointments.

"Stop looking at me like that," Janice said. Carrie was only seventeen. She hadn't lived long enough to make mistakes yet. Her daughter didn't get to claim to be her better.

But Carrie just kept looking at her until it raised her hackles.

Janice wiggled her fingers at her arrogant daughter. "Sit in judgment all you want. You don't know a thing about life. You certainly know little about mine. You think keeping lists will make you a better person, or different from me. Well, they won't. They'll just make you inflexible and unimaginative."

She'd really hit her daughter's buttons. Janice could see

the anger coiling up through Carrie's core as she straightened in her seat. But that was fine with Janice because Carrie had jabbed her buttons one too many times. Janice would bet her life that Carrie had stayed up because she'd been spoiling for a fight. Which was exactly why she had tried to escape to her bedroom alone when she first got home. But if Carrie wanted a fight, fine, she'd get one.

"I don't know a thing about life?" Carrie's eyes widened with disbelief. "I don't know a thing about life? Well, I can tell you it's not supposed to be like this. I can tell you that I know parents who are good parents, who actually care about their kids. Parents who don't think they're some stupid karaoke star. Parents who will complete a Pell Grant application for their daughter so she can go to college. Parents who don't teach their kids some messed up, twisted thought process about being underachievers, or that they are victims in a world that owes them everything. Some crazy, dysfunctional beliefs only years of crazy can cultivate. I know good people. People who don't crap on everyone else. People who—"

"People who what? You think you are so much better than us—"

"—are honest, true to their words, treat other people with respect. People who care if their kids are doing their homework, if their kids are missing and have a gun, people who correct their mistakes and don't lay in the horrible bed they make, they make new ones, and—"

"And you think you have it so bad? Life happens to people, Your Highness. Until you've walked a mile in my shoes, I don't care what you think of me. I am a good person, and I've had to make difficult choices for all of us. I've tried. Trying was the best I could do!"

"You've never tried!"

The two stood glaring at each other, chests heaving.

Of course, Carrie wasn't done. "You only care about your-self. You think you're a karaoke star, and you ignore those who could really use every ounce of encouragement you can muster. You're not a good person. A good person would make a good parent." She pushed away from the table and stared pointedly at Janice's empty hands. "And mock my lists if you want, but if you kept one, you might remember your promises. You can't even remember to bring home artichokes."

Janice followed Carrie to her bedroom and shouted through the closed door, "I said I'd bring home the treat if no one bugged me at the bar, but you all were a pain in the ass tonight. And I *am* a karaoke star! Someday when you have children, I hope you regret everything you just said. You have no idea what you're talking about, you smug little—"

"I'm not Dad. You can't badger me into fighting with you all night. We can't even have a normal argument. I just want to be normal."

"You wanted this fight! And *normal*? What does that even mean? This IS my normal. My normal is never doing anything normal, and you know what? If I was your kind of normal, I would be dead by now!"

"Oh, grow up!" Carrie shouted.

"You grow up!"

Janice closed her eyes, took a deep breath. Oil and water. She and Carrie had always been oil and water.

That girl had been screaming at her since the day she brought her home from the hospital.

Janice went back to the kitchen and walked over to the table to see what the snot had been writing. She flipped the pages in the notebook until she saw the list of books. Her books.

- *Gone with the Wind*
- *The Clan of the Cave Bear*
- *Jane Eyre*
- *King James Bible*
- *The Mists of Avalon*
- *The Thorn Birds*

Beneath the list, Carrie had scribbled, *Theme: Men leave, die, are arrogant, abusive and controlling, crippled, or perverted. And family secrets!*

How had Carrie gotten that out of the books? Those weren't the themes at all. And Carrie thought she was so smart. She was wrong. Simply wrong.

And what business was it of Carrie's? What was she doing going through her books anyway?

Especially her *Jane Eyre*. The urge to run down the hall and make sure the book was safe and sound almost overrode her curiosity.

She pulled out a scholarship essay form that read: *Review your parents' bookshelf. Identify a common theme of the books there. In one thousand words or less, demonstrate how this theme is, or is not, reflected in your life.*

Ah-ha. This should be good.

No one could guess what the stories meant to Janice, and why they meant enough to her that she had reread them several times. They meant so much that they were the few personal things she'd managed to hang on to all these years. Janice pulled out the chair and sat to read Carrie's notes.

My mom is obsessed with female protagonists who are victims of circumstance, and their choices. My mom prefers dramatic novels where the man dies in the end, is abusive, or is too selfish to stick around, allowing the heroine to burn a glorious trail of purpose via martyrdom. In some cases, the women are strong, such as Scarlett in Gone with the Wind, *who goes after what she wants, regardless of how she might hurt others—I definitely see this selfishness in my mother . . .*

Janice wished she could stop reading, but it was like looking at roadkill, she couldn't stop herself.

Ayla, in The Clan of the Cave Bear, *is forced to leave the clan and the only home she knows. It's tragic how the clan excommunicates Ayla and won't allow her to take her baby . . . I can honestly say, I do not know why my mom has this book . . . Ayla is inspiring. My mom is uninspiring . . . My mom can't even return a library book.* Jane Eyre *is over thirty years past due . . . My parents never had any goals in life. If they had, maybe my family would have had a chance. If our parents had had purpose and passion, they would have had expectations. Perhaps I'd be following my older siblings' footsteps in education instead of fighting to be the first of my family to go to college.*

Janice would've been better off not reading. Instead, she read every word, then closed Carrie's notebook.

She had had goals once. And she had a goal now—one she planned to act on, and her daughter could eat her essay.

As usual, her daughter had taken the wind out of her sails. Her earlier excitement was gonezo. Holding her purse tight, she made it to her bedroom. She grabbed *Jane Eyre* and crawled into bed fully clothed and with her purse too.

She carefully ran her finger along the tape that kept the plastic-wrapped book cover in place. Under the front cover was WJ's original birth certificate in an envelope taped to the hardback. Pulling back the sleeve, she stared at the black-and-white picture of Walter, so lovingly positioned and preserved in place. She rarely looked at his picture because when she did, she felt seventeen again, and it left her wondering what life would look like today if he'd lived. They would've been married thirty years this month.

21

JANICE

Imagine That
—Patsy Cline

Monday, January 30, 1961—Reno, NV

Allow me, Mrs. Sloan." Harry opened the Cadillac door.
"Why thank you, Husband." Janice giggled and
climbed in the front seat with WJ on her lap. "WJ Sloan,
didn't we just marry the most beautiful man? And don't you
just love the sound of our new names? Janice Sloan and
WJ Sloan."

"Names destined for fame." Harry slid into the driver's
seat, draped his arm across the wide bench, and turned toward
his new family. "It's four o'clock now. Let's drop WJ off at
the motel with the sitter and celebrate. I'll show you the casinos." His grin spread from ear to ear.

Janice liked knowing their vows were the cause of his
smile. She slid her small thumb along the inside of her

wedding finger, stroking the band, and smiled back at him. "I'd like to, but you know I'm not twenty-one."

"Won't be a problem. Just stick close to me." Harry started the car and backed out of the wedding chapel driveway. It was a converted two-bedroom house squeezed in along a strip of casinos. Bells outlined with white bulbs flashed next to the neon *Open* sign. It wasn't someplace she'd ever imagined getting married, but she didn't give a fig. She was married and on her way to Las Vegas!

Just the day before, they'd arrived in Reno after driving for three days from Minneapolis. It was Janice's first road trip, and when they'd passed the sign saying they were leaving Minnesota, she thought her heart would wind its way through her body and float up and out of her mouth, bursting into butterflies.

During Harry's courtship, she'd often wondered if Walter was their guardian angel and had sent Harry to his sweetheart and son. She still dreamed of Walter running after the red balloons, and the dread in the recurring dream had slowly lessened as hope and butterflies took its place. She was even writing a song about it, "Balloons & Butterflies."

She could hardly believe her good fortune. She and Harry had been inseparable from their first meeting at the diner six months before. Since then, he'd embraced WJ and her in his strong arms, always worrying if they had what they needed, overfeeding them, making her feel cared for and protected in a way she hadn't felt since Walter died. And when her flatmate, Stephanie, met Harry and gave Janice the thumbs up, there had been no stopping her heart. She smiled now, thinking about Harry's proposal.

It had been a beautiful September night, and she and WJ

had stood outside the diner listening to the quartet when the guys started a tune she didn't recognize.

Mama and Baby, they came to town
Big blue eyes as they looked around
Glass half full and limitless sky
They changed the life of this humble guy

So now I say to my beautiful gal
And the cherub-cheeked baby and my little pal
Will you take this ring and become my wife
And remain the songbird in my life

Because I was not happy until I saw you
No, I was not alive until I met you
I glided along, content I thought
And then, there you were, all my heart had
       sought

We can sing together and I'll love our son
You'll never doubt that you're the one
We'll travel the world and live our dreams
Please say yes, I'm down on one knee

Because I was not happy until I met you
No, I was not alive until I saw you
I glided along, content I thought
And then, there you were, all my heart had
       sought

Because I was not happy until I met you

No, I was not alive until I saw you
I guided along, content I thought
And then, there you were, all my heart had
*   sought*

Her jaw had dropped when Harry went to one knee and held out the ring. She'd squealed and nearly squeezed the breath out of WJ. "Yes. Yes. Yes."

Now they were in Reno and would continue their drive to Las Vegas in two days. They'd wanted to get married as soon as possible, but for WJ's sake, they chose a route where they could stop and rest each night. And in Reno, they could get married almost immediately.

Check. Done! They would arrive in Vegas as a certified family.

They dropped WJ off with the motel manager, Wanda, and headed down the strip. Harry knew more about Reno than she'd expected, and she smiled as he chattered, telling her how Reno was growing and had a reputation as the "Biggest Little City" in the nation. He'd asked around and was taking her to the hottest spot—The Golden Nugget. They practically skipped inside together.

"I've never been in a casino," Janice said as she leaned into Harry's side. She was afraid her head was going to snap off her neck. There was so much to look at and sounds galore. She wanted to see everything at once. Slot machines created a cacophonous song. Fingers jostled coins, and metal scraped against metal in the slots. Once released, the lever made a sound like a wind-up toy and then a *bang* as it slammed against its joint. The mechanical reels spun and clicked into place, and for the lucky players, bells chimed and coins clanked against the tin tray.

"I can't grasp it all. Slow down," Janice said, and laughter rolled from the back of her throat.

So much newness!

Harry chuckled and squeezed her hand in the crook of his arm. His index finger tapped her wedding band. "You haven't seen anything yet. This is my lucky day. You?"

She leaned into him and smiled. "Oh, I'm lucky."

"Then let me introduce you to roulette." He lifted his elbow and let her hand slide down to his palm. He veered left and led her through the crowd and tables.

"What's going on?" she asked wide-eyed when a group of twenty or so people screamed and cheered, arms waving in the air, slapping each other on the back.

"Craps."

"And that?" she asked and pointed.

"Blackjack, and this," Harry walked up to a table and pulled out a stool for her, "is roulette." He smiled at the dealer. "Minimum?"

"Two dollars," the dealer said.

Harry pulled out his wallet and removed one hundred dollars. "Chips for the lady and me. Fifty-fifty."

Janice's eyes widened. "Harry, that's too much money. We need it for Vegas. I don't even know how to play."

Harry didn't meet her eyes, but he smiled. "Baby, sometimes we just have to go for it. Here's how it works. Stack a chip, or chips, on a number, two-spot, four-corner-spot, or at the end and side of the tables here. One through thirty-six, or zero and double zero." He winked at the dealer and waved his arm over the green fabric like a magician. "See the spaces here? Even and odd numbers. And here, black or red. You have to play at least four chips each game. Okay? Then the dealer will spin the wheel and roll the ball. If it lands on your number, you'll win. It's a cinch."

Cinch? No way. She didn't even think she had grasped everything Harry had just rattled off. She hesitated to touch the pile of yellow chips. Nausea rolled in her gut. She couldn't tell if she was afraid or excited. She had never done anything like this. Three days before she had never even crossed Minnesota's state line. And fifty dollars was a lot of money. She'd rather save her share.

"What if we lose it all?"

Harry started placing his blue chips on the green felt table. She stared at his profile.

He winked. "Come on, play. The table is waiting."

For the first time, Janice realized five other people were at the table. Two men were still placing their chips, but the dealer and other three men were looking at her. She thought their eyes seemed . . . blank. Her gut tightened, and her shoulders tensed. She moved closer to Harry.

He turned to the dealer. "Roll without her."

She hated to see him peeved with her on their wedding night. "No, wait." She leaned over and placed two yellow chips on number one for January, one yellow chip on sixteen for WJ's birth date, and one on thirty for her wedding day.

The dealer waved his arm over the table, signaling all bets placed.

"Attagirl," Harry said and placed his hand on her shoulder.

She clenched her hands in her lap and watched the dealer spin the wheel and flick the ball at the seam. She felt like it would never stop spinning and then the ball dropped and bounced between and over numbers, finally settling.

"Eight," the dealer said and cleared the board. He leaned over and placed a gold dolly on the blue chips.

Janice watched in horror as he scraped the multiple chips, and all of her yellow ones, across the table. She wanted to throw up. How could Harry be cheering beside her? She'd failed them.

"We just won a thousand dollars, baby. What did I tell you! It's my lucky night!"

"What?" she asked. And then it registered. Blue chips. Harry's blue chips. "We won? We won!"

But Harry was already adding chips to the table and leaving the original winning chips in place. He glanced down at her. "Come on. Lay them out."

Janice placed her chips again on thirty, sixteen, and one. She sat back and frowned at Harry. He had placed all of his winnings on the table, including a pile on her number thirty.

The dealer made a motion with his hand above the table.

There was no going back now. Closing her eyes, she listened to the spinning of the wheel and clinking of the ball.

The dealer said, "Thirty."

Harry whooped.

Janice sucked in her breath, and her eyes popped open. "That's me!" She turned to Harry, jaw dropped. "That's you!"

Harry was doing a jig right there at the table.

"That's enough for us to get our own place in Las Vegas," she said. "We won't have to live with one of the guys, or in a kitchenette." She squeezed his wrist. The guys, minus Jim, would be meeting them there.

She glanced at Harry, but he was staring at the table. She tried to meet his eyes. He seemed dazed, like he was there with her but not there. She looked around at the other players.

They were looking down at the table. She could feel anger rolling off of their bodies.

One guy took a drag off his cigarette and glared at Janice. He blew his smoke in her face.

She coughed and leaned into Harry's arm, squeezing his wrist. "Harry."

Harry leaned forward to start placing his chips, shrugging away her hand in the process.

"Harry," she clutched his shoulder, "no, I want to go." She turned to see the angry man was still watching her.

The man snickered and slid his remaining chips on number thirty.

"Harry?" She looked back to her husband. What was happening? A dark cloud had settled upon her. Why was Harry ignoring her?

Just then, he rolled his shoulder as if to dislodge her hold.

"Harry!" She snapped at him and desperately grabbed the back of his neck—the one spot that she herself couldn't bear to have touched.

He stopped, shook his head, and looked at her.

"Are you in, or not?" One of the guys smirked and snorted. "Women."

Tears gathered in Janice's eyes. She always cried when she was frustrated. Now two men at the table were ganging up on them, and for a second, Janice was afraid she saw the same irritation in Harry's eyes. But she was wrong because he pulled her close instead.

"Dealer, we're out." Harry gathered his chips and dropped them in a plastic bucket the dealer handed him. Harry passed a few chips back to the dealer. "For you."

Janice copied his movements and took his free hand when he offered it.

Harry leaned toward the man who had blown smoke on her. "This is my wife, and she's a lady. You'd be lucky to have someone like her."

Harry led her to the cashier's cage. "Cash us out, please." The cashier counted the bills out, and Harry put the money in his wallet. He took Janice's hand and started toward the exit.

Janice glanced at him from time to time. He was not looking back at her, but she felt the pressure of his thumb sliding along her hand. Once they got outside, Harry pulled her to the side and rested his back against a brick wall. He lit a cigarette and offered her one.

She shook her head and folded her arms.

He exhaled and leaned forward to kiss her forehead. "Thanks, baby. I got a little excited in there. We won, and sometimes I just feel like I can't lose."

Janice stood on her toes and placed her hands on his chest. She could see how easy it would be to get caught up in winning. If not for the miserable people at the table, maybe she would have wanted to keep playing too. She decided to let the experience go. "Winning is exciting, but we have enough to get settled in Vegas already, only better now. And do you know why I picked the number thirty?"

"Today's the thirtieth, our wedding day. And speaking of wedding days," he took his free hand and smoothed the side of her hair, tucking it behind her ear, and slid his index finger and thumb over her earlobe, "maybe we can get you some diamond earrings to match your ring. Or we can get you a bigger wedding ring."

He had barely finished before she said, "No. I love my ring, and I never want to take it off." But earrings? She'd never had earrings before. She could get her ears pierced. Janice lifted her hands and touched her smooth lobes.

"Could we really? It won't take away from you, or WJ? Oh! What can we get WJ?" They still had plenty for a home.

Harry tilted his head to the side. His eyes softened, and he smiled. He dropped his cigarette to the ground, putting it out with the toe of his shoe.

"I love you, Songbird." He lifted her hands from his chest and kissed each one. He entwined their fingers. "Let's go home and babble our good news to WJ. Tomorrow we'll get the classified ads for the Las Vegas paper and look for a rental. And the day after, let's hit the road. Our road."

They turned and started to walk down the sidewalk, her shoulder bumping against his arm, and her skirt sashaying back and forth, dancing to the tune of her light step. She lifted their joined hands and kissed his. "I'd like to buy you a gift with my winnings too."

"Oh you would, would you?"

Janice lifted her chin and smiled at the man beside her. She glanced at all of the lights and billboards of the biggest little city and daydreamed about the choices the money allowed. This morning she had been a single mother. Now she was his wife and heading to Las Vegas to establish a home and sing her heart out. She had never felt so lucky in her life. Life had given her a second chance.

The next morning, as soon as Harry left for the gas station to fill the tank and check the tires' air pressure in preparation for their trip, Janice bundled up WJ and strolled down Main Street to a pawnshop she'd noticed the night before. She had her winnings in her purse, and she planned to surprise Harry with a new watch. Harry said he had a few errands to run afterward and would bring lunch back for them, so she only had a few hours to shop.

And maybe his errands involved the diamond earrings he'd mentioned last night. She giggled. Love was grand, and wouldn't it be a hoot if they stumbled into each other at the pawnshop?

By one o'clock in the afternoon, Janice had his silver watch and a blue leather band wrapped and hidden in the nightstand. She also bought WJ a new toy, and he was sitting on the floor slapping it with his hands.

By two o'clock though, Harry still wasn't home, and WJ was starting to whine. It was past his lunchtime, and she had nothing left on hand. She wrote Harry a note and walked down the block to a diner. WJ ate all of his cereal. On the way back to the motel, she bought a few jars of baby food for his dinner and the road trip tomorrow. It took her a while because she decided to spoil WJ by purchasing whichever items he reached for. The orange carrots and green peas caught his eye, and she grabbed some crackers. "Okay, baby, let's go. It must be three o'clock, and your new papa is probably wondering where we are."

But he wasn't. Janice frowned at the empty parking space in front of their orange motel room. Instead of going inside, she walked past their unit and went to the manager's office.

"Hi, Wanda," Janice said as she walked in, the bell bouncing against the glass door.

"Hi, sweetie. Need me to sit for you?" Wanda was in her sixties and had five grandchildren.

"No, thank you. We're leaving tomorrow. I really appreciate your help these past few days." She moved WJ to her other hip and set the bag of baby food on the counter. "Has my husband left a message for me?"

"No. Can I help you with anything?"

"No." Janice frowned. She glanced at the white-and-black clock behind Wanda. "I expected him home earlier, but I guess his errands have held him up. I'm sure he'll be home soon."

Wanda patted her hand. "Try not to worry."

Janice grabbed her bag and carried WJ back to their room. Her note still lay on the pillow.

Some three hours later when Harry came through the door, Janice was pacing the small room with a crying baby on her hip.

"Oh, thank goodness. Where have you been? We were so worried."

Harry moved slowly into the room and sat on the corner of the bed. He rubbed his face and reached for a cigarette. The box was empty.

Janice looked at his empty hands. He didn't have a gift. What of his errands? "Is everything okay with the car?"

Harry didn't answer.

Janice walked to the front window and pulled back the curtain. The car was sitting in front. "Harry, what's wrong?"

He released a deep breath.

The smell of alcohol felt like a slap in the face. What did drinking have to do with errands? "You've been drinking?"

"Janice, sit down."

She bounced WJ on her hip. "You're scaring me."

He handed WJ a pacifier. "Sit down. I need to talk to you."

Her stomach rolled as she sat next to him. "What is it?"

"Janice," Harry said. He wouldn't look at her but reached for her left hand and played with her wedding finger. "Honey, I lost it. I'm sorry."

"Lost what?" *Please, no.*

"I took care of the car and thought I would take one more try at the casino."

She sucked in a breath and reflexively squeezed WJ in her arms. "You gambled? You lost? How much?" She thought of the gift she had for him in the nightstand. With his watch and the few small purchases she'd made, she still had one hundred and fifteen dollars.

Harry mumbled.

"What?" she asked.

"All of it." He let go of her hand and put his face in his hands.

For a second, she couldn't think straight. How was that possible? She'd never seen so much money before. "But that was our gas money—money for our home."

"I know."

I know? I know? That's all he had to say. How was he going to fix this?

"How could you do that to us?" she snapped. "What are we going to do?"

"How much do you have left?" he asked but didn't meet her eyes.

"I bought a few things. Not enough to get us to Las Vegas and get a place."

"We need fifty dollars to rent this room for another week. Another two hundred, and we'll be set when we get there."

She looked around the room in dismay and shock. The room had been okay for a few days but only because it was short-term. It wasn't a home.

"We're going to have to stay here? No. I told Wanda we're leaving tomorrow."

WJ spat out his pacifier and started to cry.

Janice stood up and walked back and forth with WJ, not sure that he needed her hugs as much as she needed his. Her tears were building and starting to run over. "I don't understand. We're supposed to be a team." Janice looked over at the second bed where she had spread out the Las Vegas newspaper ads. She had circled several postings for apartments. Next to the paper was her notebook where she'd started writing more songs. She'd been giggling when she combed through the want ads. Thrilled at the prospect of her future. "Why did you do this to us?"

He didn't answer right away, and she thought of the first night she met him and his tale about Jim being addicted to gambling and having to get back to Minnesota. If it was Jim, it hadn't only been Jim, had it? She'd married someone who couldn't control his gambling. What else didn't she know about him? He'd always been so responsible and happy in Minnesota. She felt a moment of panic. They'd never be able to move to Vegas. But there was Nashville. Nashville had always been her first choice, and she didn't think they had casinos.

"I'm sorry. I had a drink and lost track. I was winning big, real big, and I thought just one more time, and I then, well, you know the rest."

She wasn't going to be able to wrap her head around his decision, and beating him up for it wasn't going to make either one of them feel better, but she needed to move forward. Grandfather had always said, "Sink or swim."

They'd swim.

"Fine then. We'll save our money and go to Nashville instead. There aren't any casinos there," she said, staring at his bent head. "How much do we need to make it to Tennessee?"

He looked at her so desperate for reassurance, she wanted to give it to him. His weakness was gambling, but together they could avoid it. He'd helped her get over Walter. She would help him too.

"I won't do it again. Believe me. Tomorrow I will go and find a job. We'll use your winnings to pay for the motel and food for the next few weeks, and then we'll be back on track."

"Good," she said. They could do this. She stood before Harry, rocking from side to side. They didn't say anything for a while. Once WJ rested his head against her shoulder, she laid him down on the bed. She turned her back on Harry and curled up next to WJ. Harry climbed into the bed behind her. He wrapped his arms around her, placed his chin on top of her head, and bent his knees up behind hers.

Even now, she loved it when his strong arms hugged her. She wanted everything to be okay, and he hadn't let her down before now.

"I'm sorry, Janice. We'll be okay. I'm a fool, but I've learned my lesson."

The stress of her day caught up to her, and her shoulders started to quake. She turned her head slightly to wipe the tears on his arm. She sniffled. "Do you promise? No more drinking? No more gambling? You're not like your friend, Jim, willing to lose everything?" A teardrop slid over the arch of her nose to join the tears in her other eye. She wanted to wipe it but didn't want to mess with his hold.

Harry kissed the crown of her head and held her tight. "I promise. I'll find a job. Any job. You'll see I'm a hard worker. We'll save our money and be in Nashville within a month.

"We need to find a new motel. This one is too close to the casinos."

"Anything."

"Can you hold me tighter?" she asked.

"Always." He pulled her close until she was cradled by his lower leg and arm. "It'll be okay."

She was happy when he got a good-paying job the next day. He admitted he was tempted to gamble, so Janice met him at work on paydays. She also took over the responsibility of paying their bills and keeping some money aside for their future. A few weeks later, she started feeling ill in the morning. Harry was worried sick about her and insisted that she go to the doctor even though the cost would delay their move to Nashville. When the doctor told them she was pregnant, her first thoughts were how happy Harry looked and how wonderful it would be for WJ to have a little brother or sister.

"We can go to Nashville once the baby is born, but I don't want to risk either one of you by traveling," Harry said. So a few weeks later when they should have been heading to Nashville, she let Harry convince her to put a down payment on an investment: a trailer on Tiger Drive in Corbett City, Nevada.

22

JANICE

Well, I'm nearly up to the moon, and I didn't need a rocket.
—Patsy Cline

Who was shaking Janice's shoulder now? Too rough for Justin or Tommy.

"You need to wake up," a male voice said.

No, she didn't. Who was that, anyway?

Someone shook her shoulder again. "Wake up."

Oh, for Pete's sake!

Janice rolled over and looked up at WJ's angry face looming above hers.

Egads! His angry face was not one she was used to waking up to. She frowned and looked around the bright room. She was still in her clothes and cradling her purse like a football player in the end zone. Thank goodness she had returned Walter's picture and WJ's original birth certificate to *Jane Eyre* before she fell asleep.

"What are you doing here?" she asked.

"You have a call. You need to take it," he said and reached

for her purse—she guessed to rush her to get up—but she didn't want him to get curious about the newspapers crammed inside.

"Let go of my purse and tell them I will call them back. What in the heck are you doing here?"

"Just get up. It's the police."

"The police? What now?" She sat up in bed and shook her head.

"They're asking for Harry."

"Oh, 'Harry,' is it now?"

"You do not want to push me right now, Mother."

Stumbling to the kitchen with her purse, she grabbed the receiver, snapped her fingers three times to get Lisa's attention, and pointed at the coffee pot. She curled her fingers except for her pinky and her thumb and gestured toward her lips in a drinking motion.

Lisa nodded and got up.

Janice looked over the cluttered island separating the living room and kitchen. The boys were watching Sunday morning cartoons, eating something, and had something all over their chins. She cringed. Blue cupcakes? Shaking her head, she put the phone to her ear and faced the hallway.

WJ loomed over her shoulder like a buzzard.

She stretched her arm out behind her to push him away. "This is Janice Sloan."

"Mrs. Sloan, sorry to call you so early on a Sunday morning. This is Detective Anderson. I need to speak to your husband. I understand he isn't home. Do you know where I can find him?"

Janice frowned. She'd never heard of Anderson. When did Corbett City get a female detective? "Why do you need to speak to Harry?"

"I have a few questions for him but nothing I can discuss with you at the moment."

"Then find him yourself."

"We would appreciate your cooperation."

"And I'd appreciate yours, Detective Anderson."

"Mrs. Sloan, we have a few questions we think he can help us with. Again, do you know where I can find him?"

Janice took the cup of coffee from Lisa, sipped, closed her eyes, and sighed. "If you did your job well, you'd know I have a restraining order against him. He's staying at the kitchenettes on Green Street."

"Thank you. If you hear from him today, please tell him we need to speak to him." She rattled off a phone number.

Janice didn't write anything down. She hung up and turned to WJ, who was now fingering her dying fern. Ignoring Lisa, who was waiting and leaning against the wall, Janice asked, "What's going on?"

"What did they want?" he asked as he turned to face her.

"Your dad. Would you know why? What happened when you saw him last night?"

"Don't," WJ said between clenched teeth, "call him my dad."

"I don't have the patience for you today," she said.

He pointed at his sister. "Stay there." He grabbed Janice's arm and steered her down the hallway.

"What's gotten into you now? You're hurting me." And she was done with men hurting her.

"I went to Harry's, but the boys were there, so I brought them home. That's it. He was drunk. Said he was going to bed. But I don't want anyone outside of us," he pointed at his chest and then hers, "knowing I was there. I had other business last night, and I don't need the police all over my ass asking questions."

There was more to this, she knew it. She shrugged away his hand. "You were expecting them to call me. That's why you're here."

"I already told you what happened. I dropped the boys off last night, and I wanted to bring them breakfast. So I did. Leave it the hell alone."

"Blue cupcakes? For breakfast?" she asked.

"You know what? Screw you. I can never do anything right. I found your kids for you last night, brought them home, and I brought them breakfast, and this is how you show your thanks."

"WJ, you don't do anything that doesn't benefit yourself. You wouldn't be here without a reason. You knew the police were going to call, and you're using your big brother card as an excuse," she said.

"That's real fucking rich coming from you. Let's talk about the choices you've made for yourself, not caring who might get hurt in the process. And the lies you've told."

Lies? Had he figured out she was leaving? But she hadn't told anyone. She didn't think Scotty would've mentioned the newspapers.

Poker face now in place, she said, "I don't know what you're rambling on about, but you know what? I don't care. Let them eat cupcakes. Spend time with them. Whatever you want. I'm going back to bed." WJ could take a flying leap for all she cared. The door bounced against the crooked door-frame as she threw it closed. The coffee cleared her thoughts and warmed her throat, which was sore from singing the night before. She pulled the newspapers out of her purse.

She locked the door and spread the ads out before her and

started circling studio apartments. She had a week to find an apartment. She didn't have time to worry about Harry, but if he did anything to screw up her plans to leave the kids with him, she would kill him. Rent was due today, so she would call him tonight if she hadn't heard from him by then.

She finished going through the papers. She had several calls to make, all long distance, and she couldn't make them while eavesdroppers were in the house. She considered waiting and calling from the bar. Scotty would let her, but then again, he was as nosy as her family. She swiped her tongue over her teeth and looked out the window.

From this angle, she could see the side of the playhouse where Harry had spray painted a white heart and cupid's arrow. He'd been drinking and painted it from an odd angle, standing in a narrow space, stretching his arm over his head. As a result, the arrow was backward and upside down. The feathers were on the bottom right-hand side, and the tip of the arrow pierced the upper left curve of the heart. Cupid wouldn't be impressed, but Janice had been.

Harry had painted, *Harry-N-Janice* in the middle.

One thing about her husband, he was one of a kind, and he'd always done little things here and there that made her laugh. For a few seconds, she allowed herself to feel what she'd felt nine years before on Valentine's Day. After he'd unveiled his clumsy art, he had taken her out for Hawaiian pizza. Just the two of them. No kids and no pepperoni. Other customers had screaming children, but not Harry and her. They found a corner table, ate their Canadian bacon and pineapple, drank draught beer, and listened to the songs they selected on the jukebox. When they stumbled home, they accidentally conceived the last of the lot, Justin. When Justin was born C-section, she smartened up and had her tubes tied.

Janice checked her wallet. Should be enough to buy her some peace and quiet.

WJ was reentering the trailer just as she walked toward the living room and offered him the money.

"Find Carrie. Take everyone out to Denny's for a real breakfast. I want the place to myself for a while."

Other than glaring at her, he didn't give her any more trouble, and he turned to the boys and gave them a thumbs-up.

They whooped and ran to their bedrooms to get dressed.

"What's this about?" He held up the money and rolled it between his fingertips. "Feeling guilty?"

Guilty on what count? If he'd somehow figured out she was hitting the road, she'd rather he just say it and not poke her with passive aggressive comments.

"Please, just take them to breakfast. I need to sort out some bills, and rent is due. I don't want them here when I make the calls. Besides, it's Sunday, and you should do something nice for someone else. Clean your conscience."

"Don't talk to me about a clean conscience," he said.

Janice watched WJ usher everyone outside. She followed them to the porch and studied WJ as he waited by his truck. What did he know? Whether it was about her plans, or about the call this morning from the detective, she knew her eldest son was up to something. She waited for them to drive away before she returned to the kitchen to make her calls. As she passed the kitchen counter, she paused and stared at the blank spot.

Her fern was gone.

But I got sensitivity an' I don't like insulks!
—Popeye

WJ pulled up in front of the trailer and hopped out of his truck. One by one, the boys jumped in his arms, and he lowered them to the ground. He shouldn't have let them ride in the open truck bed, but he was feeling bad for their days ahead, even though in the long run Harry's death was the best thing that could happen to them—he'd never lay a finger on them now.

Tommy left a maple syrup handprint on WJ's sleeve.

"Dammit, Tom, you got that shit all over my shirt," WJ said.

"Sorry." Tommy wiped his palms down the front of his own T-shirt.

Carrie and Lisa slid out of the truck cab.

"I have to babysit next door. Thanks for breakfast," Carrie said.

"Thanks, WJ," Lisa said.

"Get on with all of you," WJ said. "Call me if you need anything." He was going to have to think long and hard how he'd be able to help them now that Harry was out of the picture.

Carrie stopped and gave him a funny look. "Anything?"

Smart ass. "Just go," he said.

As soon as he was alone, he walked over to the tree next to the mailbox and picked up the dying plant he'd rescued from the kitchen counter. His mom couldn't even water a damn plant and let it grow.

He hopped into his truck and wedged the pot between the passenger side door and the seatbelt. He drove around the trailer park and down the adults-only side. He slowed his vehicle to roll over each of the four speed bumps. By the time he reached the end of the road, he decided to drive by Swan Park, where he'd left Harry's car. Then he would keep heading south and drive by the kitchenette. See if any cops were hanging out.

They'd better be, or that place was going to start smelling ripe. That damn pesky thought crossed his mind again. Should he use a pay phone and make an anonymous call to the police department?

Don't grow weak and soft. Now's not the time to get a fucking conscience. He'd given his up years ago. Weakness was Sloppy Work's idiot brother.

If he called the police, he wouldn't have to think about Harry's body decomposing—and he didn't have a crap clue why he was thinking about it—but somehow, some way, the police would end up on his ass, asking what time he saw Harry. *Weakness.*

It was suicide, so he shouldn't give a shit about being blamed for Harry's death, but if he was honest about seeing

Harry twice last night, it would blow his alibi, if needed, about the dude he and Hefty had worked over earlier. *Sloppy Work.* And he shouldn't have touched anything. He shouldn't have touched the rope, Harry, none of it. *Sloppy Work and Weakness.*

Which is why no one, especially the police, could ever find out about Harry's letter. Last night in the thick of Harry's letter and the mind-blowing fucking news that Harry wasn't his dad, WJ hadn't thought about timing or the alibi he and Hefty were supposed to be using to cover their trails. The same alibi they'd worked out with Bender. First, Hefty's meltdown had thrown it off, and then admitting to anyone that he had Harry's letter would also put him in the wrong place at the wrong time, and he'd be throwing himself under a fucking train. Not to mention, Harry had fucking outed him in the letter. Those judgmental police pricks would ruin his credibility with friends, and he couldn't be an outcast once again.

And what about his real family? The Whitworths? He hadn't decided what to do about them. It was too much too soon to take it all in, but he had a whole damn different family somewhere. A real family. In the middle of the night, he'd also started thinking he could contact them, but maybe his biological dad would be none too happy to have a drug dealer for a son, or a gay son. If the letter got out and the police contacted them for some reason, he might never get a chance with his real dad. And if Janice had taken him away from his real family once, what would she do to stop them from finding each other?

So no one would ever see the letter. Not Janice. Not the police. Harry wasn't getting the last fucking word, and the joke wasn't going to be on WJ.

WJ patted his front pocket, reassured by the tucked-in

papers. He didn't want to leave them at home: Shelly was always digging through his things. When he'd left the car at the park last night and walked to the bar, WJ had pulled out his lighter and held a flame to one end of the paper. But he'd smothered the embers and refolded the pages. *Fucking Weakness.* He almost looked over his shoulder for Sloppy Work.

But Harry's car was gone when WJ pulled into Swan Park. Who the hell took it? Sweat gathered above his lip. He flipped a U-turn and headed toward the highway. By the time he reached Green Street, sweat rings had stretched from his armpits to his lower rib cage. His body odor smelt of rancid peaches—like his life was slowly going down the tubes.

He slowed as he neared the turn for Harry's kitchenette. Three cop cars were parked in front. WJ hit the gas.

They'd found Harry. They'd take care of him. Put him in a fridge. Stop the rotting. Now he had to wait for his mom to find out. He wondered if she would have a funeral for him? Had they found him soon enough to have an open casket?

Weakness. When had he ever worried about fucking funerals?

WJ drove to the Creek Bar. He pulled around back and let himself in the back door. It was not even eleven o' clock. No need for Pete to be bouncing. There were three other customers. Except for the TV in the corner, the place was quiet. He slid up to the bar.

"Scotty, tequila," he said.

Scotty poured him a shot. "Early for you."

"The bottle. I want the bottle," WJ said. He flexed his shaking hand under the bar. *Weakness.*

Scotty held up a greasy saltshaker and a lime and then raised his eyebrows.

"No."

No one said anything as WJ slammed down shot after shot. After several, he asked Scotty if he could use the phone in his office.

Scotty tossed him the key.

Closing the door to the tiny office behind him, WJ grabbed the phone before he could think himself out of what he wanted to do. He punched in 1-775-555-1212.

He swallowed hard as the line rang.

"Nevada Directory Assistance. City and name please."

WJ had no idea what city he'd find Walter Whitworth in. Hell, he wasn't even sure if he had the right state. "Um, Corbett City. Walter Whitworth."

He drummed his fingers on the desktop while he waited for the operator to respond. Shit, he was sweating again he was so nervous.

"I'm sorry, there is no listing for Whitworth in the Nevada directory. Can I help you with anything else?"

He was just going to hang up when he figured, why the hell not try? "What's the area code for Lincoln County, Minnesota?"

He'd never met his great grandparents. His mom had told him that they'd had a falling out and that was that. But he knew they'd raised her in Lincoln County, Minnesota. No one ever talked about Lincoln, and maybe it had something to do with his biological dad. Even imagining all the lies that had been shoved down his throat made his blood boil so fucking hard he thought he might explode into a million pieces.

"The area code for Lincoln County, Minnesota, is five-zero-seven. Would you like me to connect you to Minnesota's Directory Assistance?"

"Yes."

And then a few seconds later, a new operator was asking him for the city and name.

"Lincoln County, Minnesota. Walter Whitworth."

"I'm sorry," she said.

Shit, another dead end.

"There is no listing for Walter Whitworth, but I do have a listing for William and June Whitworth. Would you like me to connect you?"

His heart was beating so hard he could hear it in his head. Swallowing hard, he said, "Yes, please."

So this is what time standing still feels like, WJ thought as he waited for someone to answer the phone on the other end of the line.

"Whitworth family," a girl answered.

He didn't know what he'd expected. Maybe he'd expected a man to answer, but not a girl who sounded the same age as Carrie. Shit, did he have a Whitworth sister or cousin? Maybe he should find out more first. He should hang up. But instead, he started talking. *Sloppy Work.*

"Is Walter Whitworth home?" he asked.

There was a long pause and the girl shouted out, "Dad? Someone is asking for Uncle Walter."

WJ heard a shuffling on the line, and a deep voice asked, "Who is this?"

WJ hung up. *Weakness.*

24

JANICE

Leavin' On Your Mind
—Patsy Cline

This was the best Sunday afternoon Janice had had in a long while, and she was celebrating with Frank Sinatra and singing and dancing to "I've Got the World on a String."

Next Sunday would be even better. Her life would improve from here on out. She glanced at the kitchen clock. It was three o'clock, but she was making the boys breakfast food as a treat for an early dinner. She flipped a pancake on the griddle in time to the music and stirred the scrambled eggs.

Justin and Tommy were glued to the TV set. The place wasn't so bad with just the three of them. Lisa was at her boyfriend's, and Carrie was either babysitting across the street or was at some do-gooders club.

See? No one really needed her to be a mother anymore.

Janice hummed and moved her hips from side to side. This time next week she would be somewhere between

Corbett City and Nashville. She tapped the wooden spoon on the cast iron pan and waved it like a baton before setting it on the stove. She giggled at her own flourish.

She had called and spoken to a few people leasing rooms in Nashville. They'd asked her a few questions, and two of them had promised to call back with an answer. She asked them all to be discrete unless they spoke to her. The last thing she needed was Carrie discovering her plans. She had a gut feeling she would get one of the apartments. Maybe she'd get a call back today, which would be perfect because she had zero plans for the rest of the afternoon except to plan her new life.

She wasn't sure how to tell Harry she was leaving, but her car would have a full tank of gas and her suitcase in the trunk when she did. No reason to give him too much notice or time to think about it. She'd learned a long time ago to throw Harry into things. She was going to drop Justin and Tommy off at Harry's and step on the gas. She'd tell Harry he could move back to the trailer. Now, if the tables were reversed, Harry would say "goodbye" or "see you later," depending on how serious he was. Harry didn't mess around with the word goodbye. Never used it unless he never meant to see a person again. But he'd never leave her, so it was a moot point.

Tommy and Justin deserved an explanation from her, though, so she was prepared to tell them about her upcoming adventure. They were young and innocent, and she wanted to make sure they heard her version and not the one a hurt Harry or an angry Carrie would spit out. She'd wait to tell them on the way to Harry's and would make it damn-skippy clear that she'd be back for them in a year if not sooner. And if in that time they decided they wanted to stay with their father, well, that was a risk she had to take. Sometimes boys needed their father (even one like Harry) more than a mother, and she had to be ready to accept their choice should it come to that.

But right now, she needed to find out if Harry had paid the lot lease. The park manager would call her tomorrow if an envelope wasn't in the drop-off box when he arrived in the morning, and he'd add on ten dollars every day they were late.

There was a knock at the door.

Maybe that was Harry now. She would let him slide on violating the restraining order if he was paying rent on time and saving her the trouble of chasing him down.

"Tommy, get the door. If it's your dad, make him wait on the porch." Janice stirred the eggs and turned off the burner. The fluffy pancakes covered the paper plates. "Justin, get the syrup and butter out of the fridge. Put them on the table."

Tommy and Justin jumped up.

"It's okay, Mom. Justin and I worked things out with Dad last night," Tommy said in a forced baritone voice.

She smiled at his freckled face. "You did, huh? I would've enjoyed that conversation."

Tommy nodded his head once, rolled his shoulders back, and stuck out his chest. "Yup." He walked toward the door with his head held high.

So serious, Janice thought, and cute too. She'd miss him.

No. There was no time or room for that stinking thinking. It was now or never and better for them in the long run too.

Janice could hear a woman with an officious tone talking to Tommy at the door. Probably some solicitor or a door-to-door Christian. She looked toward the hallway entrance. "We're not buying anything you're selling or preaching," she called from the kitchen.

Tommy stepped in her line of sight, a small child once again, looking like he was about to get in trouble. Big trouble. The space was dark behind Tommy, as if something or someone large loomed over him, blocking the sunlight from the back door.

"Well? Who is it?"

"Mrs. Sloan," boomed a man's voice, "it's Sergeant Meed, Dr. Freeman, and Detective Anderson. We need to speak to you."

Janice rolled her eyes. What now? She slapped the paper plates on the table, wiped her hands on a blue-and-white flowered paper towel, and slid past Tommy.

"Detective Anderson? I spoke to you this morning, remember? Harry isn't here. What part of restraining order don't you understand?" She nodded at the sergeant, whom she had dealt with on various occasions throughout her marriage. "Sergeant Meed." Once, she and Harry had joked they should've made Meed a godparent to one of their kids. "It's been a while," she joked.

"Hi, Mrs. Sloan," Sergeant Meed said. He didn't appear to be in a joking mood.

"I'm Dr. Freeman," the third person introduced himself, "may we come in?" He was carrying a bulky manila envelope.

Meed had never brought a doctor with him before. Detective Anderson was petite but broad shouldered. For a second, Janice was worried this might have something to do with the county or Child Protective Services. Had someone called them about the BB gun? No, not possible. It happened just last night, and she'd never known a state or county worker to work on a Sunday.

"Whatever," she said. "I've never had a doctor make a

house call," she quipped and turned; the trio followed her inside. "Boys, take your dinner outside."

"To the playhouse?" Tommy asked.

"Sure. Throw your plates in the outside garbage when you're done, and play outside until I tell you it's okay to come back in the house." She walked over and leaned against the kitchen counter. Once the boys had gone outside and shut the door, she asked, "Can we do this standing? And fast? I have a life to live."

"Why don't we sit down?" Dr. Freeman asked.

She shrugged her shoulders and walked into the living room, turned off the TV, and sat in the green corduroy La-Z-Boy recliner—Harry's chair. She looked around the room. Actually, everything would be Harry's when she left. She motioned them to the couch and waited for them to take a seat. They should be bugging Harry, not her. If Harry had done anything that would stall her departure, she was going to kill him.

The sun was spilling through the window behind her and shining in their eyes. They moved from side to side, trying to dodge the brightness. She could pull the curtains closed, but it was more fun this way. Besides, she didn't want them to get too comfortable.

"Well? My pancakes are getting cold," she said.

Sergeant Meed and Detective Anderson stared at her, hands folded.

Dr. Freeman leaned forward.

"It's about your husband, Harry. He—"

"I gathered, based on the earlier call. What. Do. You. Need. To. Know?" she interrupted.

"Sergeant Meed and Detective Anderson went by Harry's place this morning."

"And?"

He looked down at the envelope in his lap.

"Out with it, or are you waiting for me to get you some donuts?"

The doctor shook his head and frowned at her. "I'm the coroner. Harry is dead."

Later, she might remember this moment differently, but what might have only been seconds seemed like an eternity while she stared back at the group, confused by what the doctor had just said and thinking any second she'd snap out of it or they'd wave their hands at her and say, "Just kidding. Bad joke. Morbid sense of humor, you know." But they didn't. They just looked back at her like they were giving her time for her thoughts to catch up to the words: *Harry is dead.* But what was enough time to believe the unbelievable in that moment a stranger tells you your husband is gone?

Meed's face was the familiar one, so she focused on him. They were pulling her leg. Paying her back for being a little rude. She wasn't laughing.

"We found your husband this morning after we spoke to you," Detective Anderson said.

"I'm so sorry . . ." Sergeant Meed began.

The room was growing chilly, and goose bumps raced along Janice's arms just before her lips started to shake.

But she'd be leaving the boys with Harry and going to Nashville . . .

She'd never been good with surprises. She rolled her lips between her chattering teeth and squinted. "Um, I don't understand." Her knees started knocking together. She squeezed them. This was some dumb mix-up.

"I know this is shocking news," Dr. Freeman said.

Shocking? Shocking? Harry was not dead. Pete had seen

him at the bar, and the boys were with him just last night. She folded her arms across her midriff. Just a few minutes ago, she'd been picturing herself on the road. "There's some mistake. Rent is due today. He has kids to take care of. I meant *we* have kids to take care of. Here, I'll prove it." She stood up and walked into the kitchen and grabbed the phone and jabbed in the seven digits. These fools were wasting her time and stressing her out with their careless work. She'd show them, get them on their merry way, and she'd get back to planning Nashville. Someday down the road when they could be cordial divorcees, she and Harry would have a good laugh over this ridiculous blunder. The phone rested between her head and shoulder. She crossed her arms and turned toward Sergeant Meed, who had stood up.

The pretty and petite detective stopped him. "No, let her call. It's a process."

Process her ass.

"Hullo," the landlady answered. Of course she was sloshed, as usual.

"Hi, this is Janice Sloan. I'm Harry's wife. He is staying in Number Twenty-Two. Can you get him for me?"

The landlady didn't answer right away, and Janice wondered if she'd passed out drunk.

"Yeah, it's crazy how I didn't hear or see a thing. He was right as rain when I saw him. Offered him a joint, and he passed. Anyway, the police said they were going to tell you he died. He still owes rent—"

Without saying another word, Janice hung up. Her body started to shake. Leaning her forehead against the cradle, she tried to right her world. If her head could just stop spinning and help her understand what was happening here. Was this a bad dream? Maybe if she closed her eyes and opened them, the death squad would be gone. But no, when she tried, they were still sitting on her couch and staring at her with concern, or maybe it was curiosity. She couldn't tell.

Janice's legs were heavy as she returned to the living room. Funny, she'd always thought the two rooms felt more like one small room, but right now, it was the longest walk she'd ever taken. Her hands trembled as she slid them along her backside to smooth her skirt and sit down. She smoothed the front of her skirt too. Grandma came to mind.

"But he was fine. He always ends up okay," Janice said.

"I'm sorry," Sergeant Meed said again.

And he was. She could see his pity and honesty in his eyes.

"Please don't look at me like that, Meed," she said. "I don't want your pity." He made her want to start crying, and she didn't want to cry in front of them. Just because she was done with Harry, it didn't mean she wanted him gone.

"What happened?" she asked and looked toward a picture of Harry hanging on the wall. Several years ago, their eldest daughter, Michelle, had shown up with a professional photographer. She'd said she wanted to get a picture of Lisa, Carrie, Justin, and Tommy while they were still young. Michelle had said it was her idea of a Christmas gift, but since it was also the last time they'd seen or heard from her, Janice now knew it had been a keepsake for Michelle. And one for Janice now too. Harry had come home from work earlier than usual that day, reeking in his OshKosh overalls, sludge-crusted boots, red-and-black flannel shirt, and dirt-caked nails, and he'd stolen the spotlight from the kids.

As Harry had aged, his Dean Martin looks had grayed and rounded out, and he had likened himself to the comedian Jonathan Winters, and when he saw the photography set in his own home, he kicked off his boots and socks, rolled up his overall legs, grabbed a can of Budweiser, and pulled a rocking chair before the camera. His generic cap was black and white, and *HAT* was imprinted across the front, and he angled it to one side like a simpleton. He'd even had the nerve to wink at the photographer before settling into his pose, one eyebrow raised in a challenge.

"What are you waiting for?" he'd asked and laughed. "Take some pictures."

The kids had laughed, and despite her resolve to be annoyed, Janice ended up laughing too. He was so incorrigible and no longer had any shame. When the photographer snickered, the pact was sealed and pictures were taken.

In the final shot, Harry was smiling, cigarette in one hand, beer in the other, and looking quite proud of himself.

"Mrs. Sloan," someone said, breaking into her thoughts.

"Are you sure it was Harry?" She folded her hands in her lap. They still hadn't told her what happened.

"Yes." Detective Anderson leaned forward on the edge of the couch. "We need to ask you a few questions now, but we can save most of them for tomorrow."

She threw her arms up. "Well this is just great. You come over here, tell me my husband is dead. And you have questions?" She stood and began to pace from one end of the living room to the other. She hugged her rib cage. She rubbed her arms and paused before Harry's stupid picture.

"We'll tell you as much as we can at this time."

She pulled the eight-by-ten frame from the wall and held it in two hands. "Did he have rent money? Did he have any money on him?" If this picture was the only thing he'd left behind, she'd die on the spot.

Meed stood and placed a hand on her shoulder. "You're in

shock. You're shaking. Why don't you sit down?" He guided her to Harry's recliner.

She took the picture with her.

Dr. Freeman handed her the manila envelope. "Here are a few of his personal items. He didn't have any money on his person."

"'On his person,'" Janice repeated. She sat down, resting the picture on her lap like a tray. She juggled the envelope between her hands, assessing the weight. The envelope was bulky, and it reminded her of her elation the night before when the newspapers were in her purse. She blinked several times. Gripping the envelope and pushing the mouth open from the sides, she shook the contents and looked inside: Harry's watch, empty money clip, glasses, wedding ring, and handkerchief. No paper. No letter. Invisible Old Spice—Harry's staple scent—wafted across her open mouth and her nose. She swallowed and closed the envelope, creasing it shut. "Where is his note?"

"Note?" Meed asked. He looked toward the detective as if asking for permission, Janice thought.

"Harry would've left a note," she said. "For me."

Meed coughed and cleared his throat again. "You mean a suicide—"

Detective Anderson interrupted, "You think your husband was capable of committing suicide?"

Janice stopped. "Didn't he?"

Instead of answering, the detective asked, "Has he been acting peculiar?"

"Peculiar?" Janice scoffed and waved her arms around her hellhole. "He's been peculiar every day for the past three decades. But if my husband killed himself, I know he'd at least leave me a note to say goodbye."

Detective Anderson pulled out her notepad and slid forward on the couch. She pulled a pen from her pocket and scribbled. "You don't think he'd kill himself without leaving a note?"

Janice shook her head. He'd leave her a note. "Nothing short of murder or an accident would keep him from telling me goodbye." It was one of the things she'd always loved about him because he knew what it had been like for her to lose Walter and not know his last thoughts. Harry had a lot of problems, but on that one thing she trusted him; he would never leave her without saying goodbye unless he had no choice.

The detective stopped writing and looked up at her. "Mrs. Sloan, did your husband have any enemies, anyone he'd had a falling out with?"

Janice lost her breath. "Are you saying he didn't kill himself?" Frantic, she stared at Meed. "Will someone please tell me what's going on?"

WJ, she thought suddenly. He was there last night. Would he? No. Would he? Maybe. Her son? WJ? Harry? Harry was dead? He didn't leave her a note? This was going from worse to worst.

"Right now his death is under investigation," the detective said. "When did you last see him?"

She shook her head. "Under investigation?" Where was WJ? She needed to talk to WJ.

"I know this is painful and a lot to take in, and we can save the rest of our discussion for tomorrow, but I need to know when you last saw Harry."

She crossed her arms and put her cold fingertips next to her chest. She lifted her heels up and down, and Harry's enveloped belongings and the picture bounced on her knees.

She could hear his wedding ring clanking against the money clip like an old church bell shaking in a 6.0 earthquake. The noise hurt her ears.

"Have you seen him since the restraining order was filed a week ago?"

She shook her head no. Last time she'd seen him was at their fight.

Oh God. What was she going to do now?

"Are you aware of anyone in your family seeing Harry this past week?"

She looked away. "No."

"Mrs. Sloan?"

She stared them each in the eye. "I said no."

"Where were you last night?" Detective Anderson asked.

Janice clenched her jaw. "You bitch. Are you asking me what I think you're asking me? Did they teach the Miranda rights the same day they explained how restraining orders work? Get out."

Meed lifted his hands before him. "She's not saying anything, Mrs. Sloan. Miranda rights aren't required unless we are taking you into custody, which we aren't. We just need to know the last time someone saw Harry alive. It will help the investigation."

Janice glared at them all. "I was at the Creek Bar all night."

"What time did you get home?" Anderson asked.

"Around one o'clock in the morning."

"Can anyone confirm the time you got home?" Anderson asked.

She hesitated. Pursed her lips. Carrie wasn't a good person for them to question.

"We need your cooperation," Meed said.

"My daughter, Carrie, was awake when I got home."

As if she'd been summoned, Carrie opened the back door and rushed inside. "I saw the police car from across the street. What's going on?"

Janice stood to tell her to stay outside with the boys. She couldn't let Carrie stay in this room. She would say something about WJ, how he had brought the boys home from Harry's motel. She walked toward Carrie on shaky legs, pointing to the back door.

"Carrie, get out . . ." But for the second time in her life, Janice fainted.

25

JANICE

Oh, I offended you with my opinion? You should hear the ones
I keep to myself.
—Patsy Cline

Janice had to convince the sergeant, coroner, and detective that she didn't need medical attention. She still didn't know how Harry died or what his death meant to her life and her kids' lives. That wasn't true—she did know—but she couldn't bear to think about the big picture right now. If she could have stayed unconscious, she would have. The coroner insisted on sitting with her a while. Janice ignored Carrie's questions, grateful when everyone else ignored her too. Every time Carrie asked, "Is my dad okay?" they all looked away. It was a good thing because she didn't want WJ's name to come up.

As soon as they were alone, Janice told Carrie the news as gently as she could. She tried to channel Grandma sitting by her bedside after Walter died. Oh, what she would do to have Grandma beside her again, but she'd lost Grandma when she chose WJ. Janice knew she sounded robotic and insensitive sitting across from her daughter. She was just going through the motions now. There was a lot to figure out and so little information to work from. She could swear she was having an out-of-body experience, floating above the two of them and watching her shocked retelling and Carrie's shocked reception. They were like two flat paper dolls with frozen expressions and no movement. They didn't hug. There were no reassuring embraces. Carrie ran from the room, crying.

If someone were to ask her, "How are you, Janice?" she could manage, "Shattered." Shattered because, for the second time in her life, she'd lost a man she loved, and death was dictating how she would live her life. Just because she'd been planning to leave Harry didn't mean that she didn't still love him or feel a thirty-year fault line opening up in her chest that threatened to swallow her soul and spit it out all empty and useless. This time, she couldn't take her time to feel the pain and heal on the farm while her grandparents took care of her. This time she wasn't seventeen years old, pregnant, and naïve. She had to face it and deal with it all on her own.

Janice reached Lisa at her boyfriend's. "Come home now. I need to talk to you." Bobby was on his way without question even though he hadn't called or visited in over a year. Michelle couldn't be tracked down, but that was no surprise. Janice left messages where she could. She also couldn't find WJ, but Janice wasn't kidding herself. He already knew Harry was dead. He had been over for breakfast and been all nice to the kids. He was involved. She could feel it.

Justin and Tommy were outside playing, unaware. She wished she could keep it that way. At a loss for what to do next, she stared at Bobby, Lisa, and Carrie. In a rare moment of public affection, the three were hugging and comforting each other. Why did it take loss and heartbreak to bring people together sometimes? She felt lonely watching them from her chair and sitting on the outside looking in. No matter what their relationships were with their dad, people would always sympathize with them for losing their father. But what about her? Because he was in a motel and they were separated, people would say, "Well, they were separated when he died." Her loss would be watered down, and since no one knew about her dreams, they'd never understand the full extent of her pain or regrets.

Carrie's face was red, and her tears flowed. "How did he die?"

Janice shook her head. "I don't know yet. I wish I did."

"When did he die?" she asked.

"Carrie, I don't know."

Carrie just gave her that look. "But the coroner was here. Didn't you ask?"

"While I was passed out?" Janice snapped.

"Jesus," Bobby said, getting to his feet. "She was just asking. I've got to get out of here. I need a drink."

When Bobby had first arrived, he'd been rolling a chip from Alcoholics Anonymous back and forth across his knuckles. "I've got one year in now, Ma," he'd said with a shaky smile. So that was what he'd been doing with himself—trying to be healthier away from them all. She got that. After all, hadn't she been planning on leaving for a year too? Her heart had broken a bit knowing that his sobriety might change once she told him about his dad. Now the chip was nowhere in sight. Probably shoved deep into his pocket, but she hoped he'd find it again.

He leaned over and kissed her head. Despite the distance, she loved him, and she wondered if she'd ever see him again, or was Harry's death the final straw that would fracture their family forever.

"Goodbye, Mom. I can't do this."

No, no she wouldn't see him again. *Goodbye.* They all knew the rule.

He kissed Lisa and Carrie. "I'll make sure Michelle knows."

Lisa followed him out the door, saying she needed her boyfriend.

Now it was just her and Carrie: two women worrying about their futures and two small boys.

They finally had something in common.

"When are you telling Tommy and Justin?" Carrie asked.

"Tomorrow, when I have more information."

Carrie stood up to leave.

Right or wrong, Janice knew what she still had to do.

"Carrie, how much do you have in your savings account? I'm going to need help with rent until I can get your dad's final paycheck next week."

Carrie's eyes widened. "That's my college money."

"I'll get it back to you. It's just this week. You have time to save more before college."

Janice pushed what little conscience she had aside. She just couldn't give up on Nashville yet. How she would make it work, she had no idea, but she was not going to touch her winnings. No way, nohow. To do so would be giving up for good, and she might as well get busy dying if she was going to give up. Like she'd told Carrie last night when they were fighting, trying was the best she could do.

The range of emotions on Carrie's face was not easy to watch, but what was done was done. If her daughter didn't like her before, she hated her now.

"No, I don't. I have five months. And I don't have enough money yet for tuition. It's my money. I need it now more than ever."

Janice lifted her chin. "We also need a roof over our heads. You have a better chance of finding money over the next five months than I do for the rent right now," Janice said. "You'll be fine. Justin, Tommy, and I need help now."

"That's rich coming from you. If you can't find money for yourself, why do you insist it'll be easy for me to save for school? I can't even get you to help with financial aid papers! Oh my Gawd! I'm only seventeen!"

Yes, and in two months, Carrie would be graduating from high school, getting ready to live her grand life, and leave Janice wasting away in this trailer in Corbett City. This wasn't the way it was supposed to happen.

Carrie would have enough money; she just didn't know about it yet because Janice hadn't told her. She was going to. Last night actually. Her plan had always been to tell Carrie about the full-ride scholarship once she could also know in her heart that she had enough money to go to Nashville. Last night, she had that knowledge, but then there was the fiasco with the boys, the angry fight when she got home, and now Harry. Now wasn't a good time to explain all the subterfuge to her daughter.

A month ago, a packet had come in the mail for Carrie, but it had been one of those days that Carrie had gone off on Janice for being a "lousy parental unit." At that point, Janice was ready to start counting the days until Carrie would go away to school for more reasons than one. After all, Janice had her own plans in place, and the fewer children she needed to worry about, the better; and she was proud of Carrie in her own way. Had Janice left, Carrie would have always had a choice whether she stayed home with the boys and commuted to school, or if she left them with their dad and moved to Reno. Regardless, Janice had been looking forward to saying that at least one of her kids was breaking the mold and going to college.

The letter was addressed to Carrie Sloan and Parents, so she'd had a right to open it.

She wasn't sure what she expected to read when she opened it, but Carrie was receiving a full scholarship from the university. Right there, all of her daughter's hard work and focus were paying off, and Carrie would be pursuing her dreams on her own and in a way that was no way dependent on anyone else. Not a man. Not her parents. Not like Janice. She wouldn't need Pell Grants or anything else based on need.

A sad and twisted competitive streak had blown up inside while she caught a glimpse into Carrie's opportunities. Janice wanted to escape before Carrie did. Carrie had been flitting around the trailer for months, talking about her future life that would be "better than any of you have ever imagined" while Janice had kept her Nashville plan to herself.

When the letter came, karaoke had been going well for a few weeks, and Janice knew if she kept winning, she'd be able to have enough money by mid-April. (And she was right, she did). There was always a chance that Carrie might get word of the award another away, but Janice had thought it would be nice, for a change, if she could genuinely be supportive and happy for Carrie, and the only way she knew how to do that was if she could know in her heart that she was leaving too. Janice had put the envelope under her mattress. She'd slept on it, and in the morning decided she'd give

Carrie the letter over pizza, or cake, but only once she won enough karaoke contests to leave.

But now everything had changed. Carrie would still have money, still get to leave, but now was not the time to tell her because living with her would be unbearable while Janice tried to figure out her next steps.

"I've been planning for college most of my life," Carrie said. "I've saved every penny, and I still don't have enough. I'm not paying your bills instead of going to college. You should be trying to comfort me right now, not steal my hope. My dad just died!" Carrie stormed outside, grabbing the door and slamming it three times.

For the first time she could remember, Janice sat alone in her house on a Sunday evening. She leaned back in Harry's recliner and pressed the balls of her hands into her closed eyes.

If Harry had a say in dying and he didn't say goodbye, that would hurt most of all. She needed to know how he died, and she prayed with what was left of her heart that WJ had nothing to do with Harry's death.

26

CARRIE

quotidian \kwō'tidēən\ *adj 1 : daily 2 : ordinary or everyday,*
especially when mundane

Monday morning, April 10, 1989

C arrie didn't know how long her dad had been dead, but
he'd been alive Saturday night because she'd talked to
him, and WJ had picked up the boys from his place. How
long did he wait to do it after his sons left? She'd had all
night to think about it, and she knew her dad killed himself.

And it was her fault.

"Goodbye," he'd said, and she had ignored him. She
should have known when he said goodbye. She should have
been listening. She should have told someone. She should tell
someone now, but there was no one to tell, and her family
would blame her. The list of what she should have done went
on and on. She'd failed her dad, her brothers, everyone. So
unfair since she'd always meant to be a good example.

Carrie rolled to her side and turned off the alarm clock.

nity to willfully ignore him again. It was her loss, she knew, and she dashed the tears from her eyes.

She locked the bathroom door, took off her dad's sweatshirt, and looked in the mirror.

Did she look different? Did she look guilty?

Her face wasn't too puffy. The cool air of her room had helped. Classmates might not notice she'd been crying. If anyone asked, she'd say her sinuses were flaring up like they did every spring. Everyone was obsessed with their own lives and issues anyway. She placed her hands under her eyes to cover the bottom half of her face and the pimples on her chin she had picked the night before. She looked at her nose.

Some days her nose seemed wider on her face. She had the blasted Sloan nose. No one could escape it. Well, except WJ. She could tell what kind of day she was going to have based on the size of her nose. She never told anyone that, though. They'd think she was crazy. She knew it didn't make sense, but sometimes the unexplainable was true. Today her nose was red, but otherwise it looked normal. Not bloated and not flat. Normal. She turned on the shower and climbed behind the curtain. She sighed under the hot spray as the water ran over her swollen eyes and her normal nose. She had her dad's nose. She cried until the water turned cold.

Today she would show Mr. Hill the first draft of her essay. If she could just win this outstanding scholarship, she could figure out how to make college work even with a knock to her savings for rent. But it wouldn't just be rent, would it? She knew how money worked in her family.

First, Mom would need it for rent. Next week, it would be food. The following week, bills. Her savings would be wiped out. They had never been intended to support a family.

She thought about her dad's reading choices and her

She had been watching the red digital numbers change for past three hours. She shivered as she pushed her blanket aside. Goose bumps raced from her ankles and up her legs stopping at the hem of the knee-length sweatshirt she had taken from her dad's closet.

Dad—she should have checked on him—*you told me everything would be okay. Except you said goodbye, which means you were really saying nothing was okay.*

She was desperate to go to school. In her classes, she could pretend her world hadn't been turned upside down. She needed to pretend that Dad was alive and Mom wasn't going to take her savings for rent. She needed to pretend that showing up and doing her best in school would be enough to change her life and get her to college, if not this year then next. (Although the thought of waiting a year made her want to vomit and then vomit some more.) She needed to pretend that she hadn't ignored her dad's cry for help while she'd gone on and on about how he needed to complete her Pell Grant application.

She looked up, past her shooting star mobile and through the window. Nevada's blue skies were always sharpest when the air was dry and cool. What should she wear today? *What does a member of the my-dad-is-dead club wear?*

Nevada weather could be deceiving but predictable. April was the beginning of spring in the desert, with sometimes one last surprising snow, and the mornings could be very cool, but by noon it would be hot. If she wore a sweater, she would be comfortable waiting for the school bus to come, but at lunch, she would be sweating. She ran her palm along one of her shins. She would need to shower and shave her legs.

The kitchen table was empty. Her dad wasn't sitting there to wish her good morning, and she'd never have the opportu-

essay. Dad was alive when she wrote it, and her idea about his theme of justice took on new meaning. By killing himself, who was getting justice? Who was the victim? Her dad, or everyone he left behind? But she didn't want Mr. Hill, or anyone (not even her close friends), to know Dad was dead yet, so she'd still show Mr. H the first draft. Everyone would find out soon enough. Corbett City wasn't that big. But no one outside her family needed to know so soon. She'd leave his death at home today and cling to her usual routine.

She had a quiz in algebra and trig, and it was Monday-Mystery-Chemical Day in chemistry. Her afternoon job at personnel was always best on Mondays. Every Monday, she would switch out the job postings, do the weekly mailing, and scan last Friday's skill tests. She would go to her small desk pushed against the wall in a corner and check off her responsibilities. Always so satisfying. Check. Check. Check.

She climbed out of the shower, dried off, got dressed, and tightened her hair in a bun. She grabbed her pajamas and walked out of the bathroom, down the hall, through the kitchen, and past her mother, who was now sitting in her father's morning seat, so she willfully ignored her mom. It was only fair. *Sit in that chair and you shall be ignored.* She reached for the adjoining door.

"Where are you going?" Mom asked.

"To school and work."

"You can't go today," she said.

"It's Monday. I can, and I am," Carrie said and pulled open the door. She went into her room, made her bed, folded her pajamas, and placed them under the pillow. She grabbed her backpack, added her notebook, and walked back into the main trailer. She couldn't stand to be home anymore. She had to get out, and if that meant waiting for the bus longer than usual in the cold, it was worth it. She needed breathing room. Openness.

She set her backpack on the end of the couch and headed toward the boys' room. They should have been up already.

"Don't. I'm keeping the boys home today," Mom said.

"Why?"

"Carrie, come on. Your dad is dead, and he probably . . . he probably killed himself. Once I know more, I need to tell the boys. They're staying home. You should too."

Carrie's back tensed. She curled her fists. "You only think he killed himself. You don't know for sure. Did he say goodbye to you?" Oh Gawd, please let him have given a clue to her mother. Please let her pass this burden on.

But her mom shook her head and looked away. "No, he didn't say goodbye."

"Let the boys go to school and play with their friends. What's the rush in telling them?" She didn't want them to know or to have to see their sad freckled faces.

Mom said, "They're staying home. I'm their mother, not you."

"You really know how to pick your moments, Mom," Carrie said. The anger was building in her. All she had wanted was one more normal day, and her mom was ruining it.

Carrie recognized her mom's body language. It's how she looked whenever she and Dad were determined to argue with each other instead of fixing any problems.

"What kind of daughter goes to school the day after her dad died?" she stabbed.

That was a low blow even if her mom didn't know the extent of her regret.

The kind of daughter that could have saved him and didn't. That's what kind.

Now it was Carrie's turn to take a chink out of her mom's armor.

"You're not exactly the wilting widow right now. What kind of a wife pretends that she cares about her husband only once he is dead? You left him alone and lonely in that horrible motel. You kicked him out. This is your fault!"

Her mom sucked in her breath. "He hit me! I had to kick him out."

Carrie flinched. She hadn't known. She'd been babysitting at the time, and her brothers had said something about Superman and donuts. She'd thought it was just another stupid argument about drinking or money.

Oh, Dad.

"I'm going to school. I want to be around normal people and with my friends who care about me." Even if she wouldn't tell her friends today, school was where she belonged. She grabbed her backpack and headed toward the door.

She heard her mom sigh behind her. "I need you to stay with the boys while I go to the police station. And I need you to go to the bank."

Carrie's eyes started to sting. Dang it.

She'd known all night this was coming, and that in the end she'd have to bail them out and pay rent. She took a deep breath. Whenever she was mad or frustrated, she cried. She considered it her greatest weakness. She glared at her single living parent, the person to blame for putting her in this position. "I don't have a choice, do I? I'm under eighteen, and your name is on my account. If you want to ruin my life, you don't need me there to do it."

Carrie pushed through the door and rushed to the other side of the park, needing to escape. The old people always got up early but not early enough to catch her cutting through one of their yards through a hole in the fence and over to the bus stop.

Breathe. Just breathe. She was almost there.

She hopped from the cinder block down to the asphalt and let go of the cold silver fence post. Just like that, she was in a world full of possibilities. Every morning when she crossed the trailer park's fence line, she felt like she was in a different country. She swore she could feel the energy shift. She lifted her head, rolled her shoulders back, and stood tall as she walked over to the bus stop and channeled her dad.

Dad, you told me that everything was going to be okay. Help me.

This couldn't be her life. There was something better out there for her. She was not Tiger Drive. He couldn't leave her there.

27

JANICE

Got a Lotta Rhythm in My Soul
—Patsy Cline

Janice slumped in her chair as soon as Carrie left. Sometime in the sleepless night, Janice's shock and hurt for Harry had turned to anger and resentment. The grief was brewing deep, but she didn't have the time or energy to sit with it. There was so much to be done. She closed her eyes, clinging to the memory of her happiness on Saturday night. Maybe she shouldn't be surprised her life had spiraled out of control in the past twenty-four hours because nothing she'd ever wanted had gone according to plan, but how could she have gone from singing Frank Sinatra yesterday afternoon to being a widow being questioned by the police and needing to arrange her husband's funeral today?

Damn it.

Sergeant Meed had called last night to tell her when and where she needed to be today. WJ was controlling her by absenteeism and non-returned phone calls. Men were stomping all over her spirit. How could Harry have left her in this God-awful predicament? She was the one who was supposed to be leaving him!

She squeezed back her own tears of frustration. This was her greatest weakness—crying when she was angry. The only good thing about the flaw was that she'd passed the trait on to Carrie.

Why should Carrie get a normal day?

Because she wasn't going to stop Janice from paying rent. That was why.

Carrie hadn't fought her this morning, at least not about paying rent. She could banish all of Carrie's fears by admitting she had the scholarship letter. But she was a coward. She'd tell her soon enough when the time was right.

Once Carrie knew she would get to leave, Janice would be watching everyone move on with life, and Nashville would be further from her grasp. And as crazy and impossible as it sounded even to her, she wasn't ready to give up on her dream. She just needed more time to figure out how to do it or to figure out how to take the boys with her even though she hadn't been able to figure out a safe way to do that before now. She couldn't afford to take care of herself anymore, much less two boys. She needed to get a job. What kind of work would she do? Waitressing? Bartending? She'd have to do night shifts and pay someone else to watch the boys. It'd be like working just to pay a babysitter. Continuing to sing in the karaoke contest wouldn't last long, not with the younger crowd taking over.

It was all so damn depressing for all of them.

But rent could be paid, thanks to Carrie. She could at least complete the Pell Grant app so Carrie could still hope, even though she didn't really need the assistance in the long run.

Janice could use a Pell Grant for motherhood. Harry had left her with no savings or support, and she couldn't touch her winnings.

What if the Pell Grant could help them all? Maybe Carrie's extra funds could help with the boys. Maybe Carrie could stay home with her and commute to college. She could help Janice raise the boys until Janice could save enough money for the three of them to move to Tennessee safely.

Oh God.

She was sinking to new lows. She was losing her mind. Even though she'd been planning the past few months to leave the boys for a year, at least she had been leaving them with their dad. Not once had she considered leaving them with Carrie alone. Grandfather used to say, "Desperate times call for desperate measures." But she was tired of acting desperate all the time.

She should complete the Pell Grant application for Carrie —period. Carrie could come home and at least see that compromise in her mother.

By the time it was mailed and processed, maybe Janice would figure out a way to still go to Nashville, even with the boys, and she could buy some time to figure out how to tell Carrie about the scholarship without causing a huge blow-up.

But the last place she'd seen the blank application was on her bookshelf, and now it was gone. Carrie must have taken it, and now Janice would have to ask her for it later rather than surprise her with it. Carrie would be too curious about Janice's sudden interest and ask questions. Unless the school could help.

Janice looked at the clock and walked to the phone. She dialed the high school office. The staff should be there by now. "Hello, this is Mrs. Sloan. Carrie Sloan's mother. I need to speak to the principal or the counselor."

Carrie didn't want anyone to know about her dad, but now was the time to get as much help as they could. Harry had taken everyone's normal away.

"Hello, Mrs. Sloan, this is Principal Weimer."

"Hello, Mrs. Weimer. I have some sad news. Carrie's dad died this weekend. I am sure you can imagine the grief we are dealing with, but the last thing I want Carrie to worry about on top of everything is if she can afford to go to school. She hasn't received any news of a scholarship," this little lie would buy her time, "and I need help completing the Pell Grant . . ."

As soon as she finished her conversation and hung up the phone, it rang.

Better be WJ! He was the only one who did not show up last night.

"Hello?"

But it was Detective Anderson confirming her appointment and asking her to bring Carrie.

Egads! Carrie going to school was a good thing after all. If they asked Carrie to confirm Janice's arrival home, Carrie would say something about WJ bringing the kids home, and Janice had enough cans of worms to deal with. That's what WJ was—a can of worms.

"Yes, I can be there at nine o'clock. But Carrie is in school today. She has tests she can't miss," Janice lied.

When the call ended, she was tempted to leave the phone off the hook. She let it dangle from the wall mount until she remembered she was waiting for a call from the apartment managers. She set the phone down, picked it up, heard the dial tone, and reset it. She would control what she could and turn the rest over to God.

God. She snapped her fingers. It was a good time to call on God. He was always there for her when she needed Him. Him and Pastor Henry.

28

WJ

Who ya callin' lunakick?!
—Popeye

WJ shook his head and sliced his finger across his neck. His mom was the last person he wanted to talk to. She had to know by now that Harry was dead. That's why she'd be calling.

"No, Janice, I haven't seen him." Shelly listened, her ear to the receiver, and then said, "No, he isn't sitting right here. Yeah, I'll tell him you called." She hung up the phone and pointed at WJ. "I don't like lying to your mom."

"Save guilt for a good mom, not the likes of her," WJ said. He was lying on the narrow bed, staring at the ceiling and smoking a cigarette. His boots hung over the edge. He'd been hiding in his trailer ever since he'd gotten drunk on tequila and tried to call his biological dad. When would the cops come knocking on his door about Harry? They'd find his fingerprints in the car even though he'd tried to wipe everything down. He'd end up arrested, and the cops would use

Harry's letter to out him and then call his biological dad and tell him what a loser criminal of a son he had.

"Can you get me some coffee, please?"

Shelly frowned at him and turned to the sink. "You never say please. What's wrong with you?" She filled a pot with water and put it on the two-burner stove. "Why don't you want to talk to your mom?"

He looked at Shelly and then at the ceiling. "Harry's dead. Killed himself."

"Oh no, baby."

WJ slid his skinny hips over to make room for her more ample ones. He let her stroke his long bangs and tuck them behind his ear.

"When? Why didn't you say something?"

He shrugged his shoulders and turned on his side to put the cigarette in the ashtray. He curled up and laid his head on one of her jean-clad legs.

Shelly moved her hand to his back and rubbed her palm in slow circles. "I'm sorry, baby. I know you didn't get along, but that's because you loved him so much."

Shelly always knew more than he gave her credit for. Even he was at a loss with why he was both fucking grieving Harry and was happy as all shit that Harry wasn't his real dad and that he was dead. But the years he'd wasted thinking his dad didn't love him, or knowing his life could be screwed because of Harry . . . Fuck! He was tired of thinking about it. He was having a midlife crisis twenty years early.

WJ turned his head to look at her. "No one else will get that."

"It's how you love," she said.

He looked away and blinked back tears. Shelly was a

good girl. "I'm sorry I hit you the other day. I didn't mean it. Well, I did, but I didn't like how it felt. I won't do it again."

"I know. Let me get your coffee."

He rolled over and sat up in bed. He opened his night-stand and set the baggie on top. "When you're done, I need you to take your car over to Hefty's place. Tell him about Harry. Hefty will know what to do."

"I don't like him." Shelly wrinkled her nose. "Can you just call him?"

"I can't say this shit on the phone. It might be bugged."

"Our phone is bugged? That's serious crap. If our phone is being tapped then things have gone too far with those guys. Why do they need to know about your dad's death? If you did something, tell me now because if you're in trouble, those guys aren't going to stick around."

"How dare you. Those are my brothers you're talking about."

"No, WJ, they aren't. Even I can see that now. You've done too much for them, and for what? A patch and a group of junkies who love drugs more than their own kids. They're family terrorists, that's what the Knights are."

"Shut the fuck up, Shelly. If they ever hear you talking like that, they'll make your life hell, and I won't be able to stop them. You've never complained when I've given you a stack of cash. Just go over there and deliver the message. Two stupid seconds is all it will take. That's all I'm asking for. I can't be seen with them right now."

"I'll do it this once, and then I want nothing to do with them again. I mean it. Hefty creeps me out."

"Creeps you . . . did I tell you to go inside his house and sit on his fucking lap? No. I told you to go over there and tell him about Harry. Knock on the door and tell him. Don't go inside. Just tell him. Then come back here. Can you handle that simple shit?"

"I guess I have to handle it."

"Damn straight, you do. Bring back something to eat too. McDonalds. You know what I like. And go to a store and get me some Miracle-Gro, or something for my plant. And hurry, I need to get to work. I called Rudy and told him Harry died and that I'd be in late, but I can't take all day."

"What's with the dead plant anyway?"

"It's not dead. Just needs a little love."

"All right, if you say so." She closed the door.

WJ waited until he heard her car pull away. He leaned on one hip and pulled the papers out of his jeans pocket.

He laid the list on the mattress, opened the letter, and read his name out loud for the first time. "Walter Whitworth, Junior. I am Walter Whitworth, Junior. They call me Walter Junior, after my dad."

WJ stood for something. Not just WJ.

He remembered asking his mom once what WJ stood for when he started kindergarten because his teacher had asked him to learn to spell his full name.

"What do your initials stand for, WJ? What's your full name?" Mrs. Schultz had asked.

He frowned and tilted his head. "WJ Sloan."

"What name begins with 'W,' and what name begins with 'J'?" she asked.

What was wrong with his teacher? "WJ," he'd said again.

She had patted his head. "Ask your mama tonight." She moved on to the girl sitting next to him.

When his mom picked him up that day with Michelle in a stroller and Bobby strapped to her chest, WJ asked her.

"What kind of question is that? Your name is WJ," she said.

"Mrs. Schultz said they are iminitials."

"Initials," she said. "Well, she's wrong. Your name is WJ just like you told her. I'll correct Mrs. Schultz tomorrow."

"You're so smart, Mama. You could be a teacher."

"Thanks. I try." She had taken his small hand and anchored it to the stroller handle.

WJ set the letter on his legs and sucked on his cigarette.

Nice try, Mom.

He exhaled smoke rings and watched them float away.

29

CARRIE

Craving Quotidian Details

Carrie lifted her hand to wave at acquaintances as she made her way to class. She was halfway there when she saw Mrs. Peet, her junior year math teacher, heading her way. Mrs. Peet slowed and squeezed Carrie's shoulder as she passed.

Carrie stopped in her tracks and turned around, but Mrs. Peet's backside kept bobbing down the hall. Wait. An unsolicited public display of affection from a teacher? Carrie's gut twisted. *Does she know?* No way. It was barely seven thirty. Impossible.

Carrie squinted as she walked past classmates, but no one else was passing her odd looks. She reached Mr. Hill's class. She walked in just as the final bell rang and headed to her desk.

"Carrie, up here please," Mr. Hill called.

Carrie pointedly set her backpack down in her seat and walked toward him.

"Bring your bag with you," he said.

Carrie's hackles rose. Her breath thinned. Heat climbed her neck. How? How did they already know? Her eyes began to sting. She pulled her backpack over her shoulder and turned to walk up the aisle toward Mr. Hill's desk. The overhead fluorescent lights reflected off his eyeglasses.

He was watching her.

She stopped in front of his desk. "Is this about my essay? I have the first draft ready. I wrote it Saturday."

He took off his specs and stared up at her. His eyes were gentle when he said, "You need to report to Principal Weimer's office."

Carrie's eyes widened. No, no, no. "Can I go later?"

"You'll be okay, Carrie," he said. He put his glasses back on. "Bring your lunch here, and we can go through your essay."

"What does she want?" Carrie asked, but she knew.

He knew she knew. "I'm sorry, Carrie," he said. "Come back at lunch."

Carrie felt tears pool in her eyes. Blast it. She swallowed, turned, and walked out the door. What did a person have to do for some stinking normalcy? How had they found out?

The halls were empty. She glanced at each classroom she passed. Her palms were sweating. She looked for any excuse to put off facing the principal, who was going to feel sorry for her but not be able to do anything for her. What would she say, "I'm sorry"? Carrie dreaded all the sorries headed her way.

The secretary greeted her with a sympathetic smile. "Take a seat, Carrie. Principal Weimer will be right with you."

"I'll stand." Carrie walked over to the bulletin board to see if any new college scholarships were posted. She could feel the eyes of the staff burning into her back. She lifted her chin. Their pity infiltrated the air. She imagined them whispering, "Poor Carrie Sloan. Her dad killed himself."

"Carrie, you can come on in," Principal Weimer called from her office.

Carrie went inside the office and sat down. She looked at the principal and waited.

Principal Weimer leaned forward and folded her hands in the middle of the desk. "Your mother called this morning. I'm sorry to hear about your father."

Well, at least Mrs. Weimer did not beat around the bush, Carrie thought. She mentally placed her one remaining parent in a castle of hate. Bitter resentment filled the moat. Was it so hard for her mother to give her a day of routine? She tried to clear her throat as her cheeks turned red.

"Your mom is very concerned for you and how you're handling your dad's death. You told her you couldn't miss school, but of course, we can make arrangements. Would you prefer to go home? We can waive any homework for a week."

Carrie coughed. "I didn't say I couldn't miss school. I said I didn't want to miss school."

"Her intentions are good," Mrs. Weimer said.

"You don't know her. She is not concerned. She wants to control my day."

"I'm sure that's not true. This is a difficult time in your life and your mother's too. The staff and I are here to support both of you," Mrs. Weimer leaned forward again, "and I know you are concerned about your finances. I've offered assistance to your mother in completing the Pell Grant forms once things settle down."

What? Her mom had had months to do the application and sign off on it. Her only motivation could be because she'd be using Carrie's savings. Gross. It was just gross that this is what it took.

Carrie didn't need her mom. She leaned forward and surprised herself and lied. "The application is done. My dad signed it on Saturday. I have it in my backpack to mail."

"Really? Your mom was under the impression it was outstanding, but perhaps with all the shock of your dad's passing she forgot he took care of it."

"Yeah, something like that." People like the principal didn't want to believe a mother wouldn't care, but Carrie had already decided. Today she would call her dad's boss like her dad told her to, complete the application, and forge both of her parents' signatures. Her mother no longer deserved a say in her life. At every possible turn, she wanted to stand in Carrie's way.

"What exactly did my mom tell you about my dad?"

"She said he passed away this weekend."

"But how? Did she say how he died?"

"A heart attack. I'm so sorry."

A heart attack? That was as close as her mom would get to admitting she'd broken his heart.

"We don't know how he died yet." Carrie stood up.

"Carrie—"

"Can I return to class now?" Carrie stared into Mrs. Weimer's eyes. "Thank you for your concern, but if you want to help me, let me go back to class. School is all I have. Okay?"

Mrs. Weimer stood and walked around the desk. "I want to see you each day. You can come in a few minutes before school, during a class you are comfortable missing, or before the student work program. Your mom said you were still waiting to hear back from UNR on their scholarships. You should have heard by now, and we will follow up with them." She scribbled a hall pass and handed it to Carrie. "We're here for you. Let me know how we can help."

The hall pass was open for a month instead of a five-minute window. A perk of the daughters-of-dead-dads club?

"Who is 'we'? Who knows?" She held her breath.

"We've informed your teachers."

"And Mrs. Peet? She was my teacher last year. Why would she need to know?"

"Sorry, Carrie. Teachers can sometimes indulge in gossip as much as the students they teach."

Great. Just great. Adults could suck sometimes.

"It's up to you to tell your work program."

Thank Gawd for small favors. Work might be her only safe place.

"Fine. Thank you, Mrs. Weimer," Carrie said. She stood and walked out the door. She turned back and rested her hand on the doorframe.

"Actually, you can help. Can I borrow an office and a phone today at lunch?" She had a phone date with her dad's boss and a Pell Grant application. What better place to complete and forge it than at school.

"Of course."

"And I'd also like to help with the college fair in two weeks. I know you gave the slots to the valedictorians," including That Guy, Carrie thought, "but I could really use the exposure."

"I'll make the arrangements."

"Thank you."

When she returned to Mr. Hill's class, he waved her to her desk and continued addressing the class. That Guy sat behind her, and she could feel him watching her while she took a seat. She hadn't been sitting down a minute when he slid a note from behind and tapped her elbow.

Surprised, Carrie grabbed it and put it in her lap. She glanced up quickly to see Mr. Hill looking her way, but he turned away pretending not to notice the note or how they were breaking the class rule. Another pity perk. She unfolded the note: "I'm sorry about your dad."

Oh no! How did he know?

When the bell rang, she turned on him and whispered, "How do you know? Please don't tell anyone."

He was shaking his head before she even finished. "I would never. I've proven you can trust me. I'm just sorry for you and wanted you to know if you need to talk or anything, I'm here."

The last person she wanted to be sorry for her was That Guy.

"But how? How do you know?"

She thought he looked uncomfortable as he turned to put his book in his bag, but then he looked her in the eye and said, "My parents. They own the motel. But don't worry. I won't say anything."

Of course they did, she thought. Of course, That Guy's parents owned the motel where her dad died. "Then you know more than I do." She grabbed her bag and headed into the hall with her head down so she wouldn't make eye contact with anyone.

Pressing the tips of her fingernails into the palm of her hands, she managed to reach a bathroom stall before the silent, humiliating, and angry tears undid her for the world to see.

30

JANICE

Crazy
—Patsy Cline

Janice hoped she wouldn't be at the police station long. The size-zero detective had pulled her chair around to sit on the same side of the desk as Janice like they were best friends getting ready to share coffee and gossip. Janice wondered if it was some psychological hogwash, and how many people fell for it. Well, she wasn't here to play games or make friends. She just wanted to know what happened to Harry. She'd be ignoring the "friendly cup of coffee," thank you very much.

She looked at the flat white walls with scuff marks along the floorboard from people's shoes. The table had a coffee stain on the surface and a dried piece of chewing gum peeking from the bottom edge. When she was ready, and not one second before, she turned to Detective Anderson. "What do you mean?"

"Did Harry tell you how he hurt his hand recently?"

"No, I was a bit distracted with him pushing me around that day. Why?"

"So you first noticed his injuries the day you called the police, prior to filing the restraining order?"

"I didn't say that. What's going on?" Janice asked.

"Mrs. Sloan, did you first notice Harry's injured hand the same day you called the police for domestic violence?"

Janice crossed her arms across her chest. "I guess."

"Were you with Harry the night before your fight?"

"No. I went to the Creek. When I got home, he was already in bed."

"What time did you get home?"

"Like I told you before. Around one in the morning. The usual time. What's going on? What does this have to do with Harry's death?"

Detective Anderson leaned back in her chair. "A man was beaten a week ago. He's in a coma, and we have reason to believe that Harry may have been involved."

"What?" Janice shouted and stood up so fast she knocked the chair to the ground. The noise matched the ruckus of her thoughts. She couldn't handle any more surprises.

An officer standing by the door corrected her chair and guided her back to her seat.

Janice opened her mouth in surprise and then closed it. Impossible. There must be a mistake. She grabbed the coffee she'd been determined not to drink with her bestie detective. "Why? Who?"

"We were looking for Harry yesterday to bring him in for questioning. We found his car illegally parked at Swan Park, and a few items were found in the vehicle that might be linked to last week's crime."

"Isn't it illegal to search his car without his permission?"

Her new BF shook her head. "We already had a warrant."

If ever there was another chance for her to faint, it was now. A warrant? And WJ had Harry's car on Saturday night. If she had to guess—and she did—it was more like WJ and the Knights to put a man in a coma than it was Harry. Did WJ hate his dad so much he would've planted evidence in the car?

"Who is in a coma?" Maybe her skin was thick, but she was at a loss as to how to handle all this news. She thought the purpose of her meeting with the detective was to learn more about Harry's death, and instead she was finding out her husband, or son, almost killed a man? At this rate, she'd take her old life back, the one she had been trying to escape. The one she woke up to on Saturday.

Detective Anderson stared into Janice's eyes. "We have more work to do, but off the record, a guy Harry borrowed money from. A lot of money."

"How much money?"

Detective Anderson leaned forward. "Enough that he signed away the title to your trailers and cars to cover it."

Someone might as well have slapped Janice across the face. She was stunned. Harry had gambled away her frigging home?! "You know this for sure?" she had to ask.

"About the titles, yes."

Oh no, Harry, what have you done to me now?

And she had thought finding rent money would be the problem.

"I understand this is a lot of information to digest."

That was a huge understatement, but Janice nodded anyway.

"A few more questions and we can stop for today. Harry

is missing his lower dentures. Do you know where they might be, or if and when he lost them?"

Were they asking about dentures now? "He misplaced them all the time. I don't know. They weren't the best set—the prosthodontist sucked. We got what we paid for. They fell out all the time. Over time, his jaw was getting smaller—"

Detective Anderson interrupted her. "Can you give me the prosthodontist's name?"

"I can't remember. He was in Sparks on Rock Boulevard."

"Do you know why Harry's car was in the park or how it got there?"

WJ had it last. She shook her head no, and she wasn't lying because she couldn't know for sure until she talked to her son. If it wasn't Harry causing her grief, it was WJ. It was always one or the other. And this time, it was both. Now WJ was going to be tied to this coma victim because Scotty and Pete knew WJ took Harry's car from the bar Saturday night, and Carrie knew how the boys got home.

"No?" the detective asked.

"No," she said.

Anderson tossed her pencil on the desk. "If you think of anything else, please let me know."

"Where is my husband?" Janice asked. She'd almost asked, "When will I get my husband's body?" but her chest constricted. "Body" was not something she was ready to say out loud yet.

"I'll ask the coroner to call you."

The officer at the door stepped out of her way as she neared him. She walked down the hall and pulled Tommy and Justin out of the waiting room. Chip crumbs and soda pop covered their shirts. "Come on, boys."

"Sorry, we accidentally made a mess," Tommy said.

"One mess at a time, honey. One mess at a time," she said and took his sticky little hand.

"Where are we going?" Justin asked as they climbed into the back seat of her car. No, not her car because Harry had pawned the title. Holy mackerel, when would someone be coming to toss them out of the trailers and take her car?

"Crazy," she said.

31

WJ

Cops gimme a cramp, anyhow!
—Popeye

W J squinted when Shelly opened the door. Cigarette smoke was sucked out into the bright sky and fresh air.

"Leave the door open for a little while," he said.

"Gladly." She tossed the McDonald's and drugstore bags his way. "Hefty said, 'code.' What does that mean?"

WJ stopped digging in the bags. He'd been coded? What the fuck? "I told you to tell him about Harry and leave, not become a fucking messenger pigeon."

"I told him from the door, but he told me to wait. He went back in the house, and then he came back and said, 'code,' and shut the door in my face."

WJ shouldn't be surprised, but he was. *Code* was for code of silence. Code meant he was supposed to go underground and hide out until they got word to him that the coast was clear. And going underground meant leaving home and staying at associates' pads, forgetting his job, ditching his little brothers and sisters. No calls. No nothing. He couldn't bail on his job and Rudy—Rudy would need his help covering for Harry—or desert Carrie, Tommy, and Justin right now. Disappearing would make him look guilty for something he didn't do. This was all too fucking uncalled for because Harry offed himself. Cops would eventually see it was a suicide, especially once they tied Harry to the pawn-shop guy, and they'd be tipped off by records at the shop sooner than later. He'd only wanted Hefty to know because of the shitfest Hefty had caused earlier. Hefty would have to deny ever being in Harry's car and to make sure there were no signs or witnesses tying them to the car. The Knights needed to make sure WJ's people had stashes to sell, and Hefty would have to hush up Scotty and Pete. He got that he needed to lay low and avoid all things Knights right now, but holy shit, he couldn't vanish today, and they knew that, and the motherfuckers knew him better than to think they needed to remind him to be silent. But as soon as they heard he hadn't disappeared as instructed, they'd cut all ties. Thems the rules. A stupid-ass, disrespectful decision to code him. He needed to stick with a routine, act normal—not disappear like some shifty big-city sewer rat. And Hefty should be smart enough to figure all this out. No way was Bender part of this decision, and Hefty had no fucking pull to make the call.

He needed to get in touch with Bender, and this time without Shelly's poor-ass help.

"Who's Bender?" she asked.

WJ sat straight up in bed. "Where did you hear that name?" Except for Hefty, WJ never used their names around Shelly. Bender always laid low.

"I heard Hefty talk to someone he called Bender."

WJ gripped the sides of the bed to stop from spinning. Paranoia set in. Why was Bender at Hefty's? Was Hefty blaming WJ for killing their drug dealer?

WJ stabbed his finger in her direction. "You were supposed to leave."

"Don't get mad at me! I didn't want to go over there in the first place!"

"Shut the front door," he said.

"You said you wanted it open," she said.

"Shut the fucking door!" WJ threw a glass. If she'd done what he told her to do, she wouldn't have stuck around to let him be forced out. Four fucking years. Four fucking years he'd had their backs. Well, he'd show them. He'd keep his honor and stay loyal to them no matter, but he wasn't running away. They'd come crawling back and begging for him to return once this shit cleared. And then he'd pay back Hefty for his deception.

"That's it. I'm getting out of here until you cool off." She slammed the door and took off.

WJ paced the length of the trailer.

He was on his own now. Weakness and Sloppy Work were screwing with him because, after the Navy, he swore he'd never do anything to fuck up his life with the Knights. He shouldn't have trusted Hefty. *Weakness.*

A fix would help him come up with ideas, and he had to pull his shit together and get to work. He tested the weight of the baggie in his palm. His heart raced in panic. This was all he had left. By the end of the day, everyone who bought from him and all his friends would pretend they'd never seen him. He wouldn't have any resources. Hefty would get his gig for now.

He was alone. Again.

Weakness.

He was a damn sitting duck waiting for the cops to rule Harry's death a suicide and tie Harry to the beating at the river. The sooner this was cleared up, the sooner his life would get back to normal. If only Harry would have written a fucking normal suicide letter that WJ could hand over to the police. But at the same time, if he had, WJ would never have known about his name and his real dad.

WJ grabbed his keys and jumped in his truck to head to work.

As he pulled away from his trailer, two police cars and a brown Chevy were turning onto the dirt road toward him.

WJ slapped his steering wheel and slammed on his brakes. Dust exploded, and gravel flew behind him. He shoved the gear into park. Fuuuuuuucccckkkkk!

Two officers jumped out of the first car, hands on their holsters, and stared at him through his dusty cab windshield. "Put your hands where we can see them!"

WJ spat his cigarette out the window while he lifted his hands, middle fingers extended.

"Not the time to be cute. Show us your full hands."

"Sorry, fellas," he eyed the petite blonde, "and madam." WJ unfolded his fingers, turning his palms forward. Weakness could go take a shit.

Sergeant Meed strode toward him.

"Lost, Meed?" WJ asked.

"I wish I was. Keep your hands right there."

"Where do you think they are going to run off to?" He wiggled his fingers.

"Any weapons on you?"

"No," WJ lied. "Am I under arrest for something? Because I need to get to work."

"No." He nodded at the two officers, and they removed their hands from their holsters.

"Can I put my hands down yet?"

"Keep them where we can see them." Sergeant Meed motioned to the woman. "That's Detective Anderson. We need to speak with you. You can either follow us to the station now, or we can take you in."

"Sheeeeet," WJ said, leaning his elbows on the window frame, hands still extended. "I'm not climbing in that pig trap."

"Then we'll escort you. Pull up behind the other vehicle. I'll tail you."

"Escort? Well if I'm not the motherfucking President of the United States of America."

"Are you going to cooperate? If you don't want the Knights to see you talking to us, we can arrange something discreet, but it won't be on your turf."

It was all coming together now. The Knights knew he was going to be questioned, hence the code. They already knew there was trouble, and no one had warned him. His family, his brothers, had left him out to hang. Someone had given them the heads up. WJ wondered which narc had leaked the information, which narc the cops were using to cozy up with the club. He wanted to kick some serious ass.

Keeping his poker face in place, he said, "Porky, you're in the only club around here. I don't know what you're talking about."

Meed shook his head. WJ thought he heard him say "difficult" and "Sloans."

The pretty detective approached his door. "Last chance, Buzzard."

Meed and the cops had never used his club name before. Who did she think she was?

"Ah-ha, I see you don't like me saying your name. I know all about you and your role in the Right Knights. Are you going to cooperate now? You can follow us in, or we can come back with a warrant and take you in. And I won't hesitate to let the RKs know we're talking to you."

Like they don't already know, bitch. He was willing to bet her fucking narc had already made sure of that.

WJ raised his right hand to his right temple to salute the detective but at the last second pulled back all but his middle finger. "Yes, ma'am."

"Pull behind the first patrol car."

Once the WJ bacon sandwich was in place and rolling down the highway, WJ steered with one hand and removed his Buzzard belt and then his knife from his boot. He stuffed them between the bench-back and seat.

Other drivers turned to look at the center of attention of the police escort. WJ gave them his best parade wave. He was President Walter Whitworth, Junior.

32

JANICE

I've become a captive of my own ambitions.
—Patsy Cline

Janice took a seat in Pastor Henry's office while he showed Justin and Tommy the playground. The coffee-colored leather felt good beneath her legs and along her back. She caressed the mahogany chair arms with the soft inner skin of her own. The remnants of candle wax and burnt wicks tickled her nostrils. In a cozy room like this, it would be easy to make-believe her life wasn't out of control.

She had never been in the church office before. All of her interactions had been limited to sermons, some Bible classes, and standing in line to shake the pastor's hand on the way out. The pastor's office was more like a den. It had lamps and soft lighting instead of bright overheads. Three walls had built-in white bookshelves, filled with hardbacks and organized by color and height. She wondered why there was one empty shelf up top and center. She closed her eyes and imagined the smell of fresh tobacco streaming from a pipe and a crackling fire and pretended she was in the library of a mansion in Nashville.

She opened her eyes and looked at his desk. He had a note on his desk referencing the Ten Commandments. She quizzed herself but could only remember eight.

Pastor Henry joined her and sat on the other side of his desk. He moved his notes to one side. "Janice, how can I be of service to you today?"

"Why the empty shelf?" she asked. "There must be enough books about religion to complete your library."

A grin spread across Pastor Henry's gentle face. He had one of those faces that encouraged her to spill her guts out.

"I'm glad you asked. I always leave one shelf open to represent faith, hope, and opportunities."

Janice nodded. "I need an empty shelf." More like a dozen.

"So we haven't seen you at service for quite some time."

She'd been ready for him to call her out on missing church, but she didn't mind. She had always gone in spurts. She'd always been taught that "our bodies are God's temple," so why did she need to go to church every Sunday?

"I know. But I pray every day. I do," Janice said.

"And God answers every day," he said. "We would love to see you here next Sunday. You and your family."

"Do you really believe that God answers every day? That he answers all prayers?" she asked and sat forward. She hoped so because she'd been praying non-stop for the past twenty-four hours.

"Yes. Of course, He does. The answer may not always be what you want or think it should be, but He always gives the best answer."

"I don't know. Can I be honest with you? Can this be confidential?"

"Of course."

"I've been praying to God to help me win a weekly karaoke contest. I've prayed every Saturday for my best voice and to give pleasure to my fans, and I've won most times. But I've also prayed for Him to help me change my life and to follow my dreams to Nashville."

"With your family?"

"With my family." Ah-ha, that was number nine: Thou shalt not lie.

"And what's stopping you?"

Right now, everyone. "My husband died this weekend."

"Why didn't you say so immediately? I hope it is some comfort to you and your family that he is now at peace in heaven." He extended a box of Kleenex in her direction.

She took his offering and looked past his shoulder out the window. She could see Justin and Tommy on the swings. They weren't laughing much today. "I'm not facing it yet. Everyone tells me I'm in shock. I don't know, maybe I am. But we've been so unhappy together for so long, you know? I've been in love with several different Harrys over the years. He messes up. We fight. I forgive him. We fall in love again. I get pregnant again. And then the day-to-day would get to us, his drinking would get out of hand, and well, over the years the love wouldn't last as long as the hurt. You know what I mean?

"This time I didn't have time to fall in love again, not even for a day. Sometimes I worry that I don't know how to love anyone anymore. Harry took that from me. Now he's dead. He has left me to clean up his mess again. He's in heaven, I think, and I'm in hell. Look at them." She pointed toward the boys.

Justin swung high, his little legs stretched toward the sky, but he wasn't smiling. Swinging should be joyful, she thought. Tommy just sat there on his swing, staring at the ground. They'd both lost it when she told them their dad was gone, and it had hurt her heart to answer their questions and reassure them that it had nothing to do with their last "big talk" with their dad, whatever that talk had been. She wondered if Harry had considered how they'd all have to think about the last time they saw him or talked to him, and that hers had been him strangling her. How could he leave her with that?

"They lost some of their kid-shine today.

"I'm going to be honest with you, Pastor Henry. I was supposed to leave in a week to move to Nashville. I intended to leave the boys with my husband for a year until I could get settled." There, she'd admitted it to someone. If she couldn't tell a pastor, who could she tell? Getting it out there didn't make her feel much better, though. She still couldn't go to Nashville, confession or not.

The pastor frowned, shook his head, and sat forward. "I don't understand. Earlier you said—"

She stuck her lips out. Frowned. "You know, I would be more comfortable if you had a confessional booth."

The pastor raised his eyebrows. "We're a Lutheran church."

"I know. I know. I'm just saying," she said.

"What exactly are you saying? I am happy to help you, but you need to be more direct."

More direct than admitting she had planned to leave her boys? "Well, that's the first time anyone has asked me to be more direct, but okay." She took a deep breath. Opened her mouth. Closed it. Opened it again and leaned forward in her chair, tipping it on its forelegs. Goose bumps rose on her arms.

"Pastor, did you ever think your life was supposed to be different? That you were meant for greatness? That is how I feel. I've always felt my life would be, I don't know, just more." She clenched her fists and raised them in the air, shaking them. "*More*. Not where I am, but more. Yet here I am, almost fifty, and I haven't begun to live the life I'm meant to live." She had never heard her own fears out loud. Tears pooled in her eyes. Her hands clutched the silky wood of his desk. "I don't want to die here in this town, full of regrets. I'm smart. I used to be pretty too." She sat back and wiped her wet face. She wiggled her fingers. "Look at these hands. They are wrinkled, scarred, and chapped. I'm embarrassed to look at them."

The pastor offered her more Kleenex.

She took the entire box this time.

"With Harry gone, how am I going to go to Nashville? How am I going to be me?"

The pastor sat up. "God works in mysterious ways. You are going to have to take the loss of Harry one step at a time. Nashville might be several steps away. In the meantime, let God, let me, and let the church help you and your family through this difficult and uncertain time. I can arrange grief counseling for you and your family. The congregation can help you with meals this week, and of course, we will help you coordinate his funeral."

He didn't understand, she thought. No one did. "I'm not looking for handouts. I just want what I deserve. Besides, Harry was an atheist. Do you still think he is in heaven?"

"Has he always been a non-believer? Was he baptized?"

"Harry, baptized? That's funny. He believed in Jack Daniel's and Jim Beam. I think he killed himself, you know. He didn't know how to get out, so he killed himself. That's what I think."

Pastor Henry removed his glasses and rubbed the space between his eyes. "Let's pray together. Let's pray for Harry's soul, you and your family's healing, and for God's love and support during this time of loss."

"And Nashville. For a new beginning. Because, Pastor," Janice leaned forward and spread her palms wide on his desk, "if I don't go now, I'll never get to go. And if I don't, if it never happens, I will regret my life until my last breath."

The pastor dropped his shoulders and frowned. He took one of her hands and cradled it like a small child's. "Let's start praying."

Her voice wobbled. "Thank you. Thank you for hearing me." And she meant it. Never in her life had she dumped so much information about her thoughts and feelings on another person. She closed her eyes and lowered her head.

"Dear Lord—"

"Excuse me, Pastor?"

"Yes?"

"This Sunday can you ask the congregation to pray for me too?" She didn't wait for him to respond. She bowed her head.

33

WJ

Well, blow me down, I'm a gentleman!
—Popeye

WJ leaned back in the plastic chair. The police department was the worst place for withdrawals to kick in. WJ ignored the *No Smoking* sign and lit a cigarette, inhaling the smoke until his lungs burned. He'd rather get high. He hooked his thumbs in his beltless loops to keep his hands still.

"Why so many piggies?" WJ stared at Sergeant Meed, the detective, and an officer. He sucked in his cheeks and puckered his lips like a fish at the large mirror spanning one wall. "How many more behind the mirror?"

"WJ, thanks for cooperating and coming in with us without a hassle. We won't keep you long. This is Detective Anderson. She has a few questions for you," Meed said.

"I'm concerned for you, Meed. You're sweating like a mofo." And he was. "Am I under arrest, or a suspect or something? 'Cause if I am, I want you to sing me my Miranda rights, and I want a lawyer. Pronto."

Meed looked even more harassed. Good.

"You're not in police custody," the okay-looking woman detective said. "Not yet. It's up to you."

"What the hell does that mean? What's this about anyway?" Damn, he needed that fix. This place gave him the heebie-jeebies more and more. He rolled his neck. Felt like someone's eyes were drilling a hole in the back of his head. What were they using to finally get him in here? Was it about Harry? Or was it about the guy he and Hefty had worked over? Or was it about any number of other illegal things he had done? Harry was causing problems even as he was cooling in a body fridge. *Weakness and Sloppy Work.*

"Where were you Saturday night?" the detective asked.

Fuckola.

"What difference does it make to you?" WJ asked.

Detective Anderson sat back, crossed her arms over her too-small breasts—at least in his opinion—and stared him down. "The difference, Buzzard, is you weren't ditched by the Knights before now. They've hung you out to dry. No one is looking out for you except me. I'm all you have now."

Ditched? She didn't even know the right lingo. He wanted to shout in her face, "It's 'coded,' beeyatch!" but he didn't. Okay, it was one thing for the Knights to distance themselves because someone had leaked that WJ would be questioned by the police, but how the fuck did the detective already know the Knights had "ditched" him? Whoever her narc was, he spread the word fast, which meant one thing and one thing only: they had a mole planted. Not one of the Knights' dealers, not one of their users. They had someone in the ranks. They'd thought it was the dealer that Hefty went off on, but that couldn't be who was talking now because he was dead. When WJ got out of there, he was going to find the piece of shit squealer and tear him up.

What sucked was she wasn't wrong. He was alone, but he'd rather be alone than have her on his side.

"I need to get to work. I'm late. Are you done flirting with me?" WJ asked.

"Don't be cute," the detective said.

"Then stop looking at me like you want me," WJ said.

Detective Anderson turned to Meed and the other officers in the room. "I'd like a few minutes alone with this guy."

"I bet you would." WJ watched the men leave and stared at the detective.

The detective leaned back in her chair once everyone had left and stared at WJ. She unnerved him a little.

"If you've got something to say, say it. If you want to arrest me, arrest me," WJ said. "But get some balls and make the call. I need to get to work."

"Yeah, I know all about your job. The sanitation company has been a good cover for you, right? A convenient resource? It's probably why Bender first recruited you. You think he liked something about you, such as how tough you were. You never caught on to how and where he met you in a bar after figuring out you were a garbage man. Listen, I'm going to give it to you straight," the detective said.

"Wish you would," WJ said. Betrayal was rearing its ugly ass in his head wondering how she knew how and where Bender met him so long ago. Bender hadn't been using him for his job. She didn't know the first thing about loyalty, but then again, he was supposed to be in hiding and laying low. Bender had coded him. Shit.

"You and your buddies? You're small fries. You're not

any outliers of the Hells Angels. You're just a small group of idiots who got lucky or had good timing and are running a drug racket in a small city, and you're hurting—no, hell— you're killing people in the process. Don't even get me started on the lives you are destroying dealing drugs. You don't have clout, and you don't have the power of a nation-wide network. I already know that you're hoping the Angels will pick you up someday, but you're too unorganized." She nudged her head toward the door. "You're too much for these local guys, but I'm cooperating with the ATF. Together we'll dismantle your little club in a matter of months. Now, we can take you down with everyone else, or you can be a part of the bust. Either way, your little club's days are numbered."

WJ glared at the detective and ground his teeth together. His thumbs curled around his belt loops until his nails turned purple and his knuckles white. "I don't have to listen to your crap. Who do you think you're talking to? And what kind of idiot are you? I don't care if you're a detective, with the ATF, or part of a fucking zoo. And you're stupid for giving it up that you've planted a mole. We'll weed out the narcs. Your narc." WJ stood up and walked to the door. He didn't let on that he knew she had someone very close to Bender, and he couldn't help but suspect it was Hefty.

"You're not listening, WJ. You're not part of a 'we' anymore. You think you're big time, and sure, at the local bars and in your small circle, you might be some kind of notorious and scary jerk, but you're a small fish in a big ocean. Think about what I'm offering. It's your only way out, and I hold the ticket. We can dismiss the other cases we have you tied to. I'm offering you a new life."

And there it was, her fucking zinger, "other cases we have you tied to."

He turned and leaned against the door. "You don't know shit. I know what you have to offer."

"You're not who we're after. You're a pawn. You're just a gopher taking care of the crap work. I want someone bigger. Yeah, yeah, yeah, I know, I see the indignant look in your eyes. You're not a gopher, right? You were a gopher, a prospect, but now you're one of them? You're kidding yourself. All that hard work you did as a prospect? All their dirty work? It hasn't protected you one iota. So you're still a gopher. Our gopher. Our pawn. We want the top—we want Bender. Like I said, I'll have your group annihilated in a matter of time, but it would be quicker if you helped. And if you help me, I'll help you. In the past week, this police department has a man in a coma and two dead men. The guy in the coma isn't coming to any time soon. I've got a body from Saturday that was worked over really good by at least two men . . ."

Motherfucking Hefty! The backstabbing SOB.

"And you already know your father's fate, maybe better than anyone, right? We have enough inconsistencies in the scene to question his death as homicide. For example, the noose was cut away from his neck. There was no suicide letter." The detective chuckled and stood. "Funny thing is, WJ, it looks like your dad's car is a clue in all three crimes."

WJ almost shit his pants. There it was—Harry and the car were going to be his undoing.

"That's right. We found it at the park, and we've tied it to the beating last week and the murder the other night. And wouldn't you know," the detective leaned against the table, "we have a witness that saw your dad's car at his kitchenette the night he died. Twice in fact. Now, we've already confirmed that Harry left his car at the Creek Bar Saturday evening. A witness describes two men—one that sounds, go figure, just like you—showing up at your dad's in his car. We also have information that you returned to Harry's after midnight. I've got more against you, but this will do for now. Don't you think?"

WJ resisted the urge to scream. Weakness and Sloppy Work. "This bullshit you're throwing up even legal? You done babbling yet?"

The detective walked over to WJ and stopped two feet from him. "I can nail you on all three cases if I want. I'm not above doing what I need to do to take down your Knights. But you have a choice. For once in your rotten life, make a good one. You can either help us, or you can go to prison for a very long time."

"You want me to be a narc, you cocksucker?" WJ asked. The bitch didn't even flinch.

"Call it what you will. ATF calls them *informants*. You scratch our back—we scratch yours. You've got a lot to lose. Where are your fellows now? Bender is such an amateur he's not even street-smart enough to realize he is exposing himself by deserting you. Now is when you're most vulnerable, and that means the club is vulnerable. Morons. You guys go on and on about 'disrespecting one member is like disrespecting all members,' but you don't get that disassociating a member exposes the club. They should be protecting you, getting you a lawyer, helping you, or straight-out killing you. But they're not. You're here. They're not here. By now someone has told Bender you 'willingly' came into the station, something that wouldn't have happened if you'd gone underground. Whether you cooperate with us or not, they'll consider you a risk. Start looking over your shoulder. A lot. I'm your only friend right now. How does that feel? I'm your new 'we.'"

"Go screw yourself." WJ resisted the urge to shove the bitch and stormed out of the room.

The detective called after him, "I'm your only choice. You know where to find me, but don't take too long. Clock's ticking."

He lifted his hand and flipped her off.

WJ strode out of the building and to his car. What in the hell was he supposed to do? Did that female asshole know what she was talking about?

Weakness. WJ punched his dashboard until he heard a pop in his hand. He waved his hand to ease the pain.

They had witnesses linking him to everything Saturday night. It had to be Hefty. Who else could verify he had the car? Who else knew everything? Pete and Scotty, but it sounded like the police already talked to them. Nothing he could do about them right now.

His mom wouldn't say anything. Funny, but he knew he could trust her on this one thing. He wished he could call Bender, but he couldn't. The detective didn't know what she was talking about when it came to loyalty. The detective's words rang in his ear. "They'll consider you a risk. Start looking over your shoulder. A lot."

WJ shoved the idea away. He didn't want that frigid woman's voice in his head.

Would the police question Carrie? He had to talk to Carrie. He flipped a U-turn and headed toward her school. He glanced at his watch. It was almost noon. He wasn't sure what time she left school and went to work. He would have to wait outside until he saw her.

His life sucked. What in the hell was he going to say to her? Don't tell the cops I had Dad's car on Saturday night, that I brought the boys from his motel, or else? Threaten her? He couldn't. Tell her to lie or she'd be sorry? He wasn't going to be able to stop her from telling the police the truth.

He remembered when she was in seventh grade and she was going to stay the weekend with him. He had a larger apartment in Reno at the time. He was seeing some other girl then, not Shelly, but it didn't work out when she said he didn't seem like he was into her. She was right, even if she misunderstood why. After dinner, he'd set some lines of crank. When he passed the mirror to Carrie, she had started crying and ran to his second bedroom. He gave her a few minutes before he went to see if she was okay. He'd sat on the bed beside her.

"Sorry, Care."

"Why? Why would you encourage me to do drugs?"

He had shrugged his shoulders and said, "I figure it's only a matter of time before you start doing the crap. You might as well get safe stuff from me. There are kids out there getting shit laced with stuff that can kill you. If you're going to do it, get it from me."

He watched the disgust grow in her eyes. "Is this how Bobby and Michelle started doing drugs? Do you supply them with drugs? Have you given any to Lisa?"

"If someone is going to do drugs, they're going to do drugs. They might as well get a safe stash from me."

"And you make money off of them."

"It's how the world goes around," he said.

"Your world sucks. I want to go home now."

WJ had taken her home, and their relationship had never been the same. He used to feel like her champion big brother. He could imagine how she'd look at him if he asked her to lie to the police. But he didn't have a choice, did he? The detective had him by the balls, but she'd need more witnesses than a weasel like Hefty, a narc.

WJ smoked five cigarettes in the next hour waiting for Carrie to walk out of the school. By the time he saw her, he was bouncing his leg so fast and hard the truck was shaking. He opened his door and stepped outside and shouted her name.

She turned, and her nose wrinkled when she saw him. She looked over her shoulder at her friends. He thought she looked embarrassed. He'd sunk lower in her opinion than he even thought.

She walked toward him, hugging her book bag to her chest. She stopped near his truck. "What are you doing here?"

"Get in the truck. I'll take you to work." He climbed in and waited.

When she climbed in and slammed the door, she asked, "Why are you here?"

"A brother can't check on his sister? After her dad has died?" He started and revved the engine.

"Our dad," she corrected him. She grimaced and looked out the back window.

"You embarrassed?" he asked.

"No." She turned forward and shielded her face. "I didn't tell anyone Dad died, and I don't want them to ask why you'd pick me up for the first time ever. Can we just go?"

He took his foot off the brake. "Watch your tone with me." WJ looked away from the road to glance at her. "Why did you go to school?"

She sighed and slid low in the seat, placing her feet on the dashboard. "I wanted to feel normal. School is normal. But Mom ruined it for me. She called the school and told them Dad died."

WJ didn't need Carrie to explain. He understood their mother's action wasn't out of motherly concern. He'd been in Carrie's shoes, at least with their parents, his entire life too. "Sorry. I get it."

"And this guy told me today that his parents own the motel. He knew about Dad."

WJ darted a quick look at Carrie's mortified profile. "This guy, he's a friend of yours?"

"Yes. No. I don't know."

Ah, someone she liked, but even he didn't want to have that convo.

"What did he know?" he asked.

"He knew enough. He knew Dad died there. He probably knew before I did. WJ . . . Dad called me Saturday night." She looked away from him and out her window. "He said goodbye, and I didn't do anything about it. Maybe I could have saved him."

"No one could save him."

They drove the rest of the way in silence. When he pulled up outside the county building, he reached across the cab and took her hand.

"Do you remember when I used to read *Popeye* to you, and you made the scrapbook for me while I was away in the Navy?"

"Yeah."

"You know, that was the best present anyone ever gave me, and then you said that I was Popeye. That's the highest compliment I've ever received."

She was listening.

He leaned back in his seat and rested his head against the rear window. "The thing is, Popeye never gives up, does he? He just keeps going back for more. He never cares if the villain is bigger, stronger, or smarter than him. It doesn't matter how many times he gets his ass kicked. He's fucking undefeatable. He's the good guy, and he always wins in the end."

"With his fists," Carrie said.

"Yeah, with his fists, but you see, that's all he has to deal out justice. He isn't smart, and he isn't rich, but he can fight. He uses what he has to take out the bad guy. Every time. And you know who he is most protective of?"

"Olive Oyl."

"No, Olive Oyl just uses him. She can take care of herself. It's Swee'Pea. He doesn't ever let anyone lay a finger on Swee'Pea. He knows kids need protection."

"Are you saying you did something to dad to protect us? That wasn't your decision to make!" Carrie said and yanked her hand from his.

"No, no. I didn't have anything to do with Harry's—I mean Dad's—death. But listen, if the police come around and ask you if I had his car and what time . . ." He let his sentence dwindle and turned in his seat to look at her.

He watched her shoulders drop, her posture slacken, and her eyes grow moist.

Her eyes flooded with tears, and she looked daggers at him. "You want me to lie for you."

Ah, the bittersweet scent of salty tears and disappointment. It was the drug incident all over again. He was letting her down, asking her to do something she didn't believe in. He stood to lose whatever affection she had left for him. He stared at her young face, one year younger than him when he left for the Navy.

"No," he changed course, "if they ask you if I had Dad's car, you don't need to lie for me, okay? Tell them whatever you need to. Whatever you want." He waited. "And about Dad saying goodbye, we know what goodbye meant. If you want, tell the police that Dad said goodbye, tell them what that meant to him. That was his choice to say goodbye. Nothing you could've done about it. How many times did he tell us, 'You can't take back goodbye'?"

Wiping away her tears, she sighed. "I thought you wanted me to lie." She leaned over and hugged him. Hard. "Thank you, Popeye."

He hugged her tight and waited and watched her cross the street and open the glass door.

She turned and waved at him and smiled.

Weakness. But worth it. He waved back. He took a deep breath, smiled to himself, and drove away.

Well, blow me down. Sometimes right feels good.

34

JANICE

No dough. No show.
—Patsy Cline

Janice hung up the phone. Harry's body would be released tomorrow. The body. A body. He had become an It. She didn't know if she should refer to the body as Harry or It. *It* wasn't Harry anymore, or was *It*?

The medical examiner had finished the autopsy this morning and was filing the report today. Janice was surprised they had ordered a full autopsy. She wished WJ would call her. The coroner said he would call Janice back later and tell her how Harry died. Janice glanced toward the bulky manila envelope on the counter. She hadn't looked at the items again. She couldn't. When she had cracked the seal, the scent of Old Spice had permeated the air, and she could swear it had adhered to her clothing, skin, and hair. The fragrance made her eyes water. For the past several years, the scent had grated on her nerves, but at the same time, the smell was Harry's, and she was starting to miss him.

Would they wash the body? Would *It* still smell like Harry?

The coroner had asked her which funeral home to send Harry's body to, but Janice hadn't thought that far ahead. She should be looking for an apartment, planning her getaway, and packing her clothes and belongings, not looking for a mortuary, planning a funeral, and cleaning out Harry's kitchenette.

Janice looked up to the ceiling and then down at the floor. "I hope you're enjoying yourself, Harry. Are you down there? Do you hear me?"

After handing the boys cold hotdogs from the fridge, she told them they were on their own for a little while. In less than twenty-four hours, she had to have someone, or some-place, take custody of *It* from the coroner.

First, she left a message for Harry's boss to call her. Then she stopped by the landlord's office at Bengal Trailer Park. She explained Harry was dead before the landlord could be too annoyed with her about the rent. He gave her two addi-tional weeks, which meant she didn't need Carrie's savings because she could collect Harry's final paycheck in time. She climbed into her car and tried not to think about Harry's betrayal and how he'd pawned the trailer and cars. Even if she wanted to live in the trailer park, and she didn't, staying was no longer an option. The question was how much time she had before someone claimed them.

But like she'd told Tommy, she could only deal with one mess at a time. Her lifeline to sanity and the thin thread of hope she was trying to nurture were both in jeopardy of being buried under an avalanche of improbability and despair.

Once, Harry had told her that the two most consistent professions a person could choose were barber and mortician.

"Both will always have customers," he'd said. "Vanity never dies, and a person can't live forever." Harry had a point.

When Janice walked into the funeral home, she shivered. She wondered how many souls might stick to her on her way out of the building. Like Post-it Notes. She looked around the front room. Dark wood, fleur-de-lis wallpaper, dimmed sconces, and gold carpet. The musty fragrance of flowers current and days gone past hung in the air. Stifling. There was a guest book open to a blank page on the entryway table, and a set of double doors stood wide open, revealing a long and narrow room that resembled a church with a podium up front and pews for the grieving. The space next to the podium was empty, and Janice imagined a flashing red sign: *Vacancy. Vacancy.*

"Can I help you?" asked a monotone voice behind Janice.

She spun on her heel and looked down at a man she guessed to be in his midforties. He was bald and wore large glasses and a suit too large for his squatty body. He was a hopeful five-three, she guessed. The cuffs of his jacket hung past his wrists, and his tie was wider than his upper arm.

"You don't look like a mortician," Janice said before she could stop herself.

"I'm Stanley James. I'm the funeral director."

Janice stuck out her hand. "I'm Janice Sloan. I spoke with you earlier." She was startled to find his hand oddly large for his small body. She looked down and assessed his shoe size. "You're not what I expected, Mr. James."

"Please call me Stanley. Would you like a tour before we sit down and discuss your husband's service needs?"

"No, if we could just get to the point, I would feel much better."

"I understand. This way, please." Stanley led her out of

the funeral parlor and down a hallway to his office. He stepped behind his desk and spread papers in front of him. "Have a seat. Did you bring your husband's birth certificate? I will need it until the death certificate is prepared."

Janice dug through her purse and handed it to him. She fidgeted in her chair. "Isn't it funny that we get a certificate for being born and another one for dying?" This guy made her nervous. She pulled her purse closer on her lap. "Sorry, I'm babbling. I've never had to do this before."

"Please don't concern yourself. I understand. I'm sure you're in shock."

"That's what everyone keeps telling me," she said.

"Why don't we start with your wishes for the service, or your husband's wishes? Did he have a living will?"

She snorted. "God, no. He hardly made a living."

He gave her a courteous smile and tilted his head. He had Carrie's knack for conveying a million words with one look. Maybe Carrie should become a mortician.

Janice cleared her throat. "Sorry, bad joke. I'm nervous. Harry didn't want to be buried. The last time we talked about death, he wanted to be cremated and have his ashes scattered over Davis Creek, but . . ."

She paused and looked past his bald head to the shelves hanging on the office walls. They were neat, arranged by height, and filled with books about grief, transition, accounting, communication, and anatomy. No empty shelves waiting for opportunities.

"Years ago," she continued, "when we were happier, we used to have family gatherings at Davis Creek. We used to have a lot of fun there. Harry would sit with his beers and watch the blue jays for hours or walk with the kids around the pond. I liked the picnic part, but I've never been a fan of swimming. The pond was green and moldy, full of slimy frogs. But the kids liked the frogs. They'd catch tadpoles, snails, and dragonflies and bring them back to Harry as if they were some kind of trophy. Harry knew I couldn't stand the beasts, so he always *oohed* and *aahed* over them and encouraged the kids to name them and then set them free. Anyway, that's where he wanted his ashes scattered, but the creek has a few houses now, and we haven't spent any time there in years. I would've thought Harry would have left me a note telling me what to do with his remains, but he didn't. I still don't understand why he didn't write that note, and now I have to decide what to do with the body. He was an atheist, so he doesn't need a divine send-off. But I would like to have a wake. I've always believed that a viewing helps people let go." She finally stopped talking. Stanley hadn't even asked for all that information.

Get a grip, Janice.

"Yes. Many family members find the viewing helpful, and we are happy to help you during this time. However, you need to know there are local regulations for how and where remains may be scattered. It is my obligation to let you know."

"Oh. Right. Okay," she said. "Thank you."

"Based on your wishes, we can accommodate all of your needs with the exception of the handling of his ashes." He checked off items on a form and turned it for Janice to review. "Do these services look correct to you? We'll file the necessary permits and handle your husband's death certificate. We can work with the coroner's office to pick up your husband's body and transfer him to our establishment. For a viewing, we'll have to embalm him. We will also have to add a fee for renting a casket for the viewing—I'm sure you understand."

Jesus Christ. She was renting a casket now? She'd just worked out rent for the lot.

"For the cremation, we have a few viable options that are approved for cremation and the environment. We'll go over those choices next. We can have the wake and memorial service as soon as Thursday. We'll need you to supply us with a picture of your husband and an outfit for the service. On Friday, we'll transfer your husband to the crematory. We will coordinate with the crematory to have your husband's remains returned to us in the vessel of your choice, which we'll go over shortly, and then he will be in your care."

Vessel? Jeez.

"Please stop calling *It* my husband," Janice said.

"Excuse me?"

"The body—stop calling it my husband. Can I have a glass of water or something?" Janice set her purse down and fanned herself with her hands. "It's really hot in here. I thought it would be cooler with the bodies, you know?"

"Yes. Yes. Let me get you some cold water," Stanley offered and left.

"I'm not coming back," Harry's voice whispered in her ear.

Janice whipped around. No one was standing behind her. She could hear hushed voices down the hall, so she sighed with relief. She was not losing her mind. Grandfather came to mind, the way he used to say, "Hold onto your feathers."

Just hold onto your feathers, Janice thought. *Hold onto your feathers.*

Stanley returned to the office and handed her a glass of water.

Janice gulped it down.

"Better? Would you like more?" he asked.

"No. I'm okay now. Thank you. Can we finish this up? How much will the services cost?"

She leaned away from his measuring glance followed by a sympathetic nod.

"I will make a few assumptions that we can discuss if necessary." He punched numbers into a calculator, each followed by the bee-like buzz of the paper reel. When he finished, he tore the slip off and stapled it to the form. "Based on our discussion and having the service on Thursday, we can meet all of your preferences for three thousand two hundred dollars." He slid the forms toward Janice.

"What?" Now would be a good time for the floor to open up and swallow her.

"Excuse me?" he asked.

She cleared her throat. "Can you say the amount again?"

"Three thousand two hundred dollars."

"I, um, I . . ." she swallowed and looked down at her chapped hands.

Damn you, Harry. Damn you. Thirty-two hundred dollars? That was her money for Nashville. Wimpy's mantra came to mind, and she asked, "I'd gladly pay you Tuesday for a funeral today?"

"I'm sorry. I don't understand." The bald man looked concerned.

"I don't have that kind of money for a funeral. How can we make it lower? Do you have a layaway program?"

"No. We don't have a credit, or layaway, program. What is your budget? I apologize for not asking in advance."

"I don't have a budget. I didn't know he was going to die this week. I didn't know that funerals were so expensive." What was she going to do? She had to give Harry a funeral. She had to do something with *It*. But she couldn't use her money. She just couldn't. And what about when her home and car would be taken away?

Stanley removed his glasses. "If we eliminate the wake, we can eliminate the fees for the chapel, the rental coffin, and embalming. I had already applied the least expensive crematory container and urn. That would decrease the amount to one thousand six hundred dollars."

Her eyes began to sting. She couldn't afford that either. This was ludicrous. How could funerals be so expensive? She and Harry had never spent that much money on life on a good day. What kind of business was this—this death business— that they would charge so much to the people left behind? What kind of world did they live in that death was more expensive for Janice than living her dream? Her future was looking dismal and Nashville-less. Her dream was slipping away.

"I'm not coming back," Harry's voice whispered again. She spun in her seat. Nothing.

"I can't do this right now. I just can't do this right now." She shoved her chair back and left the building, ignoring Stanley's hushed call, something about time and the body. She waved her arm behind her to shoo away any spirits. She walked quickly to her car and jumped in. Her body jerked, and she wrapped her arms around her core.

"Damn you, Harry," she screamed and began to pound the steering wheel. *How could you do this to me? How could you do this to me? How dare you put me in this impossible position? This was my last chance. My last chance!*

Janice rested her head in her arms and sobbed. She sobbed for her lost dreams, her dismal future, and her lost life.

35

CARRIE

fair \fer\ *adv : without cheating or trying to achieve unjust advantage*

C arrie arrived home from work earlier than usual, thanks to a coworker offering her a ride. At first, she'd hesitated because she liked keeping her workplace and home separate, but by five o'clock, she had felt so tired that she ached from her heart to her toes. It had been one of the worst days of her life, but something awesome had happened too.

She was collating copies at work and thinking about the last time she had talked to her dad. She wanted to know how he chose to die. Was it quick? Did he have any peace in the end? Did he find comfort in knowing how and when he would die? Or was he afraid? What if he was counting on someone showing up and stopping him, and no one did?

She was still standing at the Xerox machine when her supervisor sent her to the director's office. Why did the director need to speak to her? That never happened. Had she done something wrong? Or had they found out about her dad? Oh Gawd, did her mom call them, too?

This meeting was going to be worse than the one with Principal Weimer that morning.

But when Carrie sat down, her supervisor surprised her by following her in. With a smile, she sat down next to Carrie and patted her arm in excitement.

What in the world?

Carrie felt the blush climbing her neck and cheeks as the director started by complimenting her work performance.

"As you know, Rhonda from the front desk is being promoted to a recruiting position. The team has been very impressed with your work, and we'd like to offer you a full-time position, as Rhonda's replacement, when you graduate from high school in the spring. Of course, it would mean that you couldn't attend UNR full-time, but you would receive solid wages and benefits. You could take evening classes at the community college. Take some time to think about the offer, Carrie. Obviously, I hope it will work out for you to attend UNR, but if it doesn't, you have another option."

Over the balance of the afternoon, Carrie shed a ton in worries. If she didn't have enough money for college, she still had an option. She loved the people she worked with. They recognized her efforts, her hard work. They believed in her.

When she arrived home and waved bye to her coworker, Carrie hitched her backpack high on her shoulder and opened the mailbox. Checking the mail had been the most hopeful part of each day for the past several months. And she was feeling lucky. She got an adrenaline rush when she eyed the type and width of packages stacked in the aluminum box. Each day she prayed for a nine-by-twelve-inch white envelope with her name on it. Not the gimmicky letters with green stripes and a red "Urgent" printed on the side, from collection agencies, or advertising sweepstakes offerings. She was looking for a large pristine white envelope in quality card stock, gently folded by the mailman because it would be too wide to slide in the mailbox. If there wasn't a matching envelope, she felt deprived, and trepidation would slow her movements as she removed the standard-sized envelopes. Wearing her poker face, she would fan them out like cards and read the return addresses. When it came to scholarship notifications, large envelopes were good news, and small envelopes carried bad news. So far, she hadn't gotten either. Ugh.

But between a job offer and finally submitting her forged Pell Grant application by herself, Carrie was not disappointed in the mail. When she'd called her dad's work, his boss, Rudy, was ready to help her.

She pressed the mail to her chest, ran up the back stairs, and smiled at Tommy when he opened the door for her. "Hey, kiddo. How are you?"

"Hungry."

She dropped her bag on the table and hugged him. "Where's Mom?"

"She said she would be quick and left us in charge," Tommy said.

The phone rang.

"I'll make you something to eat when I get off the phone. Hello?"

"Yeah, I'm looking for Janice Sloan," an unfamiliar voice said. Probably a bill collector, as usual. Now that Mom was making her pay rent, Carrie had a right to know about all their bills.

Carrie shooed Tommy away and stretched the cord down the hall. "How can I help you?"

"This is George McKay. You left me a message yesterday morning about the studio apartment on Demonbreun Street. Your message said to call before five o'clock, but I can't work around your schedule. The apartment is still available for four hundred dollars a month on a month-to-month basis. First come, first served. If you're interested, I'll give you the address. Once I receive the money, it's yours. So what will it be?"

Carrie clutched the phone. Demonbreun wasn't a street in Corbett City. Studio apartment? Was her mom planning to leave? Where would the boys fit in a studio?

No! Did her mom expect her to give up college and go with her? She wasn't eighteen yet—she wouldn't have any say in the matter. Her heart rate skyrocketed.

"Ah, yes. Yes. Um, let me grab a pen and paper." Her hand shook as she scribbled the address in her notebook. Nashville, Tennessee? That was more than halfway across the country. "A studio, right? One person only?" Carrie guessed.

"Yes," the man said and hung up.

Her mom was unbelievable.

Carrie's panic for herself and the boys threatened to knock her out. Her brain churned through the meaning of her mother's plan. They didn't know Dad was dead yesterday morning. Her mom was going to leave them . . . maybe not now that Dad was dead, but for sure, her mom had been planning to desert them.

Tommy and Justin were playing in the living room, quieter than usual. They were two of the sweetest boys in the world. Who could leave them like that? Even she worried about leaving them for college, but she was their sister, not their mother. The tears came easy. Her mom would've just walked away from them? Had her dad known and that was

why he killed himself? He didn't want his wife to leave him.
And if her mom was still trying to leave, how could Carrie
take care of them? Maybe her mom couldn't legally leave
them now. Would they all end up in a foster home until she
turned eighteen? Even then, she couldn't drop out of high
school to work and earn enough to support them. She had to
have an education to support them! Would the boys survive
foster care long enough for her to accept the full-time county
job in June? It would not be easy, but she could support the
three of them if it kept them together. She would find some
way to take at least a community college course. She could
stay on goal. It would just take longer. But it wasn't what she
wanted. She wanted to be like her friends, eager for UNR.
She wanted her brothers to be kids. She imagined herself
winning scholarships for UNR after all and now having to
walk away from them. Carrie had never fainted before, but
never say never. She rested her arm on the counter until she
could sit down on the floor and put her head between
her knees.

"What's wrong?" Justin asked as his small hand patted
her shoulder.

"Nothing," she said between deep breaths. "Just give me a
few seconds, all right? I'll make dinner in a minute."

She didn't know what to do or if and when she should
confront her mother. Would it make a difference or only
speed up her escape? How could her mom afford to leave?
Carrie's throat closed as she thought about her savings
account—maybe her mom intended to take it all, not just rent.
It was too late for Carrie to call the bank, but she could try the
new automated call center. She grabbed her wallet out of her
backpack. With shaking hands, she dialed the bank and
followed the prompts for her balance. Her mom would've

gone to the bank today, and her account shouldn't be missing more than the rent amount.

The full amount, including rent, was there. Now that was a surprise and a lucky break. Knowing her mother, it was only a matter of time.

Carrie needed to find a way to protect her money. She didn't know how yet, but she certainly would buy herself and the boys some time. She wouldn't give Mom the message about the apartment.

After making Justin and Tommy some supper, Carrie whipped out her Dos & Don'ts List and with great purpose, crossed out: *Don't lie* and replaced it with *Do lie if it's for a greater cause.*

When the phone rang again, Carrie yanked it out of the receiver. Probably about another apartment. "Hello?" But it turned out to be the manager from her dad's motel.

When her mom came home a half hour later with a red nose, swollen eyes, and a tired expression, Carrie felt zero sympathy.

"The motel landlord called and said you need to pick up Dad's stuff or pay his rent until you do."

"Any other calls?"

Did Carrie imagine it, or did her mom's eyes spark with hope?

"Only a bill collector," Carrie lied.

36

JANICE

Oh, I just sing like I hurt inside.
—Patsy Cline

Janice sat in her car for an hour outside the trailer before she found the strength to go inside. When she walked in, Carrie gave her the look.

"The motel manager called and said you need to pick up Dad's stuff or pay his rent until you do."

"Any other calls?" Even though Nashville seemed impossible, those apartment calls were the last tie she had to her dream. But she hoped they'd been discrete like she asked. Carrie would go crazy if she knew.

"Only a bill collector," Carrie said.

Janice sighed. Everybody wanted non-existent money.

"I'm going to the Creek to pick up something from Scotty," Janice said and turned down the hall.

Carrie called after her, "Do you know how important college is to me?"

Janice turned, wrinkled her face, and tried to mimic Carrie's voice. "Yes, I know how important your precious college is to you."

"Do you care if I can go to college? Do you want me to have a better life than you and Dad?"

"Dammit, Carrie. You always think everything is about you. You. You. You. All I ever hear from your mouth is judgment and criticism, or how you're so much better than us. You're only going to behave this way, not our way. Well, everything isn't about you. This is life. Get a grip because let me tell you something, honey, life isn't fair. Most of the time it flat-out sucks. Oh, have I already told you that? Write it down in your fancy notebook. What makes you think you deserve better than me? Huh?

"Because no, I don't care if you go to college. Right now I'm just trying to figure out how to cremate your dad and keep a roof over our heads. You know who deserves a better life? Me! I do!" Janice screamed and slammed out the back door.

Carrie didn't know her. Carrie didn't know her at all. She was halfway to the Creek before she could breathe regularly.

Janice walked through the back door and slid up to the bar.

Scotty immediately poured her a shot.

"Lady J, I'm so sorry about Harry."

Scotty's face was sober and caring.

"You know something, Scotty? Sometimes I think you're the only one who cares about me, and you're my bartender. How depressing is that?"

"How are you holding up?" he asked.

She moved her head from side to side, fiddled with the coaster. "I'm not okay. I'm really not okay. I had dreams, you know."

Scotty patted her hand. "I figured, else you wouldn't have been saving that money. Want to tell me about them?"

Janice swallowed and slid her hand out from underneath his. "Best you don't know, and I don't want to cry anymore today."

Scotty yelled over her head at the DJ. "Hey, get 'Crazy' set up for my favorite lady here."

"No, no." She didn't have any song left in her. "I can't. I can't sing tonight. I don't have it in me."

Scotty had walked around the bar and placed his hands on her shoulders, turning her in the barstool to face the stage. "Get up there. It's exactly where you need to be right now."

Janice looked around the bar. It was quiet since it was Monday, and there wasn't a contest. She recognized the few customers in the bar. She watched as Scotty leaned over and turned on the stage lights. Their brightness and warmth welcomed her. The *tap tap* on the microphone from the DJ was equivalent to someone rubbing her temples and massaging the knots in her neck.

She set her purse on the bar and walked over to the stage. No one was clapping. The quiet suited her. The stage vibrated under her footfalls. When the music began, Janice was surprised most of all how effortlessly she sang her heart out for the next hour. With no one in line, she could sing all of her favorites, and she didn't stop until she felt some semblance of herself returning.

By the time she walked from the stage back to the bar, she was wiping away tears.

Scotty handed her some tissue. "Hang in there."

She looked up. "Thank you, doctor. That felt real good."

He poured her a shot. "The police came around. That's how I found out about Harry. Pete had to tell them about Harry's car. The police already knew that Yellow Cab had dropped Harry off at his place, and the order came from here. We told them we call lots of cabs, but we couldn't outright lie. They knew the timing, and lying would have raised more questions, and I can only turn a blind eye so much and not jeopardize my bar."

"You told them WJ had Harry's car." It wasn't a question. She wanted to make sure she understood.

"Yeah," Scotty said. "Let WJ know, will you, that we didn't have a choice?"

"He's been avoiding me. You'll probably see him before I do," she said.

"Did they tell you how Harry died yet?" Scotty dropped his voice to a whisper.

"I'm waiting for the coroner to call me. You know, I think Harry just got tired and quit. By the time he died, he was half the man I thought he was when I married him, and now I know I was too naïve to see that he was never one hundred percent. I'm tired too, but I'm not going to kill myself. Once, a doctor told us Harry was suicidal, but we didn't have time to believe it. Even now, it doesn't seem real. I feel like I still need to have an argument with him about his gambling. Like he's going to stumble in here any minute and beg me to come back to him and say, 'Hey, Songbird, come dance with me.' He didn't even say goodbye, Scotty."

Scotty sighed and nodded. "I liked Harry, and I'm sad to hear it. I don't know—maybe it's for the best."

"Best for him maybe, but he really messed up my life again. Everyone feels bad about the deceased when it's really themselves they should be worried about. I don't have time to dwell on him or feel sad. There is more to do for a dead husband than a live one." Janice sipped her whiskey. She couldn't escape the expenses for Harry's funeral. And she'd have to find a new place to live in Corbett City when it should be in Nashville. She'd have to get a job. Could she last until Carrie turned eighteen and was old enough to be the boys' legal guardian, or until she could save enough money again? Her heart sank. She put her palm against her stomach. She could feel her gut twisting through the cord of her cesarean scar. Hopelessness settled around her neck like her dead uncle's iron grip. She had no choice. No choice. Stuck again and at the hands of a man. Stuck.

"I'm going to need my money, the contest money, for the funeral," Janice said. She looked away. The sympathetic look in Scotty's eyes was all it would take for her to crumble.

"How much do you need for the funeral?"

"With a wake, it's thirty-two hundred dollars. Without one, it's sixteen hundred." She put her face in her hands.

"Which funeral home? I'll take care of it. I care too much about you to see you like this, and I cared about Harry too. I remember the day almost thirty years ago when the two of you came waltzing into this bar. You've been loyal customers, and more importantly, I consider you a good friend."

Janice rolled her lips between her teeth, and she began to tremble as her eyes pooled. She shook her head. "No, I can't let you do that. I'm not looking for handouts."

"It's not a handout. Consider it a gift. Just promise me something. Promise me you'll get happy. Whatever it takes."

She couldn't believe her ears. Scotty was handing her

dream back to her. Janice looked at her old friend, stood up, and walked around the bar. She ignored everyone else as she wrapped her arms around him. She buried her face in his chest and clung to him. "I promise," she said. Her back shook as she cried silently into his chest.

37

JANICE

Death cannot kill what never dies, love.
—Patsy Cline, Epitaph

The next morning, Janice spoke to the coroner on the phone. Carrie and the boys were at school, and Janice was alone in the tired trailer. Harry's death was ruled death by hanging.

"So you're saying he did commit suicide?" she had asked.

"Only Detective Anderson knows the details of the case. You'll have to speak to her. I can only clarify that your husband's death was due to hanging. However, his body will be released today."

Janice asked that *It* be released to the proper funeral home.

Death by hanging. It was one thing to talk about Harry being dead, planning a funeral, cremating *It*, and trying to sort out her life, but it was another to be told how he died, and that his body could be picked up. Her shaking fingers poked at the phone until she had a dial tone, and she called the funeral home to let them know *It* was "ready" and that she had the money for the funeral.

The bald turtle reminded her that he would need an outfit and a photo to prepare Harry for the wake.

What photo she'd pick, she had no idea. Maybe she should give the mortician the picture of Harry in his overalls that the photographer had taken. Did they seriously think using a photo of someone alive would help him look more presentable dead?

She called the motel and made arrangements to pick up his meager belongings. His stuff couldn't take up more than a box or two. He still had most of his clothes hanging in her closet. She hadn't pushed him to come and pick them up since she thought she'd be leaving town and he would be moving back in. At the time, she hadn't cared that Harry might have mistakenly believed that his clothes in her closet meant they might reconcile once the smoke blew over. But if he had the hope, would he have killed himself? But, no, she still didn't know for sure how he had died. Only that he hanged. Death by hanging.

After she got his stuff from the motel manager, she'd have to come back home and scrounge through their basket of pictures for a photo of Harry—the more she thought about it, she couldn't risk the mortician losing Harry's one and only professional photo—and pick out an outfit from the closet for the funeral home. She would have to make a list of people to notify about the funeral but figured an announcement at the Creek would notify what few friends they had. A few of his coworkers would want to attend. Harry had been a hard worker when he worked. Harry didn't have any extended family he'd kept in touch with, so she wasn't going to worry about them. She had enough to worry about.

She pulled up to the motel and parked in front of the manager's office, careful to not look in the direction of the fateful Number Twenty-Two. She knocked on the manager's door and shook her head when she heard someone stumble and curse from the other side. It was like a motel for drunks. The door was yanked open, and Janice took a step back to escape some of the fumes.

"What do you want?" the drunken lady slurred.

"I'm Janice Sloan. I'm here to pick up Harry Sloan's belongings."

"Good thing for you, or else you have to pay rent for the week."

"Moot point. Can I have his things? I'm in a hurry." Janice couldn't wait to leave. She could feel the weight of Harry's death looming behind Number Twenty-Two.

The manager returned with a key. "I'll give you an hour. I want to show the place at noon."

Janice kept her arms folded across her chest and frowned. "I just want his things. I don't want to go in the room."

The manager cackled. "What? You think I went in there and packed up for you? Ha! One hour." She shoved the key toward Janice. "Leave the key in the lock. I'll get it later."

Janice took the key and turned, assailed by the draft of booze wafting around her as the manager slammed her door closed. Janice stared down the rickety walkway. She couldn't do this, could she? What if his ghost was inside? Would the room stink? Would there be a chalk mark where Harry's body was found, like in the movies?

Janice stood before the brown door, and the porch squeaked under her weight. She looked down and wondered if Harry had stood in this same spot. She rocked from side to side, the wood beneath her foot moaning with her movements. The key got jammed in the lock. She bent over to see the keyhole and to wiggle and coerce the key inside. She was panting, and her breath ricocheted off the door and back in her face. Goose bumps raised along her arms as she imagined Harry in this same position. She shook her head and stood straight, twisted the knob, and let the door swing open.

She stood on the threshold, hesitant to enter. She took a timid breath but smelled only the mustiness of a well-worn room. Not death. Not Old Spice. More like stale cigarettes. Dankness weighed heavily on her limbs as she leaned into the shadows of the room.

No chalk lines. But a messy bed. Funny enough, Harry used to say, "Messy bed, messy head." Making the bed was one of the only routines he kept and he'd even given that up. She stepped inside and saw dirty bowls and Top Ramen wrappers on the floor. From the boys? She pushed one bowl aside with the toe of her shoe. She turned around in the claustrophobic tomb. A pile of Harry's clothes sat on a chair in the corner. She picked them up, thankful they were clean and didn't smell like him or like the room in general. There was no closet to empty. She stepped to the desk and only found old newspapers. Nothing in the kitchen belonged to Harry.

Death by hanging. How could he have died in this small, sad room?

A scene from *An Officer and a Gentleman,* when they had found the friend hanging in his shower, flashed before her.

Time to get this over with.

She entered the bathroom but was relieved to see the shower wouldn't have been possible. There was only a bath. No showerhead or rod. The first sign of Harry was the dirt-caked yellow bar of soap resting on the side of the sink. He could never get his hands clean enough after coming home from work, and in his effort to wash them, he dirtied the soap, leaving a black scum border. She slowly opened the medicine cabinet and stared at Harry's bottle of Old Spice and a bottle of Tums. She removed both and threw them in the trash. She didn't want to smell his cologne. Once, she'd read that scents triggered the strongest memories. When the coroner had told her Harry had died, the whiff of Old Spice from the envelope had been difficult to move past.

She shut the medicine cabinet and stared in the mirror, sprayed with dots of toothpaste that Harry couldn't have made since he wore dentures. She doubted the manager would clean this place even now after someone had died.

Janice was just about ready to congratulate herself on not finding Harry in the room—other than his toiletries—when she turned and saw the bathroom door.

Time stopped, and she was rooted to her spot.

Several deep grooves of wood were missing along the top of the door, chipped away by what could only have been Harry's natural instinct and struggle to stay alive. A long crack ran down the center of the door from the burden of his weight.

"Oh my God," Janice choked, clapping her hand over her mouth to stop from vomiting. A hint of Old Spice clung to her fingertips, and she sobbed. She stumbled from the bathroom and out the front door. Her knees knocked against each other as she struggled to make it to her car. "Oh my God." She sucked in her lips and started to cry. She threw Harry's clothes through the open car window and yanked on the door handle. It was stuck.

Oh God, not now. Let me in. Let me in. Let me in. Please, God, open the door.

The door swung open, and she fell into the driver's seat

and willed her hands to stop shaking so she could start the car. She had to get out of here. When she was two blocks away, Janice pulled over until she could breathe again.

When she finally made it home, she put Harry's clothes in the large trash bin. Her mouth was oversalivating, and she was afraid she might still get sick.

That door. Oh, that door.

With wet cheeks, she walked inside in a trance and went to her room. Grabbing the manila envelope with the last of Harry's belongings, she walked to her bedroom closet. She slid the plywood door to the side and stared at Harry's shirts and slacks. Then she opened the manila envelope and looked inside. The face of the blue watch she bought him on their wedding day stared back at her. She lifted the aged blue leather to her nose, closed her eyes, and breathed deep.

Tears dropped from her chin to the front of her blouse, but she didn't wipe them away. Like when she had lost Walter, she knew there were more tears to come and that she'd never keep up with them. She stepped into the closet and sank to the floor next to his single pair of dress shoes. With Harry's shirts sweeping across the top of her head, Janice pulled her knees to her chest and slid the closet door closed.

I'm lonesome kid—I got no fren's or nothin'.
—Popeye

WJ's life was depressing. Harry was dead. Cops were crawling up his butt. His supposed friends were MIA. And he'd been fired from the sanitation company.

Thanks to the detective, he never made it to work on Monday, and he knew if he wanted to keep his day job—and he did—he needed to be there bright and early this morning. The detective hadn't been wrong; the job was an excellent resource for the Knights, not that it mattered anymore. Truth was, Harry had helped him get the job almost a decade before, and WJ liked being a sanitation worker.

Getting him that job was the only good thing Harry had ever done for him. And Harry had raised him, not that he'd done him any favors doing that, though. WJ figured he would have had a better chance being raised by his real dad. He'd never know why his mother had taken him away and given him to Harry.

Rudy was waiting for WJ when he walked in; his boss waved him into his office.

"Sorry I missed yesterday, Rudy."

"We're damn shaken up about your dad. He was a good friend and the hardest working employee this company had. I know he had his faults, but we sure will miss him."

"Thanks, Rudy. I better start my route."

"Hold on."

WJ sat back down.

"You've been here for ten years, WJ. Your dad recommended you to us, and for a long time, you did a solid job for us. But I've got to say, I'm suspicious of some of your activities with that crowd you run with. I don't like that they've been seen around here, and you just aren't the same." He handed WJ an envelope.

"What's this?" WJ asked. He had a good idea what it might be, but he prayed to God he was wrong.

"I would've given this to you three years ago, but your dad threatened to quit if I fired you. He said you just had some things to figure out. I promised Harry then that I would keep you as long as he was working here. I kept my promise."

WJ didn't know what else to do but stare at the envelope that must hold his last paycheck. So all this time, Harry had gone out of his way to make sure WJ could keep his job. Damn shit if he wasn't feeling choked up by the idea of Harry threatening to quit as a way to stand up for him. The old fucker had always been the one he'd had to stand up to. Guess if he started counting, Harry had done three things for him. Got him this job in the first place, made sure he got to keep it as long as possible, and told him about his real dad.

"Rudy, the friends you're worried about aren't going to be around anymore. I need to keep this job."

"Sorry, son. When you figure out whatever Harry hoped you would by now, give me a call, and I'll think about it. But that's not going to be anytime soon is my guess."

Great. Now WJ was an unemployed-garbage-picking-murder-suspect-narc-recruit-crank-craving-broke-bastard. He was no longer Buzzard, and he wasn't WJ Sloan either. He was a junior to someone named Walter Whitworth. Where the hell did he belong anymore?

At home, he walked past Shelly and crawled into bed, pulling the blankets over his boots. He rolled over and quadruple-checked his stash. Yep, empty. Shitola.

"Why aren't you at work?" Shelly asked.

"You better stay away for a couple of days. I'm not going to be good company for a while."

"You cleaning up again?" she asked.

"I don't know what I'm doing, but I'm not leaving this trailer," he said. He had nowhere to go, nowhere to belong.

"Are you taking leave from work?" she said.

"I got fired. Stop asking me questions. Like I said, I'm not leaving this trailer for any reason."

"Listen, I've been waiting to talk to you, but there's never going to be a good time," she said.

Shit. Shelly needed to fire him, too? No good was going to come of this, not that he blamed her. WJ pulled the blankets over his head. What he couldn't see couldn't hurt. "So talk," he said.

"We're not working out, WJ. I know it's bad timing with your dad, and now your job, but I can't do this anymore. I'll be back in a few days to get the rest of my stuff."

Great. Now he was a single-unemployed-garbage-picking-murder-suspect-narc-recruit-crank-craving-broke-bastard.

"Then go."

"I love you, you know, or at least the old you. Call me, though, if you need anything. We'll stay friends."

No, they wouldn't. WJ wondered if he could hide under the blanket for the rest of his life. "I won't be calling you."

"Suit yourself. By the way, some guy called earlier. Asked for someone with your name, but he clearly had the wrong number."

Shelly could be an idiot.

Pissed off, WJ threw the blanket back. "If someone asked for me, how can it be the fucking wrong number?"

"Well, he said he didn't know if he had the right number, that he'd called many places for a Sloan who had been in the Navy. You weren't in the Navy, so I told him he had the wrong number. Who's stupid now?"

WJ sat up in bed. He'd never told Shelly or anyone about the Navy because he never wanted to answer questions about why he didn't stay in the fucking Navy. "What was his name?"

"What?" she asked and pulled on her jacket.

"What was the guy's name?"

"Joe something."

WJ's heart jumped to his throat. No fucking way! Joe? His Joe?

"But get this," she laughed, "he said he was some pastor at a church in San Francisco, Californ-I-A. I told him there was a Sloan but not anyone who'd been in the Navy and definitely not a Sloan who would want to talk to a pastor."

WJ's palms began to sweat. "Did you get his phone number?"

"Yeah." She slung her bag over her shoulder, pushed some papers around on the table, and handed him the slip. "Are you going to call him back and mess with his head?"

WJ handled the paper carefully between his shaking fingertips: Pastor Joseph Morgan and a 415 area code. "Something like that. Hey, don't tell anyone else about this message, okay?"

"Fine by me. I'm getting out of here. I'll be back in a few days for my stuff." She set a carton of cigarettes on the bed. "You'll need these. I'll get more for myself." She stopped at the door. "I'm sorry, WJ, about your life right now."

Yeah, him too.

After she left, WJ pulled out the letter from Harry and gently refolded it with Joe's message safely inside. He put the papers under the mattress. Joe? A pastor? Father Joe? No way. He wondered why Joe was finally looking for him after all of this time. Sure as shit, he wouldn't like who WJ had become.

A gay pastor and a gay-single-unemployed-garbage-picking-murder-suspect-narc-recruit-crank-craving-broke-bastard wouldn't have enough in common to make anything work. But he wished with all his heart they did. Like he always told Carrie, though, "You can shit in one hand and wish in the other—see which one fills up the quickest."

At least he had a real name: Walter Whitworth, Junior. But that was all he had.

39

CARRIE

ubiquitous \yoo̅ 'bikwətəs\ *adj 1 : present or found*
everywhere 2 : far-reaching, inescapable

W ell, what do you think?" Carrie pushed her potato chips aside and rested her elbows on the table. She looked at her ragged nails, pretending Mr. Hill's opinion didn't mean the world to her and that his support wasn't her only hope these days.

Mr. Hill set her paper down and removed his glasses. "It's okay for a first draft."

Her heart sank. She had failed. "Just okay?"

"It's supposed to be a scholarship essay, not hate mail. Your writing is very angry, but at the same time, impersonal. Now that could be understandable given your father's death, but think through this first."

"You told me to personalize my writing. I thought I did a very good job, considering the mom and dad I had to work with." Heat climbed her neck. Darn if she hadn't been more embarrassed in the past two days than ever. She clamped her lips closed and moved her jaw from side to side. Her parents were ruining her life. Her hope. "But fine. Whatever. I'll rewrite it. Maybe I'll make it all up."

"Slow down, Carrie. There is time to improve it and be truthful. The deadline isn't until Friday. Listen, you've written a beautifully-crafted critical essay of the books, but despite what you think, it's lacking. Well, except for the one line about your parents," he turned the page, "here it is, 'their endeavor to bask in constant suffering and rudimentary thinking.' Instead, show the correlations between the books and how some of these correlations have appeared in your own life. That's what the essay is supposed to be about. Scholarship committees, people in general, don't respond well to anger. It translates as victimization. Don't be a victim. Toss the anger, and pull in your intelligence. Show them your promise, how you have learned from your parents' mistakes, and how you're a good investment."

Carrie put her head in her hands and groaned. "In one thousand words or less? I'm so frustrated. I don't want to write about my family—period. I'm *not* my family."

"Then write about your father's death and how it's impacting your family. Write about how his death further inspires and motivates you to improve your own education and future."

"But that's not what the essay is about, and you just said to avoid victimization, and honestly, I feel like I'm being screwed over by my own parents. My dad quit and left me to worry about everyone and everything. He left me with little brothers and a selfish, crazy mother, one who might be planning to desert us . . . forget it." Carrie bit her lip and wished she could hit rewind. She couldn't take the risk of creating suspicion. If her mother was planning to leave her, and maybe the boys, too, she wasn't eighteen years old and couldn't be the boys' guardian, she couldn't even be on her own. They could end up in a foster home. None of her older brothers and sisters would, or should, take them. Lisa would be their best bet, but Carrie hadn't seen or heard from her since they found out Dad died. She'd disappeared just like Bobby and Michelle. One day they lived there, and the next they were gone, absentee siblings, forever. These were the worries that plagued her nonstop. It was like a messed-up puzzle with missing pieces, and she felt helpless to put it all together. What was going to happen to her and the boys in the short-term? She mentally scoffed. Maybe she should write about her true worries. Her brothers. Her life. Being stuck in a path of destruction paved by her parents' pathetic life choices. Yeah, scintillating reading. Not.

"Desert you?" Mr. Hill asked.

"Hypothetical. Never mind. Do you ever think we all would just be happier if everyone worked together and supported each other? I feel like my parents—or now my parent—and my older siblings only take care of themselves. It's like my family doesn't think there is enough of a good thing to go around, so they all scrap for the best of the worst, climb over each other, fight over rations, and then *boom* . . . they vanish when someone needs them. And that leaves me being no better than them and looking out for myself for college and so on and so on."

She looked at him. "Do you realize I've spent my entire life trying to differentiate myself from my family? Every year of school I've suffered through teachers saying, 'Oh, another Sloan. I taught your older brothers and sisters.' I've had to prove myself each and every time. Why can't it be a critical essay about the books rather than why my parents like them?

How do I differentiate myself from my own parents? I don't know how else to write it except the way I did. I know I'm right. My mom only likes a book where the man dies in the end, and my dad was obsessed with death. His death. They both got what they wanted in real life.

"And I can't get away from my family. Everything I try fails. Every effort I make to show who I really am," she beat her chest, "*who I am*, becomes tainted by my family. I'm trying to fly to the moon, but they're everywhere, all over the place, polluting the universe, and screwing with my space-ship. They're frigging meteoroids, and I'm a shooting star. You see? Yeah, I was born into my family, and we're all made up of the same elements, but I'm someone people can wish upon."

"So write about that. That's what your essay should say. And listen, talk to me as much as you want, okay? I can help get you counseling too. Whatever you need."

"Thanks, and I know. Principal Weimer told me the same thing, and she's making me check in with her each day. The thing is, talking isn't going to change anything. It doesn't seem real, you know? I don't feel like my dad is dead yet. A week ago, I was only focused on my schoolwork and scholarship applications. Now I'm not even sure what is going to happen to all of us. And I'm really afraid. What if I can't go to school now? I have another option now. The director of personnel offered me a full-time position when I graduate, but I feel like I'm giving up on a part of myself if I take the job and settle for community college. But I'll have to if I have to help my mom raise my brothers. My mom hasn't had a job in years, and she is the most horrible, selfish woman I know."

Mr. Hill said, "We will get you to college, Carrie. I promise."

She thought about how WJ had warned her to stop caring so much about promises that were easily broken.

"I think my mom will do anything she can to make sure I don't have a better life than her. No," she shook her head when he started to disagree with her, "it's true. You know what stands between me and a better life, Mr. Hill? My mother."

"I guess you do have some things to write and talk about after all," Mr. Hill said.

"Yeah, maybe." She grimaced. "I have to go."

He walked her to the classroom door. "Focus on your schoolwork and the scholarship essay. The Rotary interview is in two weeks. I'll check in with Principal Weimer and the counselor about your applications. Given your circumstances, you'll qualify for a Pell Grant, but your mom will have to help complete the application."

Carrie spun on her heels. Good thing she'd given herself permission to lie for a good reason. "Oh. No, you don't need to talk to my mom. My dad did the Pell Grant on Saturday, and both my parents signed it. I mailed it in yesterday."

"That's good news," Mr. Hill said. "I hope it's a consolation that your dad was thinking of you before he died, and it looks like your mom is supportive in her own way."

It was all relative, she thought. Literally.

After working her afternoon job and arriving at home that same day, Carrie saw two cop cars at her trailer.

She raced into the house, wondering what else could possibly go wrong. Her mom and brothers were silent and sitting on the couch. Carrie could hear rummaging coming from her parents' bedroom.

"What's going on?" she asked.

"We're in trouble," Tommy whispered.

"They have a search warrant," her mom said.

She looked horrible, like she'd been crying all morning.

"What? For what?"

Mom lifted her hands helplessly.

"Didn't you ask them?" Was she the only responsible person in the world anymore? "Did you check the warrant?"

Her mom glared at her with such malice Carrie couldn't help but wonder if her mother would stand up and slap her if the police weren't in the house.

"Yes, Carrie, I did. Believe it or not, I was trying to protect you," she said. "Your dad may have beaten someone senseless and put him in a coma. There, happy? See how great your father was?"

Carrie's eyes darted to Justin and Tommy, who were now staring at each other with wide eyes.

"What?" Carrie asked. "Who? Why?"

"The only one who knows is your dad, and he's dead," she said. "I'm so tired of going from being pissed at him to missing him, I can't even think straight anymore."

Based on her mom's empty tone and lost expression, Carrie wasn't even sure her mom meant to say that out loud. Carrie wiped her sweaty palms on her jean legs.

Oh Gawd, was that why he'd said goodbye? He left them because he almost killed someone.

She leaned forward and put her head between her legs. How many times had she assumed this position in the past few days? Twice. She gulped for air. A second later, she saw two little shoes in her line of vision and felt Tommy's small hand at the back of her neck. He bent over and tried to look up at her face.

She sat up slowly. "Come here." She pulled him on her lap and then beckoned Justin. "You too. Come sit over here." As the two boys climbed in the recliner with her, Carrie hugged them tight. She looked over Tommy's head at her mother, who was staring at them. Her mom frowned back. For the first time, Carrie saw a flash of something in her mother's eyes. Insecurity? Loneliness? Jealousy? Fear? The look was gone before she had time to digest its meaning.

Her mom looked away from them and down at her hands resting in her lap.

Carrie was shocked to see that her mom was wearing her dad's blue watch.

Oh, Mom. Who are you?

Mom caught her staring at her wrist and quickly covered the watch with her sleeve.

Carrie sat fascinated as her mom blushed.

They sat in silence for the next hour. When the officers provided a list of items they were taking from the house, Carrie frowned and met her mother's confused expression, both too disconcerted to ask why the police would want, among other things, Harry's old dentures, work boots, a comb, and the professional photo of him that had been hanging on the living room wall. Carrie watched her mom sign the sheet of paper and hand it back to the officer.

After they were gone, her mom asked her—actually asked her—if she could make dinner for the boys so she could leave and look for WJ. Like a robot, her mom walked out of the house.

Carrie ushered her brothers into the living room and turned on the television. "Find something to watch. I'll make dinner."

Justin asked, "Isn't a coma a really bad thing?"

"It is," Carrie confirmed, "but we don't know what happened. We'll just have to wait and see. And remember, someone is innocent until proven guilty. That's what our justice system says, anyway."

"Even when he's dead?" Justin asked.

Carrie paused. She thought about the theme she had tied to her dad's books. Justice. Had her dad beaten this man? And had he then dealt his own sentence for his actions? What was their small, claustrophobic world coming to?

After they had eaten chicken noodle soup and crackers, Carrie went into her bedroom. She tugged the metal chain to turn on the overhead light. It was dusk outside. As she turned toward her bookshelf, she paused. One of the shelves had been cleared and now stood empty. She did a quick inventory, but nothing was missing, just moved to the other shelves. The police hadn't been in her room. She returned to the living room.

"Justin. Tommy. Were you in my bedroom? Did you move stuff around on my bookshelf?"

"No."

Carrie checked her brothers' room. One of the room's shelves was empty, but for all she knew, it had always been. Books and toys were strewn about the floor. She turned and walked through her trailer, noting newly emptied boards. Her mother's room was in disarray from the earlier search, but Carrie found what she was looking for—an empty tier on the bookcase. She stepped closer and recognized her parents' books, combined on the lower level.

Nothing made sense anymore.

40

WJ

Better quit insulkin' me. I hit a dame once.
—Popeye

W J lay in bed, half asleep, trying to identify the annoying noise. The worst part about crashing from crank was the bone-aching tiredness. He weeble-wobbled between deep sleep and binge eating.

But something was disturbing his sleep. A bell? Oh, the phone. And then it stopped. When he woke later, he wasn't sure what time it was, but darkness peeked between the cracked blinds. He stumbled in the pitch dark, starving. He turned on the light above the sink and grabbed some peanut butter.

The plant he'd taken from his mother was on his kitchen counter and turning yellow. "Dammit, Fern, I'm letting you down." He'd heard once that plants liked to be talked to. He squirted some plant food in the soil and then held the plant under the faucet. "You're going to be okay. Okay?" He hated how shit-poor desolate he felt.

He wondered why Joe was finally looking for him, but the baggage of Harry's death and the threat of the police smothered what little happiness Joe's effort provided. Besides, there was no point in getting his hopes up. Joe was trying to find the WJ he'd known a long time ago.

It wouldn't be long before the detective lost patience and grabbed him by his gonads. *Weakness and Sloppy Work.* His choices probably included prison, excommunication by the Knights, and/or being a narc. Not talking to Joe again. Damn depressing.

All his sloppy work wrapped around his chest and neck like a hungry python. He already knew the detective would win in the long run. Damn Hefty. Damn Harry's car. He crawled into bed and pulled the pile of blankets on top of him. He thought of how he had always liked the weight of blankets, and then he fell asleep.

Someone was banging on the door. When he was able to make his way to the door and slide the lock free, he was disappointed to see his mom.

"Go away," he said but kept an eye on her as he moved back to his bed. Couldn't trust her anymore. Guess he never did.

"You don't answer your phone. You don't call. You just disappear like every other man," she said and grimaced as she stepped inside. She waved her hands before her face. "I'm going to leave this door open."

"Good, you're leaving anyway."

"Oh no I'm not," she said. "I want to talk to you. I want you to tell me what's going on." She walked over to his bedside, lifted her red boot, and nudged his thigh. "What in the hell is wrong with you? Finally giving up drugs, I hope."

WJ grunted.

She mimicked his grunt.

His eyes followed her as she went to the kitchen, and he was satisfied when she stopped short at Fern.

"Is this my plant?" His mom poked the pot.

"Not anymore. You neglected it just like you neglected me. It's my plant now."

"Well, you're killing it with kindness. You're overwatering it." She pushed at the dirty dishes with the tip of her finger until she found an empty cup and filled it with cold coffee. She slammed the microwave closed and set the timer.

"Do you have to be so loud? Take a hint and leave me alone."

"Drink this, WJ. I'll make you something to eat. If I have to feed you to find out what your dad's last words were, then I will."

"Name is Walter," he whispered. His toes practically curled with victory when she hesitated and leaned forward.

"What did you say?" she asked and squinted at him.

He licked his lips like a cat who had just caught a mouse and watched his mom press her hand against her chest in surprise.

"You heard me."

"No, I don't think I did. Say it again."

All of the resentment he felt for her boiled inside him and oozed from his pores. His anger smelled like burnt hair, and he hoped she could smell it too. He stared at her until she turned away and busied herself with some white bread and government-issued cheese.

"Chickenshit," WJ sneered.

"Don't talk to me like that, and I don't have time for your passive aggressive crap. If you have something to say to me, say it," she said.

They sat in silence while he smacked down his cheese sandwich and drank his coffee.

"What did your dad tell you on Saturday night? My bet is you're the last one who saw him before he killed himself. The police searched our trailer tonight. I know you know something."

WJ shot up in bed. "That official? They said Harry offed himself?"

"No, the coroner said death by hanging." She paled and shook her head. "I hate even saying that out loud. I'm trying to put the pieces together because I can't believe he's gone and that he'd go without saying goodbye. The police won't say if it was suicide, yet, or if his death is still suspicious. But I went to the motel. The door . . . it was horrible."

Yeah, he remembered.

"What happened when you saw him?" she asked.

"I didn't touch him, if that's what you're really asking. I already told you, I went over there and picked up the boys. I wanted to teach him a lesson, but not with the boys there."

"So you left with the boys, brought them home, and then what? How did your dad's car end up at the park? The cops know you had his car, do you know that?"

"Doesn't matter," he said, and it didn't because the detective already had him in the palm of her tiny hand, and not in a good way. Joe crossed his mind, and WJ clung to the hope he still had a friend and then dropped it because what would Joe want to do with someone like him?

"Look at me," she said.

He looked and was surprised by what he saw. She looked softer and really fucking sad.

Her shoulders and head dropped, and she was fiddling with her hands in her lap.

Ah, her weakness. Her vulnerability. She really wanted something from him, and her betrayal about his name, the years of lies about his identity, fired him up. He was ready for revenge.

"Please. Did your dad say anything? He must have said goodbye. Somehow."

He heard her sniffle, and he could feel Harry's letter burning through his mattress and warming his ass. "Nope. Nada."

She lifted her face and looked hard at him, like he was some fucking two-year-old she could manipulate. Not today, Mommie Dearest. You took me away from my real dad. Her wet eyes sent satisfaction through his body. Her sadness and lack of control were more satisfying than crank.

"I don't believe you. I think you're hiding something," she said.

"Fine," WJ said. "He said you ruined his life. You were the worst thing that ever happened to him." He waited, anticipating hearing her chest crack open like an uprooted tree in a windstorm, but it didn't.

Instead, she stood up. "You're lying, but I'm done begging. You better watch yourself, son. If you don't want to tell me what happened when you saw your father, I can't make you, but the police are asking questions. Lots of them."

He decided to give her some truth, if only to hurt her more. "Fine. You want to know about his last moments? I went back over to his motel, but when I got there, he was already dead. He hung himself on the door, but his rope came loose or something. I found him on the chair and cut the rest of the rope from around his neck. He didn't leave a letter."

She closed her eyes. "I went by the room to get his stuff. I saw the crack in the bathroom door." She squeezed the bridge of her nose and closed her eyes.

WJ moved in for the kill. "You know what I think? This is your fault. He died for you. But that's not enough for you. You're still not happy. You think he owed you a goodbye too. You should be grateful. The idiot thought he was doing you a favor." But WJ didn't get the response he was hoping for. Instead, his mother perked up.

"How do you know he thought he was doing us a favor?"

Shit. His head was so messed up from withdrawals he'd given her a hint.

"You know something you aren't telling me. He told you he was going to do it, didn't he? You were supposed to tell me."

"Shut up. You think you know me? Some motherly instinct shit or something? Well, you don't. You haven't for a long time, and you haven't cared to know who I am. He was miserable and a failure." WJ looked around his own space. "I don't need to be a mind reader to know he thought everyone would be better off without him. And you know what? He was right. You're all better off without him, except for me because you led me to believe he had hurt one of you, and you manipulated me into hunting him down on Saturday night, and now I'm tied to a bunch of shit I didn't do. I didn't touch him. He killed himself."

She sighed. "Did he tell you he pawned the trailers and cars?"

WJ averted his gaze and rolled on his side, his back toward her. "No."

"Why don't I believe you?" she asked.

"I don't know, and I don't care. Now leave me alone!"

"Well, you better start caring," she said. "They're keeping

his car, and they searched the trailers. Something was in that car that tied him to the victim in the hospital, and that car is tied to you now too. I've already lost a husband. I don't want to lose you too." His mom grabbed her purse and headed toward the door. Before she slammed it closed, she said, "Get yourself together, WJ, and stay sober. The funeral is Thursday afternoon."

WJ waited for her to close the door. He balled his fists and roared, "My name is Walter!"

The front door swung back open.

His mother looked like an owl. The light from the sink highlighted her wide eyes. He could see her swallowing, her throat bobbing and creating shadows in the small light.

"When did Harry tell you?"

WJ pushed himself to the end of the bed and put all his loathing into his eyes.

She took a step back.

"When did Harry tell me? When did Harry tell me? Why the fuck wasn't it you who told me? Get out of my sight. I can't stand to look at you!"

He took pleasure in hearing her boots slipping and sliding against the gravel as she hurried to her car and left.

WJ grabbed his phone. If it was bugged, he no longer fucking cared. He dialed information.

"City and name please?" the operator asked.

"Lincoln County. Whitworth." WJ said.

"I have a William and June Whitworth. Would you like me to connect you?"

Yes, by damn, he would. He needed something positive in his life. He had no friends. No Shelly. And Joe was out of his league now. He needed a new family. His real family. "Yes, please."

When the ringing stopped and a man answered, WJ pushed himself to carry through this time. "Can I speak to Walter Whitworth?"

The man raised his voice. "Are you the same person who called the other day? Walter's been dead thirty years this month. Don't call here again," he said and hung up.

Holding the receiver, WJ turned against the wall and slid to the floor. In seven months, he'd turn thirty.

41

JANICE

Your Cheatin' Heart
—Patsy Cline

As Janice ran toward her car, betrayal flared in her rib cage, making it hard to breathe.

Damn you, Harry. How dare you tell WJ about Walter?

She sped away from WJ's trailer. Her leg was shaking, and her foot bounced against the gas pedal. She slammed the palm of her hand against the steering wheel. The dreaded tears of frustration began to pour down her face. If she kept on like this, she was going to get in a wreck and kill herself, and despite losing Nashville, Harry, and now WJ, she wasn't ready to throw in the towel and die.

When did Harry tell him, and why hadn't he warned her?

This final betrayal of Harry's was too much. Harry had put her in a position to be caught off guard by her own son. She hated feeling vulnerable more than any other feeling, and Harry knew that. There were good surprises and bad surprises, and she wasn't so great at either, but being thrown

under the bus was a bad one. If only Harry had told her that
he'd told WJ or wanted to tell WJ, she could have at least
prepared herself, had time to decide how and what she'd tell
him. But no, she'd had to sit there under WJ's microscope,
feeling humiliated and judged. He'd looked at her like she
was some kind of floozy who'd gotten pregnant during a one-
night stand and then stolen his birthright.

Two years after Walter died, she'd gotten a letter from
Grandma. Walter's older brother, William, had married
June Black.

Grandma had written:

> *Sorry, Janice, but the whole town thinks it's touching how
> William and June grew close and fell in love after they lost
> Walter. The Whitworths believe more than ever that June
> was the girl Walter had intended to talk to them about
> marrying. Right or wrong, sometimes people only see
> what's right before their eyes.*

What would her life have been like if she and Walter had
dated openly? What fools they'd been to think it was
romantic to share a secret love. That secret had turned out to
be a rolling stone gaining momentum. She'd never told the
Whitworths the truth. She lied to Grandfather, Grandma, and
Great Aunt about her intentions to keep the baby even though
she took and agreed to their support. She had lied to Harry
about being a widow when she met him. They lied to WJ
once the adoption went through. She and Harry lied to each
other all the time. Lied about drinking, lied about money—
hiding it here, gambling it there. And she was still lying. She
was lying to the police about being aware of Harry's injuries.
She was lying about WJ having Harry's car. She was lying

about and hiding her karaoke money. She was lying to Carrie about her scholarship. The pathetic list went on and on, and if the past was anything to go by, the list would grow.

Why had she continued to lie? Had it ever really mattered? Would the truth have been so bad? So hard? Who had she really been protecting? Herself?

The truth would have been easier. Life might have been easier.

The truth shall set you free, she thought. She'd heard these words so many times, and they had never meant anything to her before now.

Her life had become one big fat lie and would continue as one if she didn't start making some changes.

Nothing changes if nothing changes. She'd read her tattoo so many times but had never applied the wisdom before now.

She owed WJ the whole story now, no matter how afraid she was to tell him. It would be hard to explain that she'd been trying to protect him from the truth when the result was having Harry as an abusive father.

She thought about Carrie's obsessive list-keeping, the lists Carrie claimed gave her direction. She mentally ticked off the list of her lies, past and current. She mentally checked off the people in her life and realized her friend Scotty was the only one she was ever honest with, sometimes by omission only, but she hadn't lied to him about the funeral costs or wanting to leave, and because she'd told him the truth, he'd offered to pay for the funeral even though he knew about her winnings. Heck, he was holding onto her winnings for her, and he still wanted to pay for the funeral. She'd been honest with the pastor too, and thanks to him, earlier that day Janice had gone home and cleared shelves throughout the house for hope, faith, and opportunities.

By the time Janice pulled herself together and got home, Carrie was doing her never-ending homework, waiting up for her once again.

"Did you find WJ?" her daughter asked.

"Yes," Janice said and poured a glass of milk.

"Did you empty one of my bookshelves in my room?" Carrie asked.

Janice's first impulse was to lie and say no because she didn't want Carrie yelling at her for being in her room, but no more lies. "Yes."

"Why?" Carrie asked.

"Pastor Henry told me that he leaves a shelf open for hope, faith, and opportunity, and I figured we all needed some. Do you have a problem with that?"

Janice watched a variety of emotions flick across Carrie's face before Carrie looked away. Uncertainty. Confusion. Humor. At least not one of them was disdain.

"No," Carrie said. "Thank you."

Janice mentally added one line to her list of truths.

She went into her room and wrote a story, a true story. She pulled out *Jane Eyre* and removed WJ's original birth certificate and Walter's photo. She carefully added the three items to an envelope and wrote "WJ" across the front.

Janice mentally added a second line to her truth inventory. She turned off the lamp and crawled into bed.

42

JANICE

Walkin' After Midnight
—Patsy Cline

Wednesday, April 12, 1989

J anice laid in her twin bed all night, unable to sleep. For hours she stared at her husband's forever empty twin bed, reflecting on their life together. Harry had stood between her and greatness.

The thing about looking at truths and lies was she could no longer deny how she'd lied to herself. Carrie's scholarship letter haunted Janice from beneath her mattress. She was standing between Carrie and greatness.

Carrie had never messed up. She always did everything the right way. Since her birth, it seemed, she'd always gone against the family grain. She walked sooner than everyone; she learned her alphabet from *Sesame Street*; she wanted a globe for her fourth birthday; and once she started kindergarten, she had been obsessed with school. In fifth grade, when asked what she wanted for her birthday, she said, "For no one to get drunk."

And Janice had felt personally responsible, as a good mother, to show Carrie that life wasn't easy and that she'd better keep her feet on the ground and her head out of the clouds. Great things were meant for other people, not the Sloan family. Look at her as an example—she'd had big dreams, and she didn't get any of them. Giving up on them had almost killed her, and as a good mother, she hadn't wanted Carrie to have the same delusion. In hindsight, she'd thought it was best for Carrie to receive the disillusionment from someone who loved her the best she could: Janice.

Janice had been wrong. Selfish. She saw that now.

Carrie's hopes were impossible to defeat. Janice wondered if it was because she'd taken her to church more than the other kids. Janice had one stretch of faith that lasted around seven months, and they went to church every Sunday. Just her and Carrie. When Janice had stopped attending, Carrie, who'd been in the fourth grade at the time, had started walking to church on her own. Though Janice ignored Carrie's high grades and the cherry-smelling scratch-n-sniff stickers in her school folder, Carrie continued to strive, excel in her studies. She didn't seem to care about or need Janice's approval, and that was the worst betrayal of all. Janice's resentment had begun to blossom in the wake of Carrie's rising self-worth. Who did she think she was? Why should Carrie get to be happy and content? And Carrie had friends too—friends with wealthy parents and big houses. A few times, Janice drove her to a friend's house and felt the embarrassment and shame of the heap of junk she was driving.

Carrie hadn't seemed to mind one bit as she jumped out of the car, so Janice told her she either had to start paying for gas with her babysitting money or start riding her bike. She didn't care if she didn't make her other kids do the same; they weren't making her humiliate herself by exposing her to her financial betters.

As kids disappeared and Carrie's confidence grew, Janice's resentment and bitterness grew. As Carrie's awareness and disappointment surfaced, her judgment surfaced, and Janice thought she needed to be brought down a peg or two. But Carrie kept going, and Janice had been angry at her for it.

For the first time in her life, Janice recognized she'd been holding Carrie responsible for everything wrong in her own life. Her grandparents had offered her freedom, and she'd made the choice to keep WJ. She'd made the choice to marry Harry and stay with him. She'd made the choice to have every child, including Carrie. Carrie had nothing to do with any of it. Carrie had to do with Carrie. It was that simple.

As soon as Carrie and the boys left for school, Janice walked into Carrie's room and placed the scholarship letter from the university on Carrie's empty shelf.

Cross off a lie, and add truth number three.

After a shower, Janice called information to get the library's phone number in Lincoln County, Minnesota.

"Lincoln County Library, how can I help you?" a woman answered.

"Hi, I'm settling up some old debts and need to make arrangements to buy a past due book from you," Janice said. "*Jane Eyre*."

"We don't normally sell past due books. When was it due?"

Janice cleared her throat. This should be good. "April of 1959."

The woman laughed. "Well, in that case, we would have to sell you the book—you're right." After a moment, she continued, "Can I get your name? I'll be needing to run to the back room and look in our archives."

"Janice Sloan. I mean Brecker. Janice Brecker." It had been decades since she'd used her maiden name, but, of course, that was what the book would have been reserved under.

"Holy Toledo. Janice Brecker? It's me, June Black. Except I'm June Whitworth now."

Another insane surprise. Of all frigging people. June Black! Janice had no interest in talking to June. June who had lied about Walter.

"If I could just get the amount due, thank you," Janice said. She hoped her voice sounded as self-righteous as she felt.

"Oh, okay. It's just so nice to hear a voice from someone in my youth. Most people moved away. You must have been the first to leave us behind. And William and I, well, we had tried to find you at one point, but the name Sloan explains why we couldn't. Funny how your grandparents never mentioned your name had changed."

Wait, what? Why would they have tried to find her? "It's my married name. I don't understand why you would've been looking for me, though."

"Can you hold on a second while I hop on a phone in a private area?"

Janice really wanted to hang up. This truths business, including settling her old debt with *Jane Eyre*, was harder than she expected. She just wanted to pay her dues and move on. But she waited.

"Okay, I'm sorry, but I needed some privacy," June said. "Well, I was just wondering if you might have Walter's class ring?"

Janice choked and thought she might be faint again. She sat down and breathed deeply. How could June know that? "Why?"

"Listen, there's no easy way to explain this, so I'll just get to it. The day Walter died, William and I had intended to tell his parents that we wanted to get married. William told Walter first. Walter had been so happy for us, and he told William that he was in love too, and wanted to get married. But then his horrible accident happened, and we were all devastated and grieving, so we waited to tell his parents about us until a few months later, and we all agreed we should wait a year for mourning and then a year for public courting. The only hint Walter gave William was that he'd used his class ring as an engagement ring. But their parents, well, they thought Walter had been sweet on me, and it was all very confusing. We never told the Whitworths about Walter's ring. It seemed cruel to get their hopes up. Over the next several months, William and I couldn't find anyone with Walter's ring, and, well, you were the only person who we never saw again after Walter's accident."

Janice swallowed. "Walter told William he was going to talk to his parents about getting married?"

"Yes," June said.

Janice started to cry right then and there on the phone with June Black of all people. Yes, in her heart she had always known Walter had loved her and wanted to marry her, but she'd always had to work on faith alone. Now she knew.

Other people knew, even if it was only June and Walter's brother William.

"You have the ring," June said softly.

"Yes," Janice whispered.

The truth shall set you free, indeed. When she finally collected herself, Janice asked, "June, what if I told you that Walter and I have a son? His name is Walter Junior." She added a check to her truth list.

June gasped. "Oh, Janice." And then, "When can we meet him?"

Gratitude consumed Janice. "It will have to be on his terms because he only found out this week. But can I give him your number?"

"This week? I wonder if he doesn't already have our number," June said.

"Why would you think that?" Janice asked.

"Because twice this week, a man has called asking for Walter."

"He doesn't know Walter died."

June sighed. "Unfortunately, he does now."

Oh, WJ, hold on. My letter will explain everything.

Still gobsmacked by her conversation with June, Janice called Detective Anderson. She was on a roll now, and the sooner she could check the detective off her list, the sooner she could take her letter to WJ.

"Mrs. Sloan," the detective said, "I understand you were cooperative with the search yesterday. Thank you."

Janice swallowed and wrapped the phone cord around her finger, unwrapped it, and wrapped it again. "I've remembered something." She paused. Okay, so she'd noticed Harry's banged-up fist immediately, but a little fib that allowed her to tell the truth wasn't really a lie, was it? "I've remembered something about Harry, something about his hand, the morning we fought. Before I filed the restraining order. I'd like to speak to you as soon as possible. I can stop by now."

"I'll be waiting," Detective Anderson said.

43

CARRIE

dido \ ˈdī͵dō\ *n : perform mischievous pranks or deeds*

H ey, Carrie. Wait up!" That Guy shouted.

Carrie was on her way to the counselor's office after being called out of fourth period.

"Hey, where are you headed?" he asked.

Show off. He wasn't even breathing hard after running to catch up with her.

"Counselor's office. You?"

"I'm actually leaving for the day. My parents and I are driving to Stanford this afternoon. I have orientation tomorrow."

"Stanford? You get to go to Stanford?"

"Yeah."

"Wow. Congratulations. I'm impressed." She turned forward and picked up her pace. Stanford? How could he get into and pay for Stanford when she couldn't even win a scholarship? She didn't want him to ask her any more questions about school. She didn't want to admit she might be going to the community college.

"What about you?"

Ugh. "UNR." Fingers crossed.

"Cool."

So not cool if she couldn't afford it.

"Hey, can you stop walking for a second? I want to ask you something."

Carrie slowed her step. Oh boy, she thought, despite her discouragement, here it comes.

"I wanted to know if you wanted to go with me to—"

Carrie interrupted him by putting up her hand. She turned to him and sighed. "Stop. No, I don't want to go to prom. I can't afford makeup, remember? I definitely can't afford a dress. Besides, despite first impressions, I wouldn't get drunk and throw myself at you."

That Guy turned a deep red, and he looked away.

"Oh Gawd, you weren't asking me to prom." She could die. Just die.

"Erm, no, the college fair. I was going to ask if you wanted to catch a ride with me next week. Mrs. W said you wanted to work the booth, and I am working it too. It's in Reno."

"Oh my Gawd, of course not, why would you ask me to prom? Don't answer that." Carrie felt tears of humiliation. "Oh, Gawd." She hiked her backpack up on her shoulder and marched stiffly to the offices. "I have to go. The counselor is waiting."

"Carrie, wait!" he yelled after her. "I would've, you know? I tried. But I knew you'd say no."

"Right," she mumbled and kept walking. Right.

Carrie walked into the counselor's office. She could guess what Mr. Crown wanted to talk to her about. Both Mrs. Weimer and Mr. Hill had said they'd get the counselor to follow up with UNR. She prepared herself to learn that there'd be no college in the cards for her.

She'd just had one order of humiliation, but she'd take a side of utter disappointment, please.

When she saw that Mr. Hill was also in the room, she figured the more to witness her rejection the merrier. It was like her very own private support group.

"Hello, Carrie," Mr. Crown said, "have a seat."

She sat down without saying anything.

"First off, I'm terribly sorry to hear about your father."

She nodded. Let's get this over with.

"I have some good news I know you can use." He smiled and leaned forward.

Really? Impossible. "Okay," she said.

"I just got off the phone with the Admissions Office at the University of Nevada, Reno, and not only have you been accepted—they are giving you a full-ride scholarship. It will cover your tuition and housing. And the university is holding a work-study job for you to help with your incidental expenses. You can work up to twenty hours a week on campus. Now, you only need to find the funds for your books, and I am hopeful the Pell Grant will take care of that. I will follow up with financial aid next week."

"What?"

"Congratulations." Mr. Crown nodded toward Mr. Hill. "And Mr. Hill says you are working on your scholarship essay and have an interview with the Rotary Club."

"But what?" Carrie started to cry. She couldn't stop herself. Her cries took on a life of their own, and her chest heaved with her sobs. She hid her face with her hands. The stress was flowing from her body. Her hopes were uncoiling. College was the last thing she had expected to discuss with the counselor this morning and the only thing she so desperately needed to hear.

They let her cry, and she was grateful they didn't say anything during her breakdown, though she was sure they didn't know what to say anyway. When she finally stopped and looked up, Mr. Crown had set a box of Kleenex on the desk before her.

She blew her nose several times. "But I never received a letter. I've been checking every day. Every single day."

"Mr. Hill and I called yesterday, and they promised to get back to us this morning, and they did. We figured you could use some good news at this point in your life."

She nodded. "I never expected a full scholarship." Her chest shuddered.

Mr. Crown opened her file. She tried to read his scribbled notes upside down. "When students apply to UNR, all applications automatically go into the freshman scholarship pool for the university's foundation. This is how you qualified. They said you should have received an award letter weeks ago. They are faxing us a copy. And I am optimistic about the amount you'll receive from a Pell Grant."

Carrie covered her mouth, trying to stop another round of crying. She looked from Mr. Crown to Mr. Hill. "Mr. Hill, can you believe it?"

"You're on your way, Carrie. You're a shooting star," he said.

44

JANICE

Anybody that'll stand up to The Cline is all right.
—Patsy Cline

Janice flipped through the state phone numbers until she found the one for Social Security. She was hardly breathing. Why hadn't she thought of it herself? Honesty pays, she thought, honesty literally pays.

Janice had arrived at the police department hours earlier, and the detective had been waiting for her in the lobby. Instead of leading her to the questioning room Janice had been in before, the confident detective invited Janice to her private office. It was much more comfortable.

"Thank you for coming in, Mrs. Sloan," Detective Anderson said and handed her a cup of coffee while she once again pulled up a chair on the same side of the desk as Janice.

Different room, but same "let's be friends" strategy.

Janice took the coffee this time, and what the heck, she could use a friend. "Okay, so this isn't easy for me."

"Take your time," the detective said.

Sergeant Meed tapped on the door and entered. "Mrs. Sloan."

"Oh, okay. Good. I'm glad you're here too, Meed. So, when I filed the restraining order? After Harry had, um, pushed me around a bit? Well, our fight started because he'd woken up that morning before I was awake. He tried to wake me, asked me if I was okay, I was, and I went back to sleep. He'd gotten home before me the night before. When I got home, he was already passed out in his bed. He can black out sometimes and doesn't remember anything."

Detective Anderson maintained eye contact.

Sergeant Meed was taking notes.

"Anyway, since I was half asleep, I didn't really think much of his waking me to ask me if I was okay. But when I did wake up, it hit me what he had asked and, well, since he had blacked out in the past, I was concerned. I checked on my boys first, but they were gone. Harry had taken them to breakfast, so by the time they got home, I was irritated and anxious. I confronted Harry, and his fists were a mess. He'd hurt them the night before, the night you asked me about, but he couldn't remember what he'd done. I know you saw his hands were banged up when you found him on Sunday, but yeah, the wounds happened the week before on Friday night."

Detective Anderson remained silent for a few moments and then let out a long sigh and leaned forward. "Did Harry drive his car that night? That Friday night?"

Janice nodded. "He'd taken it to work and then the Creek Bar after. He left the bar without telling me. When I got home, it was parked outside. So, yeah, he had his car."

Honesty. She ticked another item off her inventory of lies

and moved it to the truth column. She answered calmly as they asked her simple questions.

Sergeant Meed was walking her out of the building when he offered, "We sent over the death record to the funeral home today. They should have the certificate for you. I'm sure you'll need it to file for your husband's social security benefits."

How in the hell had she forgotten about social security? She could've kissed Meed for reminding her. She rushed home, anxious as all get-out.

Janice's thoughts snapped back to the present when the operator answered on the third ring. "United States Department of Social Security. How may I direct your call?"

Janice imagined her heavy breathing made her sound like a pervert getting ready to ask the operator what color of underwear she was wearing. "Hello, my husband just passed away, and I need to apply for his benefits."

"One minute please."

"Survivor Benefits. This is Carol, how may I help you?"

Survivor Benefits. There might be a benefit to surviving. "Hi, my name is Janice Sloan. My husband passed away this weekend, and I'm not sure if I can receive any aid from his social security benefits?"

"I'm sorry to hear about your loss, Mrs. Sloan. We'll need to set up an appointment for you to come into the office, but I can take the details over the phone, give you some information, and then we can finalize the paperwork when you come in. We'll need to schedule your appointment after you have the death certificate. Have you received it yet?"

"I am getting it this afternoon from the funeral home. The funeral is tomorrow," Janice said. She bit into her fingernail.

Please, God.

"Okay, let me first gather some information."

Once Janice had given the woman Harry's social security number, date of birth, and a list of surviving dependents under the age of eighteen or still in school, Carol put her on hold.

Janice was worried she was going to vomit while she waited and tried not to pull her hair out while listening to the elevator music.

"Thank you for waiting. I can give you some preliminary information now, and if you can come in Friday morning at ten a.m., we can finalize the paperwork."

"Fine." Janice's teeth chattered. She sat down in the vinyl chair that Harry used to sit in each night and drink his beer after work.

"Since your husband was not yet sixty-five, his benefits are slightly decreased."

Janice knew it was too good to be true. She dropped her head. Squeezing the receiver against her face. "Okay."

She'd take what she could get. Who knew when her home and car would be taken from her, and she had the boys to care for. Ugh. One mess at a time. One mess at a time. Other things were starting to go her way, so she needed to focus on the hope, faith, and opportunity she'd opened up on all their shelves.

"Having said that," Carol continued, "as his widow, you are entitled to eight hundred and twenty-five dollars a month."

Janice could not believe what she was hearing. "Really— eight hundred and twenty-five dollars? Monthly?" Harry's take-home after taxes per month had been twelve hundred a month, and that was only if she was lucky enough to intercept him between payroll and the casinos.

"Yes, really," Carol confirmed. "And your three children

under the age of eighteen and in school qualify for two hundred and twenty-five dollars per month, but as benefits cannot exceed one thousand two hundred dollars a month, you will receive twelve hundred per month. Are the three children remaining in your care?"

Janice blinked. Several times.

"Mrs. Sloan?"

"Ah, yes. Yes. Okay. Okay." Janice ran her free hand through her hair. "I'm sorry. I'm in a bit of shock. It had not occurred to me."

"I understand. I hope you find some comfort in this information. Bring the death certificate with you on Friday, and we can finalize the application for benefits."

Janice hung up in a daze. Harry may have been horrible with money, but he'd always worked hard. She wondered if he knew when he died that he would finally be taking care of her. Perhaps it had been his way of saying goodbye. With twelve hundred dollars and her winnings, she might be able to get them all to Nashville.

Before her sons got home from school, Janice drove back out to WJ's trailer. He answered when she knocked, looking the worse for wear. He clearly hadn't left his trailer. She wished she could sit with him while he read the letter, comfort him about losing the dad he never got to meet, but that wasn't the kind of relationship they had.

"I told you to stay away from me," he said.

She handed him a bag of groceries and an envelope. "WJ, you can read this, or not. It's up to you. Don't lose the name and number I put on the envelope, but I think you probably already know it by heart. And the funeral is tomorrow."

"I am Walter!"

She started to walk away but called over her shoulder, "Well, you're also an asshole, but I don't always call you that either."

45

CARRIE

perplexed \pər-plekst\ *adj 1 : filled with uncertainty 2 :*
complicated

When Carrie arrived home from work, the boys were in the living room and playing in a fort they'd made out of blankets. "Where's Mom?" she asked.

"She's getting us a new pizza," Justin said.

"I should hope the pizza would be new. No one likes old pizza," Carrie joked.

"Good one," Tommy said. "It's called Hawaiian pizza."

"Ah, so new to you." Her mom and dad had gotten Hawaiian for themselves on special occasions. What was her mom celebrating? Even if the school called her and told her about Carrie's scholarship, Carrie doubted it would warrant her mom's favorite pizza.

"Want a tour of our fort?" Tommy asked.

"You bet I do. Let me put my stuff away. I'll be right back."

The first thing she saw was the thick envelope on her empty shelf. *It figured*—after weeks of stress and feeling down and out, of course, the scholarship packet would arrive the same day Mr. Hill and Mr. Crown told her about it. She'd even still checked the mailbox when she got home, still disappointed not to have anything she could hold in her hands. She hadn't read anything for herself and had only been told the good news. But now she could hold it all she wanted. She could memorize the letter if she wanted. Heck, she could sleep with it! It was all hers.

She threw her backpack on her bed and went for it. The heavy stock and the weight of the packet was everything she'd been dreaming about for months. "Woo-hoo!" she screamed, and the boys came running.

"What?" they yelled as they pushed open her door.

"I'm going to college!"

"Woo-hoo!" They copied her and screamed over and over. They grabbed her arms and made her jump around in a circle.

Gawd, when was the last time she'd laughed like this? And with the boys too.

She shook off their hands to open the envelope. The flap had been carefully pulled back and the glue separated. A red lipstick smudge the size of a fingertip said more than words ever could. She imagined her mom tapping her lips before she built up the nerve to not only open mail that didn't belong to her but to hide it.

Excitement over, the boys ran back to their fort.

Carrie checked the postage date on the front. Sure enough —the date was two months ago.

Her letter was never lost; it was taken, but now it was on her bookshelf. Her blank bookshelf for hope, faith, and opportunity from her mom. Carrie didn't know whether to be pissed or relieved. She lay back on her bed and watched the shooting star mobile in the window, accepting once again that she did not understand her mother at all.

46

WJ

I'm Popeye the sailor man.
—Popeye

W J read the letter from his mother for the millionth time. He turned the 1959 class ring on his finger. Perfect fit. He could've had an entirely different life and family. He could've been a different person. He rubbed his chest above his heart. Funny how he hurt for someone and something he didn't know existed five days ago.

His mom explained everything. How his dad died and why she never told his family. All these years he thought she'd ditched her grandparents for no good reason. But she'd left them for him. They gave her a choice, and his mom chose him, and from the sounds of it, Harry chose him too. Maybe he'd never totally understand what kind of parents his mom, Walter, and Harry had hoped to be.

The phone number of his newly identified aunt and uncle was written on the envelope, along with their names. It was the same number he'd dialed twice before. With it, his mom added, "When you're ready, they'd like to meet you." He would call them, but he would take some time. What had Harry told Rudy? That WJ just had "a few things to figure out." Harry was damn right about that.

His mom included his original birth certificate showing his full name, Walter Whitworth, Junior. Of all the things his mom could've given him, this was the one that had made him cry like a baby. It was just a simple sheet of fucking paper, but it was everything. It was a new beginning. A clean slate.

Walter's photo was next. He had his dad's nose.

WJ took out Harry's last words and Joe's message and spread them out next to the items from his mom.

He picked up the phone and called the police department. As soon as the detective's sissy-ass voice came on the line, WJ said, "I want to be cut loose. What information do I need to give you, motherfucker?"

47

CARRIE

resilience \ri'zilyəns\ *n : the capacity to recover quickly from difficulties; toughness*

Her mom parked in front of the trailer and turned off the engine. "Go ahead," her mom said, "I'll be in after a few."

"Okay," Carrie said, but she didn't move right away. She stared at her mother's pale face. The funeral had been draining. So many people had shown up. Carrie didn't even know her dad had so many friends or people who'd liked him. And they'd all wanted to pay their respects to her mom. Thank Gawd they'd never intended to host a reception, but Scotty invited everyone to the Creek for a beer. Carrie had been relieved when her mom had passed for now and said she'd stop by later.

"Can we get out?" the boys asked.

"Yeah, come on, you two." Carrie got out and stood between them with a hand on each of their shoulders as they walked to the back door.

"Can I go sit in the playhouse?" Tommy asked.

"Why?"

He shrugged his shoulders. "I helped Dad build it."

She squatted down before him and put her hands on his shoulders.

Justin stayed by her side and leaned into her. His small elbow dug into her shoulder.

"Not right now, Tommy. Let's stay together, okay?" she asked. She smoothed her hands up and down his arms.

He sniffled.

She stood and ruffled Justin's hair and then opened the door.

Star was waiting and ran a figure eight around Justin and Tommy's ankles.

"We can play a board game. Or do you want to watch TV?"

"TV," the boys said in unison.

"Go and see what's on. How about some ice cream?"

They nodded.

Carrie hefted the gallon plastic container of fudge marble ice cream out of the freezer. She set her hands on the counter on either side of the ice cream. Dirty dishes filled the sink. "Screw it," she said and pulled out the silverware drawer, grabbed three different-sized spoons, and carried the ice cream by its red handle into the living room. She sat down on the floor and leaned her back against the couch, setting the bucket on her lap.

"Come and get it," she said.

Justin and Tommy sat on either side of her and dug in. They all sat forward and stared at the TV.

The back door opened, and Carrie listened to her mother walk toward her bedroom.

Carrie couldn't eat more than a bite. She hadn't been able to keep much down lately.

"Dad's hair looked funny at the wake," Tommy said as he took another bite of the ice cream.

Carrie had opted not to see her dad dead and never walked close enough to the open casket.

"Yeah," Justin confirmed. "It was fluffy."

Oh Gawd, Dad would've hated fluffy hair. "They didn't slick his hair back? Like he always wore it?" she asked.

Justin shook his head. "Nope. Why didn't you look at him?"

"It's not how I want to remember him," Carrie said.

"Just looked like he was sleeping," Justin said.

"With funny hair." Tommy giggled. "I think Dad would've laughed."

Justin smiled. "You should have looked at him. It was just his body anyway. Soul was gone. He's in heaven with Jesus."

"Did you learn that the last time you went to church with Mom?" Carrie mentally ticked away the months. That would have been a long time ago. Since her dad was an atheist, the funeral hadn't been a religious service.

"Mom told me last night in bed."

"What?" Carrie asked. "I put you in your bed last night."

Justin put a spoonful in his mouth and shook his head. Ice cream oozed between his closed lips. When he was done, he licked them. "I had a nightmare, so I went and slept with Mom. We cuddled until I wasn't afraid."

"Oh." She couldn't remember the last time she'd seen her mom cuddle anyone or anything. "Here, eat your hearts out," she said and put the container on the floor. "I'll be right back."

Carrie's arms were stiff at her sides as she walked toward

the bathroom. It was the only place a person could have true privacy. Her chest tightened, and her throat began to hurt. They gave him fluffy hair? She blinked her eyes. And her mom let Justin cuddle?

Her parents'—no, her mother's—bedroom door was closed, so Carrie didn't think twice about pushing open the bathroom door.

"Oh," Carrie jumped back, surprised to find her mom there.

She was sitting on the closed toilet, face in hands and crying. She wiped her arm across her face. "What do you want?"

"I'm sorry. I thought you were in your room," Carrie said, her hand still resting on the door. "I was getting upset and didn't want to break down in front of the boys."

"Yeah, me too," Mom said.

Carrie walked in and leaned against the counter next to the sink. She crossed her arms and stared down at her mother's bent head. "I don't mean this to sound mean, and I'm not trying to be hurtful, but I thought you didn't even like him anymore."

Her mom snorted and shook her head. She grabbed some toilet paper and blew her nose. "It was never that simple."

"Did you love him?" Carrie asked.

"Yes. Many times." Her mom grabbed more toilet paper.

Carrie shook her head. "What does that mean? Many times?"

"I don't want to talk to you about it. He's gone now, and it's water under the bridge."

"I'm trying to understand." Carrie's voice shook as she tried to reason with her mom.

Her mother stood, seeming to avoid her puffy face in the

mirror, and grabbed a roll of toilet paper to take with her. "I can't explain it to you. It was many years." She headed toward the door.

"Fine," Carrie said, watching her retreating back. "I'm just trying . . . I'm just trying to know you better."

Her mom paused at the door, and she looked so spent and sad Carrie was tempted to reach out and hug her.

Her mom rested her hand against the doorframe and said, "They were hopeful."

What was she talking about? "Who was hopeful?" Carrie asked her.

"The women in my books. Your essay you're writing? I don't like the stories because the men died. It's because the women never gave up hope."

The tears came immediately, and Carrie didn't try to hide them as her mother nodded and left.

Later, after Carrie cleaned up the boys and the ice cream, she found the message from the landlord in Nashville. What her mom would do with the information, Carrie wasn't sure, but Carrie could no longer pretend she could control her mom's fate by hiding it any more than her mom could've controlled Carrie's by hiding the scholarship letter.

She might not know her mom well, but now Carrie knew her mom needed hope.

Her mom wasn't in her bedroom, so Carrie placed the slip of paper on her mom's empty shelf. Then she returned to her bedroom and started rewriting her scholarship essay.

48

JANICE

Carnegie Hall was real fabulous, but . . . it ain't as big as the
Grand Ole Opry.
—Patsy Cline

When Janice returned from the Creek Bar where the regulars had shared a parting toast to Harry, she went straight to her room. She glanced at her shelf of opportunity and picked up a slip of paper. She recognized Carrie's handwriting and the name and area code for Nashville.

At first, fury made the hair stand up on her arms, and the anger felt better than the grief she'd trudged through all day.

Carrie thought she could play God in her life and keep this from her?

When she calmed down, she realized Carrie had written a note on the back.

Mom,

I'm sorry I didn't tell you about the call. I was scared,
so I kept the message.

Thank you for giving me the college package. I am going to go to UNR and follow my dreams.

You should follow your dreams too. But please take the boys. I can't stay behind with them, and they need you. Just give me time until I can figure out how to take care of them. I'll take them back in one year after I'm not required to live in a dorm. I promise.

And I should have told you. On Saturday night, I spoke to Dad. He said goodbye.

—Carrie

Her seventeen-year-old daughter was offering to raise the boys in one year? Her daughter, who she never felt needed her or loved her was encouraging her to pursue her own dreams? Harry said goodbye?

Janice's hands shook, and she sat down on her bed. Her daughter was not standing in her way. Carrie didn't know about the social security money. The one person she had resented the most, next to Harry, was the one person aside from Scotty who believed she deserved to live her dream.

Thirty years ago, Janice's grandparents had offered to raise WJ for her, and she'd refused to be like her own mother and give up her baby. Now Carrie was offering to help raise her brothers in a year—a daughter who was Janice's age when Janice had made her first difficult life choice. Turns out that Janice and her daughter were more alike than she could have ever guessed—Harry always said they were. Janice still couldn't be like her mother, who had deserted her. She wouldn't leave the boys behind, but she would follow her dreams. She'd show all her children it was never too late.

49

WJ

Hello, my name is Walter Whitworth, Junior.

Friday morning, April 14, 1989

WJ had spent the past thirty hours answering every question the little detective had thrown at him. On the condition he'd given them all of the information he knew about the club's next deals, WJ was a free man with a bus ticket out of town.

A one-way bus ticket.

Detective Anderson followed WJ to his home in an unmarked car. After WJ packed his bag, he boxed up his *Popeye* comics with a note for the teen boy next door.

> *Billy,*
> *The comics are yours. Sergeant Meed or Detective Anderson will be checking on you every week. You tell them if your dad is giving you any shit.*
> *You're a good kid. Keep being you.*

—WJ

The kid wasn't home, but his prick of a dad was, so the feisty Detective Anderson made his acquaintance. From the looks of it, the SOB was even more afraid of the detective.

Before he slid on his leather jacket, WJ removed the Right Knight patch. It floated through the air and landed with a thud on the floor. The patch looked rough and lonely with stitches sticking out in every direction against the linoleum floor, and WJ felt a little lost and naked without it. Every single embroidered thread had been his purpose, his life, for the past four years. A dark outline of the patch remained on his black leather jacket like a scar that might slowly fade, or a bad tattoo that he'd really wanted at the time but now no longer suited him. He had some things to figure out without a patch.

He pulled out Harry's letter, list, and comic, and added them to an envelope for his mom. And then, WJ called Joe.

WJ gave his rucksack to the bus driver to shove in the storage area and picked a seat by the window. He fingered the birth certificate and Joe's message in his front pocket. Fern sat bouncing on his knee, her pot secured by a plastic bag.

Walter Whitworth, Junior, was riding one-way on a Greyhound bus to San Francisco, California. And he'd left a message for Joe asking him to meet him at the station. He was taking a huge risk going all that way without talking to Joe first, and he was scared shitless.

By the time the bus rolled to a stop in San Francisco, the weather was pouring rain, and WJ's head and heart were a twisted mess. His fear almost overwhelmed him as he

recalled a rainy day many years ago when he'd climbed off
the bus rejected, lost, and alone.

While he stood in line for the bus door, he reached to push
his long hair behind his ears, forgetting that he'd gotten a
buzz cut just before his trip. He tucked Fern in the crook of
his arm. The rain sprinkled his face as he stepped from the
bus to the sidewalk. He looked around, his eyes darting
between several unfamiliar faces.

Please, not again.

And then a warm hand squeezed his shoulder. WJ turned,
and there was Joe. Smiling. Waiting for him.

50

JANICE

A Church, a Courtroom and Then Goodbye
—Patsy Cline

Janice couldn't wait to get to the Social Security office, and she was dressed and ready to go as soon as the boys left for school. Having Harry's funeral behind her, even if only for less than a day, was a relief. She knew she had grieving to do, but she had some sorting and living to do too, and figuring out her income and the future for her and the boys was a priority.

Her next priority would be to sit down with Carrie and have a long talk. After the funeral yesterday, Carrie had said, "I'm just trying to get to know you better." Janice figured the best place to start would be at the beginning. New chapters were starting, and old ones needed to be wrapped up.

She was surprised to find WJ's empty truck parked out front of her trailer. He was nowhere in sight. He'd missed Harry's funeral, and she hadn't heard from him since she dropped off his birth certificate. She hoped he'd show up eventually, when he was ready to talk to her or ask questions. She was ready to answer.

She couldn't be late for her appointment, so she hopped into her car parked behind WJ's truck. A thick envelope rested on the dashboard, and WJ had scribbled across the front: *See you later. Walter.*

His small baby face flashed before her eyes. Too much. They'd been through too much together, and yet, he wasn't saying goodbye.

Funny how they were all having an easier time communicating via letters after all these years. Three pieces of paper and the title and keys to WJ's truck fell onto her lap. When she recognized Harry's handwriting, she gasped, and the letter shook between her fingertips. Harry. Her Harry.

Dear Songbird,

I'm a fool and a drunk. I loved you the best I could, but not the way you deserved. By the time you read this letter, I'll be gone. It won't be easy for any of you at first, but it will be easier in the long run if I'm out of the picture. I'm not trying to be wishy-washy either. You'll have a better chance in life without my drinking and gambling. I feel better about this decision than I have about anything in a long time. I was once a good man, and I aim to leave one by my last choice.

I've hit an all-time low. Hit that damn bottom AA warned me about, and I would have rather gone to my grave not letting those assholes be right about there being one. I've done a horrible thing I can't fix any other way. I hurt someone real bad. Worst of all, I screwed you over by doing it. I borrowed money from someone I shouldn't have, and I pawned the trailers and our cars. Last week, I blacked out. I beat up the pawnshop owner really bad, as in coma bad. He's been surviving on machines one day at a time. It's only a matter of time before someone comes to claim the roof over your heads, or before the police figure it out. I'm too much of a coward to turn myself in, and I can't go to prison. I'd die in there, and I'd be leaving you broke. Give the police this letter when they come knocking.

But I figured out how to take care of you. When I'm dead, you can collect my social security. Get your butt over to the social security office, apply for survivor benefits, and make all of those years of hard work mean something.

Can you grant me a dying wish? I did my children wrong. WJ most of all. Tell him about his real dad. I wish I could see his face when he hears he is Walter Whitworth, Junior. Oh, la-di-da—a junior. Let him find his family, and who knows, maybe he will become a better man than I raised him to be. You know, I never cared if he was gay. I just didn't want him to be unable to protect himself, and who better than me to teach him to stick up for himself, teach him not to trust anyone. I know this was wrong now. I was the one who couldn't be trusted. Something happened to me when I was a boy, something I'm glad to take to my grave, but I think everyone would agree with me that WJ knows how to take care of himself. No one ever took advantage of him as a kid because of me.

The comic strip I included is for WJ too. I'll be damned if his crush on Popeye hasn't finally clicked. WJ is Popeye. I'm Bluto, the bully. WJ will get a kick out of me finally putting two and two together.

I love you. Go find your dream. When I first met you,

you said you wanted to go to Nashville, and then I promised
you Las Vegas. I didn't deliver. Go to Nashville and sing
your heart out. I'll be listening, well, from somewhere, and
I'll be singing for you too.

> *Because I was not happy until I met you*
> *No, I was not alive until I saw you*
> *I glided along, content I thought*
> *And then, there you were, all my heart had sought*
> *--Harry*

Oh, would the tears never end? Her body had created more tears in her life than she could stand, but at least this time she smiled a bit through the downpour. Harry hadn't left her without saying goodbye, and he had asked her to tell WJ about Walter. He'd kept his promise.

She unfolded the second piece of paper, written to the kids, and this time she smiled hard. Carrie would like this list.

Dear Kids,

- *Do as I say, not as I do.*
- *Don't ever drink when you are too happy, sad,*
  mad, or need to make a big decision. Assume
  you're an alcoholic.
- *You're never given more than you can handle.*
- *To dream of the person you could have been is to*
  waste the person you are (I can't remember where
  I read this, but I've always liked it).
- *Only gamble spare change. Better yet, don't*
  gamble.

- *Never park by, or walk next to, white vans—avoid kidnappers at all costs.*
- *It's okay if you're gay.*
- *It's okay if you're not gay.*
- *Don't hitchhike or pick up hitchhikers.*
- *Never let anyone hit you.*
- *Nothing wrong with having your head in the clouds.*
- *Always work hard.*
- *When you make a promise, you better damn well mean it.*
- *Never doubt how much I love you.*
- *Only say sorry when you mean it.*
- *Only say Goodbye when it's final, otherwise say See You Later, because you can't take back a Goodbye.*

Love you and Goodbye,
    Dad

And WJ had added to the list:

- *Never do drugs.*
- *Stay away from gangs.*
- *Can't solve problems with your fists.*
- *It's okay to be weak. Sometimes.*
- *Never pretend to be someone you're not.*

Love you and See You Later,
    Walter Jr.

Janice drove her Ford Pinto for the last time. She laughed, remembering the tagline for the car when it first came out: *The Little Carefree Car*. With the radio on and the windows down, she sang all the way to her appointment.

51

JANICE

Hello, my name is Janice Sloan.

Thursday, June 15, 1989

J anice wanted to pinch herself. So much had happened since Harry died two months ago and WJ disappeared from their lives. She knew WJ was okay because the detective told her, "He has a chance now."

One week ago, Carrie graduated from high school with honors, and Janice had WJ's truck—well, her truck now—hitched with a U-Haul trailer, and she was ushering Justin and Tommy into the passenger side. Star jumped up behind them.

This was really happening. They were leaving for Nashville. They had an apartment in a safe neighborhood lined up and savings to get settled. The boys would have all summer to play and get used to their new life and make new friends.

As of midnight, her trailers on Tiger Drive would be hers no more, and that was fine by her. The pawnshop owner had started the long road to recovery. Janice had called on Pastor

Henry again shortly after Harry's crime became public knowledge.

"May have been Harry's wrongdoing," she'd held up a card and some flowers she picked up at the grocery store, "but I want to apologize and leave these for the owner's wife, family, and employees. I also need to talk to whoever is in charge and see if I can make arrangements to rent back the trailers until Carrie graduates. The boys and I won't leave for Nashville before then."

Pastor Henry had asked, "How can I help?"

"You could go with me?" Janice asked. She was humbled when he stood up and grabbed his keys.

"No time like the present."

Indeed.

She hadn't expected to meet the victim's wife face-to-face, but she was behind the counter when Janice and the pastor arrived. She was taller than Janice and had shadows under her eyes and wrinkles around her mouth that Janice knew she had too. Being what it was, the moment wasn't warm and fuzzy, but Janice made sure her sincere apology came across. And when the woman said she'd "have to think about" giving Janice until school was out, Janice had replied, "I will respect your decision no matter what." Within a week, Pastor Henry called.

"Someone heard our Sunday prayers for you," the pastor said. "You can stay in your home until the end of June."

Now Janice had left her keys on the kitchen counter, and Carrie would be adding her set to the pile soon enough.

"Ready to hit the road, boys?" Janice asked Justin and Tommy as she climbed in beside them.

"Yes!"

"What am I going to be again?" Justin asked.

"You're my manager, and Tommy is my agent." Janice winked and turned the key in the ignition. The truck started immediately.

She looked to her right at the small urn of Harry's ashes poking out from bubble wrap and a box on the floorboard. *Ready, Harry?*

Janice smiled, looked forward, and hit the gas.

52

CARRIE

Hello, my name is Carrie Sloan.

From the window, Carried took a deep breath and let it out slowly as she watched her mom and little brothers roll away. She'd told her mom, "No, you leave first. It will be better for the boys this way."

Her mom would be fine, but oh Gawd, would the boys be okay without a big sister? Without her? She already missed them, and they weren't gone more than two seconds.

Get a grip, Carrie.

She turned back to the book she hugged to her chest: her mom's copy of *Jane Eyre* with a receipt taped inside that read, "Paid in full." Her dad's letter marked where she'd left off reading. She'd lost track of how many times she'd read both the book and his letter.

Carrie added the book to her backpack and grabbed her suitcase and walked through the trailer. Years of their lives had been cleared out and sorted into four piles: pack, Goodwill, trash, and storage. And now the place was empty except for Carrie and her bag.

If anyone had told her two months ago that she'd be moving in with her friend, Samantha, and would have more than enough money for college in September and a job lined up, and that she would become her mother's greatest cheerleader, Carrie would have called them nuts. Yet here she was taking her last steps on the familiar creaking floorboards, out the back door, and over the cigarette-burned and tattered AstroTurf porch.

Before Samantha's parents pulled away, they asked her, "Ready to leave Tiger Drive?"

As she looked out the window at the home she'd never see again, Carrie smiled. "I was born ready."

53

THEMATIC SCHOLARSHIP ESSAY

by
Carrie Sloan

Between my parents, they had thirteen books, seven children, and too many secrets. I used to be ashamed of my family and my parents' books. I was certainly ashamed to be Janice and Harry's daughter. Instead, I am now asking myself if I ever really knew them, and what were they like when they were seventeen and had their whole lives ahead of them, believing the world was their oyster. If they were seventeen today, with an opportunity to apply for scholarships and go to college, would they? What were the dreams they dreamt for themselves as teenagers?

When I first read over my mother's books, I assumed she liked dramatic novels where the man dies in the end, is abusive, or is too selfish to stick around, allowing the heroine to burn a glorious trail of purpose via martyrdom. But who is my mother? In some ways, she is a martyr. When she was seventeen, my mother had to choose between raising a son out of wedlock or allowing her grandparents to raise him as their own, which would have allowed her to pursue her career aspirations. She did not doubt that she would learn the ropes of a radio station and someday become a country singer. Now, I will be the first to tell you that my mother has a mediocre singing voice, but I also would have been the first to tell you that my mother had never had a single ambition other than hanging out at the Creek Bar and singing karaoke. But soon my mother will travel halfway across the country to pick up the trail of her dreams where she lost it thirty years ago. She was a martyr; but now I understand she is also simply a woman, very much like the heroines in her books, who never gave up because she never lost hope.

My dad's selection was disheartening since all of his books focused on death, destruction, and elements of justice. In the end, my dad was focused on both, allowing him to be both judge and jury. He killed himself two weeks ago. I believe the books represent my father's philosophy about suicide and paybacks. He found comfort and peace knowing how and when he would die. My father was an alcoholic, father, and hard worker.

I am Carrie, proud daughter of Harry and Janice Sloan. I am seventeen, I have my entire life ahead of me, and I know the world is my oyster. I am going to college in the fall—the first person in my family to do so—and I am going to live a glorious life, and someday, I will own a library that will speak volumes about my own choices. But I'm going to leave one shelf empty, so there's always room for hope, faith, and opportunity.

I'm a shooting star. Make a wish on me.

AUTHOR'S NOTE

Book club materials are available on my website.

As much as I'd like to be historically accurate, I wanted to tell a good story. Therefore, I need to clarify a few things.

According to Wikipedia, the first karaoke machine was developed in Japan by a musician in 1971, but the karaoke machine did not become popular in the USA until the 1990s. This novel occurs in 1989. But Janice needed a means to earn and save money while doing the one thing she loved—singing. So I blurred the timing. Please forgive Janice and me.

More importantly, I want to clarify why the characters, WJ and Joe, were dismissed from the Navy in 1979 under a less than honorable and general, disability discharge. Before 1981, each "homosexual violation" was decided at an administrative level. The decision was based on opinion-driven factors such as whether someone was just being "queen for a day" and did not plan to engage in homosexual acts again; whether someone was homosexual but had not acted on their sexuality and wouldn't in the future; whether an accused could prove their sexuality; and so on. At that time, the discharge could be categorized as general, bad conduct, dishonorable, or undesirable—all of which decreased or eliminated benefits for health care and more. An honorable discharge, which would allow for benefits, would most likely not have been given, but I don't have the statistics. Additional punishment might include fees and jail time. In 1981, the Department of Defense rolled out further regulations that would eliminate the "queen for a day" plea and further imply that homosexuality was a threat to the military's mission.

I first imagined the Right Knights in 2011 and any actual gangs in this world with such a name that have cropped up since are not related.

ACKNOWLEDGMENTS

Finishing a book requires soda, licorice, yogurt covered peanuts, magazines, glue-sticks, alligator skin, earplugs, candles, walks, a timer, a door, two saw horses, a fitness ball, The Civil Wars, and olive branches. But mostly, it takes a village of believers, coaches, supporters, and collaborators.

I would not have been able to write this novel without the support and encouragement from Ted—he has opened up my world and has challenged my views in countless positive ways.

Thanks to Karsen and Adam who started the "three pages" challenge several years ago. Unbeknownst to each of us, my first three pages of this pre-internet, snail-mail exchange would become Chapter Two of *Tiger Drive*.

Thank you, Tia, for the author's new hire package that I woke up to in June 2011—you set the perfect tone for the first day of my new career. Also, thanks to Lanita, Annie, Christine, and Elizabeth for not telling me I was crazy to quit my job to write.

Detective Gonzales, the experience you shared about

lawless motorcycle clubs was most instructional (and funny and terrifying). Though I have butchered everything you told me and created a gang of amateurs (I blame my paranoia), I couldn't have created said amateurs without your help.

While writing this work of fiction (yes, that's a reminder that this is not a memoir—Hi, Mom), I felt overwhelmed with gratitude for the Stocks, Lamers, Langsons, and Huntzingers for sharing their homes and families when I needed both the most. Apryl Huntzinger and Julie Langson, I am a better person for having known you and am honored to remain close.

Many thanks to Karsen for reading each page as soon as I wrote one and for thinking each was the best it could be. Hugs to the readers on the frontline who braved reading the first craptastic drafts full of typos and insanity, and for helping me pinpoint the lines that shouldn't be drawn: Crystal, Sarah, Jessica, Tia, Kate, Gretchen, April, Stephen T., Michele, Annie, Julie R., and Ingrid, and authors Cathey Graham Nickell, Brian Peyton Joyner, Angela Alvarez, and Lisa Sinicki. Lisa—you're so patient and always believe I can write better. Brian—you worked wonders with WJ's introduction.

Chris L., thank you for sharing your creative knowledge. Steve Z., thanks for telling me to "stop worrying and get that book published already." Bridgette, thanks for reading the romance I wrote long ago (and then burned). Author Heidi Ayarbe, thanks for some synopsis sympathy.

Editors change everything. First, Deborah Halverson with DearEditor.com. You gave me advice that not only changed *Tiger Drive* but me as a writer: "Give me a reason to care about this guy." You also nailed the ending of Carrie's essay.

Lizette Clarke with Author Accelerator, thanks for the light bulb moments around POV and how to better share Harry's letters. Thanks to additional editors Carrie Ann Lahain, Kit Frick, Paige Duke, and Eddy Bay—your input gave me the confidence to charge into the publishing arena.

Online courses and masterminds with San Diego State University, Author Accelerator, Story Genius, and WeGrow-Media have taught me much about collaborating, writing, and establishing a routine.

Authors Mary Jo Hazard, Brian Peyton Joyner, Jack Schaeffer, Lisa Manterfield, and Maya Rushing Walker—you people rock my creative world, and I will continue to strive to return the favors and GIFs. Rupert Davies-Cooke and Gemma Glover, our micro-group has created macro results from day one. Cheers!

"Kicksass" creator, Kelsey Browning, you are the best (and most relentless) coach and Say-It-Like-It-Is friend out there. That you introduced me to Mrs-Can-Do-Anything-Reva is a bonus.

Dear newsletter subscribers, thank you for being you and for joining me almost weekly. I'm grateful to all of the Tiger Drive Squadsters, especially Mary Jo Hazard, Mary Incontro, Donna Barker, Lorraine Watson, Crystal Case, Aimee Strathman, Susan Murray Kurilla, David Prater, and Lisa Sinicki. Donna, one call with you and the squad was born. Validation? Check!

Mr. Thompson, as you'd say, "BOOM!" Thank you for our *We-Can-Write-Books-Right?* calls. Answer: YES, WE CAN.

A book is judged by its cover. Thank you cover designers Olya Vynnychenko, Estella Vukovic, and LancelotZ01 for taking on the challenge. Colleen H., thanks for being my nonreader who judged the covers and description. And author Carlen Maddux, thank you for suggesting a subtitle. Thanks to Buffalo Books and Short Stories Bookshop & Community Hub for your feedback on my book covers and media sheets.

Thank you, King Features Syndicate for supporting my use of E.C. Segar's *Popeye*. And Patsy Cline, thanks for being ahead of your time and for inspiring Janice and me.

Finally, thanks to Crystal for picking up the phone every time I call (excluding nap time).

ABOUT THE AUTHOR

Teri Case is a native Nevadan. Her alcoholic father, bipolar mother, and nine siblings taught her to watch and learn from others and that laughter can lighten any load. She often travels—watching, learning, and writing about people who want to matter. Teri authors the *Vitality Stories* newsletter and is the founder of the Tiger Drive Scholarship.

Author photo by Gretchen LeMay Photography

To follow or contact Teri:
https://www.tericase.com
teri@tericase.com

Made in the USA
Middletown, DE
04 August 2018